Praise for
The Winemaker Detective

**Twenty-two books
A hit on television in France**

"Alaux and Balen offer intrigue and plenty of good eating and drinking... this book and its successors will whet appetites of fans of both *Iron Chef* and *Murder, She Wrote.*"

—*Booklist*

"Unusually adept at description, the authors manage to paint everything.... The journey through its pages is not to be rushed."

—*ForeWord Reviews*

"I love good mysteries. I love good wine. So imagine my joy at finding a great mystery about wine, and winemaking, and the whole culture of that fascinating world. And then I find it's the first of a series. I can see myself enjoying many a bottle of wine while enjoying the adventures of Benjamin Cooker in this terrific new series."

—William Martin, *New York Times* bestselling author

"A fine vintage forged by the pens of two very different varietals. It is best consumed slightly chilled, and never alone. You will be intrigued by its mystery, and surprised by its finish, and it will stay with you for a very long time."

—Peter May, international bestselling author

"An excellent mystery series in which you eat, drink and discuss wine as much as you do murders."

—Bernard Frank, *Le Nouvel Observateur*

The Winemaker Detective

An Omnibus

Treachery in Bordeaux
Grand Cru Heist
Nightmare in Burgundy

by Jean-Pierre Alaux and Noël Balen
Translated by Anne Trager and Sally Pane

LE FRENCH BOOK

First published in France as
Mission à Haut-Brion, Pour qui sonne l'angélus
Cauchemar dans les Côtes-de-Nuit
by Librairie Anthème Fayard 2004

English translation ©2013-2014
First published in English in 2013 & 2014
by Le French Book, Inc., New York

http://www.lefrenchbook.com

Translators: Anne Trager & Sally Pane
Translation editor: Amy Richards
Proofreading: Chris Gage
Cover designer: Jeroen ten Berge

ISBNs:

Trade paperback: 9781939474568
Hardback: 9781939474582
e-book: 9781939474575

BOOK 1

Treachery in Bordeaux

A Winemaker Detective Mystery

Translated from French by Anne Trager

"A bottle of wine contains more philosophy than all the books in the world."
— Louis Pasteur

1

The morning was cool and radiant. A west wind had swept the clouds far inland to the gentle hills beyond the city of Bordeaux. Benjamin Cooker gave two whistles, one short, the other drawn out, and Bacchus appeared from the high grass on the riverbank. He had that impertinent look Irish setters get when you remind them that they are dogs. Benjamin liked this clever and deceptively disciplined attitude. He would never roam his childhood landscapes with an animal that was too docile. The Médoc was still wild, despite its well-ordered garden veneer, and it would always be that way. In the distance, a few low wisps of fog were finishing their lazy dance along the Gironde Estuary. It was nearly eleven and time to go home.

The Grangebelle's graceful shape rose among the poplar trees. The building would have seemed bulky, were it not for the elegant roof, the lightly draped pergola, the delicate sparkling of the greenhouse, and the old varnished vases set out in the vegetation with studied negligence. Elisabeth moved silently among the copper pots in the kitchen. She shivered slightly when he kissed her neck. He poured himself a cup of Grand Yunnan tea with slow and precise movements. She knew he was tired. She was perfectly aware of his nights of poor sleep, the deleted pages, the files he relentlessly ordered and reordered, the doubts he had when he completed a tasting note, his concern for the smallest detail, and the chronic worry that he would deliver his manuscript late and disappoint his publisher. Benjamin had worked in his office until five in the morning, taking refuge in the green opaline halo of his old

Empire-style lamp. Then he had slipped under the covers to join her, his body ice-cold and his breathing short.

Who could have imagined that France's most famous winemaker, the established authority who caused both grand cru estate owners and unknown young vintners to tremble, was, in fact, a man tormented by the meaning of his words, the accuracy of his judgments, and an objectivity that he brandished like a religious credo? When it came time to hand over a manuscript, his self-doubts assailed him—the man whom the entire profession thought of as entrenched in certainty and science and masterfully accomplished in the fine art of critiquing wines. Benjamin Cooker knew that everyone, without exception, would be waiting for his book to arrive in the stores. They would be weighing his qualifiers and judging his worst and best choices. It was essential that the publication of his guide never blemish his reputation as a winemaker and a sought-after, even secret, advisor in the art of elaborating wines. He made it a point of honor and proved it with his sometimes scathing criticism of wines he himself had crafted. To him, moral integrity stemmed more often than not from this astonishing faculty of uncompromising self-judgment, even when it was forced and terribly unfair. He sometimes thought it belonged to another century, a faraway time, when self-esteem and a certain sense of honor prevailed over the desire for recognition.

He closed his eyes as he drank his tea. He knew that this moment of rest would not last long and that he should make the most of it, appreciating these slow, spread-out seconds. Elisabeth remained quiet.

"Send him to me as soon as he gets here. I need to have a few words with him before lunch," he said, calmly setting down his cup.

Benjamin Cooker dragged himself back to the half-light of his office. He spent more than an hour examining his tasting notes for a Premières Côtes de Blaye and finished by persuading himself that there was nothing left to add. However, his preamble about the specific characteristics of the soil and the vineyard's history was a little short on information, despite his in-depth knowledge of every acre. There was nothing wrong with what he had written, but nothing really specific either. He would have to draw a more detailed picture, refine the contours, and play with an anecdote or two to clarify the text. He did not even lift his eyes from his notes when the doorbell rang out in the hallway. He was nervously scribbling some poetic lines about the Blaye citadel when Elisabeth knocked at the door. She knocked three more times before he told her to come in.

"Our guest has arrived, Benjamin."

"Welcome, young man!" the winemaker said, pushing his glasses to his forehead.

An athletic and honest-looking young man with short hair honored him with a strong handshake that left Benjamin wondering if his fingers would still work.

"So you're Virgile Lanssien," Benjamin said, lowering his reading glasses to the tip of his nose.

He invited the young man to sit down and observed him over the top of his lenses for a minute. His dark, pensive good looks would have been almost overwhelming, were it not for the spark of mischief in his eyes. He was dressed simply in a pair of slightly washed-out jeans, a navy blue polo shirt, and white sneakers. He was smart enough not to feign a laid-back attitude when everything about him was on edge. Benjamin appreciated people who did not posture.

"I have heard a lot about the time you spent at the wine school. Professor Dedieu was unending in his praise for your work, and I have to admit that I was rather impressed by your thesis. I have a copy of it here. The title is a little complicated, *Maceration Enzyme Preparation: Mechanism of Action and Reasonable Use*, but your reasoning was straightforward and clear, particularly the section about blind tasting an enzymatic treatment of cabernet sauvignon must. Well done, very well done! Please do excuse me for not having been part of the jury when you defended your dissertation."

"I won't hide my disappointment, sir."

"In any case, my presence would not have changed the result: You greatly deserved the honors you received. I had an emergency call that day to care for some grapevines in Fronsac, and it couldn't wait. The flowering was tricky and required quite a bit of attention."

"I understand, sir. Did you save them at least?"

"More or less. There were enough grapes for me to offer you a bottle," Benjamin said, smiling.

The young man settled into the armchair and relaxed a little. He knew that these formalities foreshadowed a flow of questions that he would have to answer with candor and precision. Benjamin Cooker was a master no cheating could fool. Virgile had read everything written by this man, whose reputation stretched as far as North America and South Africa. He had also heard everything there was to know about the "flying winemaker"—all the scandal mongering and bitter words, along with the passionate commentaries and praise. Everything and its opposite were the usual lot of exceptional people, the ransom paid by those who had succeeded in imposing their singularity.

Virgile Lanssien tried to hide his apprehension and answered the sudden volley of questions that descended on him as distinctly as possible. They covered so many topics—layering, copper sulfate spraying, sulfur dioxide additions, microclimates, grand cru longevity, aging on lees, filtering and fining, gravel or limestone soils, fermentation temperatures, primary aromas, and degrees of alcohol—in such disorder, yet Virgile managed to avoid the traps with a skilled farmer's cunning.

"Well, Virgile—I can call you Virgile, can't I? I think that after these appetizers, we have earned the right to a meal."

Elisabeth, wearing a checkered apron tied at her waist, welcomed them into the kitchen.

"We will eat in the kitchen, if that does not bother you, Mr. Lanssien."

"To the contrary, ma'am. May I help with anything?"

"Why don't you set the table. The plates are in that cupboard. The cutlery is here."

Benjamin was surprised to see his wife accept the young man as if he were already part of the family. But Elisabeth knew her man well enough to guess that the job interview was going well.

The winemaker grabbed three stem glasses and poured the wine he had decanted that morning, before the walk with Bacchus.

"Taste this, Virgile."

Benjamin observed his future assistant while he cut the bread and placed the even slices in a basket. The boy knew how to taste. He used his eyes, his nose, and his palate in a natural way, with the attitude of someone who knew more than he showed.

"Wine can be so good when it's good!"

An amused smile crossed Benjamin's lips. The young man had a talent for finding the truth beneath the surface but also a certain guilelessness. Virgile was a cultivated ingénue with enough freshness and spontaneity to compensate for the long years he had focused entirely on his studies.

"I will not be so cruel as to subject you to a blind tasting," Benjamin said, turning the empty bottle to display the label.

"Haut-Brion 1982!" the young man said with a note of rapture. "To tell you the truth, I've never tasted one of these before."

"Enjoy it then. It's harder and harder to grab this vintage away from the small-time speculators who are complicating our lives."

"I made something simple," Elisabeth interrupted, putting an old cast-iron casserole on the table.

Virgile paused, unfolded his napkin, and gave the pot an apprehensive look. Large chunks of eel floated in a thick greenish sauce filled with so many herbs, it looked like a patch of weeds.

"I know, at first glance it does not look very appetizing, but it is a recipe that deserves overcoming your first impression."

"I think I know what it is."

"Lamprey à la Bordelaise. It's a classic," said Elisabeth.

"With this dish, you should always drink the wine that was used in the cooking," Benjamin said, dishing out generous portions. "And nothing is better with lamprey than a red Graves."

Virgile stuck his fork into a piece of eel, dipped it in the sauce, and nibbled at it.

"It is first rate, Mrs. Cooker! Excellent."

"And now, let's try a little of this Haut-Brion with that," Benjamin suggested. "Just a swallow, and then tell me what you think."

Virgile did as he was told, with a pleasure he had some trouble hiding.

"It is beautifully complex, particularly with the tannins that are very present. Rather surprising but not aggressive."

Benjamin remained silent and savored his lamprey.

"It leaves a very smooth sensation in the mouth," Virgile continued. "And yet it has a kind of grainy texture."

"Very perceptive. That is typical of Haut-Brion. It is both strong and silky. And what else?"

"It's fruity, wild fruits, with hints of berries, blackberries, and black currant fruit."

"True enough," Benjamin said. "You can taste cherry pits later on, don't you think?"

"I didn't notice, but now that you mention it."

"Beware of what people say. Some may not find that hint of cherry pits, and they wouldn't be wrong."

The guest took the blow without flinching. Benjamin had no trouble pushing his interrogation further. The Pessac-Léognan grand cru loosened Virgile's tongue, and secrets slipped out in every sentence. He recounted his childhood in

Montravel, near Bergerac, where his father was a wine grower who shipped his harvest to the wine cooperative and had no ambitions for his estate.

"You'll take over the business one day, won't you?" Elisabeth asked.

"I don't think so. At least not as long as my father is in charge of the property. My older brother is all they need for now to take care of the vineyards."

"That's too bad. Bergerac wines have come a long way and could certainly benefit from your talent," Benjamin said.

"Perhaps one day. I rarely go back, truth be told. Mostly to see my mother, who accuses me of deserting the nest, and my younger sister, who is the only one I can confide in."

He talked a lot, not so much because he wanted to monopolize the conversation, but rather to satisfy his hosts' unfeigned curiosity. To earn his future boss's trust, he felt it was appropriate to answer the Cooker couple's unspoken questions. The winemaker needed to know what was hidden in this excellent and dedicated student. Never had he experienced a job interview that was so informal and piecemeal. He disclosed himself without ostentation, without mystery, and without immodesty. He talked about swimming in the Dordogne River and playing for the Bergerac rugby club, but only for one season, because he preferred canoeing and kayaking. He mentioned his first medals when he joined the swim team, his years studying winemaking at La Tour Blanche, near Château d'Yquem, before he did his military service, and his studio apartment on Rue Saint-Rémi, from which you could see a little bit of the Garonne.

Between two anecdotes, Benjamin went to get a second carafe of Haut-Brion and allowed himself to share some of his own personal memories. It pleased Elisabeth to see her husband finally relaxed and able to forget the tribulations of his writing for a while. Benjamin recounted the crazy, hare-brained ideas his father, Paul William—an antique dealer in London—had and his mother Eleonore's patience. Her maiden name was Fontenac, and she had spent her entire youth here in Grangebelle, on the banks of the Gironde, before she fell in love with that extravagant Englishman who collected old books in a shop at Notting Hill.

Virgile listened. His handsome brown eyes were wide open, and he looked like a slightly frightened child as he began to fully comprehend that this was the famous Cooker, *the* Cooker, whose books he had devoured and who was now sharing confidences. The oenologist enjoyed telling the young graduate about his chaotic career. He had studied law for a year in England, spent a year at the Paris Fine Arts Academy, worked for a year at the Wagons-Lits in train catering and sleeping-car services, and then bartended for a year at the Caveau de la Huchette in the capital before being hired at a wine shop in the fifth arrondissement in Paris, where he worked for three years while taking wine classes.

"The year I turned thirty, I started my wine consulting business," Benjamin said. "Elisabeth and I ended up moving here after my maternal grandfather, Eugène Fontenac, passed away. Since that day, I haven't been able to imagine living anywhere other than Bordeaux."

"That's an unusual career path," Virgile said.

"Yes, it is atypical. I had been around wine since I was a kid, when I visited my grandfather in Grangebelle during summer vacations, but I needed a little time for all that to distill. I had a lot of doubts during my Paris years, and I spent a lot of time searching. I have followed a rather roundabout path, but I do not regret any of the detours."

"It's intriguing, like the path a drop of Armagnac takes before it comes out of the alembic."

"That's a fine image," Elisabeth said. "But sometimes it is better not to know all of the mysteries lying in the dark."

"This is one area in which my wife and I differ. I believe you should always seek to uncover secrets."

"I don't really have an opinion on the subject," Virgile said, studying the bottom of his empty glass.

Benjamin Cooker stood up and folded his napkin.

"My dear Virgile, from now on, consider yourself my assistant. We'll discuss the conditions later. I hope that this wine cleared your mind, because I believe you will need all of your faculties. We have a particularly delicate mission awaiting us."

"And when will I be starting?"

The winemaker took a last sip of Haut-Brion and set his glass down slowly. He slipped a hand into his jacket pocket, looked Virgile in the eye, and handed him a set of keys.

"Right now."

2

A few expertly negotiated bends in the road were all it took
to assure Benjamin Cooker that he had made the right choice.
His new assistant handled the old Mercedes 280 SL convertible with tact. He hadn't needed much time to adjust to it.
Virgile had no doubt that handing him the wheel was less
a sign of trust than a test. He felt his employer eyeing his
slightest moves with a distant vigilance barely masked by the
drowsiness that was beginning to slow him down. As they
drove through Bordeaux, Benjamin did not regret having let
Virgile drive. He was beginning to feel the night of insomnia,
and he let the comforting purr of the six cylinders soothe him.
The accelerations were smooth, the braking soft, the turns
balanced. The boy had to have some hidden fault!

As they approached the limits of Médoc, traffic slowed
little by little, until it stopped entirely. The city of Bordeaux
was mired in construction. The disfiguring yellow-orange
signs looked like they belonged in a cheap carnival. Cranes
with empty hooks stood silent, while aggressive insect-like
bulldozers lumbered all around them. The tramway—silent,
shiny, and bright—would soon rise from this tangled mess. But
for now, motorists could do nothing but wait. Some irritated
drivers honked without any illusions of being able to move
along, while others just put up with it silently.

"We're trapped," Benjamin grumbled. "Take the first street
to the right, and let's head to Pessac."

"Are you sure?" asked Virgile.

"Go on. I know a shortcut."

The driver put on his blinker and turned onto a lane lined
with gray shops whose scaly facades could have used a serious

facelift. The city was being transformed, but it would take much work to restore the gleam of years past. Stonework blackened by pollution would have to be cleaned, and long-neglected facades would need to be uncovered for Bordeaux to find its glory again. Only then could the city open up to the Port of the Moon once more, having shed its rags and come into its own.

Benjamin dictated directions. "Take the second street to the right, then the first left, followed by another left. Straight ahead to the sign. Watch out for the speed bump. To the right. Now, a little farther along, after the blue signs, keep right." Bordeaux's suburbs filed past in a confusion of cubical houses dropped there during the happy-go-lucky nineteen fifties, ugly sheet-metal warehouses and deserted workshops, faux rustic houses with small well-kept yards and mocking gnomes, storefronts, and nineteenth-century working-class homes with stylized figures, sculpted friezes, and zinc festoons.

"We're not far from the wine school," Virgile said, surprised.

"Indeed, it's nearby. At the next light, take the small road that heads downhill. We're almost there."

Benjamin asked his assistant to stop the convertible in the parking lot at the entrance of a large estate that was drowned in greenery and surrounded by a stone wall; shards of broken bottles lined the top to dissuade dishonest visitors. Virgile, who had not asked any questions during the trip, could not contain his curiosity any longer.

"Is this already Pessac?" he asked. "I'm a little lost."

"Yes and no. We're at the Château Les Moniales Haut-Brion. The estate is situated where Pessac, Mérignac, and Bordeaux meet. It is the only vineyard still found within greater Bordeaux."

"Is that so? I thought that there weren't any more on the registry."

"You are quite mistaken! This is one of the intriguing facts about the Moniales Haut-Brion."

"So, it's the last vineyard planted *in* Bordeaux itself?"

"Or the first, depending on how you see things, Virgile," said Benjamin. "Most important, it is owned by one of my best friends."

Before going through the heavy wooden gate that opened to the grounds, the winemaker glanced around, and it seemed that the landscape had changed once again since his last visit some eight months earlier. The estate was locked in by suburban housing developments dating from the happy time before the first oil crisis tarnished illusions. A little farther north, blocks of white subsidized housing rose in stripes against the blue sky, insulting the eye.

Now, right in front of the main Moniales entrance, there were new two-story buildings that already looked like they would age poorly. The architects who designed this tidy, soulless complex clearly lacked taste and culture but had shown a very advanced knack for economy. It was easy to detect the second-rate developer's stinginess in the hastily built structures. No consideration had been given to the families that would take out twenty-year mortgages on homes in this suburb, where the tiniest concrete block was accounted for, the piles of sand measured to the last grain, the woodwork negotiated at the lowest cost, and the gates put up without any grace.

Benjamin entered the estate and immediately headed toward the cellars, which were at the other end of the grounds. He felt at home. Virgile followed three steps behind, not daring to walk beside him, still wondering what they were doing here.

A man of stature was walking in their direction. Benjamin waved at him and turned to his assistant. "Denis Massepain, the estate owner."

Massepain's steps were heavy. But his bearing was that of a natural gentleman farmer devoid of all affectation. He wore a white herringbone shirt, putty-colored pleated dress corduroys, a tweed jacket, and English shoes. Benjamin and he could have had the same tailor. Both had the elegant bearing that comes from being born into well-to-do families. Nearing the age of fifty, neither had concerns about fleeting trends. Denis was an old friend, one Benjamin did not need to see often to feel as close to as he had the day they had met. From time to time, they crossed paths, getting together with their families for an evening in Grangebelle, meeting for a long lunch, just the two of them, at Le Noailles in town, or seeing each other briefly during a tasting among experts. Luckily, Elisabeth got along well with Thérèse Massepain, the daughter of wine merchants from the Chartrons neighborhood. She too had highborn elegance and reserve.

They were a charming couple. Their children were educated, and their company was always pleasant. Benjamin was pleased that Denis had married so well. It was as if Thérèse's smile and the pearl necklace she always wore brightened him up. He had studied to be an embryologist and had worked for a long time for a large pharmaceutical company in Castres before he took over operations at Moniales Haut-Brion, which belonged to his in-laws. Denis had finally put away his test tubes and potions to dedicate himself to presses and oak barrels. He worked hard, was blessed with a pragmatic approach, and was extremely rigorous in his winemaking. It took him only a few years to make this wine one of the most prestigious in the appellation.

"Benjamin, it's a disaster!"

"Hello, Denis."

"A total disaster!"

Benjamin knew his friend had an abrupt nature, but to not even greet him?

"Smell that!"

The winemaker carefully sniffed at the vial that Denis held out. He paused.

"I'm going to be very honest with you," the winemaker said right out, wrinkling his nose. "This is the worst kind of smell. It's a real mess, and you never know how the wine will turn out."

"Are you thinking the same thing I am?"

"I'm afraid so," Benjamin grumbled, moving his nose away from the flask.

"*Brettanomyces?*" the estate owner stammered with a worried look that seemed to refuse the answer that he already knew was obvious.

"I'm not going to hide anything from you. And it seems to be very advanced already."

"I don't understand. It happened all at once. I went to Germany for a week, and when I came back, I found four barrels like this."

"Denis, you are not the first to be the victim of this kind of thing. But it is rather rare to find a Brett infection in a winery of your standing."

"That's why I called you so early this morning."

Absorbed as he was, Denis Massepain had been oblivious to Virgile's presence. Now he took notice and glared at him with suspicion.

"Virgile Lanssien, my new assistant," Benjamin said to re-assure his friend before going into the cellars.

"Pleased to meet you," Denis muttered.

"The pleasure is all mine, sir," the young man said, forcing his voice a little.

They followed the winemaker, who had already started ferreting among the barrels. The cellars, which had recently been renovated and enlarged, were kept remarkably clean. There were small one thousand- to two thousand-gallon tanks used to ferment grapes from each parcel separately. The wine was then aged in oak barrels for about eighteen months before being bottled. The small Moniales estate had long lingered in the shadows of the prestigious Château Haut-Brion and its neighbor, Mission Haut-Brion, yet it could now easily rival the best vineyards in the Pessac-Léognan appellation.

Denis Massepain was aware of the challenges and duties the Haut-Brion name imposed on him, so he had called on the advice of experts, notably André Cazebon, an eminent researcher and dean of the Bordeaux Wine School. Benjamin had great esteem for this specialist in monitoring phenolic maturity. He had perfected a technique that made it possible to precisely determine grape maturity so that the fruit could be harvested at the optimal time. With this, the winemaking process could be adapted for each tank, and unique results could be obtained from each parcel.

"Did you tell your wizard?" asked Benjamin.

"I wouldn't have bothered you if he had been around. I think he is in Lyon for a conference."

"We'll need his opinion. I'd like to talk it over with him."

"I haven't been able to reach him."

"We'll take samples from all the barrels, and we also need—"

"It's done already," Denis interrupted. "I prepared a sample from each barrel."

"In that case, I'll take everything to my lab and ask them to fast-track the tests."

"I would like this to stay between us," the estate owner said with a sigh.

"Who do you think we are? It seems to me that Cooker & Co. has a reputation for being more than discreet!"

"I'm sorry, Benjamin. That's not what I meant."

"Virgile and I will be the only ones who know. We won't use any labels or names, so nothing will leak out. Don't worry."

Benjamin gave Virgile a nod, and the assistant effortlessly hoisted the crate full of numbered flasks from the small stainless-steel table. Virgile followed his employer, who continued to talk with the master of the Moniales, as they left the cellars and walked up the central drive on the grounds.

"Virgile will come back tomorrow to take further samples from the barrels that are still healthy. In the meantime, you have to isolate the four contaminated barrels," Benjamin advised. "That is a basic measure, and it needs to be done quickly. Better safe than sorry! You don't have to walk us to the gate. I know the way."

The two friends shook hands without saying anything further. His arms around the wooden crate, Virgile took leave of the estate owner with a nod and a smile that tried to be encouraging.

"This estate is really magnificent," the young man said, looking around at the large trees dotting the grounds that had been designed by Michel Bonfin, the landscaper who did the Chartreuse Cemetery in Bordeaux.

Virgile did not hide his admiration. He stopped for a moment to contemplate the Moniales Haut-Brion manor house, built on a hill in front of the cellars. It was surrounded by rows of grapevines and dominated the landscape without arrogance. The château was not huge, but the balance of its slate roof, the curve of its front steps, and the proportions of its facade, with wings that had white Doric columns on both sides, gave the building elegance. A creek called the Peugue flowed at the foot of the knoll, ending among the loose moss-covered cobblestones of a fountain. A small Baroque chapel, built in the seventeenth century, with a pink marble-encrusted pediment, stood in the shade of a chestnut tree. Flocks of birds chirped in the pale April light, and leaves rustled in the breeze.

"It is hard to imagine such a place in the middle of the city."

"It's a small piece of paradise, my dear Virgile, with a whiff of sulfur in it."

"I get that impression too, sir," the assistant said, arranging the samples carefully in the trunk of the car.

Benjamin drove back. They had to move quickly. Very quickly!

3

Benjamin rubbed his eyes. Once again, the night had been short. He gulped down half a teapot of Grand Yunnan, took a very hot shower, splashed on a healthy dose of Bel Ami aftershave, and dressed quickly, not really choosing his clothes. He had spent the entire night rereading his tasting notes, and he had a sharp pain in his lower back.

Elisabeth was still sleeping when he let Bacchus leap into the convertible. The setter sat in the passenger seat, his nose to the wind, a proud look in his eyes, and his ears perked to the understated accents and streamlined drama of a Gluck opera. Benjamin whistled the first measures of *Iphigenia in Taurus*; he was out of tune, but his heart was in it. This was his favorite opening of all, not because he thought it greater than the major works by Mozart or Verdi, but because it was concise. Benjamin had a predilection for openings, prologues, and introductions, whether they were symphonies, oratorios, or lyrical works. He had recorded many tapes and enjoyed them the same way he enjoyed a bottle of wine: for the pleasure of tasting, without feeling obliged to finish it.

The drive was short between Saint-Julien-Beychevelle, where Grangebelle was nestled, and the pier in the small port town of Lamarque. Benjamin drove the nine miles slowly to savor the crisp morning air and make the most of the always-comic show his quivering dog put on, his impertinent snout up to take in the view. The car was quickly loaded on the Médocain, a modern functional ferry stripped of all poetry. Benjamin felt nostalgia for the old captain, Commander Lemonnier, who skillfully piloted a straight-from-the-past boat called Les Deux Rives, an ancient potbellied tub whose curves became graceful when, in the hands of a real sailor, they caressed the sea foam. Lemonnier, a former Cape Horner and a formidable master mariner, had started piloting this freshwater crossing between inland Médoc and the Blaye citadel when he was well beyond seventy. He was capable of steering his boat through fog and dark nights without using any sophisticated navigational instruments. All he needed was a compass, a chronometer, and a tide schedule to avoid the mud banks and skirt the treacherous islands of Île Verte and Fort Pâté, with its headlands. It took him barely twenty minutes to reach the other bank, and it was a pleasure to watch him in the wheelhouse, examining his little black Moleskine notebook, where he had noted maneuvering speeds and course durations, giving orders with an authoritative voice, and landing at the pier without even lifting his eyes from his chronometer's silver box.

The other side was a foreign land, a place that you could reach with a cannon ball, if not with the lob of a slingshot. Like the kids from the Médoc, young Benjamin had dreamed of bloody attacks, galleys in distress, pirate raids, toothless buccaneers, and wild mutinies when he had spent summers here. And after a stormy night, when the current carried knotty peat, empty containers, and puffed-up plastic bags, he could still imagine combats and skinned corpses, their bellies filled with saltwater.

As soon as Benjamin landed on the right bank of the Gironde, he had the same feeling of adventure that had captivated him when his grandfather Eugène had taken him to visit Blaye. He parked the convertible in a downtown lot and headed toward the citadel. Bacchus barked and had already gone through the king's gate when Benjamin started over the bridge leading to the ramparts.

Their walk continued for two full hours. Dog and master explored the fortress at great length: the Minimes Convent, the barracks, the prison and the powder magazine, Dauphine counterscarp, Liverneuf gate, the central pavilion, and the fortified flanks. Benjamin perched on the Cônes stronghold, pausing for a long time to watch the estuary's slow-moving muddy water. He stared at a swirling eddy in the distance, then set his gaze on a sailboat before eyeing some lone branches washing against the foot of the cliff. Afterward, he climbed the Eguilette tower and took out his spiral notebook. He unscrewed the top of his fountain pen and jotted down some notes in his precise, swirled writing:

Vauban, a man from Dijon (develop this idea)... the two visits from the King (check the dates)... Fort-Médoc kids... fishing for freshwater river shrimp... plaice fillets, court-bouillon (recipe with fennel)... Roland de Roncevaux (be concise)... do not forget Ferri, layout of Fort Pâté... arms factory, troop housing... the water is yellow, brown even, flowerbeds of the houses on the right... shops without giving any details, clock above the bridge, stone watchtower.

He crossed out "stone" and replaced it with "suspended."

It was nearly noon when he turned back toward the middle of town. Bacchus was thirsty and was beginning to show signs of fatigue. Benjamin walked over to a cast-iron fountain and knelt beside the running water, cupping his hands to catch it for his dog to drink. They had enough time before the next ferry to visit an antique shop downtown. As soon as they passed through the beaded curtain, a lean man greeted them. He had the profile of a wading bird, as though he were an ancient hieratic sculpture carved in dry boxwood and lost among the shop's odds and ends.

"Mr. Cooker, I was just going to call you."

"You say that every time, my good man. One of these days I'm going to end up believing you," teased the winemaker.

"No, I mean it. I just received some marvels that have your name all over them."

"Show me your latest finds, but let me warn you, I did not come to Blaye to hunt for antiques. I do not even have a checkbook on me."

"Who even mentioned money?" the shopkeeper asked with a wily look in his eye. "Take a look, just for fun. And of course, if you have a little weakness for it, you can pay me later."

"Who says I have weaknesses?"

The secondhand-goods dealer unlocked a storage trunk lined with tarp and took out a brightly colored enameled-metal plaque depicting a wine from Saumur. Benjamin was among his best customers, or at least one of the most loyal, and the dealer knew he collected all manner of objects having to do with vineyards and wine. He had already sold him some fine pieces, notably still lifes full of bunches of grapes brightened with tin pitchers, well-made seventeenth- and eighteenth-century paintings, several mythological engravings of Bacchanalia, and various antique corkscrews from all over, some of them very rare. Among Benjamin's finest acquisitions were two well-preserved posters from 1937, one drawn by a certain A. Galland for the Ministry of Agriculture, which touted French wines for "health, gaiety, and hope." The other one was created by Jean Dupas and glorified the city of "Bordeaux, its port, its monuments, and its wines." It had a naked woman standing between the steeple of Saint-André Cathedral and a column generously endowed with clusters of grapes, from which emerged an ocean liner ringed with steam and an old sailboat. These posters brightened the winemaker's offices at 46 Allée de Tourny in Bordeaux.

"I already have this plaque," the winemaker said, somewhat disappointed. "It is very beautiful and typical of the period between the two wars. It looks a little less rusted than mine, but one is enough."

"Well then, I also have a magnificent tun barrel lock that could interest you."

"Magnificent! A *barre de portette*. This was used to keep the small opening at the bottom of a large cask closed. It is really beautiful!"

Benjamin brushed the bronze plate lightly with his fingers. It was decorated with two stylized fish crossing their fins and rubbing their scales in a wavelike movement. The bolt was attached to a wooden support that had the patina of age, but it worked perfectly.

"Are you going to charge me too high a price for this, as usual?"

"I haven't shown you everything yet," the salesman whispered with a mischievous look.

He slid his tall, emaciated body between two armoires and came back with an average-sized painting he placed in front of Benjamin.

"And what do you say about this?"

Benjamin remained silent, although there was much to say. He had been looking for this type of representation for quite some time. It was clear that the canvas dated to the end of the nineteenth century. A stocky winemaker armed with a glass pipette was standing next to a line of oak barrels. A candle on a stool brightened the cellar. The simple balanced composition, the fluidity, the blended colors, and the steady strokes gave this work a timeless feel while placing it in a clear framework. The man's clothing was the only element that spoke of the period, while the entire scene had the scent of eternity. How many times had Benjamin found himself in exactly the same position, among the casks, pipette in hand, sampling wine in nothing but candlelight?

"Do you even dare put a price on this painting?" the winemaker inquired without looking up.

The antique dealer dared and even quoted an amount high enough not to bear repeating.

"You know I don't like to haggle. I have always found that to be somewhat vulgar, but nonetheless…"

"Neither do I, and there is no discussion," the salesman said with a tact that Benjamin appreciated. "That is why I'll give you the barrel lock if you take the painting."

There would be no more bargaining. Benjamin left carrying both items and promised to send a check within the week.

The crossing home seemed longer than it had on the way over, but as usual, the ferry took only twenty minutes to reach the Médoc embankment. Had he gone by land, the drive to the Aquitaine Bridge would have cost him an hour and a half.

Benjamin was eager to show Elisabeth his purchases. She liked the painting but made a face when she saw the bronze lock. Still, she was glad that he had not come back with yet another grape-harvesting basket, wooden topping-up utensil, or silver tasting cup.

The evening was pleasant. Bacchus recovered from the day's excitement in front of the fireplace, where a fine blaze was crackling. The couple enjoyed a tête-à-tête with a meal that was simple enough to allow them to get to bed early.

When his wife had finally fallen asleep, and he felt her calm breathing, the winemaker got up quietly, put on a robe, and went to his office. He checked the ink cartridge in his fountain pen, placed a blank piece of paper at a slight angle under his left hand and began to write about the Blaye citadel.

"History sometimes has an irony that's worth recalling. The land of Bordeaux owes its salvation to a child of Burgundy. When King Louis XIV ordered Vauban, who was born in 1633 in Saint-Léger-de-Foucheret, to build a fortress, several projects had already been…"

Benjamin sighed. A bad start. Not entirely useless, but a little heavy-handed. The city of Blaye had already made it through several centuries before the man from Burgundy unrolled his plans. Yes, Vauban did leave behind a ninety-four-acre fortress with a 2,640-foot-long wall around it and underground passages to protect two thousand people, but violent confrontations had reddened both estuary and dry land before Vauban had built the rough-and-ready bastions.

He opened the cigar box at the corner of his desk and lit up a sweet San Luis Rey robusto, drawing in a deep puff with great pleasure as he leaned back on the headrest. The vitola immediately delivered spicy flavors of green pepper and cinnamon. The smoke, which was not too ample, rose up, round and light. The tobacco was not strong, but developed an aromatic richness in which he could easily discern honey, caramel, and cacao. Benjamin remained in the same position for over half an hour, his mind elsewhere. Then he returned to his pen.

"Blaye is called Bordeaux's first rampart. Much is said about this rocky headland. Many popular legends and a few invented stories surround it. Some say that its name comes from the Latin *belli via* (translation: war road); others affirm that a Gallic warrior named Blavos (Blavius in Latin) founded it; people also talk about Blavia, a Celtic word that landed here on the battle path. In any case, Blaye's history is above all..."

Benjamin started yawning. The muscles in his back were sore, and his eyes were stinging. He set down his pen without capping it, crushed out his half-smoked Havana in the ashtray, turned out his lamp, and joined Elisabeth, who, snuggled in the warmth of the comforter, grumbled when she felt his cold body.

4

After answering a few letters from some persnickety readers, filling out a check for the antique dealer in Blaye, checking with his secretary to make sure that the invoice registry was updated, and planning several meetings for fall with Beaujolais estate owners, Benjamin Cooker left his office on the Allée de Tourny and walked to the laboratory he had set up on the Cours du Chapeau Rouge. Virgile was early and had introduced himself to the staff. By the time his employer came in, the assistant was already deep in discussion with Alexandrine de la Palussière, who was in charge of biological testing.

"I see you did not waste any time getting to know each other," Benjamin commented, catching his breath.

"Hello, Mr. Cooker. You didn't take the elevator?" asked the young woman.

Virgile Lanssien shook Benjamin's hand, taking care to control his grip.

"Don't worry, Alexandrine, I'll survive," the winemaker said, still panting, his hands on his lower back. "It will be my only workout for the entire month."

Alexandrine de la Palussière was a discreetly elegant Bordeaux woman who often wore clamdiggers, showing off her tanned calves. She was around thirty, of average height and delicate, with a small upturned nose, green eyes, and bob-cut auburn hair held back with a clear mother-of-pearl headband. On this day, she was wearing a white blouse with the first two buttons astutely undone and a pair of beige leather flats. She was the last child in a line of fallen aristocrats and was not afraid to depart from the rules of her rank by pursuing advanced studies and working like a common mortal. In times past, her family had owned several acres of vineyards in the Haut Médoc, dominated by an enormous château. Her grandfather had ended up squandering this inheritance in Biarritz casinos and the posh bedrooms of high-class prostitutes. Unlike some penniless petty nobles who clung to appearances, this young woman bore no resemblance to the "dying race" that could still be found in Bordeaux. She was bright, pragmatic, and unpretentious, satisfied to contribute her scientific knowledge to the world of wine that had for so long enriched and nourished her family.

"Where do things stand, Alexandrine?" the winemaker asked when his breathing had returned to normal.

"I need five to eight days to get a reliable colony count."

"That is way too long!"

"But that is the time needed to correctly isolate the yeast and take a count."

"You've gotten me used to miracles. We need to find a quicker solution, even some sort of emergency response, if possible!"

"I can't make any promises, but we could possibly get quicker results by combining plating with a direct colony hybridization. We'll need to use a specific sporulating Brettanomyces probe coupled with peroxidase. After membrane filtration and culture, in forty-eight hours I should be able to tell you if I can detect the micro-colonies."

"Please, Alexandrine, make things simple!" Benjamin cut in.

The young woman's green almond-shaped eyes showed a trace of irritation.

"Mr. Cooker, you know well enough that it is never simple to make things simple!"

"I'll grant you that," Benjamin said in a softer tone.

"What I can tell you is that there is no doubt about the nature of the contamination."

"There's no mistaking that smell of horse piss," said Virgile.

Alexandrine ignored the comment and continued. "The smell of ethyl phenol becomes clearly perceptible once you reach six hundred micrograms per liter. I believe there's an even greater concentration in the samples you brought."

"Do you need more samples?"

"It would be interesting to follow any changes on a daily basis while we are waiting for the first results."

"Virgile will take care of that."

"With pleasure," the assistant murmured without turning his attention away from Alexandrine.

"If I use a consistent approach, I should be able to get a rather reliable quantification, although I won't be able to discriminate perfectly between the living and dead cells, but it would be a good start. An increase in the concentration of phenols would certainly allow me to determine the threshold of alternation, and we could come up with a response strategy," she said.

She perceived worry underneath the winemaker's imperturbable stiff upper lip. In response, she shrugged and shook her head, telegraphing that she wished she could say more.

"The only decision you can make today is to isolate the contaminated wine."

"Thank you, Alexandrine. I would like you to be the only person working on this case. Handle it personally, and make sure that it stays confidential."

"Of course, Mr. Cooker. You can count on me. I do not know the owner of this estate, but tell him that we will find a solution."

"I will try to reassure him."

"In any case, insist that he do nothing until I have defined the exact pH of the wine, the oxidation, and the colonies. He needs to avoid sorbic acid at all cost. It is totally ineffective in red wines, because it is very unstable in the presence of the high levels of lactic acid bacteria found in reds."

"Call me as soon as you have something new," the winemaker concluded.

Then he quickly made the rounds in the offices to greet the other staff members and introduce Virgile Lanssien. He couldn't help pausing for a moment at the windows that opened onto the port, and then he reviewed the results of ure-thane-concentration tests that had been done on stone-fruit brandy. He scanned the report without going into the details, which covered the carcinogenic risk linked to urethane and fruit purees.

When it came time to leave the lab, he found Virgile doing his best to engage Alexandrine. He signaled that it was time to leave and walked out to the landing. His assistant was quick to join him.

"I understand your attraction, Virgile," Benjamin said in a low voice. "But you would be wrong to pursue her."

"Is that so?"

"I think that boys have little effect on her."

"Are you saying she's…"

"I think that she is more moved by my secretary."

"I never would have thought it. And I usually have a nose for detecting that kind of woman."

"Virgile, think about getting your nose out of the glass from time to time."

The Rue des Faures smelled of lamb. The heavy aroma of spices and grilled meat rose up in thick swirls from the hodgepodge of Arab shops, suitcase stores, and faded bistros. Benjamin pretended he was lost in the small streets weaving through the Saint-Michel neighborhood, lingering a little to take full advantage of the moment and enjoy the few stolen hours away from the upscale atmosphere in the Quinconces quarter.

Virgile had returned to the Moniales Haut-Brion with instructions to carefully monitor the sample-taking process. They would meet around ten in the morning to come up with a battle plan to fight the yeast, whose presence the winemaker was having trouble explaining.

Benjamin was holding the painting he had bought in Blaye against his chest. He had wrapped it carefully in brown paper and was on his way to Pascale Dartigeas's restoration workshop near the Passage Saint-Michel. He pressed the doorbell and was greeted by the recorded croaking of a tree frog, which had replaced the original chimes.

"Come in, Mr. Cooker!"

Pascale Dartigeas appeared in a long white smock, a dainty paintbrush in her hand and a rebellious lock of hair hovering on her forehead. She was a beautiful forty years old. When she smiled, crow's-feet appeared at the corners of her blue-gray eyes, and pretty dimples emerged in her cheeks. She showed the signs of a woman who had experienced a lot of unrestrained, selfless love, along with intense joy and periods of abandonment. She had certainly been disappointed by the thoughtlessness of men.

"Hello, Pascale. You look well today."

"Thank you," she said, brushing the hair off her forehead. "I hope you are not here for your overmantel panel. It won't be ready before the end of the month, if all goes well."

"Don't worry. Take your time. I only came to show you my latest extravagance."

"Extravagant people feel very much at home here."

Benjamin carefully removed the brown paper and showed his painting with a satisfied smile.

"What do you think of that?"

"I have nothing to say, Mr. Cooker. It is more than charming. It is—"

"—just what I love," the winemaker interrupted.

"I have no doubt about that, but mostly, it's surprising. I mean, it's very curious. Have you noticed the man's face?"

"What's in the man's face? Is something wrong with it?" Benjamin grumbled, suddenly worried.

"Nothing serious, but it doesn't look like it was part of the original painting. I think it has been repainted. It's a rough job and not very recent, but it was added by another painter."

"Are you sure?"

The art restorer called out to her intern, who was working in the back room, and asked her to bring a black light.

"Let me introduce Julie, who is doing her apprenticeship."

Benjamin nodded at the young blond with big blue eyes. The cleavage of her small breasts and her long legs molded into a pair of tight jeans would certainly have driven Virgile wild. The apprentice flashed an ambiguous smile that threw the winemaker off a little. Pascale Dartigeas took the Wood's lamp from her and ran it above the canvas. A dark stain appeared. All three of them leaned over the painting as she repeated the operation several times.

"There is no doubt. It has been repainted. I propose that we clean it up and see what's underneath. Julie can start on that later today. Of course, that is if you will allow her to get a little behind on your overmantel, because she is the one who is working with solvents right now. For the time being, I'm touching up the wings of this Baroque angel you see over there, and I don't have time to do the cleaning myself."

"No problem, Pascale. I trust your judgment. And my overmantel appears to be in good hands."

The apprentice, who was either timid or just reserved, ran her tongue over her teeth. She seemed ready to say something but was second-guessing herself.

"What is it, Julie?" Pascale said.

"Have you talked to Mr. Cooker about the second overmantel?" the intern asked in a soft voice.

"Oh, of course, what was I thinking?" said the art restorer. "I almost forgot to tell you that Julie worked on an overmantel that was identical to yours when she did her internship with my colleagues on the Rue Notre-Dame."

Benjamin appeared irritated by this news. He had been certain that it was unique. He would demand an explanation from his antique dealer in Blaye soon enough, but Julie's steady voice and blue eyes calmed him. There was grape harvesting, with people in the rows of grapevines, a small creek and rather tall, very green trees on the side, along with a manor with ocher-colored walls at the bottom. Yet even though the cracking and snail-shaped scaling were similar, the paintings were not exactly the same. No doubt the same painter had done both overmantels. The aging, impasto, traces of mold, gaps, and colors she had to regenerate all corresponded.

When she finished talking, Benjamin had trouble detaching himself from her blue eyes, which seemed to grow brighter and brighter as her face became more animated.

"Do you know the owner of the overmantel, Mademoiselle?" he asked, visibly excited.

"It belongs to Dr. Bladès, an ear-nose-throat specialist who works in the Saint-Gènes neighborhood. I think his office is on the Cours de l'Argonne."

"I'm curious to see this overmantel. Can you see the little chapel near the manor house?"

"No, and it is just that detail that gives character to yours. Particularly the edge of the facade, which is especially delicate," Julie said.

"It is the Mission Haut-Brion chapel. Monks dedicated it to the Virgin Mary toward the end of the seventeenth century. There is no mistaking it, and I agree with you, it gives the painting character."

"I took a picture of your overmantel before we started working on it, if you are interested," said Pascale Dartigeas. "I'll lend it to you, but you'll have to remember to bring it back for my records. In the meantime, what do we do with this repainted face of your cellar master?"

"I don't know. Do your best, as always!"

"In that case, I have a proposition for you. We could do a portrait of you and replace the man's face with yours. This was what people used to do, and I'm sure that this man has taken on the various identities of each one of the painting's owners."

The winemaker found the idea amusing and promised to come back with a picture for the restorer to use as inspiration. Then he asked if he could consult one of the eight volumes of the *Benezit Dictionary of Artists* to determine who was behind the painting's signature. It was a certain T. Roussy, whom he found quickly on page three ninety-five of volume seven covering artists with names between "Poute" and "Syn," as shown in gold lettering on the spine of the book, which was the color of wine lees. Benjamin removed the cap of his fountain pen, took hold of his spiral notebook, and leaned over the table to jot down the information.

"Toussaint Roussy, born in Sète (Hérault) in 1847 (French School). Studied at the School of Fine Arts. Curator at the museum in Sète. His career began at the 1877 Salon. The Sète museum has the following works: *The Fiddler's Lunch, The Swiss Church, Entry to the Port of Sète, Beer Hour.* The museum in Béziers has *The Cooper's Refreshment Stall.*"

The winemaker closed the thick volume and took leave of the two women with the courteous deference that spoke of his traditional upbringing and good British manners. When he left the workshop, he crossed the Place Saint-Michel and bought a lamb kebab from a tiny take-out. Then he went to sit at the base of the bell tower facing the church.

Around him, a group of acne-faced teenagers were playing with a soft-drink can. Another group of young Kabyles from northern Algeria was shooting hoops on an outdoor court near the Gothic bell tower. On the steps in front of the church, a couple of lovers whispered to each other. Nobody paid any attention to Benjamin Cooker. The sun was warm, and no heads turned to see him savor his too-fatty, too-spicy overcooked sandwich that should have ended up in the first garbage can he found.

5

Dark clouds swept in with the tide change in the early afternoon, and a light, damp wind began to blow. The shrieking of the seagulls dissipated along the docks, a reminder that the ocean lapped right up to the city gates.

Before returning to Grangebelle, where he hoped to work on his manuscript, Benjamin Cooker made a detour to the Moniales Haut-Brion. He found Virgile busy in the cellars with two of the estate's workers. The contaminated barrels had been isolated, and they were preparing to decant them into stainless-steel tanks. The winemaker's visit was not particularly appreciated when he announced that two other barrels needed to be set apart as quickly as possible. Alexandrine de la Palussière had left a message on Benjamin's cell phone, indicating the numbers of the barrels in which she had detected worrisome quantities of the yeast.

"The full scope of this hasn't hit me yet," Denis Massepain said with a sigh.

"Keep your spirits up. We will find a solution," Benjamin said. "I can't guarantee that we will save the entire production, but we will limit the damage."

"Six barrels! Do you realize what that means? Six barrels are already ruined."

Benjamin quickly calculated the extent of the disaster. It represented about eighteen hundred bottles, as each barrel held just over fifty-nine gallons. If they didn't find an effective parry, this would be a serious loss for the winery, which had only 12.85 acres of vineyard. He was not the full-time winemaker at this estate, but he knew its ins and outs perfectly. They left nothing to chance here, and the Moniales could have served as an example for any winemaking school. They set their planting density correctly at ninety-five hundred plants per two and a half acres. They grew grape varieties that corresponded to the Appellation d'Origine Contrôlée for Pessac-Léognan, with forty percent merlot, fifteen percent cabernet franc, and forty-five percent cabernet sauvignon. The average age of the vines was thirty years. They neglected none of the necessary steps in caring for the vines' development, with experienced personnel removing shoots, pruning buds, and thinning out leaves and plants. Hand harvesting meant that each parcel got the greatest care. Each batch spent a reasonable period of fifteen to twenty-four days in tanks. Barrel aging lasted around eighteen months, favoring the most traditional malolactic fermentation. And nobody could reproach sanitation on the premises.

"I just can't figure out what's gone wrong. This is very strange indeed," Benjamin said.

"What can we do?" Denis asked, running a nervous hand through his hair.

"Okay, so we have three new barrels and three others dating from last year. Is that correct?"

"Yes, you know that I renew half of the barrels each year. That is exactly what I can't explain. It can't come from the wood!"

"I know your supplier. He produces superior barrels. My secretary called the cooperage, and they checked their orders and delivery dates. None of the other estates have had any problems. But I don't agree that it doesn't come from the wood."

"Why? What's your idea?"

"Wood is the only vector that facilitates such a quick contamination. You know as well as I do that it harbors and protects all kinds of contaminants. One slip in monitoring or a sulfur dioxide addition that's a little shy and—"

"Let me stop you right there," Denis Massepain interrupted. "If the wood were contaminated, it would not be limited to a specific number of barrels. The whole production would be polluted, if only because of handling and the cross-use of cellar equipment."

"Virgile!" Benjamin shouted in the direction of the fermenting room. "Come here. I need to ask you something."

The assistant appeared without delay, his face sweating.

"Can you decant the six barrels?"

"Right now?" the assistant asked, a little taken aback.

"Why? Are you in some hurry? Do you have a date?"

"No, sir, but, uh, that could take some time. We won't finish before the middle of the night."

"In this line of work, you need to know how to stay up late, young man. And now you are going to experience your first night nursing the sick."

"I can ask my two workers to stay," said the owner. "And I'll change, because I think we'll need at least four people."

So Denis Massepain returned to the manor house to change out of his city clothes, and Benjamin took his assistant aside to talk to him quietly. He reviewed each of the steps involved in decanting the barrels and asked Virgile to make sure he eliminated the lees and deposits, to do it in a sheltered place, and to reference the metal tanks using the barrel numbers. He also asked that each of the empty barrels be set outside the cellar and covered with tarps.

"Do you have any questions?" the winemaker asked, looking at his watch.

Virgile promised that he would follow his instructions exactly and reminded Benjamin that it was a bad time to take the beltway or the main streets. He would end up stuck in traffic with everyone coming home from work.

"You're right," Benjamin said, making a face. "I had better not return to Médoc right away. I'll drop in on someone who is not expecting me."

Dr. Pierre Baldès had cleverly distributed the folds of his shirt in a vain attempt to hide a slight paunch. He had a plain elegance found in men who have been established for some time and a certain bearing despite his growing portliness and skin exposed too often to the sun. Benjamin nodded a greeting as he entered the office, feeling a little sleepy after spending two hours in the waiting room browsing the mundane gossip in the magazines and listening to annoyed patients snort.

"Please sit down, sir. What can I do for you?" the ENT doctor asked with the particular indifference found in older clinical practitioners.

"Well, I'm quite healthy. My nose is intact, and my palate still alert. I do not have any problems to speak of, Doctor."

The doctor stared at Benjamin, wondering if he was dealing with a joker or someone who was chronically depressed.

"Please excuse me. I have not introduced myself. Benjamin Cooker here. I have come to discuss something that is, well, uh, personal."

"I'm reassured. For a minute there, I thought I had a crazy one on my hands." Pierre Baldès smiled, pinching his lips a little.

"I would like to talk to you about a painting," Benjamin said, getting straight to the point.

"A painting? Correct me if I'm wrong, you are Cooker, from the *Cooker Guide*?"

"Yes, and as it turns out, we both bought the same painting. Well, nearly the same. Let's just say that we have two paintings that look very much the same."

"I don't understand what you are talking about," said the doctor. "We have two paintings that are the same, but they're not really the same? And what work of art are you referring to?"

"A late-nineteenth-century overmantel that you had restored on the Rue Notre-Dame. It is a rural scene showing grape harvesting under a blue sky, with a building in the background."

"Yes, I have that painting. And you are telling me that you own the same one or nearly the same one? I am very surprised.

It is a rather minor work. Well done, yes, but fairly naive. I do not think that it could have been interesting enough to copy."

"That is what I think, as well," interrupted Benjamin. "And that is why I have come to see you. Would it be too much to ask to have five minutes of your time to see your overmantel? I won't be long. The time of an appointment, no longer."

"An appointment that's not covered by your insurance?" the doctor joked. "In that case, it could end up costing you a lot."

"I don't want to impose on you. I could stop by another day."

"No, not at all. Follow me."

They went through a hidden doorway and climbed the stairs to Baldès's apartment. It was well appointed, elegant but conventional. It looked like a spread in an interior design magazine, with just that touch of originality, that fanciful detail and hint of color acceptable and necessary to justify the decorator's fee.

The overmantel reigned over a white marble fireplace in front of two large purple sofas. The frame had been restored with gold leaf, and the original mirror seemed to be just as mottled as Benjamin's. There was no doubt about it. They had been done by the same artist. The same soft light, subdued by dark leafy vegetation, bathed the scene. The rows of vines formed waves descending toward the bottom of the hill, giving an identical perspective, although the people here had their backs to the painter and were harvesting in small groups of two and three. In the distance, it was easy to make out the stout silhouette of the manor house, whose roof could belong to none other than the Haut-Brion château.

"Just what I thought," Benjamin murmured, moving closer to the painting.

"And that is?"

"You see those two square towers on the left and the projection on the right wing, with its two pointed roof turrets? It can be none other than Haut-Brion."

"I confirm," Baldès said in a near whisper, as if he did not want to disturb the winemaker's thoughts.

"That is a very fine surprise. Very fine, indeed! I own your painting's twin, except that mine represents Mission Haut-Brion."

"And it is a harvest scene, as well?" the doctor asked.

"With just a few minor differences. It has the same perspective, the same tones, the same characters, and the same trees. I have a snapshot from before it was cleaned and restored."

Benjamin stepped back a couple of feet and took out the picture that Pascale Dartigeas had lent him. He closed one eye and held it at arm's length toward the overmantel.

"Yes, I'm under the impression that these two painting belong together, Dr. Baldès. Look closely. Yours is on the right, and the trees on the left side fit perfectly with the trees on mine."

The doctor took the photograph and lifted it to see it in perspective. He half-closed his left eye and looked perplexed.

"Focus on the left side of the painting," Benjamin advised. "After a while, it will jump out at you."

"You're right. The two scenes go together. It's incredible. There is a perfect continuity between the poplar trees, the cloud, the little pond, and the rows of grapevines."

"Do you know where yours came from?" Benjamin asked.

"I bought it from an antique dealer in Maynac. For next to nothing, I must admit. But the restoration cost me quite a bit."

"I found mine in Blaye. The price was not particularly excessive either, but quite a bit of restoration work is needed to fix some serious tears and fly specks, and the sky needs touching up."

"They must have been stored under terrible conditions."

"I have to admit that I am curious about where they came from."

"Probably a local château or some bourgeois home. You'll need to ask an art specialist or historian. I know of only one person who could tell you, if he were willing to talk to you."

"And where would I find him?"

"In Pessac. His name is Ferdinand Ténotier, and he lives in the Cité Frugès. He's easy to find, and you can't mistake him. A strange fellow, but he has a brilliant mind. He used to teach at the university, which apparently fired him over some serious issue. He's been retired for as long as I've known him, and there is no telling how old he is."

"A historian?" Benjamin asked.

"Better than that. He has no specialty but is an expert in everything. You can always try to see him, but I wish you luck with that."

Before taking his leave, Benjamin offered to buy the doctor's overmantel, making it clear that he was willing to pay a nice sum for it. The doctor gave an evasive and polite response.

"Perhaps," he said. "I'll have to think about it."

Benjamin could tell from Pierre Baldès's tone that he would never sell his painting. He hid his disappointment and agreed to autograph a copy of the latest edition of the *Cooker Guide,* which the doctor had on his shelf.

6

Benjamin Cooker drove slowly through the town of Pessac and then parked his convertible in the shade of a scraggly pine tree. It did not take him long to find the old Ferdinand Ténotier in the Cité Frugès, a working-class neighborhood designed in 1925 by Le Corbusier at the request of industrialist Henri Frugès. The homes were made of reinforced concrete and had angular facades and suspended decks. A few had been renovated over the years, their original blue and green hues covered up. On the whole, however, the modernist garden housing development was a chaotic landscape, with blocks of eroded buildings emerging from sickly vegetation.

When Benjamin asked where he could find Ténotier, some people tensed up, while others joked. All agreed that the former professor was crazy and dangerous. He lived at 12 Rue Le Corbusier, in a ramshackle building where the dreams of the great visionary architect were showing a number of cracks. Benjamin planted himself in front of the structure and observed the leprous walls, the original wooden shutters all askew, the rusted drainpipes, sheet-metal roofing that was falling in on one side, and the large patches of mold that marbled the gray cement.

He knocked several times before a red, somewhat bitter-looking face deigned to appear in the half-open doorway. Benjamin Cooker introduced himself, smiling pleasantly and saying his name in a clear voice that didn't seem overly ingratiating.

"I know who you are," the man said curtly.

"Thank you for seeing me. I need your insight, Mr. Ténotier. I was told that you are the only—"

"Who's talking about me?"

The interview was going to be touch and go. The man was suspicious, but Benjamin had expected this. Ténotier had an extremely piercing look and poor teeth behind thin lips. He had gone several days without shaving. His greasy hair hung under the collar of a grimy shirt. He had neglected his nails. His nose was spongy, his cheeks hollow and full of blotches. His back was hunched, and his breath was bad enough to asphyxiate a herd of buffaloes. He reeked of solitude and hatred, intelligence and abandonment. A man to avoid.

"Dr. Pierre Baldès told me that you most certainly could—"

"That one still thinks about me, does he?"

"He had nothing but good to say about you."

"Compliments are cheap."

"I assure you—

"Will it take long?" the old man spit out in a wine-dripped hiccup.

"I'll be quick, no more than a quarter of an hour," Benjamin said with a composure he often called upon in prickly situations.

"In that case," Ténotier grumbled, disappearing to let the winemaker pass.

As soon as Benjamin entered the main room, a violent smell of ammonia stung his throat and nose. A cat brushed between his legs, followed by two others, and then came a whole drove of raw-boned felines he could vaguely make out in the darkness. A shredded blanket covered a picture window, and weak rays of light filtered through the torn fabric.

"Sit down," Ténotier muttered, pointing to a chair where a tabby, as scrawny as all the others, was sleeping.

Benjamin preferred to sit on a heavily clawed stool. The old man set two sturdy glasses down on the table, grabbed a cardboard pack, and poured some red wine.

"We'll drink together. I'm sure it's been quite some time since you tasted a wine like this one," Ténotier threw out, with a hint of provocation in his raspy voice.

Without letting himself be disconcerted, Benjamin lifted the glass to his lips and swallowed a mouthful of revolting plonk that burned his throat.

"That's true. It has been a long time," he said, making a face.

"Everything is going to hell! I drink something that doesn't deserve to be called wine from square packs and cardboard kegs. I drink shit because I'm poor, sir, but I'm not ashamed to be poor. I'm only ashamed of the times we live in, of what people throw to guys like me. I'm ashamed that people actually dare to sell crap like this on the pretext that others like me can't afford anything else. It's shit, I'm telling you!"

Despite his advanced state of alcoholism, his dirty fingernails, and the havoc and feverishness on his face, Ferdinand Ténotier had a lyrical disillusionment like that of a wise man who had probed humanity until he reached self-disgust and hatred. He seemed precipitously near the end of his rope.

"This is the first time I've been here. I had no idea that the development was so spread out," Benjamin noted, thinking it best to change the subject.

"It's a ghost town, a concrete cemetery. That's what it has become! And the middle classes get off on moving into a historical area. It's all being bought up by architects, doctors, lawyers—people who think they know something. They invest in cultural heritage. Some heritage. Just junk!"

"It is a surprising place, though. Have you lived here for a long time?"

"Fifty years. A little more even. My parents lived here before me. They were real working-class people. Good people. Nothing in their heads, but huge hearts. We're all screwed. The working class is all gone."

Ferdinand Ténotier downed his glass in one shot and poured himself another, a lost look in his eyes, his head down.

"It was a pioneering idea in the nineteen twenties," Benjamin said. "This concrete housing development with large picture windows, private bathrooms, and gardens."

He regretted his words as soon as they came out. The old man threw him a ferocious look and spilled his wine on his shirtsleeve.

"Le Corbusier was just a bunch of theories. He was an ideological con artist, a communist asshole who sold his body to patrons to build dumps for the proletariat. I shit on those illusionists who preached social justice, humankind, and all that crap, who filled their pockets until they burst. And above all, sir, they continue to sermonize, to give us lessons about how to live.

"Mediocrity killed off all the real thinkers. Nobody ever listens to people who really think, because thinking is harmful. You understand, nobody will lend an ear to anyone who says what we really are and where we are really headed. We should blow up all the universities and schools where they don't even know how to speak Latin anymore, where everyone thinks that Roland Garros was a tennis player. They harbor soft asses, ignoramuses, little neat and clean people, career-minded shit eaters who will go on strike only when it doesn't interfere with their schedules and their vacation leave. They want to pretend to carry out a revolution, but only if it doesn't threaten their mortgages, their lawnmowers, and their savings accounts. They are dying of comfort, with empty heads and full stomachs.

"Le Corbusier loved glory, medals, and money. The bastard hated the people. He knew nothing about the little people. Because they stink, they smell of sweat, they shit out kids by the truckload, they use bad words, the people! Mind you, Le Corbusier had at least one thing going for him, his first name was Charles Edouard, and that nobody could take away from him. He had a very French first name, a small saving grace."

He drank two glasses of wine, one after the other, wiped off his mustache with the back of his hand, and stared at his visitor. His eyes were bright, very black, and it was impossible to make out the pupils.

"Why are you here?" he asked, rubbing his stubble-covered cheeks.

Benjamin took out the picture of his overmantel and gave it to the old man, who slid it under a ray of warm light.

"Ah, you too," Ténotier chuckled.

"You certainly know that Pierre Baldès has a similar painting. I guess he also came to see you."

"Yes, he came, and he refused to drink my poison. Spineless!"

Benjamin took this as a compliment.

"Come on, let's drink to all those delicate doctors! Bottoms up! Raise your glass to all those savant monkeys who can't read Hippocrates in the original." Ferdinand burped and filled up his glass.

He loudly clinked Benjamin's glass.

"Your painting is Mission Haut-Brion. The doc's represents the Château de Haut-Brion. I have nothing else to tell you."

"That I knew already," Benjamin said, without showing any impatience. "But what is most astonishing is that they go together. The right side of my painting joins up perfectly with the left side of Baldès's. They must be part of a two-paneled work made for some sort of mural."

"Probably," grumbled Ferdinand.

"And I am curious to know where they come from, since the theme is rather rare."

"Your lousy paintings aren't famous. They're hackwork."

"I think they are rather well done for that kind of painting," Benjamin said. "A little naive, yes, and rather broadly drawn, but they are not lacking in character. And the lighting is well mastered, particularly where the sky meets the trees. They have a nice brushstroke to them."

"Well, sir, I believe that everyone should be held accountable for his own taste. Only the spineless say the contrary. But I don't have time to waste on two worthless sketches just because they were painted locally."

Benjamin caught the reference as it flew by.

"You are sure that these works were painted by an artist in the region? Perhaps a painter from Pessac?"

"When the doc came to see me, he brought his painting, and I admit I had the feeling I had seen it somewhere before. But at the time, I couldn't for the life of me remember where."

"And has it come back to you since?" the winemaker asked, trying not to look too insistent.

"I think so."

Ferdinand Ténotier filled up their glasses again. He threw the empty cardboard carton to the back of the room and leaned over to grab another one from the floor.

"These overmantels were in the reading room at the Château de Vallon," the old man said. "I saw them at the beginning of the nineteen fifties, when they were still hanging above the fireplace, which was made of Pyrenees marble."

"The Château de Vallon?" the winemaker said, surprised. "I seem to recall seeing a label with that name on it on an old bottle."

"If you still have that bottle, guard it with vigilance. It's a relic!"

"I don't have it in my wine cellar, but I certainly saw it at an auction or something like that."

"Those damned urban planners made their way through there!" barked the old man. "The Château de Vallon was totally destroyed in 1966, and you'll find a housing project where it stood. Isn't the republic a beautiful thing! Always ready to trash what belongs to us! The châteaux in Pessac that have been torn down in recent years all belonged to us, to you, to me, to everyone! We all own our history! The people of France. I tell you, it all belongs to the people of France! What a wretched shame. A handsome château like Vallon. It was built in 1777 by Victor Louis, the same architect who built Bordeaux's Grand Théâtre. It had a sloping roof, a large flight of stairs, huge grounds, and then there were the vineyards. Several acres that produced a fine red Graves. If my memory still serves me, I believe it got a silver medal at the Bordeaux fair in 1895."

"I can check my archives, if you're interested," Benjamin offered.

"You want archives. I'll show you some you'll never see again."

Ténotier had trouble standing up, then staggered to the greasy buffet and brought back a shoebox full of sepia-colored photographs and ancient postcards. His hands trembled.

"Look at that! Château Fanning-Lafontaine, torn down in 1980. The grounds were remarkable, with rare tree species, including some Louisiana cypress that the Baron Sarget imported. There were acres and acres of vineyards right next to the Haut-Brion estates. There was a workers' clinic there before it got sold off. If you go there now, you'll find a housing development. Here, this is a picture of the Château Condom, which belonged to Dr. Azam, the father-in-law of the great historian Camille Jullian. Another housing development. In 1921! They drew a road right through the middle of the estate, right there where you see the orange trees. It's sickening. What a waste!"

He gulped another glass of wine as he continued to go through his documents. His commentary became harsher and harsher. There was sadness mixed with violence in the pathetic drunk's voice. Benjamin couldn't help feeling something himself in seeing these images of a time that had already been forgotten, lost in gravel and cement blocks. The Château Monbalon, an estate that spread over one hundred and twenty acres, including twelve with vineyards, five with prairies, five more that were farmed, and eighty-nine with pinewood forest and private hunting grounds. There, in 1927, the Mirante housing development grew up like a wart, before the château itself was destroyed in 1982 because it had fallen into disrepair. The same thing happened to the Domaine de Macédo and the Château Haut-Bourgailh. Just like the great estate of Haut-Livrac, one of the oldest noble homes in Pessac, which produced fifteen barrels of fine wine annually before urbanization devoured it. The same destiny was reserved for the Château Haut-Lévêque and its six barrels of red wine, the Château Bersol and its fifteen barrels, and Château Halloran, which produced twenty-six barrels of well-structured wine before being turned into a hospital. All these elegant monuments, surrounded by landscaped grounds and domesticated vines, disappeared at the dawn of the 1960s to create an industrial zone.

Ténotier had a few words, a date, a reminder, a legend, a political allusion, a sharp comment, or a mean statement to make for each photo. This man's bad-mouthing and his endless knowledge began to seduce Benjamin, who enjoyed listening to the point of sipping his cheap wine without balking.

"Here is a postcard I always have a hard time looking at," the old man continued. "The Château Saige-Formanoir pissed out fifteen or so tanks of red wine at the end of the nineteenth century, and then the fifteen acres of vineyards were pulled out in 1956, the same year the Garonne River froze over. That was the beginning of the end. Starting in 1970, they built eight eighteen-story buildings on the estate. All that so that four thousand idiots could have hot water, an elevator, a tiny balcony, and the opportunity to hear their neighbors fart.

"But the worst was the university, with its thirty thousand students who arrived in 1979. Are there really thirty thousand kids capable of reasoning and writing a dissertation without any spelling mistakes? Do we really need all those fact-stuffed brains to keep the country going? They tore down the Château de Rocquencourt to set up a sports complex on the campus: nearly six hundred and twenty acres of intellectual desert for brats who buy soft drinks and don't give a shit that it wrecked acres of vineyards!"

There was already a serious dent in the second carton of wine when old Ferdinand began telling the story of the Haut-Brion domaine. Of course, Benjamin knew the basic outline, as he had become interested in this exceptional spot very early on, but he was dumbfounded by the fallen professor's encyclopedic knowledge; the institution must have judged him as disreputable as he was cumbersome. Ténotier was a smooth drunk. His hesitating elocution and crimson face showed his fatigue, but he babbled with panache and made theatrical gestures as if inspired. His presentation was littered with anecdotes, details, dynastic successions, historical perspectives, religious references, risqué episodes, obscure testimonials, legal cases, pertinent trade analyses, climate vagaries, and vintages.

"Do you know *The Pessac March*? The Saint-Orens family wrote the song, the music by the father and the words by the son. A fine piece of idiocy," he shouted out as he began to sing with all his heart.

> Pessac, jewel of the 'burbs,
> Making Bordeaux ever more superb,
> Eastward, on for some miles,
> Can be seen its gleaming roof tiles.
> All around its aging church
> And the old town's ancient birch
> Dressed with pretty, stylish flowers
> Are rising practical, modern towers.

His voice was quaking, both fluty and hoarse. He caught his breath between two stanzas.

> Both farmers and winemaker manors
> Pushed away by town planners
> As outward grew the city,
> With no nostalgia and no pity.
> Yet Pessac held tight in its bosom
> A gem worthy of its wisdom,
> That source of ever-grand wine,
> Moniales Haut-Brion and its vine.

The last note was prolonged, suspended in the air of sour wine.

"And it goes on like that for eight verses. Those were the days," he said, looking into the distance. "Today, if you want to dabble in bagpipes, you have to confine yourself to the Pessac Accordion Club in a concrete music school. You'll never make good musicians by locking them up in an old factory. They need to breathe, to fill their lungs. There's also the Pessac ditty by Edouard Trouilh. The melody is not very complicated, only one flat in the key.

He blew his nose into his fingers, cleared his throat, and began to hum an approximate melody.

Two things keep me alive,
The only reasons I survive,
Haut-Brion and my Belle
Nothing could be so swell,
One for its drunken charms,
The other to hold in my arms.

"It's all bunk, trivial, but it was a time when you could still sing after a meal without being considered an idiot. The girls were trusting, and the boys as voracious as they are today, but things were less formal. There used to be education in this country, before we lost the colonies. Education is very important, Mr. Cooker. It has nothing to do with breeding. You are an educated man. It shows. You are capable of putting up with a washed-up old man like me for more than an hour, and you are not just pretending to listen. I could almost end up liking you, if I still believed in people."

Benjamin remained silent. The old man's cheap wine had started to go to his head and upset his stomach.

"I'm going to tell you something, Mr. Cooker," Ferdinand muttered, his voice pasty with alcohol.

"Your two overmantels, well, the truth is, there were three of them."

Benjamin's eyes widened.

"You mean it was a triptych?"

"Yes, three panels. Not one more, not one less. You weren't expecting that, were you?"

"And the other painting completes the scene, I suppose?"

"Evidently. And the solution, well, you'll find it in water. For once, that will be a change for you."

"In water? What do you mean?"

"Today, Mr. Cooker, you shouldn't invest in wine. If you want to become rich and hold everyone by the short hairs, sell water. Soon enough, you'll have to beg to get a cup of water, and when it comes to that, well, we're on our way out! Water's a gift from God! It's all going to hell, I tell you. It's all going to hell!"

Ferdinand Ténotier yawned, belched several times, and placed his hands flat on the greasy wine-stained table. A black and white cat jumped up and rubbed against his right cheek. The old man swiped at it, sending it to the other side of the room. Then he placed his purple face on his crossed arms and fell asleep.

7

A cement truck rumbled in the distance, drowning out the birds that were nesting in the trees. As Benjamin walked across the grounds, he looked to the top of the century-old cedar tree, where a turtledove was grooming its feathers. He followed the thin flow of water in the Peugue. The creek slowly made its way between patches of herbs and around large roots that had grown out of the ground, blocking its passage and forcing it to make detours.

Benjamin Cooker was exhausted after his meeting in the Cité Frugès. The old Ténotier's awful cheap wine had left his mouth cottony. The smell of cat piss was still stinging his nostrils, and after spending so much time in the shadows, he had to keep blinking his eyes. Those two hours were enough to wipe out a tasting career and compromise his reputation as a winemaker. People were busy at work near the Moniales Haut-Brion cellars, which quickly brought him back to reality. He greeted the assembled crowd from a distance so as not to burn himself in the steam coming out of the barrels. They had started washing the contaminated casks early that morning. Virgile left the team to pursue the work while he reported to his boss.

"Everything went perfectly, sir. We finished decanting around one this morning. We attacked disinfecting at seven, and we should be finished soon."

"Is everyone following the instructions?" Benjamin asked without showing concern for his assistant's fatigue.

The young man was clearly strong and well built, spoiled by nature even, yet his face was pale and wrinkled from the lack of sleep. He had deep purple bags under his eyes.

"I followed your instructions closely," the assistant said. "I added the same amount of ozone to each barrel, and I raised the water temperature to two hundred degrees."

"Did you use constant pressure?"

"Yes, but then I prolonged the treatment time and spent a quarter of an hour on each barrel. I think that should do it."

"You still have to be wary of ozone. It's an effective disinfectant, but it causes oxidation that could promote certain volatile substances that influence the wine's aroma and the wood's quality."

"We rinsed at high pressure, sir. Long enough. I really followed your recommendations to the letter."

"Very good, then. Don't change anything," Benjamin said, waving at Denis Massepain, who was walking toward them from the château.

The assistant disappeared into the thick white steam rising from the barrels being rinsed with the high-pressure stream of hot water. Virgile was demonstrating a lot of energy and concentration. He was also showing a natural authority that allowed him to give orders to the workers without being arrogant.

"Your new employee seems quite good," Denis said, giving Benjamin a tired handshake.

"Yes, he's a good recruit. He works hard and keeps smiling. Those are two qualities that are hard to find these days."

"Is everything okay, Benjamin?"

"I think so. We'll proceed with sulfiting tomorrow. Doing it today would have been ideal, but my lab manager has to finish something urgent and cannot make it earlier."

"Did you tell her?" Denis asked with a worried look. "Does she really need to be here?"

"I had to. But you have nothing to fear. Alexandrine de la Palussière can be trusted. I need her here to adapt the sulfur dioxide dosage. She is the one who recommended that we use ozone to clean the barrels, and I think it's the best technique. Chlorine could accelerate the formation of trichlorophenol, which would then break down into trichloroanisole. Don't ask me for the specifics. I don't know anything more, but from experience, I can guarantee that we will avoid any moldy aromas this way. And it's better to forget any chemical detergents and fungicides, such as quaternary ammonium compound, because they always leave a residue after rinsing."

"I'll leave it up to you. I don't have a choice, do I?" sighed Massepain. "I haven't slept since this whole thing began, and I prefer not to say too much about it to Thérèse. She worries enough as it is."

"You're right. The best thing to do for now is to stand by your team and wait until the end of next week. I think that in a few days I'll be able to tell you where things stand."

Benjamin and his friend took a short walk on the grounds, making small talk that was not entirely futile. It relaxed Massepain a bit. And the winemaker took advantage of the moment to get a closer look at the new cabernet franc stock that had just been planted on a small parcel. Tender sprouts were starting to bud; they would not give clusters for another two or three years. He glanced over the meticulous rows of vines, quickly judging the state of the soil composed of thick Gunz gravel, sand, and clay and noted with pleasure that the vineyards had just been plowed. His eyes stopped for a moment on the Haut-Brion estate hilltop that dominated the neighborhood. Then he cupped his hands around his mouth and called out to his assistant. "Are you almost finished? We're off in five minutes, Virgile!"

The two men dropped the newest samples at the lab and by some miracle found a parking spot between two construction-site fences near the Place de la Bourse. Then they walked up the Cours du Chapeau Rouge, passing the Grand

Théâtre's massive columns and then turning on the Allée de Tourny to reach Noailles. Benjamin had the near-daily habit of lunching at this elegant brasserie, where he was greeted with somewhat affected nods from Bordeaux citizens of note, although they never dared to disturb him.

The table for the esteemed Mr. Cooker had been held for him, as usual, and the two men were welcomed with the polite friendliness given to long-time regulars. They were ravenous and opted for two quick starters followed by grilled fish served with a dry Pessac-Léognan white. Benjamin let his assistant choose the wine, which took quite some time, as he hesitated between a Château Carbonnieux and a Château Ferran before finally deciding on a 1998 Château Latour-Martillac.

"You deserve it, Virgile!"

"I have to admit that there's no time to get bored with you!"

They talked about this and that, trivial things and insignificant memories that were nonetheless important, because the two of them were getting to know each other. At the end of the meal, Benjamin offered the young man a cigar, but he declined politely in favor of an espresso. Then the winemaker suggested a digestive walk under the Jardin Public's blue cedar trees. Before going to the park, Virgile asked to stop at his studio apartment on the Rue Saint-Rémi, so they made a quick detour along the top of the Rue Sainte-Catherine. Benjamin waited outside, and his assistant came back down quickly, holding a large plastic bag.

"What are lugging around in that sack?" Benjamin asked.

"Stale bread. I keep it to feed the ducks and the fish in the park."

"Do you do that a lot?"

"I'm a country boy, and where I come from, nothing goes to waste. I can't get myself to throw bread away."

"I feel twenty years younger in your company, my dear Virgile," Benjamin said, clearly moved. "I often brought my daughter to the park, and every time, we had our stash of stale bread."

"I didn't know you had a daughter."

"Ah, Virgile, if you only knew Margaux. She is pretty as a picture, twenty-four years old and now living in New York."

"What is she doing there?"

"She is in the import-export business, specializing in regional products."

Benjamin said nothing more on the subject. He didn't like his life to be an open book, and he made it a habit to never give himself away in the first chapters. Virgile asked no other questions, and they walked in silence to the gilded gates opening onto the public park's bouquet of trees.

Gravel crunched under their heels. They passed a bronze bust of the French writer François Mauriac, sculpted by the Russian-born artist Ossip Zadkine. The sculptor had given the writer an eagle's profile, high cheekbones, a sharply carved chin, an excessively hollowed neck, and the face of a mystic ascetic, showing a deep understanding of the Malaga writer's dual nature. At the end of the central walkway, they passed the small Guérin family puppet-show stage. Its wooden shutters were closed. They stopped on a metal footbridge that crossed over one of the branches of the large pond.

"When I was a kid, I was scared to death of falling in among the carp," Benjamin said, looking dreamily at the water. "Later, I was even more frightened when Margaux leaned over the railing."

"Well, it is teeming with fish!" Virgile said, tossing in some stale crumbs.

Hundreds of fish rose to the surface in a single movement and then launched into a violent combat. Benjamin and Virgile observed this sticky carpet of open jaws, bulging eyes, and knife-like fins with distaste. The carp made a ghoulish clicking sound as they swallowed the pieces of bread. Some ducks tried their luck in the fray, in vain. They floundered in the whirlpool of viscous scales without managing to collect anything but the crumbs of the feast.

The two men then crossed the playground to reach the other part of the pond, where they spread out breadcrumbs for the numerous sparrows that nested near the spillway. Two blond mothers appeared on a walkway. They had the elegant air of the well bred from the Quinconces neighborhood. But their desperate shouts contradicted their sophisticated looks. "Jean-Baptiste! Eugénie!" they yelled as they peered into the bushes and scanned the flowerbeds.

A uniformed park officer with a wild mustache joined them and also started looking through the bushes. Other mothers in straight dark-blue skirts and white blouses joined the search, as well, followed by a stream of children in English-style clothing. There was something terribly chic about the chaos.

"Can I be frank with you?" Virgile asked suddenly as he scattered crumbs on the grass.

"I don't expect anything less of you," Benjamin answered.

"Well, okay, uh, I really think that, well, you might think I'm paranoid, but this spoilage thing, it just doesn't make sense. Not in an estate like Moniales Haut-Brion. Particularly Brettanomyces. Especially not in a cellar that is maintained so well. I've been hanging around with the team for a few days now, and I assure you, they are very serious."

"I know," Benjamin said.

"And Denis Massepain knows the business. He doesn't let anything get by him and has an eye on everything. He's a real winemaker, and I don't see how he could have let a contamination of this scope happen."

"I agree."

"As far as I'm concerned, there is only one possibility, but it's hard to voice such a thing."

"Go ahead, Virgile. Don't beat around the bush. Say what you have to say."

"Someone had to slip those spores into the barrels," the assistant said, tossing a small slice of bread to a turkey with a low-hanging wattle. "I've thought it over and over, and I can't think of any other possibility."

"You are not alone. I've been thinking that for a while now."

"Do you know if he has any enemies? Someone who is angry enough to ruin his life?"

"Not to my knowledge. Denis is loyal, calm, and correct. But I am not a good judge. He's my friend."

"Who knows? Maybe something happened with a member of his staff?"

"His workers and cellar master have been there for years, and the atmosphere at the estate is relatively serene. He is surrounded by motivated people. No, I doubt it's an inside job."

"Maybe one of his competitors wants to throw him off balance? Someone who is jealous and wants to cast a shadow on the estate? Someone full of envy who wants to put him on his knees?"

Benjamin took the final chunk of bread from the bottom of the plastic bag and threw it near a swan, which barely stretched its neck before continuing on its way with disdain.

"If the profession had to resolve its differences with biological warfare, where would we be, my dear Virgile? You know the wine world. It's a milieu where people observe and watch each other, sometimes with fear but always with respect, and everyone knows how to recognize his colleagues' value. Estate owners even help each other to a certain extent. You have to admit that the professional groups set up for each appellation bring the harvesters together and make them stronger. Or at least that is what we all pretend to believe! When there are hostile feelings, they play out in the trading halls. Nobody gives any gifts when it comes to selling one's stock. But everyone is always courteous. May the best man win!"

"I want to believe you, but I am convinced that there is someone around the Moniales who visited the cellar and who knows perfectly well how to taint a barrel of wine. I don't know how he managed, but he knows the premises and how to get in. There must not be that many people who have the keys and know the alarm code. Denis Massepain is the only one who can tell us for sure."

The two worried mothers had wound up finding their children. A crowd had formed around a bush where the little Jean-Baptiste and Eugénie were hiding, trying to strangle a mallard.

"Your reasoning is sound," Benjamin said. "Have you read Montesquieu?"

"No, I haven't read any Montesquieu, nor have I touched Montaigne, and I never finished a single book by Mauriac. I've done none of the local writers. I guess I should be a little ashamed, living in Bordeaux and all."

"Mostly, it's too bad," Benjamin said.

"And what does he have to say, your Montesquieu?"

"If my memory serves me, he says, 'I prefer the company of peasants, because they have not been educated sufficiently to reason incorrectly.'"

8

Virgile steered the car with his left hand and scratched his head with his right. He looked preoccupied. His lips were pursed, and his eyebrows were knotted.

"That Montesquieu wrote some bullshit."

"Who hasn't?" Benjamin sighed.

"I remember one of my French teachers telling a not-so-glorious story about him."

"Is that so?"

"In one of his books he wrote that King François I had refused gifts offered by Christopher Columbus, but François I wasn't even born when Columbus discovered America!"

"Just goes to show you, my dear Virgile, that you should always check your sources. That said, I've always been suspicious of the philosopher. In fact, Montesquieu seriously gets on my nerves. I shouldn't tell you that, because in this town it is not seemly to criticize local heroes, particularly when that glory reaches beyond the nearby Libourne hills."

"Mum's the word, I promise!" Virgile smiled.

"Lesson givers have always exasperated me. Montesquieu spread all kinds of holier-than-thou theories about slavery, none of which kept him from stuffing himself when Bordeaux's slave traders invited him over. The world is filled with moralizers who forget to sweep in front of their own doors. Are you interested in history? You know, in those things that often bore young people your age?"

"When you're born in Bergerac, you can't escape the past. Take my word for it," Virgile responded. "I've always found it fascinating, but sometimes I feel crushed by all those old stones and a little overshadowed by the illustrious dead and memories of grand battles."

"Battles that had no reason for being," added Benjamin. "But we have to know about them to keep history from repeating itself. Yesterday, I met an amazing fellow. One day I'll take you to see him. If you like the little stories that make up the big picture of history, you'll spend an enriching, albeit slightly frightening, time with him."

Benjamin told Virgile about Ferdinand Ténotier, sparing no detail, including the overpowering cat smell, the cheap wine, the sorry state of the apartment, the singular atmosphere that reigned in the small Cité Frugès streets, the postcards, and the terribly destiny of Pessac's châteaux. Virgile listened carefully, and the drive seemed short, despite the traffic on the boulevards and the inevitable bottleneck as they neared the Barrière de Pessac intersection. He asked a few questions about Le Corbusier, whose name he vaguely recognized, although he had never seen any of his work. Benjamin offered an explanation that he tried to make impartial, without any value judgments. The young man would have to make up his own mind, and the winemaker did not want to influence him, as he admittedly was no authority in the area of architecture. Le Corbusier had left his mark in the Aquitaine region, from the first experimental houses he built in Lège-Cap-Ferret in 1923 to the futurist buildings constructed in Pessac two years later. Benjamin did not feel especially moved by these structures, but their innovative spirit deserved respect.

During this meandering discussion, Virgile learned of his employer's passion for antiques and painting. The assistant became all the more attentive when Benjamin brought up the two paintings of the Château Haut-Brion and the Mission Haut-Brion, especially when he mentioned the mysterious third painting. The young man did not comment, though. He finally admitted that he didn't know exactly what an overmantel was. Benjamin was happy to explain.

"It's a painting or a decorative panel. At the beginning of the seventeenth century, these panels were often set in moldings and had mirrors. Overmantel used to refer to the decorative woodwork that complemented the artwork, but now it has come to mean the entire piece, which often hangs over a fireplace. Painted canvases most often have a frame with a small mirror underneath. In French, it's called a *trumeau*, which comes from the old French *trumel*, which meant leg fat or, for a butcher, a beef shank. The word evolved to mean the part of the wall between two windows."

"That's wild," Virgile said. "You could make a fortune on game shows!"

Benjamin smiled and asked him to slow down when they entered Pessac. They crept along the Avenue Jean-Jaurès, a ribbon of pavement bordered on both sides by waves of vineyards whose undulating movement broke the monotony of the suburbs.

"Turn at the next gate to your right," Benjamin said.

"Are we going to—"

"Yes, we are," Benjamin said, suddenly curt.

Virgile skillfully maneuvered the car and drove slowly under a brown stone archway, stopping in the shadow of Château Haut-Brion. Still gripping the steering wheel, he looked up, awestruck at finding himself in the heart of an estate whose prestige had long been the thing of dreams. Benjamin was barely out of the car when a tall, thin man who was wearing a twill suit and appeared to be in his forties greeted him with notable respect. Benjamin asked if it was possible to disturb the steward.

"I am sorry, Mr. Cooker. He is absent, but you are always welcome at Haut-Brion. Is there anything I can do for you?"

"I won't be long. I just need to make a topographical check for the next edition of the guide, and I need to take some notes from the top of the plateau."

"Would you like me to accompany you?"

"Thank you. That will not be necessary. I know the way."

The winemaker and his assistant took off on foot amid the rows of grapevines, climbing the hump of greenery without saying a word. It would have been like being in the countryside, were it not for the incessant dull humming from the north. It sounded like a distant storm brewing in the heat, but in reality it was the barely muffled sound of Bordeaux, mixed with the peripheral grumblings that spread across the suburbs.

They reached the top of the hill in no time. Benjamin caught his breath while he scanned the urban landscape that extended below. He knew immediately that his intuition was correct and that he had finally found what the old Ténotier was referring to. Why hadn't he figured it out sooner? Virgile registered his employer's satisfied nod of recognition without understanding what was going on.

"Of course," Benjamin muttered. "It jumps out at you!"

He approached the water tower that stood in the middle of the Haut-Brion estate, an enormous concrete wart planted right in the vineyards, like a constant reminder that here nature was on shaky ground, barely accepted, and on borrowed time. Benjamin looked up. It was not so much the structure's ugliness that caused him to despair, but all those cubic meters of water standing over one of the most prestigious wines in the world, like a vulgar form of provocation.

"This is the water the old man was talking about!" the winemaker said, touching the tower's roughcast.

He took out the picture of his overmantel and looked toward Mission Haut-Brion dozing at the foot of the hillock. It was all there: the dormer windows in the slate roof, the chapel with its stone cross, the two columns at the front gate, the barn transformed into a cellar flanking the building. Of course the trees had changed. Some were gone, others had grown. The lines of the vineyard had also evolved somewhat, and now the surrounding area bristled with buildings and electric poles. Modern housing encumbered the horizon, but the perspectives fit perfectly, only slightly transposed and compacted by the artist. More than a century earlier, a local painter had set himself up with his easel in this very spot, prepared his paints, drawn his sketches, and placed his spots of color amid a group of grape harvesters.

All he had to do was turn his head a little to the right, toward the south, and Dr. Baldès's overmantel appeared in turn, with the emblematic facade of the Château Haut-Brion, its two conical turrets transported to the wing as if to lighten the main central square of the building. The earth was combed as straight as a die, and not a single rebellious plant intruded. Benjamin paused for a moment. He already knew what he would discover but waited a few seconds to better enjoy the instant when he would find the landscape of the third painting.

A quarter turn to the right, toward the west, and he saw it by just looking at the bottom of the hill. The Moniales Haut-Brion was there, yes, hidden behind the plants, but very much there. It was so obvious. He would have realized it earlier, had he taken the time to think about it. Benjamin kicked himself for not being more perceptive, and he silently thanked Ferdinand Ténotier. The third painting was right there under his nose, and, unlike the other two, it had to be the only one that didn't correspond exactly with reality. The Moniales château was now obscured by greenery the landscaper Michel Bonfin had planted at the beginning of the nineteenth century. The painter had enjoyed a clear view, as the trees were less filled in and shorter, and he had been able to make out the flow of the Peugue, the moss-covered stone fountain, the small pink marble chapel, and the grapevines. With a little imagination, it was easy to picture the scene.

Virgile was standing off to the side, but he quickly picked up on his employer's speculation. He walked up and squinted, examining the landscape and forming a frame between the right angles of his thumbs and index fingers.

"In my opinion, sir, if you pretend the strip housing, apartment buildings, and suburban homes around the estate are not there, you can almost believe that..."

Benjamin imitated him, closing one eye to focus.

"Indeed, all that's missing are the grape harvesters," he said, as he was sure that the third painting had workers in the vineyards, like the others.

"So there you have it, your third overmantel. It's the Moniales."

"Unfortunately, that is not so. Reality is just an illusion, my dear Virgile. Only the artist's eye captures the truth, even if it seems distorted or interpreted. Do you see what I mean? I would really like to know where that piece of truth is hiding."

"We're not really going to hit up all the antique dealers in the region, are we?" the assistant asked with a little too much familiarity.

"Watch what you say. I'm perfectly capable of doing that," Benjamin replied. There was no joking in his tone.

Virgile rubbed his neck and felt it best to keep a certain distance. He regretted overstepping his bounds and saying something that could have been interpreted as a lack of respect.

"There is something bothering me, sir. What's the link between the Moniales and the Haut-Brion estate?"

"There isn't one today, except that they share the same *terroir* on the Graves plateau. The Moniales estate belongs to the Fonsegrive-Massepain family, and it has since the beginning of the nineteenth century, when it was purchased by Aristide Fonsegrive, a wine trader in Bordeaux and a direct ancestor of Denis's wife, Thérèse. During the French Revolution, when all the land belonging to the Church was confiscated, the estate became state property."

"It once belonged to the Church?"

"To the Order of Our Lady of the Moniales, for two centuries. At first, there was nothing but a small watermill surrounded by prairie and vineyards. Toward the end of his life, Jean de Pontac, who was the true founder of the Château Haut-Brion, thought he could gain a foothold in heaven by giving this parcel to a religious order. He was a bourgeois Bordeaux merchant and had bought the manorial rights. He was born in 1488 and died in 1589, was married three times, and had fifteen children. He was a busy one."

"He lived to be one hundred and one?" asked Virgile.

"Don't you count fast. Jean de Pontac did, in fact, live under the reigns of kings Louis XII, François I, Henri II, Charles IX, and Henri III. Some years are good and age exceptionally well," Benjamin sighed. "I have tasted some wines that have crossed the century and lived through a dozen French presidents."

The winemaker sat down on a small pile of stones at the foot of the water tower and invited his assistant to do the same. He then recited the full details of the Pontac family dynasty. Arnaud II, the fourth son of the centenary, was the bishop of Bazas, and his funeral procession was over nine miles long. Geoffroy, president of the Bordeaux parliament, lived in the Daurade, a private mansion overflowing in gold and mirrors. Arnaud III wallowed in the same luxury as his father and became the first president of the local parliament. And finally there was François-Auguste, who also headed up the Bordeaux parliament and was the last direct Pontac descendent to own Haut-Brion.

"From then on, things became terribly complicated," the winemaker continued. "François-Auguste lived in such luxury, the château was seized twice to pay his debts. When his sister, Marie-Thérèse, inherited the estate in 1694, the land was split up, and she managed to keep only two-thirds of it. I'll spare you the details of who slept with whom and who was the widow of whom."

"Too bad! That's often the most interesting information!" said Virgile.

"You'd be disappointed. There is nothing very spicy, just stories of alliances and marriages for money. No small favors or pillow talk, I fear. At this stage, François Delphin d'Aulède de Lestonnac, Marie-Thérèse's son—she had married the owner of Château Margaux—inherited both Haut-Brion and Margaux. And that explains a rather astonishing tradition.

Haut-Brion, which is in the Graves, is still classified as a Médoc premier cru, in accordance with a very ancient formulation that did not take into account its geography, but rather its age-old noble codes of usage."

"And that's still the case today?"

"Don't forget that Bordeaux is a land of traditions. Never forget that! So, stop me if it gets too complicated, okay, Virgile? This François Delphin, marquis of Margaux and owner of Haut-Brion, died in 1746 and passed down his land to his sister, Catherine d'Aulède de Lestonnac, the widow of Count François-Joseph de Fumel, who had a son named Louis, who would die at a very young age. Are you still with me?"

"Yes, yes. I'm closing my eyes to concentrate better."

"In the end, it was the grandson, Joseph de Fumel, who developed the estate, adding an orangery, operational buildings, and very large grounds. He also contributed greatly to the renown of Haut-Brion wine abroad, trading with England and Sweden. He was guillotined in 1794. From then on, the same lot was reserved for the Moniales. The estate was sold as state property, and Charles-Maurice Talleyrand bought it in 1801. At the time, he was Napoleon's minister of foreign affairs, as you know."

"Is he the one who limped? The one Napoleon called 'shit in silk stockings'?" Virgil asked, knitting his eyebrows.

"The description is terse but rather well summarized. Tallyrand was a grim man but brilliant. He is said to have given this advice about Haut-Brion, and it's guidance that people should heed more often. 'Before raising such a nectar to one's lips, hold the glass high, and look at it, sniff it at length, and then, set your glass down, and talk about it!' Very perceptive, isn't it?"

"Well put," Virgile said, nodding.

"Tallyrand did not stay at Haut-Brion for long. He sold everything in 1804. He had other things to do, and he didn't have a farmer's soul. You have to be a little bit of a farmer to love a land like this one, even if your coffers are full of gold, and you're chock-full of honors. As was the Larrieu family, which was next in line. They were a dynasty of jurists with a number of more or less happy successors throughout the nineteenth century. After Joseph-Eugène Larrieu and his son, Amédée, came Eugène, who inherited in 1873 and went on to impose a near-military discipline on his winemakers. This was an important step, as the Larrieu family bought the third that belonged to the countess of Vergennes and united the domaine again. They always had energetic stewards, and you have to admit that were it not for Eugène Larrieu's authoritarian determination, the estate would have suffered more from the Phylloxera and mildew epidemics that ravaged all of Bordeaux's vineyards. He managed the estate with an iron fist until 1896, but he had no heir. His vines were prolific, but he was dry."

The ups and downs of Haut-Brion's history had loosened Benjamin's tongue, and he was in brilliant form. He enjoyed initiating Virgile into this world, with its codes that were sometimes difficult to decrypt. He went on to talk about the various problems linked to the joint ownership of the property and the Compagnie Algérienne, a bank that owned the château for a time before selling it to the extravagant André Gibert. He was a stickler for rules but loved experimenting. He also lacked an heir, so the estate ended up in the hands of the American financier Clarence Dillon after several months of harsh negotiations. On May 13, 1935, the Château Haut-Brion was transferred to the Dillon family. Over time, the majority of its heirs were attached enough to the estate to forget the bustle of New York and show an interest in its operations. Some even settled there.

"Okay, I'll stop there! I think I've overwhelmed you," Benjamin said, getting up.

They returned to Bordeaux at dusk. Benjamin dropped his assistant off at the Place de la Victoire and drove down the Cours de la Marne to reach the Saint-Jean train station. He double-parked and ran to the departure hall to get some pictures made in a photo booth. The harsh flash surprised him as he tried to put on an impassive, dignified expression. The result was astonishing, to say the least. The four small pictures showed just three-quarters of his face. One eye was half closed, the other was red from the flash, and he had a splotch of white light running across his forehead. Benjamin was quite amused by his startled look. "Clearly, reality is nothing but an illusion," he thought, slipping the photos into his inside jacket pocket. He was sure that Pascale Dartigeas would be talented enough to rework his portrait and reproduce his features accurately.

The end-of-April evening breeze was warm. As he left the train station, he removed a parking ticket from under the windshield wiper of his Mercedes and tossed it onto the back seat. Benjamin Cooker had just spent an excellent day.

9

Do you think you can suffocate on your own vomit?" Virgile asked, folding the newspaper.

"Spare me the details, please," the winemaker said, looking disgusted.

The winemaker hadn't read more than the first paragraph of the article in the latest edition of the *Sud-Ouest* before setting it on the edge of the table.

It was late morning, still chilly, and there were only a few scattered patrons at the Régent's outside tables. A handful of regulars, comfortably sheltered by a large red awning and ensconced in their rattan chairs, were taking in the city's moods. Some were deep in their newspapers, not paying any attention to their neighbors, while others were sipping their coffee in seats at the front to better observe the comings and goings on the Place Gambetta, with its buses swerving along the Cours Clemenceau and young women hurrying between stopped cars.

Virgile had joined Benjamin a little late. He sputtered an excuse and immediately started talking about the story in the paper. The headline read, "Pessac loses its living archives." The story took up two columns but didn't have any pictures.

The quiet Cité Frugès, a modern architectural jewel designed by Le Corbusier, is in mourning. Mr. Ferdinand Ténotier, a professor of medieval history at the University of Bordeaux for thirty years, was found dead yesterday morning in his apartment. The postman, who was delivering his pension payment, discovered the old man slumped on his kitchen table, his face lying in the remains of a meal he had regurgitated. This solitary, sometimes extravagant man, once married to an aristocrat from Andalusia, was a leading expert in Pessac history. Mr. Ténotier studied at the École des Chartes and had a comparative literature degree from La Sorbonne. He spoke Latin, Greek, Hebrew, Armenian, and several other languages. In addition, he received many honors for his 1954 annotated translation of Don Quixote from sixteenth-century Spanish. He was also the author of a popular pamphlet on the history of Pessac, which, unfortunately, is out of print. No stone in the town was a secret to him, and his tragic death at the age of seventy eight is a great loss for our region.

"It's strange. The funeral arrangements aren't mentioned in the article," Virgile said.

"I'm not surprised."

"They're not going to bury him like a dog, are they?"

"You never know. I suppose they'll do an autopsy to make sure his death was accidental," Benjamin said, getting up from the table.

"You think so?"

"What I think is that it is high time we get to Moniales and check some things out. Don't you agree, Virgile?"

"If you say so."

Alexandrine de la Palussière was already at work when they arrived at the cellars. She had checked the steel tanks, taking a few new samples before intervening to treat the contamination. She was wearing beige leather espadrilles, plain linen pants, and a sky-blue cashmere sweater. She looked like someone fresh and ready for a golf resort or a sailing club for indulged teenagers. Her bob cut, held back by the never-changing mother-of-pearl hairband, brought out the best in her smooth face.

She carefully descended the stepladder she had been perched on to join her employer, who was fretting at the door of the building, his face pale. Alexandrine put on a smile as she walked over to him with a lightly swaying step. She shook the winemaker's hand and gave Virgile a look-over. She thought he might actually be nice, but his good looks were a little too impertinent. Denis Massepain had just arrived from his office, where a phone call had tied him up for an hour.

"Excuse me," he said, uncomfortable. "I didn't even have time to greet Mademoiselle de la Palussière. I was on the phone with some American buyers. Business must go on."

He said hello to the young woman, who accepted his apology immediately and introduced herself. The owner apologized again and thanked her for coming. She thanked him for his trust and said she was sorry, in turn, for not introducing herself earlier.

"Where are we, Alexandrine?" Benjamin asked, putting an end to the unproductive civilities.

"I considered two different approaches. I didn't have the time to discuss them with you, but I quickly abandoned the idea of using diethyl pyrocarbonate in its new dimethyl form. It is not stable enough, because it is too quick to hydrolyze into ethanol and carbonic gas. In my opinion, that could leave minor secondary products that might give the wine an overly fruity aroma. In addition, we would have to use over two hundred milligrams per liter to totally destroy the infection."

"That's unthinkable!" Benjamin said. "It is absolutely impossible, and it's forbidden by European regulations."

"In that case, I think that we should fall back on the more traditional sulfur dioxide treatment. It's the only alternative."

Denis Massepain listened attentively. He had been trained as an embryologist and had spent years working in the pharmaceutical industry, so he understood what the alchemist was saying. Virgile, however, found it too esoteric for his taste.

Alexandrine continued her presentation as if she were addressing only her employer. "Cleaning the barrels was crucial. Now the wood should be healthy, which will prevent any yeast proliferation in the cellars. We are doing a residual analysis of the cleaned barrels, but if the work was done properly, there should be no problem."

Virgile did not falter.

"I have no doubt about the results," Benjamin said dryly.

"I hope not," Alexandrine responded. "All we have left to do then is to add the sodium dioxide, and I think that will be done in an hour or two. I used the most recent readings to determine the pH of each lot to adjust the dosage. I won't use wicks, because they are not precise enough."

The biologist was referring to a technique dating from the eighteenth century that was still in use. Sulfur candles, introduced by the Dutch, were nothing more than wicks dipped in sulfur that produced a sanitizing gas when burned in wine barrels. The winemaker had often used them to eliminate germs and minimize their effect. He knew the advantages and limitations of this system, which had been used to save some great wines while preserving their purity and aromatic characteristics.

"What method do you suggest?" he asked.

"I will use effervescent sulfur that allows for more precise dosing. It is easier, although the trouble with metabisulfite discs is homogenous distribution of the sodium dioxide. We'll have to stir from time to time. Mr. Massepain can make sure the lees get in suspension on a daily basis."

"Virgile will stop by and do it, don't worry," Benjamin said. "He will also take samples from the tanks and bring them to the lab so you can monitor the treatment."

"As you wish," Alexandrine answered without looking at the assistant.

Benjamin wished his biologist luck and then motioned to Denis and Virgile to follow him.

"That woman is a gem," he said softly. "But honestly, I prefer sparing you another presentation on yeast dosing, active ingredients, gauging antiseptics, and all those damned molecules. They are enough to make you hate wine."

The Moniales estate owner would have chuckled, were the situation not so serious, and Virgile held back a quiet laugh himself for fear of appearing mean-spirited. "Denis, I'm going to talk to you as a friend and certainly not as a client," the winemaker said suddenly. "In any case, you're not a client, and you never will be. Don't even expect to get a bill!"

"But I insist!" Massepain said firmly.

"We can talk about that later. We have another matter to discuss. I would like you to tell me very frankly if you have had any trouble with a member of your staff."

"No, not at all. I even gave some raises not so long ago. Overall, my employees are not complaining, and I must say that I have been very touched by their reaction to this problem."

"Are you absolutely sure there hasn't been any problem?"

"No, I told you. You have seen their attitude. Everyone is working late and not counting their hours."

"Who is responsible for the cellar keys and the security system?"

"Why are you asking me all these question?" Massepain asked.

"Answer me. Who has the keys? Who knows the code to the alarm?"

"Two of us: the steward and I."

"Nobody else? Not even your secretary?"

"No. And I don't even want to hear what you are trying to insinuate. Jean Laborde has been my steward for years. He's a wonderful man and has my total trust. It sounds like you—"

"I have to, Denis," interrupted Benjamin. "We are more and more convinced that this infection did not get here on its own. I don't want to make any accusations, but it could be an act of treachery. Virgile agrees with me, isn't that so?"

The assistant nodded.

"But you've seen infections like this in other cellars, haven't you?" Denis Massepain asked. "This is something that happens to others. It was my turn."

"This is true," acquiesced the winemaker. "And I won't disclose the names of the estates where I've had to intervene.

But each time, it was the result of negligence or questionable sanitation. That is totally impossible here."

"What do you plan to do then?"

"Have there been any recent visitors who have had access to the cellars? Reporters? Salespeople? Interns? You get the picture. Any outsiders coming and going?"

"There was a magazine reporter this winter, with a photographer. They interviewed me for an article, but we only went through the cellars to take some pictures. That's all."

"Have there been any other visitors?"

"Very few, and they stayed mainly in the tasting room. I don't like to have people in the barrel room. Most of the time it is locked, as you know."

"Have there been any interns from the wine school? You must get some in from time to time."

"I've had four since last year, each for a month and no longer. You know that if you really want to train young people, you need to take time, and I don't have a lot of it to spare. We don't have enough staff."

"What became of these interns? Have you seen them since?"

"I haven't had any contact with them. Some must have graduated, and others are probably still at school."

"Could you give me their names, along with the names of all your usual staff and their addresses?"

"My secretary will have all that information. Follow me."

They went to the reception area near the entrance gate. They climbed the stairs, consulted a large green notebook, and made several photocopies that Benjamin gave to Virgile.

When they got back to the Mercedes, they heard thunder. In the distance, the skies over the ocean were rumbling, and a west wind was carrying in dark, threatening clouds. A few heavy drops of cold rain came down on the two men, who hurried to put the convertible top up. The assistant held the handful of photocopies over his head to protect himself. Benjamin grabbed them out of his hands and shielded them under his jacket. The pavement gave off the sweet aroma of wet dust.

"Hurry, Virgile! Get this car covered up. This is good weather for winemakers. Here you could say 'April showers, good for wine and flowers.' "

10

Grangebelle glistened behind the flowing shapes of the poplar trees. Elisabeth had lit tens of small candles and placed them along the windowsills at the front of the house. Benjamin parked his convertible near the wine cellar, checked the date on his watch, and suddenly realized that he had turned fifty at exactly 12:15 that afternoon. He had crossed that critical threshold of a half a century, which he had long worried about. Bacchus celebrated his arrival as he did every other evening. He jumped up and put his muddy paws on his master's light blue shirt. Benjamin brushed him off and hurried to the house. His wife was waiting for him in the hallway with an amused smile. He hugged her and whispered in her ear, "I can't believe it. The big five-zero, can you imagine?"

"Happy birthday, my Benjamin. I can't wait to open that 1953 Gruaud-Larose that you've been hiding away all these years."

"We're going to enjoy that one," Benjamin said, sniffing the aromas coming out of the kitchen. "It smells like the seaside, like we're on vacation, my love."

"I prepared you an Arcachon stew. The sea scallops were superb. And I invited the Delfrancs."

"That's an excellent idea. I haven't seen them in ages. I'll bring up a few bottles of white too. We'll start with the Gruaud-Larose."

He went down into his sanctuary, a small, well-ordered cellar, meticulously—almost compulsively—arranged, where he kept his best stock, the rare vintages, bottles from prestigious estates and exceptional wines few people ever got to taste. Alain and Chantal Delfranc were among the privileged few who could appreciate such an honor. The couple had recently moved to Saint-Estèphe and opened a bed-and-breakfast whose reputation had quickly spread across the Médoc. Alain had worked for years in the French intelligence service. He had taken an early retirement so that Chantal and he could leave Paris and launch the venture they had dreamed about for years. The two men had met in the 1970s, during the carefree days when Alain was still a police intern, and Benjamin was tending the bar at the Caveau de la Huchette. They had remained in touch, and when Alain's project took shape, the winemaker helped the couple find an old manor house that they transformed into an upscale guesthouse before opening one of the best restaurants in the area.

Alain was a refined epicurean and an inventive cook who grew unjustly forgotten heirloom vegetables and loved promising small-estate wines. In his new role as guesthouse owner and restaurateur, he spent much of his time in the cozy warmth of his kitchen, convinced that a passion was not fully experienced until it was shared. Chantal followed along, bringing with her a perpetual good mood. She decorated the premises with a clear taste for simple furniture, worn leather, and metallic accessories, balancing beige and chocolate brown to produce a rare, authentic feel and old-world charm. Chantal was graceful, despite her plump waistline, sassy nose, and mischievous eyes. She lived life with a candid sensuality that threw some people off—those who couldn't see beyond appearances. What could be construed as easy virtue was simply a genuine, open interest in all the pleasures that came her way.

Benjamin grabbed two bottles of a dry white Château Haut-Brion. It was criminal to open this 1989 now, but to hell with expert recommendations! Life was too short, and he would not wait another fifty years before tasting it. When he came back up from the sanctuary, the Delfrancs had just arrived. Bacchus was barking. Elisabeth was untying her apron, and Chantal was already joking about Benjamin's respectable age. Alain smiled as he set his raincoat down on one of the chairs in the entrance.

The bottles of white wine went into a bucket of ice, and everyone sat around a coffee table in the living room to taste the illustrious 1953 Gruaud-Larose that the winemaker had decanted much too late. This evening, every sacrilege was permitted. Benjamin slowly unwrapped the gift the Delfrancs offered him. He was intrigued by the medium-sized flat box, undid the ribbon, and was careful not to tear the wrapping paper. He slowly opened the cardboard and discovered a bright ink drawing dating from 1933.

"You're out of your mind! You shouldn't have!"

"Of course I had too!" Alain said. "I'm no crazier than you are opening that Gruaud-Larose as old as your arteries."

"You're mad," Benjamin said again, holding the sketch along its edges. "I can't believe it. An original from the Nicolas catalog illustrated by Jean Hugo. You can't find these anywhere."

"That's proof you're wrong," Chantal said, lifting the glass to her lips. "You know that Alain can find anything, any-where, whenever, and, well, however!"

Benjamin seemed almost uncomfortable and did not know how to thank his friends. He took a sip of wine, with the full tasting ritual, because he had to find a way to calm his emotions. Elisabeth disappeared and returned with a steam-ing tureen.

"Let's eat. It's hot. I made a stew, so there are no starters."

"I've been waiting to taste this famous stew of yours!" Alain said, rubbing his hands.

He immediately asked for the recipe. Elisabeth didn't hold out on him and told him every detail: the puree of carrots, leeks, tomatoes, onions, and shallots that she cooked over low heat for twenty minutes before she strained it through a fine sieve; the salt, pepper, and saffron dosed with care, along with the hint of cayenne pepper; the mussels cooked in a white Graves; the juice strained before the addition of the delicate langoustine tails; the sea scallops sautéed in hot butter; and the crème fraîche used to thicken the sauce, which was then reduced for at least three minutes.

Everyone got a generous serving, and there was a moment of silence before the compliments started flying. As usual, Elisabeth accepted her triumph with modesty and raised her glass of white Haut-Brion. They toasted Benjamin and then talked about all manner of things, about time flying by too quickly, about children living too far away, about vacation memories, bottling in Bordeaux, about wine, as always, and about gastronomy too, about old English cars, unreadable books and boring movies, about all those little essential and useless things that strengthened the bonds among the four friends a little more each time they met. They ignored politics, however, not because they weren't interested, but mostly because they didn't want to chance miry paths where friendships could get stuck. Spiritual concerns were also only mentioned in passing, with just a few allusions tainted with irony. Benjamin knew his friend was resolutely atheist, and he himself believed that one could not reasonably talk about God with a flute of Champagne in his hand.

Dessert was sumptuous, without any candles or ritual song. Benjamin hated those childish manifestations. Elisabeth knew him too well to commit that faux pas, which would have ruined their enjoyment of the Bavarian cream presented on a caramelized sheet of puff pastry and covered with roasted chopped pistachios. They drank coffee in the living room, and no one wanted an after-dinner spirit. Alain lit a pipe of Amsterdamer, and Benjamin dug around in his little rosewood box to find a Lusitania from Partagas, which he then lit with relish. The women stayed at a distance, complaining about the smoke that kept them from enjoying the perfume samples they extracted from their handbags. Benjamin took advantage of the moment to remove a piece of paper from his jacket pocket. He unfolded it and held it out to his friend.

"Do you still have any contact with your former colleagues in intelligence?"

"With some, yes. I've got a friend from Paris who was transferred to Gironde. We see each other from time to time."

"Could you get me some information about these people?"

"What kind of information?"

The winemaker briefly summarized what had happened to Denis Massepain, and without going into the details, he shared his suspicions. He didn't want to incriminate the employees on the list; he just wanted to make sure there was no doubt about their integrity. He insisted that any inquiries be made with complete discretion in a totally unofficial way.

"I'll call you tomorrow," Alain said. "Don't tell me anything else, or I'll end up becoming interested."

The following day dragged out. It was both lethargic and feverish. Benjamin waited for Alain's phone call and couldn't concentrate on his writing. He had gotten up rather late and had drunk his tea mechanically, nibbling on a few broken pieces of Melba toast. Finally, he holed up in his office to outline the *n*th draft of his text about the citadel.

"The rocks of Blaye have seen many battles. This city, perched on a steep cliff one hundred and twenty feet above the Gironde Estuary, has been the object of everyone's desire. Since the time of the Gauls and the Romans, the Visigoths, the Vikings, and the Plantagenets, there have been bloody battles, distant echoes of which..."

"Elisabeth," Benjamin shouted down to the living room, "Don't stay on the phone long. I'm waiting for a call."

He walked out to the deck that overlooked vineyards and played with Bacchus for quite a while, showing a clear lack of enthusiasm as he threw and threw again an iridescent blue plastic bone that Margaux had brought from the United States the previous summer. Then he tossed the hideous object into the garbage can as his dog looked on in disbelief.

Elisabeth offered him a light meal, which he refused. He chose to close himself up again in his office, where he reread some juicy passages of *Le Chic Anglais*, James Darwen's precious guide for the perfect gentleman. The author's sharp witticisms, peremptory precepts, and delicious bad faith failed to make Benjamin laugh. He set the work down with exaggerated nonchalance in an attempt to control his nervousness. Then he tried to force himself to relax. After five minutes spent drifting, his feet up on his leather Empire desk, he decided to waste away the afternoon of waiting by focusing on the upkeep of his footwear. A John Lobb lover, no matter how wealthy he was or how many people he employed, could never entrust his shoe polishing to anyone else. What could be more personal than shining his black leather Oxfords and buffing his brown loafers? He had selected each pair with great care on trips to Paris, and he never missed an opportunity to visit the shop on the Boulevard Saint-Germain to explore new collections and find old classics. He preferred, however, the store on St. James Street, which he visited every time he went to see his parents in London.

Benjamin spent more than three hours polishing his Lobbs, tirelessly massaging the leather with a light concentric movement that accentuated the shine. He took pleasure in observing the fullness of the grain, the hue, and the amber transparency of his shoes, a harmony just as subtle as the one experienced by his eye, nose, and mouth when he tasted a grand cru wine. The winemaker was almost calm when the telephone finally rang.

"I handled your list," Alain said. "My former colleagues still remember me, and they took care of it in a day. Maybe you could send them a case of Médoc."

"I'm listening."

"I don't have much to say about the staff members. The steward got a speeding ticket, and one of the workers has filed for divorce, but other than that, there is nothing on record. They all lead rather calm lives."

"And the four interns?"

"No problem there, either. None have records. They work hard and don't make any waves. Edouard Camps is still in school and is preparing his dissertation. Antoine Armel found a job on an estate in the Touraine, where he is assistant cellar master. Sébastien Guéret took over the family's printing business after his father had a car accident, and David Morin works in sales for a Cognac merchant."

"So there's nothing that stands out, then?" Benjamin said, disappointed.

"Sorry, bad luck."

Benjamin hung up after promising to stop by the Delfrancs place to taste his sweetbreads cooked in a Bordeaux sparkling wine. Then he tried to rewrite the piece on the Blaye fortress, although he knew the end result would not be the best.

"Some say that the body of Roland de Roncevaux lies under Blaye. Charlemagne's troops transported his corpse in a gold coffin on the back of two mules to the Saint-Romain de Blaye basilica, which was buried in the seventeenth century by Vauban's landfilling work. Were you to dig, you would perhaps find Durandal's sword and the valiant knight's ivory horn that was immortalized by the song…"

Benjamin threw the paper into the trash and finally joined his wife, apologizing for being so disagreeable.

11

Benjamin and Elisabeth could barely hear the bustling Place Saint-Michel on the other side of heavy church doors. They were kneeling near the central aisle, observing the sanctimonious in Sunday dress desert the benches. The Mass had been mediocre. The sermon had lacked verve, and members of the flock had either dozed or been distracted. The Cooker couple waited until the organist's last notes fell silent. Then they walked out into the square in front of the church. A flea market had invaded the space at dawn. A colorful crowd moved around the dozens of improvised stands. A huge variety of objects was laid out on the ground: coffee grinders without handles, scratched vinyl records, Louis-Philippe armoires that had been too well restored, stolen car radios, garden ironworks, dusty engravings, windproof lighters, and military medals. Benjamin nosed about but didn't find anything that caught his eye, with the exception of a corkscrew with a brass handle shaped like a pair of legs, one of them with a garter belt. He paid next to nothing for it. Elisabeth followed him, looking detached, and then stopped in front of an Art Deco sugar bowl that she bought without bothering to haggle.

"I need to stop in to see the art restorer," the winemaker said. "Her workshop is open on Sunday mornings."

"Let's be quick about it, Benjamin. I'd like to get home."

Pascale Dartigeas greeted the couple with a smile that lit up her face and highlighted her blue-gray eyes. She was standing in front of a seascape whose colors were in dire need of cleaning.

"Mr. and Mrs. Cooker! To what do I owe the pleasure?"

"You asked me for a picture to redo that cellar master's portrait on the Toussaint Roussy."

"Indeed, show me."

The winemaker held out the photo-booth pictures and waited for Pascale Dartigeas's reaction.

"I don't mean to be rude, Mr. Cooker, but you look horrible in these pictures. Don't you agree, Mrs. Cooker?"

"I haven't even seen these. Show me," she said. "Yuck, it would have been hard to make you any uglier."

"What can I do with a face like that?" Pascale said, a little vexed.

"I'm counting on your talent to tidy it up," Benjamin said with a laugh. "You speak the truth, so paint me with the same honesty."

"I'll work from memory," she said, looking him straight in the eye, as if she wanted to grab her client's mischievous expression and natural distinction.

Elisabeth had wandered to the back of the workshop and was examining the soft pink flesh of a Baroque angel that was flying in the swirls of a long purple scarf.

"Have you made any progress on the overmantel?" Benjamin asked. "I don't see your intern."

"Julie is not here today, but she is working on it. Don't worry," the restorer said. "It will be finished at the end of the month. Your overmantel is intriguing. I just talked to a man who was examining it and said he owns one just like it."

"Say again?"

"A rather corpulent man in a wheelchair who came in not more than ten minutes ago."

"Do you know who he is?" Benjamin asked, suddenly nervous.

"Not at all. It was the first time I'd seen him. He just told me that his was in better shape and that all he had done was clean it by rubbing a cut potato on the varnish. A heresy! That's an old wives tale that never worked and could ruin a canvas."

"When did he leave?" Benjamin asked.

"I told you. Ten minutes ago. He went toward the bell tower. His wife was pushing the wheelchair. They can't be too far."

The winemaker quickly said good-bye, promising to come back during the week. He grabbed Elisabeth by the wrist, tearing her away from the flying angel. "Quick. It's important," he whispered into her ear. She barely had time to say good-bye to Pascale Dartigeas before she found herself outside the store, gripping her husband's arm. They walked quickly through the stands along the sidewalk in front of the Passage Saint-Michel, stepping over piles of old mechanical parts spread on the pavement, bumping into a grandfather clock, and nearly knocking over a very kitsch psychedelic lamp.

"What's happening, Benjamin?" Elisabeth asked, out of breath.

"We're looking for a man in a wheelchair."

"And you think we'll find him at the flea market?" she asked.

This was not her husband's first flight of fancy, and she was used to even more comical situations, but she felt completely lost. Benjamin summed up the conversation she had missed while she was contemplating the celestial creature.

"We absolutely have to find this fellow," Benjamin continued, using his hand to shield his eyes from the sun.

His wife did the same and slowly turned to examine the surroundings in a broad circular movement.

"Over there, to the right. That looks like a paraplegic," she said calmly.

"Where?"

"Near the café, on the other side of the square. His wife is helping him get in the car."

"I don't see anything!"

"To the right, I said. She is folding up the wheelchair and putting it in the trunk. It's a white station wagon with an antenna on the roof."

"I see it. By the time we cross the square, they'll be gone already. Follow me."

The couple ran to the convertible, which was parked on the Rue des Allamandiers. Benjamin started it with a six-cylinder roar that scared a crowd of bystanders, who stepped aside like a single person. Elisabeth held onto her seat as they sped around the church and came out on the Rue des Faures. The station wagon was already on the street that led to the Capucins market. Benjamin slowed down a little, reassured that he would not lose the car now. They drove up the Cours de l'Yser, after running a red light, and cut across the Cours de la Marne. When they arrived at the Place Nansouty, the white station wagon had already disappeared behind the clump of flowers in the center of the roundabout, having turned onto the street leading to the Saint-Jean train station.

"What the...?" Benjamin spit out, stopping behind a delivery van that was blocking the road.

"They turned left. Calm down," his wife said, putting a hand on his arm.

Benjamin impatiently drummed the steering wheel with his fingers as he waited for the van driver to deign to start up again. Then he rushed onto the Rue Pelleport and slowed down to look into the side streets.

"There they are," Elisabeth cried out. "They parked on the Rue de Cérons. On the left. She is unfolding the chair."

"It's one way. I'll have to take the next street and go around the block."

It took them only two minutes to drive around the block, but they arrived too late. They barely caught a glimpse of the wheelchair as it disappeared into a dull-looking building, and the entrance door clacked shut. Benjamin stopped his convertible in the middle of the street without turning on his blinker or turning off the engine. He walked up to 36 Rue de Cérons and read the enameled sign above the doorbell: "Yvonne Soulagnet. No soliciting."

"It's not right to disturb people this early on a Sunday afternoon. I'll come back tomorrow," he said to his wife. "Since we're in the neighborhood, let's go buy some *cannelés* from

Laurent Lachenal's bakery, and we can pick up some of his sesame bread. I'm starving after this little adventure."

Benjamin felt a little muddled after spending two hours in traffic jams. He had just driven across greater Bordeaux without putting the top of the convertible up, breathing in gas fumes and collecting a layer of dust from the ongoing construction the entire way. When he finally turned onto the Rue de Cérons, he had no trouble finding a parking spot in front of number 36. He rang the bell several times before an elderly woman stuck her nose through a crack in the door, which was held firmly in place by a safety chain. He introduced himself, using a fake name. He didn't bother to provide any lengthy explanations, preferring to get directly to the point.

"I'm looking for a disabled man who was here yesterday. I know that he likes paintings, and I would like to talk to him about a canvas that could interest him."

"I live alone," the woman mumbled.

She had a husky voice that didn't seem to go with her frail body. Her wrinkled yellow complexion resembled a baked apple, and she had sparse hair and hunched shoulders.

"Excuse me for insisting, Mrs. Soulagnet, but I am sure that he will be happy to meet me. I have a painting that I'm certain will interest him."

"Another lousy painting that serves no purpose," the old woman said. "The house is full of them."

"I promise you that Mr. Soulagnet will really—"

"That's not his name! He's my son-in-law. Unfortunately. My poor daughter fell in love with a good-for-nothing, instead of his brother, who knew how to make money. It's a good thing my grandson was able to take over the business. Paintings don't feed the family!"

"You are right, Madame, but please, allow me to insist."

"You are stubborn, aren't you," the old woman chuckled.

"At least give me his name and address so that I can get in touch with him. I won't bother you anymore."

"Gilles Guéret. He is a printer in Bègles. You'll find him in the phone book. The *Béglais Pratique* free sheet is his. My grandson's Sébastien Guéret. He's in charge there now."

Then she let out a grumble in the guise of a good-bye and slammed the door.

Pensive, Benjamin slowly walked back to his Mercedes. He turned the key, began to leave the parking space, and then cut the engine. He grabbed his cell phone and called Virgile.

"Where are you?"

"Hello. I'm at Moniales. I'm finishing up with the samples to take them to the lab."

"We can see to that later."

"But, sir, Alexandrine is waiting for them."

"I said later! Does the name Sébastien Guéret ring a bell?"

There was a brief silence.

"He was an intern on the list. We went to the same wine school, but I didn't know him very well. He wasn't in my class. He is two years younger than I am. We talked to each other occasionally."

"Excellent. You will need to get in touch with him right away."

"How?"

"I don't know. Figure something out. He runs a printing business that publishes an advertising circular. Find something to sell, and go there now. It's in Bègles, the Guéret Press. It's not that complicated. I'm sure you'll find it in the industrial park."

"Something to sell?"

"Anything, it doesn't matter. Be there in half an hour."

"Maybe my car? It's a rundown Renault 5. I don't have any idea how much it's worth."

"It doesn't matter, I told you. Run an ad and try to talk to this Sébastien Guéret. Dig around, ask questions, and bring back what you can."

"So I don't even go to the lab?" Virgile asked.

"It's urgent! You should be on your way already!"

"I'd say, sir, that things are picking up."

"It's about time!"

12

The printing firm's office was functional, with a clinical ugliness that reflected the tastes of the entrepreneurs who had
located in the industrial park. Virgile approached the counter,
looking somewhat timid, and grabbed an ad form. The secretary flashed a big smile.

"Mademoiselle, I'm not sure how to fill in this form."

"I'd be happy to help you."

"Well, I'd like to sell a, well, a somewhat old car. Actually,
a really old car. Let's just say it's not in such good shape, and I
don't exactly know how to describe it without scaring potential buyers away."

"That is a little difficult. You could say, 'Average condition.
Passed inspection.' Or 'Sold as is. Price negotiable.' That's
what people usually put, but I don't know anything about
mechanics."

The conversation continued in a tone of flirtatious banter-
ing. Virgile was playing for time, talking while he watched
staff members come and go behind the window at the reception desk. A surly and sad-looking secretary was yawning as
she made photocopies. A man was pushing a cart of newspapers, and a worker in blue overhauls was on his way to the
employee restroom. After fifteen minutes, Benjamin's assistant
had barely filled in ten lines of his ad form and was still chatting with the secretary, with no end to topics he cared nothing
about. They talked about the Aquitaine Bridge project, the
thirty-five-hour work week, the point-based driving license,
the teachers strike, traffic jams at the Place de la Victoire, the
next Johnny Hallyday concert, taxes, the bad season for the

Girondins soccer team—so many things that reassured people about their ability to judge the state of the world.

He was beginning to feel desperate when he finally caught a glimpse of Sébastien Guéret's chubby cheeks. Their red hue betrayed poorly contained anger. The woman doing photocopies suffered a volley of reprimands and disappeared into the restroom, presumably to compose herself. Sébastien looked like a prosperous employer. An extra twenty pounds had been enough to settle him in life, giving him the self-satisfied look of a manager. When he approached the secretary, he took on an entirely different tone.

"Corinne, my dear, don't forget to bring in my signature book after lunch break," he said in a tender voice.

"Hey, we know each other, don't we?" Virgile said, sounding almost enthusiastic.

Sébastien Guéret looked up and saw him. Dimples appeared on his blotched chubby cheeks.

"That's right. You went to the wine school. Lanssien, isn't it? Mr. Virgile Lanssien!"

"We were not so formal back then."

"Sorry. It's a habit. What are you doing these days? Still in wine?"

"Oh, here and there. Some seasonal work on the estates when they need extra workers."

"I'm through with that. For a while, I thought I liked it, but after my father's accident, I had to take care of the business. And in the end, this is where I belong. If you've got some time, I can show you around. It's all brand new. We moved in last February. It was a lot of work but was worth it."

Sébastien wasn't exactly boastful, but he couldn't hide his pride. He invited Virgile to follow him and gave him a detailed description of each of the offices, starting with his, paneled in faux cherrywood veneer, followed by the accounting department, the invoicing computers, and the storage room. He went on about the growth in advertising revenues, thanks largely to the chamber of commerce and other institutions, paper he bought by the ton, rising prices, and storage issues. Virgile listened and nodded, pretending to be impressed. The personnel began to disappear for lunch.

"Don't forget to lock up after yourself!" Sébastien yelled out.

Then, lowering his voice without dropping the haughtiness, he added, "You have to keep a tight rein. Otherwise they'll be the end of you. Jerks! Believe me, it's not easy to run a business like this."

"I'm sure," Virgile said, giving him a knowing look.

"Some of them miss the old man and try to make things hard for me. I'll end up firing them one day or another, believe me. For that matter, I want to build an entirely new team."

"Times change," the winemaker's assistant said, thinking that might be an appropriate comment.

"If I had listened to my old man, we'd still be in the old neighborhood with run-down offices, only thirteen hundred square feet, crappy orders, and no potential for growth. His accident and his dead legs are really sad, but to be honest, he had turned down the wrong road awhile ago. No pun intended. He put all his money into printing catalogs for regional artists, for Sunday painters nobody knows about. His passion for lousy paintings cost us a lot of cash. Not to mention all those paintings he felt he had to buy to help out the freeloaders who didn't have enough cash to buy their own paint."

"He was like a patron."

"Patron, my ass! It almost ruined us, and my mother was happy when I finally took over the business. It's not always easy for her. She has to take him around in his wheelchair like a kid, wash him, and help him to the bathroom. You get the picture. But he leaves us alone now. We give him enough to buy one or two paintings from time to time, and that's all he asks. Come on, let me show you the best part yet."

He opened double doors that led to the machine room filled with shiny new rotary presses. Sébastien explained how each one worked, talked about the ten-year loan, the write-off, and how he had to keep changing the equipment for the graphic designers, particularly since *Le Béglais Pratique* had tripled its print run. Virgile was unable to stop him. Only the constant ringing of Sébastien's cell phone could get him to consent to a break.

"Excuse me. I'll be just a moment," Sébastien whispered. "If you want, you can wait for me in the hallway and have a coffee. I'll be right there."

"No problem. Take your time," Virgile said.

Once Virgile was alone, he walked around the deserted offices and looked under some piles of papers without really knowing what he was looking for or even if there was anything to find. He put a euro into the coffee machine and continued his tour with a burning-hot cup in hand. Sébastien Guéret's office was open. The lights were on, and his computer was snoozing. Virgile hit a key, and the screen lit up. He clicked on the "mail" file and scanned the list, which he judged to be of no interest, and then he opened the file called "projects." Several files were arranged under small colored icons. Virgile shuddered when he saw one called "Moniales" at the bottom of the list.

Without thinking, he clicked on the web browser icon and pulled up the Cooker&Co.com mail. It was taking forever. He logged in and sent the file to Cooker's address. His heart was pounding, and his shirt was suddenly damp. If only Sébastien could keep talking on the phone! The seconds dragged on. When the file was fully transferred, he opened the privacy settings window and erased any traces of what he had done.

He immediately returned to the lobby and had time to finish his coffee before Sébastien came back, excusing himself for being so long. Virgile told him he had an appointment in town and promised to stop by again. They said good-bye with an emphatic handshake.

As soon as he got into his rundown Renault 5, Virgile called his boss. "Sir? Are you at the lab? I'll be at the Allée de Tourny in fifteen minutes. Wait for me in your office. I just sent you an e-mail."

The Cooker & Co. inbox had several messages in it, including one from the owner of Vistaflores in the Argentine Pampas, where Benjamin was expected for the next wine-making season. There was also a note from Margaux, who wrote with news from New York, but Virgile immediately clicked on the Moniales file. It took a while to download, but when he was finally able to open the document, Benjamin had a totally unfamiliar reaction.

"Holy shit! That can't be!"

The third overmantel was right there, lit up on the screen. Occupying the entire page was the Château Moniales Haut-Brion and its perfectly balanced facade, its rounded steps, its Doric columns, and its dark slate roof. The little chapel's tympanum was depicted in heavy brushstrokes. The painter had portrayed the building correctly, without respecting the enclosure's proportions. The vineyards appeared larger and spread beyond the walls. Because the overmantel had been photographed and scanned, the colors were exaggerated. The graphic designer who had laid out the accompanying information had been careful not to cover any part of the château's imposing structure, because it illustrated the significance of the announcement:

Moniales Residence
A corner of paradise two steps from central Bordeaux
Thirty upscale apartments just minutes from downtown
Near the university and shopping centers
Pool, tennis courts, playground, quality facilities
Treat yourself to country luxury in the heart of the city!

"Well done, Virgile! Well done!"

They opened another file. This time it was a spreadsheet with construction costs, profitability thresholds, supplier estimates, and financial prospects that were a little difficult to decrypt. They scrolled through several dozen pages, a cold

succession of measurements, percentages, and sums. Enough
to make them dizzy.

Benjamin picked up his telephone and immediately called
Alain Delfranc. At this hour, he had probably finished the
lunch service and was quietly smoking his pipe at the window
of the kitchen.

"I have news in the Moniales Haut-Brion case. We just discovered something huge."

"Where are you calling me from?"

"From my office on the Allée de Tourny. I'll admit that this
is a little too big for me to handle all by myself."

"Okay, don't move," Alain ordered. "Starting now, don't
touch anything else."

13

Taste that!"

Benjamin Cooker lifted the glass to eye level. Then he low-ered it slowly, tilting it slightly in front of the white tablecloth to judge the wine's dark color and slightly oily texture as it slid slowly down the side.

"It's good," he said without showing any enthusiasm. "Very good, even. What is it?"

"Is the fabulous Cooker, the imperial winemaker, afraid of losing face?" Alain teased him gently.

"Not at all, my friend. I can tell you that there is sun in it. It's from the South. Perhaps it is made with syrah."

"You're getting warm. You're even quite close."

"Or rather, it's grenache noir and carignan. In any case, it is a blend like that. There is also some mourvèdre and perhaps a little cinsault."

"You're almost there."

"Its attack is not so subtle. It is well structured. You can feel the tannins. There are hints of berries and a slight touch of warm spices. It's well done."

"So?"

"Perhaps a Côte-du-Roussillon. You can smell the terraces, the stone, and the *tramontane* wind."

"You're burning hot."

"I'd say a wine from Collioure, with a characteristic per-sonality and a very concentrated licorice finale. Perhaps it's Les Espérades from the Vial-Magnères domaine. It resembles that kind of wine."

"Damn. How do you do that?"

"You do your job, and I do mine," the winemaker said, drinking another mouthful. "And what if you told me a little about yours."

"The one that used to be mine," Alain Delfranc corrected, lifting his index finger, "and that I was right to run away from, considering how rotten the world is!"

"Regardless, you did me a great service by taking the Moniales case to the police. Thanks to you, everything was handled quickly and efficiently."

"I think that if you had brought it to their attention yourself, they would have passed it from department to department," Alain admitted. "And they would have taken longer to order the search."

Benjamin poured himself another glass of Collioure and lit up a Villa Zamorano—a falsely rustic robusto from Honduras that he had heard about but had yet to taste. He settled into his armchair and let out a thick puff of gray smoke.

"So, now you can tell me exactly what he confessed to, our Guéret."

"Everything, absolutely everything! He didn't try to deny any of it. He was working for his uncle, Robert Guéret, who is, well, an unscrupulous real estate developer. The man helped his nephew when Gilles Guéret had his car accident. He invested in the printing presses and got bank loans to help Sébastien. In exchange, he asked for some small services. The kid wasn't a hard one to corrupt. He was a little snot who wanted to get ahead and, most of all, to prove to his mother that he could succeed where his father had failed."

"So it was Uncle Robert who planned the whole thing?" Benjamin asked, leaning back on the headrest.

"When Gilles Guéret had his accident, Sébastien's uncle got involved with the advertising circular. Sébastien was still an intern at the Moniales Haut-Brion, and the uncle wanted the kid to quit his oenology studies and take over the family business. Obviously, he put out some cash to persuade him. Before Sébastien left, however, the uncle saw his opportunity and asked his nephew for a favor. He had the kid make a wax imprint of the cellar keys. Apparently it is not very complicated. Sébastien took advantage of a moment of inattention on the steward's part to take the keys from his jacket, which was hanging near the door of the tank room, and he simply molded them in a special wax. Then he used the impressions to have the keys made. "

"So this wasn't something that Uncle Robert had spent a long time planning?" Benjamin said, setting down his empty glass.

"Not at all. One day when he was picking up his nephew at the château, it dawned on him that he could ruin Denis Massepain's life and offer to buy the estate at a rock-bottom price. Then he could build luxury apartments. No kidding. An estate of that standing, with several acres of trees and a small brook, has great appeal to developers. But that you saw on the documents."

"Yes, I saw. But that doesn't explain how they managed to get past the alarm."

"Guéret Jr. had overheard a conversation between Denis and the steward. One of them had mentioned a year, but it seemed out of context. Guéret realized that it was actually the code to the alarm. When he returned to put that damned yeast into the barrels, he entered the four numbers, and the alarm was turned off. He's not dumb! In fact, he's quite clever, because he specifically chose to pollute only some of the barrels so it wouldn't look like a malicious act."

"Absolutely. For the uncle and the nephew, it was just the first part of a strategy designed to drain Massepain's morale and put a proverbial knife to his throat. In any case, they intended to go as far as they needed to get their hands on the Moniales. They were ready to act as soon as their attacks succeeded. You saw how the uncle used Sébastien to build his marketing campaign for the luxury apartments even before the yeast had done its job. It was all in perfect order—starting with the overmantel used in the initial advertising. The whole campaign included posters, brochures, ads, and other promotional materials, all produced free of charge by the Guéret presses, of course!"

"And the overmantel..."

"That is another story. It is, for that matter, exclusively your story. Had you not gone out looking for that painting and then instinctively put two and two together when you discovered the connection to Sébastien, this crime would have played out. Nobody would have known. For that matter, I would like to know how many dirty deeds of the kind have been carried out in the Pessac and Talence areas! Behind all those buildings, luxury apartments, and suburban houses there must be some pretty sleazy politicking, scheming, bribing, intimidation, and power plays."

"Better not to imagine them. What good does it do? But how did they get their hands on that overmantel?"

"That was just by chance. Sébastien's father had bought the painting some time ago, and it had been lying around in a back hallway. The son had known about it since he was little, and he thought it would be good for the marketing campaign. Very chic! Even small-time swindlers can have class."

"Alain, I have to admit that I have been dishonest about something."

"It's time for the great confession!" the innkeeper said as he lit his pipe again.

"Yes, I must confess that I did something really ugly. It was a dirty trick you should never, ever pull on a friend."

Alain Delfranc started to turn pale.

"Are you serious, Benjamin? Or are you joking?"

"No, I'm serious. And if I tell you, promise me you won't tell anyone."

"Okay, okay."

"Your Collioure. I knew what it was with the first mouthful. I wrote about it last week for an English magazine."

"Cheater! And on top of that, you dragged out the pleasure, just so I'd wonder if there was a tiny chink in your winemaker's armor?"

"No, no. Just to make fun of myself."

He made the decision when he woke up. He would use the first introduction to Blaye he had written. Just to be sure, Benjamin reread his new attempts to describe it and ended up throwing them away. He then called his editor to tell him there would be no modifications, with the exception of three words he absolutely had to change: "milksop" for "coward," "bloody" for "bloodthirsty," and "diverse," which fit better than "contrasted." When he hung up, he did not feel all that self-assured and was afraid that his final instructions would not be followed. He drank two cups of tea and decided to take Bacchus on a walk to clear his mind.

He didn't return until lunch, his boots caked with clay and his face damp with perspiration. The dog was in no better shape than his master. His tongue was hanging out. He was dragging his paws, and he didn't even bother to bark when Virgile's Renault 5 came speeding up Grangebelle's gravel drive.

"Hello, Mr. Cooker. Your friend Denis has sent over four cases of Moniales Haut-Brion to thank you for what you did."

"Of course you told him that tomorrow I'm off to Burgundy and that I would stop by to see him when I get back."

"I'll be sure to do so. When you are gone, I'll drop in to make sure everything is going well, but we can already say for sure that this year's wine has been saved. Alexandrine is sure of that."

"Keep the cases, Virgile. You deserve them as much as I."

"Mr. Massepain gave me four, as well."

"He's a gentleman. Let's go in. Elisabeth must be waiting for us to eat. I think she prepared a beef *estouffade* with olives, mushrooms, and a good red wine—a Canon-Fronsac she managed to steal from me."

Before sitting down, Benjamin grabbed a book from the shelf and handed it to his assistant.

"Here, Virgile, it's a pleasure for me to give you this. You may not care to read Montaigne, and you might frown on Montesquieu, but you must read François Mauriac."

"*Maltaverne.* That's an intriguing title."

"It's a fine text. I'll be honest with you. I would give anything to have never read it, so I could enjoy discovering it again. Indeed, that is the only advantage of youth."

"Thank you. I'll start reading it tonight."

"Read it whenever you want, Virgile. Tonight, in a week, in a year. It doesn't matter. Great writing is like a great wine. It finds those deserving of it."

BOOK 2

BOOK 2

Grand Cru Heist

A Winemaker Detective Mystery

Translated from French by Anne Trager

"Finishing off a bottle of wine together
is a fine sign of friendship."
—Jean Carmet

1

Paris finally returned to its splendor at dusk. Lights from the cruise boats caressed the buildings on the Left Bank. The bridges cast wavering shadows on the waters of the Seine. At the corner of the Rue Dauphine, a few patches of half-melted snow, curiously saved from the passing footsteps, were shining under the streetlights.

Benjamin Cooker had felt deprived of light all day. He awaited this miraculous hour, when everything could be reborn in the fleeting glow of night. As he got older, he had less tolerance for the unchanging leaden sky that covered Paris in winter. Everything, from the pallid faces of café servers to the hotel concierge's waxy complexion, the bare trees in the Tuileries Gardens, and the homeless camping out on the subway grates, seemed dull and gray. He had loved this city in his happy-go-lucky days, and now he found it suffocating.

Here, even the snow was hoary, dirty, and reduced to mud in a few hours with the constant comings and goings of the city. He missed peaceful Médoc, and he was impatient to return to his home, Grangebelle, the next day. The vineyards would be superb, all white and wrapped in silence. The cold would be dry and refreshing, and the sky nearly royal blue. He would go for a solitary walk along the Gironde just to hear the snow crunch under his boots. Elisabeth got cold easily and would probably remain in front of the fire in the living room, her hands around a steaming cup of tea.

Benjamin Cooker drove slowly, letting his gloves glide over the steering wheel while he whistled along with a Chopin nocturne on the radio. According to the too-ceremonious radio host, it was *Opus 19*. He was comfortable, settled into the leather seat of his classic Mercedes 280SL. He turned onto Pont des Arts to get to his hotel, which was near the opera house. The red light was taking forever. He lifted the collar of his Loden and turned up the radio as someone approached the car, flicking his thumb to mimic a lighter. Cooker squinted to get a better look at the man's face. It was hidden under a hood, but he seemed young, despite his stooped, somewhat misshapen form. Cooker shook his head and waved his hands to indicate that he did not smoke.

The light turned green, but Cooker did not have time to accelerate. His car door opened suddenly, as if it had been ripped off, and cold air rushed in.

"Take that, rich bastard."

The man pulled out a switchblade. Cooker did not move. *Don't panic. Stay calm. Breathe slowly. Think fast.* He felt the tip of the knife on his Adam's apple and gulped. A second man opened the other door and searched the glove compartment.

"Get rid of him," he said, unbuckling Cooker's seat belt.

The hooded man hit Cooker twice in the jaw, grabbed him by the tie, and dragged him to the ground. Then the thug kicked him in the stomach, head, and ribs—"Take that, asshole." The taste of blood and thick grit from the pavement burned his lips—"Your mother's a bitch." A final glance, a few notes of Chopin—"Eat shit, dirtbag!"—and screeching tires. Then nothing.

Staff hurried through the corridors at the Pitié-Salpetrière Hospital. The warm aroma of hot coffee filled the ward. Benjamin Cooker was trying to look at the small corner of white sky that was attempting—in vain—to light up the room, but he could barely turn his head.

"Don't worry, sir. You're safe here."

The nurse had bright green eyes. A gold cross was hanging from her beautiful freckled neck. She had a soft voice; it was almost tender and sleep-inducing.

"You should get some rest. You are still in shock, Mr. Cooker. Your wife will be here soon."

She spoke the way a child would speak to her father. Cooker thought about his daughter, Margaux. He hoped that Elisabeth had not told her what had happened. There was no sense causing worry. He could barely remember anything from the previous night, except the 1961 Latour he had shared with Claude Nithard, his publisher, at the Tour d'Argent.

The nurse took his pulse, explaining that he had been found unconscious on the sidewalk and rushed to the emergency room.

"What about my car?"

"Stay calm, sir. It is only a car. You are lucky to be alive."

A tear rolled down Cooker's cheek. He closed his eyes and sighed deeply to expel the feeling of powerless rage and isolation that tightened his chest. His old convertible also carried his tawny leather briefcase, which held the fountain pen Margaux had given him. A jeweler in New York had engraved his name on it. The briefcase also held some bank statements, his agenda, and the thick dog-eared notebook he was very attached to. Year after year, the winemaker had jotted down his impressions of all the wines he had tasted the world over, along with who had what stocks of the best vintages. How many pages had he filled with his meticulous handwriting? At best, the document would end up in some garbage can in the projects or the sewer.

Elisabeth would be here in a few hours, sitting on the edge of his bed. He would tell her everything. Well, what he could. The truth was, he couldn't remember much. It had all happened so quickly.

"Yes, my love, the light had just turned green."

His wife put a finger to his lips and said, "My poor darling, look at what they've done to you."

Sadness filled his face. He stared at her and said nothing more. Then he looked down. He was disappointed with himself. He had fallen into a trap and had not even put up a fight. He felt like a coward. She knew the words to reassure him and make him feel better. She told him that she was thankful he was alive, that he should let the police do their job. Elisabeth then whispered a few sweet nothings. And they crossed their fingers and hoped for the best, as they always did when they faced life's hardships.

"They'll find your notebook, Benjamin. Don't worry. I'll call your editor."

"No, I'd prefer that you didn't. Don't tell anyone but Virgile."

Of course, Virgile Lanssien came with Elisabeth. He would not have left his employer's wife alone in such a crisis. Elisabeth went to find him in the hallway.

"Boss, how's it going? They really crushed you, didn't they?" Virgile teased, trying to lighten the mood when he saw the winemaker's bruised face.

Cooker smiled at the vineyard humor. His jaw hurt terribly, but he felt better with Elisabeth and Virgile at his side.

"I don't remember anything. Can you believe it? Nothing! Except that 1961 Latour. I wish you could have tasted it."

The nurse came in to change the bandages on Cooker's swollen face and caught Virgile's eye. He gave her a once-over, from neck to ankles, while Elisabeth hung up some clothes she had brought for her husband. Virgile winked at his boss.

"The snow has already melted," the young woman said, clearly sorry about that.

Cooker's eyes were half-closed. He winced when the nurse ran a damp cloth over his eyebrows to remove the dried blood.

"What handsome blue eyes you have, sir," she said, trying to divert his attention from what she was doing.

"I believe they are why my wife married me. Isn't that so, Elisabeth?"

"I won't argue with you today, not with what you've been through," Elisabeth said, kissing his hand.

Virgile seemed a little uncomfortable. He turned to the window. "I think it's going to snow again," he said to fill the silence.

The nurse looked at him and smiled with something less than innocence. To the impish grin she added, "From your lips to God's ear."

Virgile looked her in the eye and said, "If that were the case, the snowflakes would be angel feathers."

"You are a lucky man, Mr. Cooker, to have such a spiritual son," the nurse said.

The week passed slowly, punctuated by bandage-changing sessions, lukewarm meals, temperature checks, and long periods of sleep. Christmas was a few days away. Large snowflakes were falling, as if covering the ground with a layer of protection. Carole was thrilled. The nurse had disclosed her first name to Cooker, perhaps in the hope that the information would get to Virgile.

"So he's not your son?"

"No, he's my assistant. He is very good at what he does."

Carole blushed and quickly changed the subject. "You are healing nicely. You were incredibly lucky. The man was that close to slitting your throat. If he had, you wouldn't have made it."

When she leaned over the bed, Cooker couldn't help staring at the three beauty marks on her chest. *This is ridiculous*, he thought, reproaching himself for his moodiness. *My face is not disfigured. It's just bruised.* He felt old, even though he was just fifty. Admittedly, the graying temples, a rebellious lock of hair, bushy eyebrows, and crow's-feet gave him a dignified charm. But was he still attractive? And why was he wondering this after having a narrow brush with death?

"Life is all about seduction," his father would have said. It was a maxim the man had practiced until his later years.

Still, Cooker was regaining some of his appetite for life, despite the anxiety attacks he suffered in the middle of the night. He would wake up in a sweat, pursued by hooded teenagers who threw insults and lighters at him. Cooker knew he would need time to process the trauma.

Carole, who clearly had a thing for Virgile, was helping with her disarming innocence and the childlike euphoria she expressed when she saw snow on the rooftops.

"I hope it lasts until Christmas," she said continually, like a child repeating a prayer without really believing in God or Santa Claus.

Cooker used whatever ploys he could to keep her in his room. They would look out the window and watch the snow swirl between the zinc rooftops and chimneys.

One afternoon, the winemaker loosened up enough to tell her a personal story. He wasn't positive it was true, but that didn't seem to matter.

"My father rarely left London, but one day before the war, he went off exploring southwestern France. He ended up in Toulouse, visiting the Basilica of Saint Sernin. He stayed at Le Grand Balcon, the hotel where the famous aviators Jean Mermoz and Antoine de Saint-Exupéry had met."

"I loved Saint-Exupéry's *The Little Prince*," Carole said, slipping her cross back and forth on its chain.

"At the time, my father dreamed of being a pilot. He was only twenty. He stayed in Saint-Exupéry's room, where there was an old radio. He tried to tune into Radio London but got distracted by Radio Toulouse and the advertising slogan 'Dubo, Dubon, Dubonnet.'"

The nurse laughed at Cooker's attempt to imitate the nasal tone of old-time radio hosts. He exaggerated it to please her.

"From his room, my father could see the Place du Capitole. Have you ever been to Toulouse?"

The nurse said no and mentioned her roots in Grenoble.

"The sky was gray, the weather uncertain, and Radio Toulouse announced, 'Dear listeners, direct from the Toulouse-Blagnac weather station, ninety-nine flakes of snow have fallen on our fine city, and the temperature is freezing. We are expecting more snow tomorrow, so get out your mittens. And now, Jean Sablon will sing '*Vous qui passez sans me voir.*'"

"Ninety-nine snowflakes. That was news in the day," Carole said.

"That's when my father said it was best to watch out for the French. He wrote his mother a letter to tell her about the ninety-nine snowflakes, and she told him to come home to London as soon as possible. She thought he was losing his mind. He even admitted to standing at his hotel window and counting snowflakes until dusk, coming up with far more than ninety-nine."

"I don't believe you," Carole said.

"It's true. I promise you it's true," Cooker answered in a deadpan voice. "My father did eventually get an explanation, something about how at the time, nobody improvised on the radio. They just read from notes. The radio announcer confused some shorthand for nine centimeters for ninety-nine snowflakes. He apparently got a good reprimand from his boss."

Cooker puffed up when the nurse laughed at his story, showing her flawless teeth. Then Virgile burst into the room. Carole turned around quickly, smoothed out her scrubs, and nearly knocked the winemaker's IV bag off the stand.

"Your torture is nearly over, Mr. Cooker. You should be getting out tomorrow."

Virgile watched the way Cooker and the nurse looked at each other as his assistant handed over the morning paper with a mischievous grin. The front-page story in the newspaper *France-Soir* caught the winemaker's eye immediately: "Grand Cru Heist. A hundred bottles of the famous 1989 Angélus premier grand cru classé were stolen last night from the renowned cellar at the Place de la Madeleine in Paris. The burglar stole only this internationally acclaimed Saint-Émilion and selected the very best vintage, which received top ranking in the *Cooker Guide*."

Cooker pulled out the latest edition of his guide, which Virgile had brought him, and read his tasting notes in full.

"Who could want anything more for Christmas than some 1989 Angélus?" he asked.

Behind the attempt at humor, there was concern in his voice. He was thinking about his friend Hubert de Boüard de Laforest, who owned the premier grand cru mentioned in the article.

"How are you feeling today, sir?" Virgile asked.

"Like an ass who wasn't brave enough to fight and ended up in his shorts on the sidewalk." Cooker suddenly felt enraged. He tensed his jaw and pushed out his chest, as if he could not breathe. "They took everything, Virgile. Everything! All my notes. My entire guide. And my memories, my pride, my honor."

Virgile stared at his boss. Cooker pulled himself up on the bed and grimaced when he tried to turn to the window to hide the sob he felt coming on. Carole touched his shoulder.

"It's nothing, Mr. Cooker. Calm down. You'll be home tomorrow. You'll forget about it over time."

"And you've got all those notes in your head," Virgile added, also putting his hand on his boss's shoulder.

Just then, a cell phone rang.

"It's probably Elisabeth worrying about me," Cooker said. "Oh, it's you, darling? My little Margaux. I'm happy to hear your voice."

A smile came over his face. Virgile and Carole caught each other's eye and left Cooker, who was already looking more optimistic.

2

At the bottom of the valley, the Indre River flowed through patches of reverent willow trees. It was January, but it felt like an aging autumn in this part of the Touraine region. Lazy cows grazed in the pasture, just as they had in the summer. From the terrace of the Château de La Tortinière, Benjamin Cooker stared at the blurry lines of the landscape. In the distance, the Montbazon castle showed off its tower from another era. The Virgin Mary that rose above the edifice would have been demoralized by the ruins of the fortress. Recently, city workers had pulled off the ivy that had overgrown the fortifications, perhaps offering some redemption to the copper statue.

"Rest." Everyone—his doctors, of course, but also Elisabeth, Margaux, Virgile, and the others—kept saying the same thing. Sometimes Benjamin Cooker showed worrisome symptoms, with long silences that nobody dared to interrupt.

"This kind of attack is a violation, Mr. Cooker," a psychiatrist had told him in the hospital. "You will need weeks, perhaps even months to move on."

Cooker had closed his eyes. He was not convinced that Grangebelle, his retreat-like home in the Médoc, was the ideal spot for his convalescence. He needed new surroundings and new people.

He told Elisabeth and Virgile that he had chosen the Touraine because he still had a lot to learn about the wines in that region. He had visited the Loire River valley several times in the past. Vouvray, Bourgueil, and Chinon had pleased his palate, and he had often promised himself that he would explore this area further. It was known as France's garden, and the vineyards grew in the shadow of stone lacework castles. His stroke of bad luck had actually become an ideal pretext to wander the vineyards, even though they were bare at this time of year.

Cooker intended to stay until January 22, Saint Vincent's feast day. It was a symbolic choice. Saint Vincent was the patron saint of winegrowers, and with a little luck, the day would be "clear and beautiful" for "more wine than water," as the saying went. Elisabeth arrived with him and spent a few days, but she had to return to Grangebelle to take care of their dog, Bacchus, who did not appreciate it when they were away too long.

"Can't you come home, Benjamin? I don't like the idea of leaving you alone. You're going to be bored in that hotel during the off season."

"Me, bored? With everything there is to see and drink? Don't worry, my love. I need to get my head together before I go home. If I set one foot in Grangebelle, I'd have to go to the office. I couldn't resist."

Aware that Elisabeth was not particularly reassured, Cooker saw her off on the bullet train from Saint-Pierre-des-Corps to the Bordeaux-Saint-Jean station, where Alicia Santamaria, the Spanish immigrant who lived with Grangebelle's gardener, came to get her.

Elisabeth called her husband to say she had arrived safely and told him that Alicia had once again railed against France's lax immigration policies. Alicia blamed them for the country's rise in violent crime. In her mind, the assailants were probably North African.

"*Por Díos*, I can't believe what happened to monsieur!" Alicia had said, her Spanish accent tinged with Gascon. "They let everyone into France. *Qué misería*."

At Château de La Tortinière, Cooker knew he would find the solitude he needed to get over his fear of driving in cities and people asking him for a light. But he didn't quite know how he would get through the weeks ahead of him.

He dropped into a rattan chair that beckoned in front of the balustrade. He wasn't feeling faint, but he did need to catch his breath. Cooker was about to ask for a glass of water but thought better of it. The concierge, Gaétan, was right there, looking concerned.

"It's nothing. I'd like a Bourgueil from the Domaine du Bel Air. Do you have some?"

He felt better when he saw Gaétan rush off, taking the stairs two at a time and then returning promptly. Cooker seemed to regain his sense of self before the wine glass was even full of the dark red liquid. He lifted the glass to his nose, while Gaétan, looking like a dignified Greek statue on a spacious estate, held the bottle, waiting for a verdict that would be brutally honest. The winemaker sniffed aromas of berries and spices and picked up a few woody notes before bringing the glass to his lips. He savored the Bourgueil with the mannerisms of an experienced wine taster. He rolled the mouthful like a billiard ball on a pool table, lining his palate so as not to miss any of the full, round, ripe tannins in this excellent wine. From time to time, he clicked his tongue to refine his judgment. The concierge waited for the final decision. Cooker patted the chair next to him, beckoning the young man to sit down.

"I cannot enjoy this pleasure alone," Cooker said. Gaétan looked flattered by the invitation.

Cooker was the only guest at the hotel, so they could enjoy this luxury. La Tortinière would close for the season shortly, and the staff had been cut back.

Cooker shared his impressions of the wine. The concierge was hardly a novice and had a fairly refined palate himself. Cooker had found an ally, not unlike Virgile. Gaétan and Virgile were both about the same age, with expressive faces, a sense of humor, and a little clumsiness that made them charming.

Cooker and Gaétan chatted until the sun had disappeared behind La Tortinière's turrets. Cooker could no longer see Montbazon, and the cows had disappeared from the pasture as if by magic. The winemaker felt a chill and returned to his room. He would order dinner from room service before calling it a night. Tucked in his pocket was the hotel chef's recipe for saffron honey ice that Gaétan had gotten for him. Elisabeth would enjoy it.

Cooker went to sleep with Madame de Mortsauf. He had stopped at an antique book stand in the city of Tours and picked up a leather-bound copy of Honoré de Balzac's *The Lily of the Valley* that, curiously, had been used to dry flowers. Yellowed linden leaves and flower petals garnished every chapter, like exquisite bookmarks. The book gave off faded floral aromas, and Cooker devoured the novel. La Tortinière was his. He was alone in this manor that smelled of wax polish and holly. The owners lived in another building a hundred yards away.

"You're the master of the house," owner Anne Olivereau had said with a genuine charm that impressed the wine expert.

He had no bad dreams that night. Cooker was healing. The next day, he would get back to writing his guide. He had not told his editor what had happened and did not intend to. Saying nothing about it was a matter of pride.

When Cooker woke up, he spotted a Morgan Plus 8 parked majestically in front of La Tortinière. It was deep green, very English, and gleamed on the white gravel. The winemaker smiled and left his room to admire the sports car. Such a jewel deserved respect. He was sure that its owner was a subject of Her Majesty the Queen.

The license plate proved Cooker correct. He caressed the chrome, as he would a sleeping tiger. He walked around the car several times, peering in the windows to examine the convertible's interior.

A Morgan! He had dreamed of this car since he was a kid. The mechanics were way too fragile, but nothing could top it for luxury and elegance. Twenty years earlier, he had almost bought a very fine model that had belonged to French novelist André Malraux's son. But by the time he had convinced the bank to lend him the money, the beautiful English car had been snatched up by some fifteen-minute celebrity. The winemaker had never gotten over it and had fallen back on his Mercedes 280SL, which he now missed.

The concierge came to greet him and listened to Cooker expound on the car: how it could hold the road, the custom interior, the fine cylinders, and the specific sound its exhaust made. Gaétan was not particularly passionate about vintage cars but nevertheless asked a number of questions that Cooker was happy to answer. In exchange, Gaétan gave Cooker the name of the owner, a certain Sir Robert Morton, a middle-aged man accompanied by a gorgeous young blond woman who spoke "approximate" French and seemed to come from some Eastern Bloc country.

"They arrived at dawn, demanded a copious breakfast served with champagne—he wanted nothing but Moët—and asked not to be disturbed under any circumstances," Gaétan said, lifting an eyebrow.

The young man looked up at the lovers' room, where the shutters were closed. Cooker imagined the couple intertwined under wrinkled sheets. Surely, it was some secret liaison that had found refuge in this isolated hotel.

"I'll take my tea in the small dining room," Cooker said, rubbing his hands in anticipation of meeting this Mr. Morton.

He was impatient to see the mysterious owner of the Morgan and his conquest. He wolfed down two croissants and drank three cups of tea. Then the winemaker had to go see the car again. The air was brisk, but the sight of the chrome reflecting the January sun revved Cooker's imagination. With his British background, he would find the right civilities and some common ground with these people, who shared his passion. He was already imagining himself riding through the countryside behind the wheel of that convertible. But the shutters remained hopelessly closed.

The concierge told Cooker about the pleasant walks in the area, down by the river. He opted for just a short walk around the hotel grounds, which were covered with moss and ivy. A number of trees watched over the La Tortinière manor. Lebanese cedars, Japanese pagoda trees, sequoias, and several varieties of evergreens formed a huge nave that even bright sun had trouble penetrating. The solitary walker tried to see the tops of each, but clearly the trees that surrounded the hotel were much older than the building.

The winemaker remembered what Gaétan had told him the evening before. La Tortinière's architect had been inspired by Charles Perrault's legendary *Sleeping Beauty*, even though the author had set his fairy tale in the Château d'Ussé, which was not far away. Cooker, however, refused to transform Mr. Morton into Prince Charming. He imagined him plump, slightly potbellied, wearing designer clothes. His Gold Card had to be the source of unimaginable charm, capable of seducing a Lolita who had managed to escape the streets of Budapest. But this Morton fellow did get the benefit of the doubt. He could not be completely lacking in taste if he drove a Morgan Plus 8.

Cooker walked deeper into the vegetation. Frozen leaves crackled under his shoes. A squirrel caught his attention and then took off on a path festooned with red berries. A slate-roofed farm appeared among the trees. Leading to it was an old drive lined with what looked like two-hundred-year-old holly bushes. Cooker was about to investigate when he heard steps behind him. He winced before recognizing a familiar voice. "Mr. Cooker, Mr. Cooker. There's a phone call for you."

Gaétan was out of breath, and his nose and cheeks were bright red from the cold. He asked Cooker to return to the hotel. The caller hadn't given his name, but he wanted to talk to the winemaker right away.

"It's urgent and personal," the young man said. "That's all that he told me."

Walking quickly, Cooker followed Gaétan but soon had to ask him to slow down because he couldn't keep up. When they arrived in front of the hotel, Cooker was disappointed to see that the Morgan was gone.

"Have Mr. Morton and his protégé already run off?" he asked.

"Rest assured, he's just gone to Tours in search of cigars, leaving his princess to sleep," Gaétan answered with a wink.

Cooker was liking this Morton more and more. Not only did he appreciate English cars and pretty women, but he also had an affinity for cigars. The man had to be an epicurean. With so much in common, they were destined to meet.

Cooker took the phone that sat on the marble reception desk.

"Hubert? What a surprise."

Cooker was happy to have his friend on the line. They hadn't spoken since some international tycoon had the gall to make an offer on his estate. Hubert had refused, of course. Château Angélus had been in the family for eight generations.

Hubert asked him how he was feeling. Yes, Cooker told him, he was feeling better. Yes, he was recovering his appetite for life. No, he had no news about his convertible, nor about his briefcase, but he still hoped to get his tasting notes back. They were of no interest to anyone but himself.

"But tell me, Hubert, what wouldn't you do to get people talking about your wine? I read in the paper that your Angélus is popular with thieves. Great publicity!"

Cooker noticed Gaétan listening discreetly as he arranged bottles of brandy on the shelves behind the bar. But he continued to speak loudly, as if he were alone in the hotel.

"It's a strange thing that happened. What is that you said?"

After every pause, the winemaker responded, "No! That's unbelievable."

Cooker saw that the concierge was even more curious about his mysterious half-sentences.

"It's a joke! Someone sent you a cryptic play on the Angélus devotion to the Virgin Mother—'Hail Hubert, full of grace. The Lord is with you, but your wine is not.' Whoever it is, he has a wicked sense of humor. I'm surprised he didn't send a bell, along with the card. It's too bad I only write guidebooks, because this would make a great novel, my friend."

The winemaker was now sitting in the golden leather arm-chair, as if to better enjoy the comical story his old friend Hubert de Boüard de Laforest was recounting.

But as Cooker continued to talk, he realized that Hubert didn't think that this was anything to joke about.

"Really, Hubert, it's just a prank. Why are you taking it so seriously?"

The two friends spoke for a long while, until an elegant figure made a noisy entrance in the château lobby. Cooker supposed it was the infamous Mr. Morton and gave him a slight nod while continuing the commentary on his friend's story. Then he cut the conversation short. "All you can do now is wait. If more of your wine is stolen, I suggest that you go talk to the police."

Cooker was still amused after he hung up. He had to share the story with someone. He would tell Gaétan, or maybe he would confide in the lanky Morton, who turned out to be as tall and dried up as a Tuscany yew tree. He was savoring a Cohiba and reading the *Herald Tribune*.

As soon as there was silence in the hotel lobby, the Englishman abandoned his reading and slipped his thin glasses into the inner pocket of his jacket. Then the owner of the Morgan got up and headed toward the clearly uninhibited guest whose telephone conversation had been all but public.

"*Excusez-moi*, sir, are you not Mr. Cooker, the well-known winemaker and critic?"

The man spoke broken French mixed with Oxford English. His diction was a little precious, as were his gestures. Cooker confirmed his identity with a smile and shook the Englishman's hand.

"Let me introduce myself. Robert Morton. I work in London for a wine brokerage."

"So, we share three passions," Cooker was quick to point out.

"I have no trouble imagining the first, but I must admit that I don't know what the two others could be, Mr. Cooker."

"From what I can tell, there are cigars, and are you not the happy owner of that dream car that's perfect for taking in Loire Valley's castles?"

Morton grinned. He rubbed his chin and asked the wine-maker if he'd like a cup of tea. "Unless you would prefer coffee."

"With pleasure," Cooker said. "Thank you."

"A cigar?"

Robert Morton opened his shagreen case and took out a cigar with a band that Cooker recognized. He handed the Havana and the guillotine cutter to Cooker, whose friendship he seemed keen to nurture.

"So, Mr. Cooker, you like English beauties? I truly understand."

"Not always English, but I would go to Rocamadour on my knees for a Morgan."

"Where's that?" the Brit said.

The winemaker gave Morton a lesson in the history of that town in southwestern France that had attracted pilgrims for centuries. Smoke swirled above their heads, as the two men sized each other up. When Gaétan asked if they wanted more tea, they were speaking in English. There seemed to be no stopping them. Between two thick curls of smoke, they discussed New World wines, convertible sports cars, French and English rugby teams, Médoc wines, the cost of real estate in Périgord, southwestern French gastronomy, Charles de Gaulle, Churchill, Lady Diana, Charlotte Rampling, and Lord Byron, not to mention Cooker's recent misadventure in Paris.

Toward the middle of the day, the young woman who shared Morton's bed showed up, yawning. It looked like she had just climbed out of bed and thrown on a pair of jeans and a tight T-shirt. She was beautiful, tall, and had a lofty neck. With her full bust, she almost looked like a naïve and mischievous cherub—or a fallen angel whose steel-blue eyes said much about the pain they hid. Her elegant bone structure accentuated hollow cheeks and sensual lips.

"Did you sleep well, Oksana?" Morton asked in a flat voice.

Cooker was convinced that she meant little to this dandy, who pretended to know more about life than his age seemed to imply. For that matter, it took skill to guess the slender man's age. His flashy signet ring did, however, betray new money. That did not make the man any less likable. The new friends jumped at the idea of going to lunch at the Château d'Artigny. But the Morgan had only two seats. Oksana would be sacrificed on the altar of machismo.

"Go back to bed, darling. Tonight, we have a long drive. We have to be in Bordeaux before midnight." Robert Morton pecked her on the forehead.

Gaétan dried champagne glasses behind the bar and Cooker saw him looking her up and down. She pretended not to notice and walked out, swaying her hips in a way that was both seductive and rejecting.

3

Morton and Cooker finished off two bottles of Vouvray. Their meal was copious, with a coriander-flavored *nage de langoustines*, mullet filets sautéed with endive, veal tenderloin with morels, and a slow-cooked carrot and orange dessert. Then Artigny's sommelier dug up some aged rum that called for two cigars—double coronas from Partagas. After everything he had been through in Paris, nothing was more important to Benjamin Cooker's morale than savoring the present.

The two men were in brilliant form and raised their glasses to life, love, and their respective success. By the time Mortan revved up his sweet engine to drive back to La Tortinière, neither of the two men could even pretend to be lucid. The aged rum from Martinique had definitely cheered them up, and the road from the restaurant back to the hotel seemed to have quite a few more bends and curves than it did earlier in the day. Even the chill in the air was not enough to nip their euphoria. A frowning Gaétan met the two staggering men in front of the hotel.

"Did you have a fine lunch, sirs?" he asked and then stammered, "Um, Mr. Morton, the young woman accompanying you preferred to call a taxi and asked me to tell you not to try to contact her. Uh, that's what she said."

The Englishman swore under his breath. Cooker looked down and said, "I'm terribly sorry. It's my fault."

"Not at all, Benjamin. It's perhaps the best thing that has happened to me today."

"If you say so," Cooker said, looking doubtful.

"Gaétan, a double rum, please."

"Right away, sir," the concierge responded. "And for you, Mr. Cooker?"

"The same," the winemaker said, keen on not abandoning his partner in crime.

Robert Morton collapsed in an armchair. It swallowed him up. His bony knees and the wounded-bird expression on his face were all that Cooker could see. Morton emptied his glass in one gulp and asked for his hotel bill. This bothered Cooker. Morton was evidently more concerned than he had said. The winemaker tried to dissuade him from driving in his state, but in vain. The Englishman insisted that he could not be late for his appointment in Bordeaux and waved a weak good-bye.

"Business, my dear Cooker. You know what our line of work requires."

Cooker nodded. He finished his rum, and, from La Tortinière's front steps, watched Morton zoom down the drive in his vintage Morgan. *Well, that was a short-lived friendship,* he thought. Not wanting to be alone, he headed to the bar and ordered another rum from Gaétan, who said nothing.

Mr. Morton was a strange man. *This* Cooker knew. Otherwise, he knew very little about him, although he was sure their paths would cross again. He intuited it as he examined the bottom of his glass, like a fortune-teller reading tea leaves. Alas, the hotel's rum was more rustic than the one at Château d'Artigny, and Cooker did not finish his glass. He huddled in a chair for a long time, missing Morton already. He would have liked to see Oksana in her tight jeans again, and he would have loved driving that Morgan, even just around the grounds or on a short trip to Montbazon. *Had it all been a dream?* The rum was making him doubt the very existence of the eccentric and enigmatic Morton.

He ended up falling asleep in the armchair. The crackling of wood and the pungent aroma of smoking vine shoots awakened him a short time later. Gaétan had lit a fire. Cooker apologized to the concierge, as if he had been caught red-handed being lazy.

"Would you like to have dinner in your room tonight, Mr. Cooker?" Not giving the winemaker a chance to gather his thoughts, Gaétan added, "I can make you a truffle omelet, if you'd like."

"Nothing," Cooker said dryly.

Then, changing his mind, he added, "Please, bring me a glass of water and two antacid tablets."

Gaétan made a teasing face and removed the glass of rum from the table. Cooker pulled himself out of the armchair and walked over to the fireplace. Heat was beginning to spread throughout the dark lounge. He thought about Grangebelle and Elisabeth, who was alone in that large house with nobody but Bacchus. At this hour, they would be able to see strands of light from the Blaye power station rippling on the silt-laden waters of the Gironde.

Cooker couldn't sleep that night and took a sedative. When he woke up, a young waiter who looked nothing like Gaétan brought a tray into his room at the promised time: Grand Yunnan tea, bread with butter and apricot jam, just the way he had it at Grangebelle. The famous winemaker was not a man to change his habits. He had asked that they find him an English-language paper, *The Herald Tribune* if possible, but there was only the French daily, *Le Figaro*, on the tray. The teenager apologized, as if he had made a serious mistake. Cooker stopped himself from snarling and said, "It's not important."

He then informed the boy that his shirt was buttoned wrong. The boy looked down, horrified, and apologized again, "Don't hold it against me, sir. I had to replace Gaétan at the last minute. Nobody knows where he is."

Cooker started questioning the replacement, who turned out to be the owners' nephew.

"Perhaps he's sick and can't answer the phone?"

"I don't know, sir. We knocked on his door, but nobody answered. Mrs. Olivereau said he never sleeps anywhere else."

Cooker, who was both surprised and impatient to find out more, plopped his toast back on the plate.

The boy looked like he had said too much and asked to be excused. Cooker pulled a ten-euro bill out of his pocket and handed it to the teenager. Then he stood silently in front of his window. He heard the door close behind him and tried to focus on the distant statue of the Virgin Mary. A layer of milky fog covered her from head to toe. Cooker put on his glasses, as if it would help him glimpse the Madonna's thin smile.

It was nearly eleven in the morning when he finally decided to leave his room. Reading *Le Figaro* was not enough to remedy the disagreeable sensation of being hung over. He wasn't nauseous, but he was definitely grumpy.

When he started down the stairs, he was surprised by all the activity in the lobby. Four local police officers were questioning the hotel owner, who appeared to be saddened by what she was hearing.

"Yes, that's her," Mrs. Olivereau said, pointing at the dog-eared picture the officer showed her.

A young cop was jotting down everything that his superior officer said. He was squeezed into a uniform that was too tight, and his face reddened when the officer started talking faster.

"You say she arrived with a certain Mr. Morton yesterday morning? What was he like? Can you describe him?"

Cooker stopped on the stairs, his hand on the rail. He held his breath, not wanting to miss a word of the conversation.

"Can we see the couple's room?" the detective asked, sounding somewhat satisfied with the way things were going.

"The room was cleaned immediately after Mr. Morton's departure. I fear you won't find anything there," said the château owner, who now seemed very distraught.

"It's a formality," the captain said without looking at her.

As he stood on the stairs, Cooker knew the investigators would eventually notice him, and they did. It was hard to tell if they looked at him with scorn or suspicion. They turned back to the reception desk, as if it were the hotel owner's responsibility to announce the identity of this very distinguished guest, who was wearing an impeccable suit but still seemed a bit disheveled from the night before.

"Ah, Mr. Cooker. Did you sleep well?"

"To be honest, not at all."

"I'm so sorry to hear that," the owner said. She then explained the presence of the police with a short sentence. "These men are here to ask some questions about the young woman who was here with Mr. Morton yesterday."

"Oksana?" Cooker asked.

"Do you know her?" the captain asked.

"I would have liked to know her better, if you see what I mean," he said with a mischievous smile, trying to cover his sudden concern that something had happened to her.

"What was her name again?"

"Oksana. That is how she was introduced to me. I didn't ask to see her ID. I'm pretty sure that she was not French. Isn't that so?"

"You are right," the captain answered. "She was born in Minsk."

Cooker slipped his hands into the pockets of his flannel pants. "I'm not all that sure she was over eighteen," he said.

"Nothing escapes you, does it, Mr., um, what was your name again?"

"Cooker. Benjamin Cooker," he said, handing his card to the captain, who looked suitably impressed.

"You look familiar. Have I seen you on television?"

"I rather doubt that," Cooker said.

The young officer who was taking notes looked at Cooker with wide eyes. The winemaker suspected that he wasn't used to seeing people standing up to his boss.

"Mr. Cooker, what do you know about Robert Morton? I believe you had lunch with him yesterday."

"Nothing. I know nothing," Cooker said before adding, "That is, nothing I have had time to verify. I can only tell you about his car and his supposed business as a wine broker. I could tell you everything about his Morgan but zilch about him."

The telephone at the reception desk rang. The hotel owner grabbed it.

"It's for you, Mr. Cooker. It's Chief of Police Fourquet from Paris."

"Please excuse me," Cooker said, slipping between the officers to take the phone.

"Yes, Chief. Some good news?"

The lead local officer at the reception desk was obviously hanging onto every word Cooker said and seemed irritated by how easily the winemaker took charge.

"Where is that you say? In Leipzig?"

Cooker's face suddenly lit up.

"What state is it in? Good, good. How did you find it? Aha! German intuition, perspicacity and rigor! I never understood how they lost the war." Cooker laughed.

"What's my new license plate again—1955 JO 6I, you said? I didn't know all the subtleties. Do I owe you a Château Latour? A 1961, of course. That was a fantastic year. No, really, it's my pleasure. It won't be at La Tour d'Argent, though. Too many bad memories."

Had Cooker been in the same room with Chief Fourquet, he would have kissed him on both cheeks. After thanking him again, he hung up the phone, looking thrilled.

"Captain, if you stopped a navy-blue Mercedes with a French license plate reading 1955 JO 6I and found an Albanian wearing an Orthodox cross and sunglasses behind the wheel, what would you do?"

The captain stared at him. He didn't seem to appreciate how familiar Cooker was being with him. *He probably considers me insolent,* Cooker thought.

"Uh, I would check his identity and his driver's license."

"Wrong answer, Captain! Europe does not have any borders anymore, and you should know, my friend, that the car was stolen, and the plates were faked by someone who did not know that the letters 'O' and 'I' have been banished from European plates."

The captain blushed. Cooker grinned.

"Champagne, Mrs. Olivereau! Champagne for everyone. My car was just found in Germany. Which, for a Mercedes, you must admit, is not out of the ordinary."

The waiter from breakfast was lining up the champagne flutes on the counter. Cooker summarized his recent experience in Paris. The winemaker's relaxed approach seemed to have an effect on the foursome of local police, and they took off their caps and sipped a little champagne.

Cooker went on to praise the hotel and its owners, along with the staff that was so attentive to detail and able to react so quickly. But he added that he had hoped to see Gaétan. That is when Cooker, realizing he still had questions about Oksana, asked the captain why he was inquiring about her.

"I'm sorry, Mr. Cooker. She's dead," the captain replied. "A jogger found her body this morning on the banks of the Loire."

Cooker frowned as the captain explained that the prostitute from Minsk, who was barely seventeen years old, had been strangled with copper wire, which was also found on the riverbank. It didn't appear that she had fought back. She still had her clothes on, and they weren't dirty or torn. She wasn't wearing any jewelry. The only thing she had with her was a card from the Château de La Tortinière. It was in the back pocket of her jeans. Scribbled on it was a cell phone number.

Nobody at the hotel, not even Cooker, had spent any time with her. Morton had treated her like some kind of plaything that he wanted to keep all to himself.

"The only person who could perhaps tell you anything, Captain, is Gaétan, our concierge, but he didn't show up for work today," Mrs. Olivereau said, obviously not in the mood for the Deutz, whose fine bubbles were quite out of place, considering the circumstances. It was clear to Cooker that nobody felt like celebrating.

"It's not like him," Mrs. Olivereau said. "He's a real asset here, and he's always available."

"Did you try to call him at home?" the captain asked, setting down his glass as well.

"He lives on the grounds, but he didn't answer his door when we knocked. We finally opened it with our own passkey. He wasn't there."

"Doesn't he have a cell phone?"

"We thought of that, but it just goes to voice mail."

Cooker, who had listened without saying anything, set his champagne flute on the fireplace mantel and turned to the hotel owner. "Would you mind giving us his cell phone number?"

"Of course, Mr. Cooker."

Mrs. Olivereau wrote down her employee's number on a piece of paper. She held it out to the winemaker, who approached the captain.

"Would you mind comparing this number with the one you found in Oksana's pocket?"

The captain scowled but followed Cooker's suggestion.

The silence that followed confirmed Cooker's hunch. The atmosphere in the room grew heavy. The hotel owner could not believe that Gaétan, her loyal employee, could possibly be involved in such a sordid affair. Not him! It was not possible.

"You don't think that...?" Mrs. Olivereau stammered.

The winemaker let the captain answer.

"I'll have to put out an APB immediately. You must admit, ma'am, that the disappearance of your concierge does coincide with the young girl's murder."

"Yes, I understand," the hotel owner said, clearly reluctant to admit the obvious.

The bottle of Deutz stood in the bucket of ice, and nobody even considered pouring more. The four cops had put their hats back on. La Tortinière was in a state of shock. Even

Benjamin Cooker could not imagine the young man he had just met was a murderer. This quiet retreat on the banks of the Indre wasn't turning out to be so restful.

4

A day had not gone by without a phone call from Virgile. Cooker suspected that it was a feeling of helplessness, rather than thoughtfulness, prompting his assistant's calls. He sensed Virgile worried that the convalescence would drag on and that he couldn't carry on all by himself. After all, Cooker was overly sensitive, as much as he tried to hide it behind an easy-going attitude or the opposite, a foul temper. He was also impulsive and never went half way. This supposed retreat in the country, which he had decided on without really consulting Virgile, would inevitably have some repercussions.

And to be quite frank, rest and relaxation were not Cooker's strong points. The sooner he got back to his office on the Allées de Tourny in Bordeaux, the sooner he would return to his usual witty, strong-minded self. Furthermore, over the past two weeks, samples had been piling up in the lab, and a number of his loyal customers had been trying to get in touch with him. He was being summoned not only to South Africa and Argentina but also to Burgundy and near Rasteau in Provence, where, according to his lab tech Alexandrine de la Palussière, there were a few pending emergencies. Without Cooker, day-to-day business was turning into a mess.

"Sir, you're wanted all over the place."

"That's giving me too much credit. For now, I'm doing a Vouvray cure. Once I've gotten through it, perhaps, my dear Virgile, I will focus on the small concerns of Cooker & Co. As for Rasteau, you should go, my good man. And give me a report."

Before hanging up, Cooker added, "By the way, Virgile, from now on, you are forbidden to say anything bad about the police. This morning, I learned that they found my convertible. It got picked up in Leipzig!"

"Where's that?"

"In Germany."

"You can't expect me to know the names of twenty-five hundred grape varieties and also be skilled in geography," Virgile said, clearly pleased with the news.

"I agree, but you could improve very quickly by taking the first plane to Berlin and bringing my favorite toy home, if you see what I mean."

"Which implies that I swing by the Loire Valley to pick you up, I gather."

"You're a quick learner. Go strut your stuff across the Rhine."

"What about Rasteau?"

"Rasteau can wait. They are as close to paradise as you can get. Nature serves them well. Isn't patience the mother of all virtues? Use that as an excuse when you talk to the head of the co-op. He's a friend of mine, another one of those winemakers who left Bordeaux, selling his soul to the devil in Provence."

Virgile laughed. He seemed to be pleased with the turn of events and the tone of the conversation. "I'll be at La Potinière in under two days."

"It's Tortinière, Virgile. Clean your ears, for God's sake."

"And what about your notebook? Still no news?"

"Don't even mention it."

Changing the subject, Cooker asked, "Anything new in Bordeaux?"

"Yes, in fact, the shop La Vinothèque de Dionysos on Cours de l'Intendance was robbed last night. It was weird. Just like in Paris, they took only the Angélus."

"I'm surprised my friend Hubert de Boüard has not called me yet. How many bottles?"

"I don't know, but it's your friend Mr. Delfranc, the former cop from Saint-Estèphe, who called the office to tell you. He asked after you and wants you to call him when you have a chance."

"Nothing else?"

"Oh, yes. Someone broke into Alexandrine de la Palussière's apartment."

"What did they take?"

"Nothing. That's what's strange about it."

"It's not a thief, then, but one of her exes," Cooker said, sure of himself.

"That's going a bit far, sir."

"Women are ghastly to each other, my dear Virgile. You're too young to know that."

"Excuse me for being so naïve."

"I'm not interested in Ms. de la Palussière's private life. But before you get your ticket for Germany, go sniff around La Vinothèque de Dionysos. I want to know which vintages were stolen, how many bottles, and, for that matter, how the thieves pulled off the heist."

"Fine, Mr. Cooker," Virgile said, sounding excited.

"Perfect. I'll let the authorities in Leipzig know that you are coming, and before you leave, send Alexandrine some flowers from me."

"Roses?"

"Whatever you like. After all, you're the one who knows how to communicate with women."

Cooker cut the conversation short when the hotel owner told him a certain Hubert de Boüard was on one of the hotel's lines.

"I'll take it right away," he said.

An impish look was returning to his eyes.

"Hello, Hubert? I need to give you my cell phone number again so you don't have to keep calling the front desk. I just heard the news from Virgile. You've devised a very clever publicity campaign, my friend. Your wine will be all over the papers tomorrow."

"Oh... Why do you say that?" The man from Saint-Émilion spoke in a hushed tone, his anxiety seeping through.

"Benjamin, I got another one of those messages in the mail today."

"A message?" Cooker asked, just a bit impatient. "Explain yourself."

"This morning, I got another card. It was the same as the other day. But this one said, 'Your Angélus is gone, and you don't stand a prayer.' And after that, well—"

"And after that, what?"

"It said, 'Two from you.'"

"Nothing else?"

"Nothing."

"Where was it sent from?"

"Spain. Madrid to be exact."

Cooker paused. "Two from you? This has to be connected to the heist that took place last night at La Vinothèque de Dionysos in Bordeaux. I can't say that I'm happy to be the one to break the news."

"This is unbelievable," Hubert de Boüard said.

"As was the case with the Place de la Madeleine in Paris, the thieves took only your Angélus. I bet the investigators are going to think you're behind this. I hope you have a good lawyer."

"But, Benjamin…"

"I'm not kidding. This is very curious. Do you have any enemies? Be honest with me, Hubert."

"I swear, Benjamin, I don't understand this at all. I just hope it's some kind of prank, a practical joke."

"This could very well be a practical joke, Hubert. There's no reason to panic. Let's just wait and see."

Cooker promised the Angélus estate owner that he would stop by as soon as he was back in Bordeaux, perhaps as early as the following week.

"What about you, Benjamin? How are you feeling after what happened?"

"Helping out friends like you is restoring my appetite for life. You wouldn't believe it, but one of the guests at the hotel where I'm supposed to be resting was found murdered on the banks of the Loire, and the concierge has inexplicably disappeared. It's alarming, isn't it?"

"My mysterious cards must seem dull in comparison."

"Don't be so sure. I wouldn't let anyone sully the image of Angélus. You know how highly I regard your wine. Actually, I think it's polite of your robbers to inform you every time they commit a break-in. And, as far as I know, they take only the best years. Connoisseurs. You should be happy, Hubert, at the quality of the people who are getting your fine wines into the news."

"Is that how you see it?"

"Frankly, you would be wrong to think of them any other way," Cooker said.

"Perhaps you are right," the Château Angélus owner said, still a little bit skeptical. "Do you think I should tell the police?"

"Wait for the next card. That way you'll have ample evidence, and you can minimize the possibility of being treated badly by some dismissive rules-obsessed detective."

"Before this is all over, I might be saying a few extra prayers myself—I don't care what the card said."

"I see you have recovered your sense of humor. Sleep soundly, Mr. de Boüard."

The winter sun had barely won the duel it had been fighting since the early hours of the day with the layers of fog spread over the Indre. Now its pale rays were sparkling on the lazy river. The winemaker felt like walking to escape the grim atmosphere in the château. He was starting to really miss the Médoc. And he could not get his mind off the Angélus case.

Cooker was used to taking long walks in the vineyards and pine groves in the company of his impertinent dog, Bacchus, but he had underestimated the distance that separated La Tortinière from the banks of the Indre. The path he took—it was the one the concierge had liked so much—ran through the woods, the moor, and pastures where cows grazed nonchalantly. He had dressed warmly and had picked up a hazel tree branch to use as a walking stick, as well as a weapon. Since his attack, he was always on guard. He turned to the right and followed a wall bordering a battalion of poplar trees filled with noisy birds. Otherwise, everything seemed peaceful. Cooker sat down on a worm-eaten fallen tree trunk between two weeping willows whose flimsy branches dipped into the slack waters of the river.

The church bells in Montbazon rang out at noon. Cooker was getting hungry, and his stomach was beginning to growl. High up on the top of the hill, La Tortinière was nothing more than a rock formation surrounded by a luxuriant English garden. Gray wisps of smoke were floating out of the chimneys. The winemaker followed them until they melded with the clouds. A sudden desire to eat roasted perch renewed his energy, and he decided to cut across the fields. He was a little winded and trying not to slip on the wet ground when he saw a tall form under a gnarled apple tree.

Wearing dark pants and a white shirt spattered with mud, Gaétan was staring straight ahead, a hemp rope tight around his neck. There was a surprised look on his bluish, nearly purple face. His mouth was open, and his swollen black tongue was hanging out. At the foot of the tree, the winemaker noticed footprints, as if the boy had hesitated at length before putting an end to his life.

5

I didn't think I would see you again so soon," the police captain said, sounding almost pleased when he saw Cooker holding his hands in front of the fireplace to warm them.

"We are going to end up being regular fixtures here at La Tortinière," Cooker said, trying to sound friendly.

"I would gladly have skipped that honor considering the circumstances," the captain responded. "I must say, though, the investigation is moving along."

"Is it?"

"It's all clear now. Don't you think, Mr. Wine Expert?"

Cooker figured the detective wasn't going to let him get the upper hand again.

"Not really. I think it's an even bigger mystery."

"How is that?"

"For now, nothing proves that Gaétan murdered the girl."

"Yet you are the one who clued us in."

"I know, but we need, oh, sorry, *you* need more solid evidence."

"Remorse, Mr. Cooker. Remorse. Perhaps there was no pre-meditation to get rid of the girl. But you know, this is a classic case. A prostitute refuses to submit. They have words. There's the excitement, the violence, the rape perhaps, and in the heat of the moment, the irreparable. Then his conscience takes over, and he doesn't want to be judged by others. He is horrified by what he has done and needs to pay the price."

"If I may toss a little sand into this well-oiled machine, Captain. Do we know if the killer took advantage of his victim?"

"The girl's autopsy results won't be in for another hour, but it is highly likely."

"Haste makes waste, Captain."

"I'll grant you that."

"I presume you will order an autopsy on the concierge."

"Of course, that's procedure, even though it is a fairly obvious suicide."

"I recommend that you visit the site where he was found. The view of the Indre is very picturesque."

Cooker spoke without too much sarcasm. This police captain was friendlier now than he was the first time they had met. "Didn't you notice the mud on his clothes and the scratches on his arms?"

The captain did not give Cooker the opportunity to continue his argument. "It's likely that the girl tried to fight him off. Maybe she even bit him."

"If I remember correctly, there was no sign of a struggle. At any rate, you'll compare the DNA, I suppose."

"You're not trying to tell me how to do my job, are you?" the captain asked, smiling.

"That is not at all my intention."

"In any case, although the two deaths are most certainly related in some way, the first scenario might not be the right one."

"The only connection between the concierge and the girl is the concierge's phone number," Cooker said.

"Now that we're on that, I'm wondering if it was his handwriting," the captain said.

"You didn't check?" Cooker asked.

"You're being a nuisance, for God's sake. Do I ask you if the wine you make is watered down, or if you take kickbacks from certain estates listed in your damned guide?"

The winemaker did not bat an eye. He stood up calmly and headed toward the armchair, where he had left his jacket. He took out a small notebook and scribbled a few notes in pencil. The detective watched without saying a word.

As Cooker wrote, the flashing blue and red lights of the police cruisers and ambulance began sweeping the walls of the lounge. Cooker heard heavy footsteps and dull voices.

He went out to the front to watch the ambulance leave, taking Gaétan's body to the morgue in Tours. Cooker remembered the question that Gaétan had asked him not that many hours earlier. The naïveté had moved him: "Tell me, Mr. Cooker, how do you become France's most famous winemaker?"

"You know, Gaétan, I am just an amateur, but I don't settle for anything less than the best. The rest is just luck."

"Luck?"

"Yes, luck," Cooker had said.

Fatigued and demoralized, Cooker returned to the hotel lounge. The captain had vanished. The hotel staff, meanwhile, had red eyes and long faces. The winemaker went to his room to rest, but he could not find sleep. Virgile would arrive the next day, before this tragic story could be cleared up. The girl's murder had shocked Cooker. She had seemed so vulnerable. And what part had Gaétan played in all of this? He had been such a conscientious hotel employee.

There was a knock at the door. Two shy knocks.

"Leave me alone," Cooker grumbled.

"It's Captain Guilhem."

Cooker got off the bed and opened the door.

"By all means, come in."

"I wanted to apologize for earlier."

"No harm done."

"I should hope not," the captain said.

"Let's say the case is closed. I wasn't too polite to you either. What would you like to drink, Captain?"

"No alcohol. My day's not finished yet."

Cooker opened the minibar tucked inside a sturdy wood cupboard. He set two cans of orange juice on the table he used for writing. "With or without ice?"

"Never any ice," the captain said, having recovered some of his self-assurance.

"You're right. I hate ice myself."

"I was right! You're not the kind to put water in your wine," the captain said, setting his cap on the bed.

"Too bad I'll be leaving tomorrow, as I think the two of us could have gotten along," Cooker added, sloughing off his grumpy attitude.

"Your contribution would, in fact, always be welcome."

"Consider it yours, Captain."

"You will return to your wine, and the day after tomorrow, you will have forgotten the misadventures that occurred at La Tortinière."

"So you call a double murder a misadventure?"

"You don't believe Gaétan's death was suicide?"

"Not any more than I believe Oksana was raped," Cooker said.

"Yes, we did get the autopsy results after you went upstairs: there was no sign of sexual abuse, but hairs found on the girl belonged to the concierge."

"Do you have the hotel business card that you found in the girl's pocket?" Cooker asked.

"Yes."

"Would it be possible to see it?"

"Of course."

The winemaker took the card and went over to the bedside table, which was piled with wine-related publications and a few glossy wine-auction catalogs. Gaétan's recipe for the saffron honey ice cream was sticking out of one of the magazines. Cooker compared the writing against what was on the card.

"It's an ice cream recipe," the winemaker told the captain. "Gaétan was kind enough to ask the chef for it."

"And?"

"See for yourself, Captain. There are enough numbers in the list of ingredients to prove that it was not the concierge who wrote down his phone number on that business card."

"That doesn't change anything," the captain said.

"True. One could also imagine that she gave herself to the boy and then wrote down his number."

"How poetic, Mr. Cooker. I myself am pragmatic. That is certainly why we are not in the same line of work."

"In the name of that pragmatism, you should know that in prostitution, the john reveals more of himself than the woman who pretends to be enjoying it."

"Mr. Cooker, you seem to have experience in this area that I, alas, cannot claim."

"Now, now, it's human nature. You're a bit of a prude, Captain. Yet the card was found in Oksana's jeans and not in his."

"I'll give you that. If she didn't write it down, and neither did her friend, or lover, or customer, whatever you want to call him, then who did?"

"Quite simply, someone who wanted to point the finger at him," Cooker said.

"You are Machiavellian, Cooker."

"No, just pragmatic," Cooker said, smiling.

The captain studied the woodwork while he finished his orange juice, making a face with his last swig. Then there was a knock on the door.

"What do you know. I should open an office here," Cooker said. "Come in."

A deputy came into the room. He approached his superior officer and whispered a few words in his ear. The two men then stared at Cooker's shoes.

"Would you like to know where I get my Lobbs?" the winemaker asked without a trace of sarcasm. "I don't want to disappoint you, but they are not Berluttis."

"Excuse me?" the captain said, "I believe this is more criminal than it is political." After chuckling, he added, as if to polish off his adversary, "Pardon my nosiness, Mr. Cooker, but could you please tell me what size you wear in—what was it now—Lobbs?"

"Well, what a fine idea! Forty-two and a half, European size. I'm partial to that half. At my age, even a demi-measure matters. I see that you have finally decided to analyze the footprints under the apple tree, which I thought were suspicious from the start."

The captain interrupted him. "Roussin, you can speak freely in front of the gentleman. We are beginning to share the same views on this strange case. I get the feeling this is not our last surprise."

"We found size forty-one, which corresponds with the concierge's shoes, and a few between size forty-two and forty-three. I suppose those are yours, Mr. Cooker?"

The winemaker did not answer.

"We also found size forty-five footprints. Actually, they were closer to forty-six. They led down to the river. That's a lot of people for one dead man," the captain said, sighing and rubbing his neck.

"I'm pleased to see you're coming around to my point of view, Captain. If you aren't susceptible to heartburn, you deserve a second orange juice."

"You are very kind, Mr. Cooker, but one should never overdo a good thing."

"Really? I will not insist. I admire your restraint."

6

To celebrate Virgile's arrival, Benjamin Cooker uncorked a bottle of Bonnezeaux from the Petits-Quarts estate, a 1997 Le Malabé. The honey-colored wine was just as sweet as it should be, full of fruit and flowers. It was the perfect accompaniment to convivial conversation. Virgile admitted that he knew nothing about this wine, which came from three small shale hills overlooking the village of Thouarcé.

Cooker just had to slip outside, his glass in hand, to admire his car. The convertible had not suffered during its absence. It was as shiny as it had been the day he bought it. There was just a little scratch on the right side.

"I had to show my credentials to get the keys, and I almost came back empty-handed," Virgile recounted, clearly satisfied with having brought his boss's wheels back.

"The Germans are a bit persnickety, to say the least," Cooker said, still delighting in his car.

"Worse than that, I'd say, more like pains in the ass."

"A true German can't stand the French, but he gladly drinks their wines. I'm not the first person to say this. I'm quoting a German writer. Who do you think it is?"

"Um, I'd say Goethe," the assistant guessed, looking a little embarrassed.

"Congratulations, Virgile. You always surprise me."

"I don't deserve any praise. He's the only German writer I know. By the way, you have forty-eight hours to change the license plates, or else you'll have more problems on your hands. There's a special permit from the Leipzig police in the glove compartment."

"It'll be done tomorrow," Cooker said.

"So we're not hitting the road tonight?" Virgile asked.

"I wouldn't ask that of you, considering all the miles you've just driven."

"I don't feel tired at all."

"But I do," Cooker said firmly.

"You're still recuperating, sir."

"True, but that isn't the only thing that's been on my mind," the winemaker said, knitting his bushy eyebrows. "Strange things have been happening here."

"What kind of strange things?"

"Two crimes in under twenty-four hours."

"And that's all?" Virgile said, whistling. "Yes, strange things, as you say."

"And I haven't told you the half of it."

"Well you have either told me too much or too little. Two crimes—that's something."

"I agree."

The wrinkles on Cooker's forehead deepened, making him look even more pensive, and then he added, "The Bonnezeaux awaits us. We don't want it to get too warm."

"In the meantime, you're teasing me. What's the weapon? Who are the victims? Is there a motive?"

"To tell you the truth, I haven't the slightest idea."

"That doesn't seem like you."

"And yet that's the way it is. But this is not a conversation to have without a drink. Quick, let's go in."

They stopped at the reception desk, and Cooker reserved a room for his assistant. Then they found a small lounge where they could discuss Oksana's murder and Gaétan's supposed suicide. Virgile listened attentively. He looked perplexed. Then he said, "I really like the aromas of ripe, almost candied fruit, the citrus and exotic fruit, along with a hint of toasted…"

Cooker was surprised. This was not what he expected to hear from Virgile. Then he thought better of it and followed his assistant's lead. "I wonder if I don't prefer the following year. It's in the same range, with flattering aromas, concentrated flavor, and a fine finale. It is very representative of the appellation—both intense and light, refined and flowery, without being diluted. It is always refreshing but with a kind of warmth. Bonnezeaux is a sure bet, like the Coteaux du Layon, and they age well. One day, we will come back to explore the Anjou wines under circumstances that are, well, calmer. I am sure you'll like it here."

"You are in brilliant form, Mr. Cooker! I'm happy to see you like this, after what you have been through. But I still don't know if you invited me to the Loire Valley to get your car back or to help you unravel this strange case of an Eastern European whore who was bumped off for who-knows-what reason."

"You wouldn't talk like that if you had met Oksana."

"Which means?"

"The Virgile I know would have been all over her in a minute and not too long thereafter in her bed."

"No, that is for other men. For an inexperienced concierge, perhaps, or a lonely hotel guest suffering from midlife lust. That's not my style. You understand, don't you?"

"Not exactly," Cooker said, clearly goading Virgile.

"I never was very good at drawing pictures."

"Then I'll let you off the hook. But follow through on your thoughts. I'm interested."

Cooker had picked up the bottle of wine and was preparing to fill Virgile's glass. The young man stopped him.

"I'm no cop, but I'd bet a case of your Bonnezeaux that this has something to do with Morton, the Morgan Man."

"What makes you so sure of yourself?"

Cooker was not ready to accept this suggestion. Robert Morton, the refined and cultivated dandy who had been his well-mannered compatriot for a day, had to be an honest man. He would bet on it. He was prepared to stand up for Morton's integrity. Except that he knew absolutely nothing about this person, who said he worked in wines but had no business card to show for it.

"He said he had to leave right away for an important meeting in Bordeaux," Cooker said without much conviction.

"In Bordeaux. Well, well."

"There's nothing unusual about that for an international wine broker."

"If you say so," Virgile said. "Then we just might run into him. You can't cross the Aquitaine Bridge in a Morgan Plus 8 without being noticed. So, sir, tell me, do you know a lot of English brokers who drive across France in that kind of convertible, when vintage car collectors are hard pressed to take that kind of car out of the garage once a year?"

The winemaker did not like the young man's tone, but he had to admit he had no arguments to counter Virgile's line of reasoning. With his innocent air, Virgile had once again found faults in a pristine picture.

For the first time since he had arrived in the Touraine region, Cooker had no trouble falling asleep. Calm had returned to La Tortinière. They departed at the first light of dawn. Cooker left a thank-you note at the reception desk while Virgile put their bags in the car. Then the winemaker slipped into the beige driver's seat. He rubbed the leather-covered steering wheel and the walnut dashboard. Then he adjusted the rearview mirror. Finally, he turned the key and revved the engine. Virgile was already asleep by the time they got onto the A10 highway.

Cooker turned the radio down low, so as not to disturb his sleeping assistant, who had a smile on his lips. He appeared to be having a sweet dream.

Cooker was enjoying the pleasure of driving and the anticipation of seeing Elisabeth and returning to his offices. Yet as the day went on, his anxiety began to rise. His retreat in a setting as refined at La Tortinière was meant to provide him with needed rest, but he was not feeling rested at all. He thought he could heal himself, but had he chosen the right remedy? The time spent in pampered elegance had only put off the fear of once again being in crowds and dealing with the everyday realities of life. Quick, nervous questions shot through his mind. They were choppy, like the white lines on the highway.

Cooker grew tired of the radio commentator's conventional analysis of the Israel-Palestine situation. He preferred listening to a CD of Marianne Faithfull that was in his glove compartment. The first track was his favorite. It was called "Sleep."

Virgile had curled up on his seat. He grumbled, sounding just like Bacchus, and crossed his arms. Cooker turned up the heat. He, too, was getting cold. Marianne Faithfull's throaty voice reassured him. It was warm and vibrant, melding smoothly into the orchestration.

Virgile mumbled, "Where are we?" He fell back asleep before Cooker had time to answer.

Large clouds rolled over the Charentes region, and a hard rain began to fall. The windshield wipers had trouble keeping up. A sign announced "Next Exit, Saint-Jean-d'Angély." They would be back in Bordeaux in two hours.

When the Mercedes began to shake, Virgile rubbed his eyes, looked at his watch, and then glanced at his boss, who was clearly alarmed. The vibrating was becoming even more pronounced.

"Shit!" Cooker shouted. "What did those bastards do to my car? Was it shaking like this when you drove from Leipzig?"

"No, it was fine, boss," Virgile responded. "Maybe we blew a tire. We should check."

Cooker pulled the car to the side of the road and got out to inspect the tires. All four seemed to be okay.

"We'd better find a service station," Virgile said.

Cooker glanced around and said, "Let's get off at the Saint-Savinien exit. It shouldn't be far now, and I've heard it's got just about the only roadside restaurant worth consideration on this road to Bordeaux. At least we could make the best of a bad situation."

The shaking didn't let up, and the two men stayed alert while Marianne Faithfull kept vigil. To be safe, when they reached the exit, Cooker took the first road after the tollbooth.

They found a service station that no longer sold gas but did do repairs. A rusty sign read "Dollo et Fils." A man in dirty overalls pulled himself out from under a rusty van. He was ageless, wore a felt beret too small for his head, and had an engaging smile.

"What can I do for you?"

"Everything!" Cook said, sounding like he believed in miracles.

"What a week. All of Europe seems to be stopping by, and like they say on TV, most of it is breaking down. Yesterday, I saw an old Italian clunker from Fiat. Earlier an English car drove by, right before that a Porsche came in and now more German wheels."

An apprentice with a shaved head was fixing a tire in the corner. There were huge holes in his gauged earlobes. Cooker had seen these outlandishly stretched piercings on other teenagers in Bordeaux. The boss probably didn't like it, Cooker thought, but cheap labor was cheap labor. In this corner of Saintonge, they were not even making good cognac anymore, and customers had to be rare. The winemaker tried to explain the car's symptoms, imitating the wobbling car.

"Is that so?" the mechanic said, brushing his beret to the back of his head. "I bet it's the alignment. Hit a hole in the road maybe?"

Cooker looked accusingly at his assistant. "Did you run into any potholes on your way from Leipzig?"

Virgile shrugged. "I don't think so, boss."

"No worry," the mechanic said. "It's easy to fix. But you're in no hurry, I hope. With a car like that, you must have all the time in the world."

"That is not really the case," Cooker retorted, looking at Virgile. The assistant stood by in silence as the winemaker undertook negotiations that required some diplomacy.

"I don't mean to pry, but what exactly do you do?" the mechanic asked.

Cooker realized that things were turning sour, and he would not be seeing Bordeaux's Tour Pey-Berland so soon.

"I'm a winemaker," Cooker said.

"Are you making those garage wines everyone is talking about these days? You have to tell me how you do it. Maybe it's the wave of the future for *garagistes* like me," the mechanic said with a wink.

Mr. Dollo's face was purple. He clearly liked the fruit of the vine.

"Come on, tell me how you do it, and maybe I'll become a Saint-Émillionnaire and drive a Mercedes myself."

Cooker and Virgile both laughed, and the winemaker saw an opportunity to advance his cause. If he wanted this bizarre individual to focus on his car, he would have to uncork one of the bottles of Vouvray he had picked up in the Loire Valley. The trunk was full of them, and the winemaker liked the idea of using it to grease the mechanic's palm.

"But, sir, before I get to the Mercedes, I gotta finish off the Porsche. The guy's in a hurry and was here before you. It shouldn't take long. Just the belt and the hose. He gave me a nice tip to have it ready this afternoon at four. Know what I mean?" the mechanic said with another wink.

"I believe I do," Cooker said, taking a Taille aux Loups 1993 Clos de Venise from his trunk.

The mechanic grinned and wiped his hands on his overalls.

"I won't say no to that. You're not the kind to run out of gas, that's for sure."

7

At the back of the garage, behind dirty windows and walls decorated with old calendar pinups, sacrilege was occurring. The precious Clos de Venise was foundering in red plastic cups. Virgile had trouble making out the aromas of mangos and pineapple that had enchanted Cooker during the blind tasting some time ago in Amboise.

As rough as he seemed, the mechanic was jovial and even likable. He had improvised a cocktail hour in his office, where oil cans and old tires mixed with a jumble of papers. He thought it polite to serve up stale peanuts in a promotional ashtray.

The mechanic emptied his plastic cup three times, wrinkling his nose and clicking his palate to mimic an expert right under Cooker's nose. The winemaker found it amusing but did not react, hoping that his knowledge of mechanics would surpass his talent as a wine taster.

The mechanic raised his voice and waved a dark, greasy hand to invite his apprentice to join them for the shipwrecked dry Vouvray.

"Come on, taste a little. It'll make a man of you."

The teenager came over and waited for the mechanic to fill his cup. Virgile tried to make conversation, in vain. The boy lifted his cup and emptied it. In one gulp, the clear Vouvray from Montlouis-sur-Loire disappeared. The apprentice held back a burp as he put his cup down. Cooker asked him how old he was, and the mechanic was quick to answer for him. "Sixteen and nothing in the noggin. Just gigantic holes in the ears for the birds to fly through."

The apprentice lowered his head. He managed a small smile as if to apologize for not belonging to the world of adults, and then he made his way behind a wall that served as a closet.

Now that the bottle was empty, and introductions were over, would the mechanic finally decide to get his calloused hands on the convertible? This side trip was taking an unexpected turn. The Cooker-Lanssien team was no longer in a hurry.

The mechanic promised to look at the sick car at the beginning of the afternoon but would not get down to surgery until later in the day, as the Porsche had to get done first.

"He had no wine for me, but he's not too tight-fisted, if you get my drift."

"Oh, yes, I do," Cooker said, adding, "Tell me, my friend, isn't there a place to eat around here of some repute? I can't remember the name."

"Here, all you've got is the truck stop, the Platanes. It's just over there at the intersection," the mechanic said, pointing in the direction of the restaurant. "It's run by Yvette. Nothing fancy, but the steak *à la bordelaise* is good."

"That's the place, Virgile. I recall now, there's not much choice, but they apparently make a mean red wine sauce with just the right amount of bone marrow, butter, and shallots."

The apprentice, who had come out from behind the wall, opened the enormous garage door, which made a loud and annoying squeal as it went up. He had taken off his overalls and was wearing a sweatshirt with English writing on the back. It read "Fuck the boss."

Cooker called out to him, as if he wanted directions, "Hey, kid, what's your name?"

"Rodolphe, sir."

"Nice name," the winemaker said, accompanying the compliment with an unexpected and substantial tip, in another attempt to get the repairs done before day's end.

"Thanks, sir. Have a good meal. You'll see. Yvette is really cool."

As they made their way to the restaurant, Virgile walked with a light step and lifted his nose to sniff the heady odor of wet earth. Cooker stomped along, his head down and his hands deep in his pockets.

Cooker didn't look up until they reached the restaurant parking lot. And parked right in front of him was the beauty with shiny chrome.

"That's Morton's car," Cooker said to Virgile. "I'd recognize it anywhere."

"What did I tell you, boss," Virgile responded. "I said we'd probably meet up with him. But here, in this little hole in the wall, now that's a surprise. And days after he was supposed to be in Bordeaux? I mean, seriously, how does that happen? We break down, take the car to a garage that doesn't sell gas, waste a bottle of Clos de Venise, and find the Morgan at a truck stop."

"Coincidence, my dear Virgile, coincidence. And besides, there really isn't any other place to stop for a decent meal on this road between Tours and Bordeaux. Is it that surprising?"

"What will you say to him? Do you think he knows his girlfriend Oksana is dead?"

"I don't know, Virgile. Why don't we go inside and find him first."

Walking into the restaurant, Cooker scanned the bar and then the dining room, where a waitress was flitting from table to table. Robert Morton was not there.

"Two?"

"Yes, please, miss."

"Near the fireplace?"

"No, next to the man over there."

"As you wish, but you'll be near the door. There are drafts."

"That's fine."

The waitress smiled at Virgile as she handed him the menu.

"A drink, perhaps?"

Having failed to spot Morton, Cooker was in a foul mood. "Two steaks, *à la bordelaise*. How's that, Virgile?"

It was not a good time to contradict his boss, so the assistant responded, "Yes, perfect." Then Virgile tried to smooth things over. "Perhaps he's in the restroom. He'll be out in a minute."

Cooker grumbled.

"Some wine?" the waitress asked. "I could recommend something from the Loire Valley."

"God forbid, no Loire wine," Cooker mumbled under his breath.

"A Château de La Salle, then?"

Virgile nodded at Yvette, who smiled at him in return.

Cooker paid no mind and just complained about the water, which wasn't cold enough. He took a pen out of his pocket and started scribbling on the paper tablecloth. His assistant sat in silence. Cooker imagined that he was just trying to get along.

All things considered, Rodolphe had been right. Yvette was cool. She had long legs, accentuated by shiny heels. Her hips were full, and her heavy breasts swung freely under her shirt.

From where they were sitting, they could hear shouting in the kitchen and smell the hot oil. Cooker examined the other diners, as he kept an eye on the restroom door. He tried to intercept bits of conversation and decrypt their ways of eating, drinking, and speaking. He made a face. Nobody here matched the man who had so appealed to him on the banks of the Indre. Especially the person with the large mole on his left temple who was sitting next to them. The gangly fellow was reading *Le Figaro* and drinking a glass of rosé from Provence. He was wearing tortoiseshell glasses, had a signet ring on his left hand, and he was decked out in a sweater with a horrible multicolored geometric pattern.

Virgile kept following the waitress with his eyes. Cooker couldn't help thinking that the place had gotten its reputation as much from her shape as the steaks.

Their steaks *à la bordelaise* arrived, and Morton was still nowhere to be seen.

"Tell me, Virgile, what do you think of that man drinking rosé next to the wall? No, not that one, to the left."

Virgile remained silent for a while and then said, "Married, around fifty, four children, Catholic, a little noble blood in his veins. He sells corks made in Portugal, has never cheated on his wife, bought a lot of Eurotunnel shares, and is still trying to convince his wife that he's going to earn his investment back. She doesn't really care, because she is sleeping with one of their oldest son's friends. Yes, yes. Gontran's best friend, who teaches her to play golf every Saturday afternoon. She just finished rereading *Ripening Seed* by Colette and says that her husband is a loser and a bad lay, that she has the right to some pleasure, that tomorrow she will definitely leave him, and that her mind is made up. He's entirely preoccupied with the stock market, which is slow to rise, the promise of a vacation with the Arteuil family in their dusty old château in the Poitou, and Eléonore, who is doing her first communion next Sunday. He's a nobody. He can't lie. He doesn't even like nice cars. I bet he drives a Japanese rig that he's still paying off."

Cooker broke out laughing and nearly choked on his Château de La Salle. Some of the other diners, hacking away at their solitude as they emptied their plates, looked at him with disapproval. Cooker felt like he had just become the center of a number of conversations in this lapse from his usual reserve.

Their neighbor on the right got up to leave. Like a fussy old bachelor, he brushed the bread crumbs off his sweater. Cooker noticed his slender fingers and long nails. The man buttoned up his cardigan, adjusted the silk scarf stuffed into the collar of his pale pink shirt, and left a ten-euro tip on a cracked dish. He then carefully folded the receipt and slipped it into his wallet.

Cooker watched him walk out the door and across the parking lot. Then, to Cooker's amazement, the man in the colorful geometric sweater got into the Morgan and started pulling out of the parking lot.

"Quick, Virgile," Cooker yelled, pushing himself away from the table and racing toward the door. By the time they reached the parking lot, the Morgan was speeding down the road.

"That man just took off in Morton's car," Cooker said, out of breath.

"What could have happened, boss? Do you think he stole the car, maybe even before Morton got to Bordeaux? And if he did, what happened to Morton?"

"We're not going to get the answers to those questions now," Cooker said and sighed.

Cooker and Virgile went back into the restaurant, a little embarrassed by the scene they had made when they ran out without paying their check. They returned to their table, figuring they had time to kill before retrieving their car at the Dollo garage. Cooker ordered a cognac and offered his assistant a cigar. Virgile accepted, for once.

"This one should be gentle enough for your delicate palate," Cooker said, carefully cutting off the top of a light-colored and slightly veined wrapper and lighting Virgile's cigar.

"Did you say it was a Santa Damiana?"

Virgile seemed slightly drunk on the cut-hay and dried-alfalfa aromas of the cigar. Just as they did with wine, the smells of his childhood came to the surface.

"Undergrowth, humus, ferns."

Cooker nodded, as he did when he pulled the first olfactory sensations from a glass of wine. Virgile was no longer his assistant, but an applied and determined student.

Virgile continued, hitting his stride. "Pepper, leather, horse manure."

"So far, I agree," Cooker said, puffing his Lusitania. "I think you may be ready for one from Cuba."

"Should I take that as a compliment?"

"Let's just say that you've lost your innocence. Yes, that's it."

A young man in a white toque and stained apron came out of the kitchen and put his arm around the waitress's waist. Yvette adjusted her shirt and simpered at Virgile. Her lipstick had lost some of its shine, and her tight black skirt was hiked up a bit.

The restaurant was now nearly empty, abandoned to the swirls of gray smoke that seemed to stick to the still blades of an old fan. Two cigar butts sat on a blanket of ashes in a shell-shaped ashtray. At this time of day, Cooker and Virgile were no longer wanted here. The cook had removed his toque and had cleared his throat a number of times before saying, "We're closing."

Yvette puckered her lips. "It's not that we're chasing you away or anything, but—"

"It's fine," Cooker said with an amused smile. "It's time for a nap."

Outside, the rain was working the fields again. Cooker walked quickly in an effort to stay dry, and Virgile kept pace. When they arrived at the garage, the Mercedes was right where they had left it. Cooker felt his temple begin to throb as he faced the prospect of spending even more time waiting for his car. The mechanic came out of his office. He wiped his forehead with the back of his sleeve.

"Don't get worked up, now," he said. "The Porsche is done, and I can get going on the Mercedes. Out of alignment. I knew it. Must have been a hole in the road, like I said, eh?"

He went back into his office and came out again, carrying a grimy dog-eared book with "Mercedes" written on the cover.

"You're in luck, my friends. I still have the manual for your vintage car."

He opened it, and Cooker watched as he checked the calibrations for the wheels.

"Two hours, and you're on the way back home. One hour, if you must hurry. The Porsche owner, he was in the hurry, and he was not cheap."

8

In Bordeaux, the Place Saint-Michel was the site of an odd makeshift setup that morning. Antique vendors fought gusts of wind to raise their gigantic green-and-yellow parasols. Large drops of rain coming from the west jeopardized an improvised Oriental carpet sale. Cautious vendors covered their goods with see-through tarps. There were few passersby, and little chance of making a deal.

Cooker made his way quickly through the flea market without even glancing at the stands. He nodded at a few vendors with whom he sometimes haggled for still lifes, winemaking tools, old postcards, and mismatched crystal glasses.

His coat collar was up around his ears, and he took care not to slip on the cobblestone walkways in the Saint Pierre neighborhood. He turned on the Rue Saint-Rémi, stopping at the Grand Théâtre newsstand, where he intended to get back into his old routine.

"Hello, Mrs. Camensac," he said. "I'd like the *Sud-Ouest, Le Figaro*, the *RVF,* and the *Herald Tribune*, please. Nasty weather, isn't it?" And then he headed up the Allées de Tourny.

He paused when he reached number 46. The copper plaque that read "Cooker & Co." was dripping in the rain. The bronze doorbell was still shiny, but he would have to paint the door next spring. He pushed open the porte-cochère.

Nothing had changed. Benjamin Cooker had not been in his offices for over a month. The staircase felt steeper, and he had to stop on the landing to catch his breath. He would not admit it, but he was nervous about getting back to work. It took his secretary Jacqueline's candid smile, purple suit, and perfect education to dissipate his anxiety. How could he have forgotten the heady smell of beeswax that always hovered in his somewhat quaint offices? And the discreet whistle of the kettle that Miss Delmas used for her god-awful herbal teas? If only he could convert her to regular tea.

"Mr. Lanssien will swing by around ten this morning," Jacqueline said, helping her boss with his rain-logged Loden.

"Mr. Cooker, I arranged all your mail in file folders on your desk," she said, spreading his jacket over two coat hooks.

"Thank you, Jacqueline. What would I do without you?"

Several piles of letters awaited him on the Empire-style desk. A carefully tied package was sitting next to his old Napoleon III inkstand. A felt-tip marker had been used to write "Personal" on the outside. The handwriting was thick and contorted. Cooker looked for the sender's address but found nothing. He ripped off the brown paper wrapping. Inside, he found his notebook.

He examined the packaging again and found a postmark. It was the only clue: the notebook had been sent three days earlier from the Champigny-sur-Marne post office. In the end, it did not really matter, now that he had recovered his car and his precious notebook. He called Elisabeth right away. She suggested that they celebrate the event at noon at the restaurant Noailles.

"That is, unless you invite me to the Saint James in Bouliac."

"Done deal," Cooker said, rubbing his cigar box before pulling out a D Number 4 from Partagas.

The wall clock hanging above the mantel had just announced ten o'clock when Virgile barged into Cooker's office. His coat was too big for him, and he looked pale. He wore a colorful turtleneck, and dark bags under his eyes indicated that his night had been too short. He plopped into an armchair in front of the desk and registered his boss's good humor.

With gray cigar smoke encircling his head, Cooker was busy putting checkmarks on some of the letters encumbering his desk. He removed his reading glasses, which gave him a certain professorial look, and told Virgile about the fine surprise that had been waiting for him. The winemaker had to cut his story short, though, when an unexpected visitor stuck his head in the door.

"Hubert! What brings you to Bordeaux?"

The owner of the Château Angélus did not look his best.

"Come in. You know Virgile, my assistant, don't you?"

Hubert de Boüard shook the young man's hand. His friendship with Cooker was longstanding, and there had never been any snags. Angélus got fantastic notations in the *Cooker Guide*, especially after the premier grand cru heir took on the services of the renowned winemaker Michel Rolland while also following the less official advice of his friend Cooker. The two men had a very cordial friendship and shared a passion for Cuban cigars.

"What are you smoking at this hour of the day, old devil?" Hubert asked.

"A D4, as you can see. It's a bit strong, but the day has gotten off to a good start. My tasting notes that were stolen in Paris came back to me in the mail. I don't know if it was the thief or a Good Samaritan who found it somewhere. I suspect it's the latter. It's comforting to know that someone, somewhere took the time to wrap it, stick postage on it, and drop it in a mailbox. And to do so without asking for a dime, but just because it was the right thing to do. You see, Hubert, acts like that make me believe in people."

"I'm really very happy for you, Benjamin."

"I can assure you right away. Angélus got a good rating in the new guide," the winemaker said. "You, of course, know how highly I regard your 2000 vintage. Perhaps you would like to know the final score I gave it, unless you've come to tell me you got another mysterious message."

"That's exactly it," Hubert de Boüard said, holding the white envelope out to his friend.

Virgile leaned in as Cooker examined the address. Biting his lip, he said, "This friend of yours might be a neighbor. The card was sent from Saint-Émilion yesterday."

"That is what worries me," Hubert said.

The tick-tock of the clock was the only sound in the room. With just enough affectation, Cooker set his cigar down in a white porcelain ashtray. He removed the card from the envelope and read the terse message: "Cave de l'Angélus. Does that ring a bell?" Then, in all capital letters, "AND THREE FOR ME."

Cooker quickly closed the card, as it was clearly disturbing his friend, one of Saint-Émilion's most emblematic winemakers.

"Now, Hubert, I'm afraid you have no choice. You have to tell the cops. When did you get it?"

"In the morning mail."

"Virgile, were there any break-ins on the news last night or today?"

"Not that I know of, sir."

"Did you listen to the radio this morning?"

"Yes, well, no, I mean, not exactly."

"So actually, you aren't really awake. Go home and take a good shower, and this afternoon I want a detailed list of all the wine auctions planned for the next month."

"Throughout France?"

"France and beyond, including London, New York, and Geneva. Is that clear?"

"Yes, sir."

"Oh, and I almost forgot. Tell your lady of the moment to give you a break. Don't forget to mention that your boss is back from vacation."

Cooker's sudden frivolity seemed to cheer Hubert de Boüard up a bit. He put his cigar back in his mouth and took two puffs before reading the morning newspapers with his friend. The Angélus gang had not struck again. Or at least not yet.

An hour later, Elisabeth Cooker walked into her husband's office without knocking. Cooker knew that she rarely did this, and it reflected just how happy she was that he had recovered his notebook. She greeted the Angélus estate owner with effusive kisses on his cheeks.

"What? Where's the champagne?"

"True, after all, why not?" Cooker said affably.

"Jacqueline, please, four champagne glasses. Let's uncork that Dom Pérignon that's been waiting in the storeroom refrigerator."

They all raised a toast to Cooker's health, the returned notebook, the rating given to the 2000 Angélus, and all others who praised that exceptional wine. Hubert forgot his worries and promised to drop the three cards off at the Libourne police station. Cooker invited him to join them at the Saint James for lunch.

"Hubert, I'm sure it's just some bad joke. You need to get your mind off it. A good meal is exactly what you need."

"I don't want to get in the way of you two lovebirds."

"Oh come on, you're like family."

The three friends crossed the Allées de Tourny under a golf umbrella to reach Hubert de Boüard's Range Rover, which was double parked on the Rue de Sèze. A soppy, barely legible parking ticket on the windshield did not even dampen the trio's mood.

"Some more mail," Cooker said with a smirk.

Lunch at the Saint James lasted well into the afternoon. It was a pretext for the head sommelier to get the famous and expert diners to taste some of his wines. Elisabeth listened, tasted, and added her two cents. She seemed happy to see that her husband's enthusiasm had returned. In the restaurant parking lot, Cooker contemplated not returning to his office and going home to enjoy Grangebelle under the rain. He pictured a fire in the fireplace, Bacchus at his feet, a call to Margaux—it was only noon in New York—and a cup of Nepalese tea, the one his tea-loving friend Gilles Brochard had sent him.

Then he changed his mind. He had too much work to do. Hundreds of tasting samples awaited him, and he needed to swing by the lab and make sure Alexandrine de la Palussière was on those cases of eutypiosis in the Côtes du Marmandais and the Entre-Deux-Mers. The vines were rotting, and radical treatment was needed. New regulations forbade the use of sodium arsenite. Virgile would have to monitor the endemic proliferation of the damned fungus that was eating away at the vine stock. No French vineyard had been spared. And the recent rain was not helping. It was pruning season, and shears propagated the infection. Naturally, Cooker & Co. recommended the intensive use of a fungicide like benomyl to at least contain the spread, but that required time and a lot of meticulous work. His office was drowning in calls for help, and dawdling at home would be criminal. Cooker was starting to feel guilty.

He gave Elisabeth a tender kiss and reassured her that he would be all right. On the left bank of the Garonne River, behind a curtain of rain, Bordeaux looked like a bad watercolor. Cooker would have to face the traffic on the Pont de Pierre. When would the work be done on the tramway?

Cooker did not recognize him at first. Wearing an off-white raincoat, a long woolen scarf, and a checked hunting cap, the man looked like a wading bird emerging from a marsh. He was waiting in the reception area. When he saw the wine-maker, he smiled to hide his discomfort.

"This gentleman has been here since the beginning of the afternoon," Jacqueline was quick to say. "He would like to see you. He says he knows you."

"We do know each other, in fact," Cooker said. "Please come in, Mr. Morton."

The visitor had clearly left behind the self-assurance and elegance that had so appealed to Cooker at La Tortinière. He seemed hesitant. He talked in starts, and his outfit was ordinary, to say the least.

"Please, do sit down," the winemaker said, with a touch of condescension. The man looked clearly bothered by something.

Cooker examined him, his gaze lingering conspicuously on Morton's shoes, which were very well-polished loafers with worn-down heels. He guessed the size to be forty-three, perhaps forty-four.

"Would you like a whisky, my dear man?"

"No, thank you," said the intruder, who did not remove his raincoat.

"It's been a while since our stay at La Tortinière. I'd say a lot has happened since, hasn't it?"

Morton sank into the armchair. He was very pale, and his features were tense.

"What about a Macallan 1946 from my personal collection?"

"That would be hard to refuse," Morton said.

Cooker filled two finely chiseled glasses.

"Thank you, Benjamin. Do you mind if I still call you Benjamin?"

"Why would I mind?"

"Because you must think that you have a murderer sitting in front of you."

"Why would I be thinking that?" Cooker asked, barely sipping his whisky. "As far as I'm aware, you drove off in your Morgan long before Oksana's body was found. And, by the way, I spotted your Morgan in a small town about two hours from Bordeaux. Someone else was driving it. Was it stolen?"

Cooker noted the surprised look on Morton's face. He seemed to be fumbling for an answer.

"Why, uh, yes," he said. "It was stolen. I've reported it to the police. You spotted it? I'll have to tell them. But I'm not here about the car. I'm here to convince you that I had nothing to do with Oksana's death."

"I'm listening."

The Englishman took a swig of the Scottish malt, and it seemed to revive him. He unbuttoned his raincoat and untied his scarf.

"I didn't kill Oksana or the concierge—and yes, I do know that he was found hanging from a tree. Please, Benjamin, don't doubt what I'm saying."

"I would like nothing more than to believe you, Robert. But your name is not Robert, is it? Nor is it Morton?"

"How do you know?"

"I'm not one to confuse a Bordeaux wine with a Burgundy. The same goes for my friends. I'm quick to separate the wheat from the chaff."

"Where do you put me?"

"For now, among people who need help. That is, if you give me some proof of your good faith, starting with your real identity."

"My name is James Welling and—"

"You were not born in London, were you?"

"That's right. I come from Canterbury."

"That might explain your ease at telling tales."

The Englishman smiled. He had never read Chaucer, confessed his ignorance, and promised to remedy it someday.

"I won't ask that much of you," Cooker grumbled. "Did you know that Geoffrey Chaucer was the son of one of London's largest wine merchants?"

"No, I didn't."

"Are you at least a wine broker?"

"Well, yes and no."

"If you want to stay friends with me, you had better start giving some straight answers."

"Let's just say that I work in wine, but more with collectors and enlightened connoisseurs."

"I had noted that vinegar is not your cup of tea and that you don't wipe your mouth with your sleeve when you eat."

"I get it from my father. When I was a teenager, he let me taste great wines like Château Haut-Brion, Romanée-Conti, Pétrus, Cheval Blanc, and even Ruster Ausbruch."

A man who knew that intriguingly sweet, refreshing, and elegant Austrian wine could not be all bad. Morton—or rather Welling—was starting to look just a bit better. Cooker put his glass of fifty-year-old Macallan to his nose and listened to the man, who was going on about the wines he had sampled during his formative years.

The list was long. For each estate, Welling supplied the vintage without any hesitation. He had an infallible memory. "1961 Margaux, 1967 Yquem, 1955 Mission Haut-Brion, 1959 Lafite-Rothschild, 1982 Pétrus, 1983 Montrachet."

Cooker's eyes glistened as Welling enumerated the mythic vintages. He was having a hard time concealing his jealousy. They ended up finding a shared memory, a 1961 Hermitage La Chapelle.

"It was as dark as ink, but what fruit!" Welling said.

"I remember aromas of cooked prunes," Cooker said, excited to be recalling these sensations.

Welling became more animated, and his sentences were sharper. A rebellious lock of hair on his forehead made him look mischievous and even a little precious. His signet ring shone in the glow of Cooker's desk lamp. Dusk was spreading across the city.

"You deliberately left the Loire wines off your inventory. That would certainly bring us back to the reason for today's visit, would it not? Didn't we say we'd share a Bonnezeaux

when we were at Château d'Artigny?" Cooker asked, wink-
ing to look sly.

"I always honor my promises, Benjamin."

And like a magician, Welling slid his hand into the inside
pocket of his gabardine and pulled out a bottle of the golden
liquid.

"Les Deux Allées, Château de Fesles, 1995. How's that for
you, grand master?"

"A lesser bottle would have done the trick. I like that you
keep your word. That's a sign of integrity. Speaking of which,
I'm curious about what you did when you left La Tortinière
after learning that your companion, or should I say, your
plaything, had taken off."

The Englishman looked down, cleared his throat twice,
swallowed a mouthful of Macallan, and held his glass in the
palms of his hands, as if he were trying to warm it.

"That is exactly why I am here."

Welling stood and started pacing without looking at
Cooker. He told his story from start to finish without omit-
ting any details, which seemed to give some credence to what
could have appeared unseemly.

Yes, that night, he was supposed to go to Bordeaux. The girl
had been a prostitute, but she had wounded his ego by leaving
him, and he didn't feel like driving all the way to Bordeaux
right away. So he drove his Morgan to Tours. He parked not
far from the police station and took a long walk along the
Quai d'Orléans. He ended up in the Jardin François Premier.
From there, he went into a sordid cabaret, where strippers were
putting on such a pathetic show, he had no choice but to down
five or maybe six brandies. That was when one of the other
customers came up to the bar and started looking for trouble.
They called him damned Rosbeef and son of a bitch. They
slapped him around. Afterward? He did not really remember.
He woke up groggy in front of some townhouse, with blood on
his face and a sore back.

Cooker felt like lighting a cigar but decided to play with his pen instead. He did a sketch of Welling in blue ink. Sketching was a skill that dated back three decades to the one year he had spent at art school in Paris. When his visitor fell silent, he encouraged him.

"And then?"

"Then I wanted to go back to my car, but I couldn't remember where I had parked it. So I paced up and down the street along the river until I was exhausted. I was devastated. That's when I saw them locked in an embrace on the embankment. He was kissing her neck, and she was responding. I just stood there. I didn't curse or threaten. I tried to yell, but nothing came out. I was speechless. I was trembling. I was freezing to death."

The winemaker was concentrating on getting Welling's slightly protruding chin just right, when he noticed that the man was shaking. His monologue was not as smooth anymore.

"Then, after giving me one of her looks—you remember Oksana's looks, right?—she said to the guy, 'Let's get out of here. There's another drunk.' I can still hear them laughing as they made their way down the steps toward the river. They started to run and disappeared under the bridge."

Welling was now looking out the window. Cooker knew his back was turned because he was hiding his tears.

"Was it the boy Gaétan, the hotel concierge?"

"I couldn't tell, really. I barely saw them."

"What about his size and his hair?" Cooker pressed, growing just a little annoyed by the show of emotion.

"Yes, I think it was him."

"And then?"

"And then? Two men approached me. One was small, and the other one was brawny, I would say. They asked me if I knew the girl. They had a thick Central European accent."

"What did you tell them?" Cooker asked.

"I shook my head."

"Why?"

"I don't know. Maybe I was afraid for her. Or for me."

"They took off down the stairs and disappeared under the bridge."

"What did you do then?"

"Nothing."

"Did you hear screams?"

"Nothing, Benjamin, I swear."

"I'm not the one you should be swearing to. It should be the police. And quickly. You know you're a major suspect, right?"

Welling finally turned around. He wiped his tears on his sleeve and mumbled, "First, I had to confide in you. You are the only friend I have in this country."

The winemaker did not like being a confidant in this way. He set aside the pad where he had drawn the very touching Welling, who did not look at all like that dashing Morton from La Tortinière. He then poured some more whisky in Welling's glass.

"1946. Can you imagine, Benjamin, that's the year I was born."

"Should I believe you?"

Welling showed him an old, dog-eared passport with a picture of a man wearing glasses. Next to it was his very British pedigree: James Cornelius John Welling. Date of birth: 15 August 1946. Place of birth: Canterbury, Kent.

Now that the Englishman had revealed his real name and shared his memory of all those fine wines, Cooker liked him again.

"So, should we open that Fesles?" Welling asked, as if to test Cooker's trust.

"No, tomorrow evening, at the same time, once you've told the police everything."

9

Virgile resigned himself to completing the task assigned to him. The job was painstaking, enormous, and thankless, but he could not disobey Benjamin Cooker. With the boss back, excitement was returning to the lab on the Cours du Chapeau-Rouge and the offices on the Allées de Tourny. Virgile retired to a small room to make a systematic list of wine auctions, beginning with those in Bordeaux's Chartrons neighborhood. He called the heads of Dubourg, Cazaux, Dubern, Bricadieu, Courau, and Le Blay. They were all overly courteous and gave him a list of the stocks they would be auctioning. He did the same with Mr. Poulin and Mr. Le Fur in Paris. He also consulted Tajan et Artus Associés, along with Catherine Charbonneaux, who was one of Cooker's friends. In his zeal, he made the rounds of France's other wine auctions, estate by estate, château by château. He did not think he would get through it in a day. The man who assigned him the tireless task did, however, refrain from harassing his "secretary." Gratitude was not the least of Cooker's qualities.

The next day, Virgile set a thick stack of papers on Cooker's desk, like a bearer of bad news expecting to be shot.

"No stocks of Angélus anywhere?" Cooker asked.

"Just six bottles by Mr. Galateau in Limoges, twelve at Sabourin in Châtellerault, and two cases of six with Besh in Cannes. Nothing to get excited about," Virgile responded, reading disappointment on the winemaker's face.

But Cooker paused as he went over the list. He put on his reading glasses and underlined one item twice. Then, after a long sigh, he smiled at his assistant and said, "Tell Jacqueline to call in an offer on the 1961 Pape Clément for, say, a hundred euros a bottle. Add the case of six 1985 Mazis-Chambertin for, well, two hundred euros, give or take fifty. Okay?"

"You got it, boss."

"At least your work wasn't a total waste of time."

Virgile scowled, took his papers, and started walking away. He was not wearing the kind and attractive expression that had worked so well on Elisabeth Cooker the day he had arrived at Grangebelle for his job interview.

"What's bothering you, Virgile? A heartbreak?"

"Just a break, that's all."

The winemaker did not want to pry. He knew he could put his foot in his mouth. He decided to stand up and survey the activity on the Allées de Tourny, where carnival workers were taking down a merry-go-round. Having second thoughts, he moved closer to his assistant.

"Nothing serious, I hope."

"It's my little sister, Raphaëlle. She—"

Virgile stared at the empty carousel that no longer had its wooden horses. His eyes filled with tears. Cooker put a hand on the young man's shoulder.

"What is it?"

"She's got cancer. Colon cancer. It doesn't look good."

Virgile started sobbing. "Tell me she's not going to die."

"Virgile, I can't tell you what you want to hear. I will pray for her."

"Like that will help."

"Would you rather resign yourself to her dying?"

"That's not what I mean, Mr. Cooker."

The two men looked at each other. The telephone rang twice, and Cooker ignored it. His secretary knocked on the door.

"Just a minute, Jacqueline, please."

At that moment, nothing was more pressing than the needs of his distressed assistant. This worthy son of a winemaker with such an earnest look seemed ready to collapse. Cooker knew that at twenty-five, death was not a looming prospect, but instead a far-off eventuality.

"Come on, Virgile. I think we have better things to do than pour out our feelings to each other. I don't think Raphaëlle would like that. Actually, I'm sure she wouldn't."

After a long silence and a gesture of tenderness that could have been that of a father to a son, the winemaker added, "I have hope for her."

Virgile dried his cheeks, the way he must have on winter mornings when he walked to school in Montravel, and the cold wind stung his eyes until he cried. He looked like a little boy again. The same little boy who used his sleeve to wipe blood from his nose when he fought like a devil in the school-yard with a bully who cheated at marbles. Virgile always said that in the Lanssien family, there was "no sniveling, even when you bury your mom and pop." How many times had his father called him a pussy when he crawled into his mother's arms to cry? Would he cry on his father's grave one day? This was the same father who had not seen Raphaëlle since she had taken up with a divorced man who was fifteen years older than she.

When Cooker and his assistant left 46 Allées de Tourny, the merry-go-round had been completely dismantled. Shy rays of sunlight were trying to revive a city mired in winter. One could barely make out Lormont through the thick fog that refused to lift off the Garonne, rusting its pontoons and barges. The two men slipped into the convertible that was parked on the quays. The tramway had opened up recently in this part of town and now reigned over public transportation in Bordeaux. Virgile took it frequently, but Cooker refused. "Perhaps one day," he had said without an ounce of conviction.

"Head to Saint-Macaire" was all that Cooker said. For once, he refrained from turning on the radio or playing one of the opera openings that exasperated Virgile.

"Mission?"

"Château Fayard."

"Isn't Jacques-Charles de Musset one of your favorites in the upcoming guide?"

"Exactly. It's a small estate, just over seventeen acres and about a dozen barrels of a dry white every year. Beyond reproach," Cooker said.

"Yes, I tasted a few samples at the lab," Virgile added.

"And?"

"Sweet."

"Virgile, what is this hip language you're using? Sweet. You don't call a dry white wine 'sweet.' That's like saying a wine is 'good.' If it's not good, there's no reason to talk about it, and if it's good you drink it and *describe* it."

Cooker was getting worked up, as only he knew how to do. He could throw a fit at a moment's notice and then get over it just as quickly. Truth be told, Cooker was just trying to divert Virgile from his sad thoughts, and he wondered if his assistant was fooled by the tactic.

"In Fayard, there are vines that are over sixty years old, with yields of—"

"Around five hundred and twenty gallons every two and a half acres. And the vines are fertilized with horse crap."

"How do you know that, Virgile?"

"Four years ago, I harvested there. It was, well, let's just say it was more than good."

"Well then, say it was outstanding." Cooker saw his assistant smile for the first time that day.

Layers of fog covered the river as the elegant Château Fayard rose from the rows of vines that winter had transformed into sad, bony skeletons.

Virgile dug up his memories from the harvest and shared them with Cooker. The laughter among the grapevines,

T-shirts splotched with red, hands stiff from intensive use of pruning shears, and backs stooped from days of going from row to row, heads down and cutters in hand.

Virgile seemed very happy to see Jacques-Charles de Musset again. Of course, he remembered Virgile. He even remembered that the young man had followed around a Swedish girl named Ingrid. She had aquamarine eyes and hair as golden as Semillon grapes. It was one of a thousand flirtations that had no tomorrows. It was just the way of the harvest: hard work, schoolboy pranks, girls in tank tops, boys in their prime, juicy clusters of grapes, sweet lips, and uncalled-for gestures covered up by the laughter of old-timers who made sure nobody dawdled. That was four years ago, the year Raphaëlle fled Montravel to live her life in Périgueux. Virgile loved his sister. And to think that...

"No, that is very kind of you, but we have other plans. Another time, perhaps. Thank you for the case."

Cooker said good-bye to the head of Fayard with a firm, friendly handshake that Virgile clumsily tried to imitate. His heart was not in it. That was too bad, because he had fond memories of the Saint Macaire harvest, mixed with a few regrets. Why had he not bedded that beautiful Ingrid?

As they drove back to Bordeaux, Cooker tried to find out more about the pretty Scandinavian who had captivated his assistant. Virgile refused to answer his questions and remained silent, looking out over the dark waters of the Garonne.

On the way, Cooker made a sharp turn to the right. The tires screeched, and Virgile gave his driver the evil eye. Cooker did not blink as he stepped on the clutch and changed gears. A few minutes later, the Mercedes stopped at the Place du Verdelais. There was not a soul on the walkways, which looked like they belonged in an old spa town where people went to treat melancholy as much as rheumatism. The village looked dead. What inhabitants remained must be working or napping this afternoon. All around the square, abandoned shops had bygone signs. The only hotel had given up. A gigantic basilica seemed to crush the houses that pushed against its base. A golden Mother Mary perched on the steeple overlooked the whole. Cooker thought about Montbazon.

Virgile buried his chin in his jacket. A cold wind whisked brightly colored papers off the ground. They announced a raffle in Saint Maixent: "Win a wide-screen TV, ten fat ducks, two stag legs, and other prizes. Do not litter."

"What are we doing here?" Virgile grumbled.

The winemaker did not respond and walked toward the basilica. Virgile followed in silence.

The smell of melted wax floated in the dark air. The walls were covered with ex-votos dedicated to Our Lady of Verdelais, known for miraculous healing and miraculous good works. Cooker made the sign of the cross and walked down the central aisle, illuminated by a few flickering candles, past a woman who was praying.

As he knelt at the front of the church, Cooker recalled the Angélus devotion. He wondered how many times the homage to the Blessed Mother and the Annunciation had been recited in this ancient place. How many times had the Angélus bell rung at six in the morning, noon, and six in the evening? It was a ritual followed in Catholic churches all over the world.

Cooker thought Virgile would be lurking somewhere in the back of the church. And, in fact, his assistant was hovering like a naughty imp near a confessional that had probably not seen a sinner in decades. From this observation point, Virgile watched his boss's somewhat abstruse actions. He seemed impressed with Cooker's devotion, although he himself did not believe in God anymore than he believed in himself. Nobody had taught him how, not even his mother, who had been raised by nuns.

Cooker buried his face in his hands for a long time and then stood up and lit a votive candle. Virgile, still huddled near the old confessional, stared at the flame. He shivered. He must be thinking about Raphaëlle, perhaps saying a clumsy prayer, begging the plaster Lady of Verdelais statue, which was dressed like some Oriental doll as she looked down on him from her pedestal. The church bells broke the frozen silence. Cooker made the sign of the cross again and joined Virgile on the square outside the church. The young man's eyes were red.

"I don't believe in that stuff, sir."

"You're lying. I saw you praying near the confessional."

"I wasn't praying. I was crying."

"It's the same thing," Cooker said. "You cry when you think God has abandoned you. Even Christ experienced doubt on the cross. You have no reason to doubt, or you might as well just change jobs, my dear Virgile."

"Never."

"Show the same faith in the unknown as you have in things related to wine."

This was one of the occasions when student and teacher dared to explore the meandering path of religious belief. They talked for what seemed like hours about philosophy and theology while following the stations of the cross that rose above the Garonne Valley. The two pilgrims braved the west wind and the light rain that seeped into their bones, and for a while, they forgot their ages, their health, their ambitions, and perhaps even their own convictions. Then the Verdelais church bells struck five.

"Oh dear," Cooker said. "I forgot to call Hubert de Boüard. Come on, let's go to Saint-Émilion."

10

Along the ridge, the thick forests of the Landes blocked the horizon. The ashen sky darkened suddenly in a call for night to come. Cooker was happy to let his assistant drive the Mercedes. Their long discussion had exhausted him. He asked Virgile to put on the high beams. "The roads are treacherous here," he said.

Saint-Émilion was only three-quarters of an hour away. As they drove through Saint-Germain-de-Grave, Cooker pointed out the former Sisters of the Assumption convent, which had been converted to a wine estate a century earlier.

"The Château des Mille Anges—château of a thousand angels," Cooker said.

"Did you count them?" Virgile asked.

"A lot of them didn't show up, apparently. But you know as well as I do that angels never miss out on taking their share of drink."

Virgile rolled his eyes at this vintner reference to the portion of wine that evaporates in oak barrels. He stepped on the gas pedal.

"Virgile, we're not in any hurry. Stop here, would you?"

Before the shadows took hold of the hills and valleys that outlined the Bordeaux Premières Côtes, Cooker pointed his elegant index finger at the line of cypress trees that led to Malagar, a home that author François Mauriac had held dear.

"Look, there is the Maromé castle, which Toulouse-Lautrec liked so much," Virgile said, glancing at Cooker with a smirk.

Cooker was blown away. *Who was being the professor now?* His assistant was no angel and took an evil pleasure in rebuffing people who were too full of themselves. Virgile continued:

186 J.-P. ALAUX & N. BALEN

"And there is the Domaine du Cheval Blanc, which shouldn't
be confused with the Château Cheval-Blanc, which belongs
to your friends Bernard Arnaud and Albert Frère. Isn't that
right, master?"

"It won't be so much fun if I have nothing left to teach you."

"But you did teach me a lot today."

Virgile looked up at the sky, which was sadly lacking stars.
But lights were shimmering at Génisson, Grand Housteau,
Âtre Étoilé, and Grang Garron, estates whose wines Cooker
knew well, not only because he had tasted them, but also
because he had made some of them. The winemaker had a
respectful word for each of these domains shining on the hills.
As the night slowly took possession of the acres of vineyards,
they shared a moment of wordless private pleasure. Was it still
a decent hour to be visiting Angélus?

Cooker's cell phone rang, interrupting the moment of
grace and satisfaction the two men were enjoying.

"Cooker here."

"It's Welling. Am I bothering you?"

"Yes, I mean no. What's new?"

"I have to see you. It's urgent."

"Okay. In my office, tomorrow, around, say, eleven."

"What about tonight?"

"Listen, James, I'm in the middle of an assessment."

"Can I come and join you?"

"Well, actually—"

Virgile could see that his employer was becoming entan-
gled in ridiculous lies. Annoyed, Cooker finally said, "Okay,
listen, be at the Café Français in an hour. No, I will not be
alone. Yes, that's right, my assistant will be with me."

He hung up, angry with his caller. "What a bore."

Virgile waited for his boss to give some explanation. It was
long in coming, but then Cooker told the story of Welling's
visit to the office, from beginning to end. He recounted every
detail. The winemaker had believed what the strange man
had said.

"Why, then, did he lie to you at La Tortinière?" Virgile asked.

"For love of wine!"

"That's a little simplistic."

"He's a collector, Virgile. A fabulous collector. He has tasted the best wines the world has to offer. I suspect he is rich and passes much of his time traveling the globe, putting together the best wine collection one could ever imagine."

"Is that an end in itself?"

"You're becoming philosophical, Virgile."

"You're contagious, sir."

Cooker furrowed his brow, which in him was an indication that he was pleased. He liked the compliment.

"What exactly is he doing in Bordeaux?" Virgile asked.

"I admit that I didn't ask him," Cooker confessed, uncomfortable at being found out by his own student.

"It can't be an auction that's on his mind. That's for sure," Virgile said, still a little annoyed by the previous day's assignment.

"We'll know in less than an hour."

"Unless he serves up another one of the stories he's so good at when he sits down to eat," Virgile said.

"I promise you, Virgile, you'll want to make his acquaintance."

"If you say so, sir."

Cooker wondered why he didn't go to the Café Français more often. This Bordeaux brasserie had the kind of old-world charm that had captivated him when he was an art student in the capital, cultivating refined idleness on the Boulevard Saint-Germain. The copper work was as shiny as it could get. The booths were comfortable, and the staff was friendly without overdoing it.

As an aesthete, Cooker chose the moleskine booth without hesitation. He could see the proud Saint André cathedral from there. Each of its dizzying pinnacles was lit up like a Christmas tree. In the middle of this extravagance of light, the Tour Pey-Berland was not to be outdone. The statue of the Virgin Mary on its steeple had been covered in gold leaf. This stone theater was outrageously flashy. Bordeaux had suffered far too long from the plague that had eaten away at its eighteenth-century façades and had every reason to be happy with its recent face-lift. The city shone anew and was experiencing a renaissance. Cooker was among those who were pleased. The city was like its wines and deserved to have its reputation supported at all cost, even if it meant a little artifice.

Welling did not spoil the scene. He was wearing a duffle coat that, with his graying hair, made him appear somewhat lost in the modern world. He removed it with such a pronounced British flair, the effect was almost theatrical. Welling gave Virgile his best smile and shook Cooker's hand warmly. They each said they were dying of hunger and unrolled their napkins without waiting. Straight out, the Englishman ordered a 1988 Canon la Gaffelière. Then the waiter sent an order for three *entrecôtes*, rare, to the kitchen.

"Perhaps some mineral water?" the waiter asked.

"I think I was clear, young man," Welling answered.

"Could there be a teetotaler among us?" Cooker added.

The waiter put on a poker face and held up his order pad.

"A what?" Virgile asked, hardly fooled by his boss's act.

"A teetotaler," Cooker pontificated. "A race of individuals not to be recommended, incapable of communicating about wine, with a natural repugnance for alcohol."

The three diners broke out laughing. The waiter timidly joined in.

He filled their glasses with Saint-Émilion, which exhaled Oriental spices. Cooker noted aromas of cooked cassis. Virgile added cedar, while Welling, who chose his words carefully and spoke with affectation, mentioned smoked oak. What followed was a tasting by experts that intrigued the couple sitting to their left. The woman looked like she was soaking up Cooker's words. She and her companion did not appear well-suited for each other, but this evening, they shared curiosity. Restaurants always seemed to be full of bored couples who enjoyed eavesdropping.

"Welling, you are looking well since you gave yourself up to the police."

"Did you know that they weren't even looking for me? I wasn't even a suspect."

"Thanks to your feet," Cooker said.

"What do you mean?" Welling asked, pausing his knife above his steak.

Virgile was wolfing down his shallot-topped meat between mouthfuls of grand cru classé. The winemaker, distilling his deductions like an old rusty alembic, did not say much. His astuteness excited Welling, who emptied his glass of Canon-la-Gaffelière rather quickly. As Cooker explained how he had been exonerated in the Oksana case and then in the disguised suicide of the concierge, Welling tossed in "that's right" after each forkful.

"There's no hiding anything from you, Benjamin. It's as if you were there when I talked to the cops. Do you know the captain?"

"A little," the winemaker said evasively, eyeing his seemingly passive assistant. "But tell me, James, you didn't really invite me here to tell me what I already know."

"No, but to let you in on a good deal. It's the least I can do for you. A private sale tomorrow. Nothing but treasures. Marvels, I assure you."

"Like what?" Cooker asked.

"For starters, 1955 and 1975 Pétrus, 1983 Margaux, 1989 and 1995 Latour, 1995 Ducru-Beaucaillou, 1989 Cos d'Estournel,

1998 Calon-Ségur, 1996 Pichon-Longueville, 1970 Conseillante, 1977 Pape Clément, 1990 Talbot, among others."

"Stop, stop, my cellar is already full," Cooker said, trying to conceal the disillusionment in his voice. This list was worthy of a forger. "A private sale, you say?"

"Yes, I'm in cahoots with the Belgian broker I stood up on the night Oksana walked out on me. We have an appointment tomorrow morning at the Hôtel de Villesèque."

Virgile, who had so far been quiet, nervously pulled off his sweater, as though the Canon-la-Gaffelière was making him too hot. He asked the waiter for water.

"Mineral water, please."

Welling and Cooker both stared at him. Virgile responded, "Sirs, I now am joining the teetotalers."

"You know, Virgile, that could get you fired," Cooker said.

"Wait until tomorrow afternoon before doing the paperwork," Virgile said with youthful arrogance. "Mr. Welling, could I tag along tomorrow?"

"Why would you like to do that?" the Englishman asked.

"To see those labels."

"I'm afraid that will not be possible," Welling answered, looking very sorry. "This kind of event requires the greatest confidentiality, and Mr. Wolvertem, my Belgian broker, would certainly not want you there."

"Tell me, James, how did you meet this, well, this broker of the finest and rarest wines?" Cooker asked, articulating each word.

"On the Internet, Benjamin. I may be driving a Morgan, but I am a modern man. I take only the best from the past. That is my philosophy."

"I have no doubt," Cooker said.

"How many customers like you does your Mr. Wolvertem have in Bordeaux?"

"I'm his only one."

"You mean he came here just for you?"

"Sort of."

"Tell me, Mr. Morton," Virgile said, "sorry, Mr. Welling—I can't get your name straight. Please excuse my ignorance, but how does a private sale like this work?"

"It's really very simple," the Englishman explained. "You go to the host's hotel suite. You tell him what you would like to order and how much, and so on. He gives you a price. You can sometimes negotiate a little, but not always. There's a man in the hotel parking garage who will have what you purchased in a vehicle."

"You get it on the same day?"

"About an hour after you've made the purchase."

"Nothing written."

"We are among men of honor, Virgile."

"Certainly, but we don't know this Mr. Wolvertem, and apparently he plans to keep his identity a secret."

"You're right," Welling said, looking a little embarrassed.

Cooker was relishing this discussion. But only a tremor in his nostrils divulged his delight.

No, he would not have any dessert. "Just a coffee. A double espresso for the young man."

Welling declined an after-dinner drink proposed by his friend. He was very focused on satisfying Virgile's somewhat aggressive and unrelenting curiosity.

"What do you intend to buy Mr., uhm, Welling?"

"Ask Benjamin. He knows my weakness for Saint-Émilion. I won't forbid myself a few Médocs or Pomerols."

"So you'll buy out the Angélus."

"Yes, for sure. If there is any, I wouldn't hesitate. Generally speaking, the prices are a good deal, compared with what I've seen recently at the auction houses."

"Which means?" Virgile asked.

"Fifty to sixty euros a bottle for very good years. More, of course, for historic years," Welling whispered.

Cooker took a pen from his jacket and jotted a few figures on the paper tablecloth. Then he ripped off the corner and slipped it to Welling.

"I'll take all the Angélus for the years noted, no matter how much. Then we can split them fifty-fifty if you want."

Welling rubbed his chin, then sighed and sneaked a self-righteous look in Virgile's direction before giving Cooker a wink.

"Do you want a check tonight?" Cooker asked.

"I believe Mr. Wolvertem prefers cash. Actually, I'm sure of it."

"That should be expected, considering his job—if you can call it a job," the winemaker said, drinking the last of his coffee, which was now cold.

"It's what I said, nothing written down," Virgile said, slightly irritated that his boss was condoning this black market.

"Virgile, I'll see you at the office tomorrow around noon," Cooker said, turning to address Welling. "That is, unless you change your mind and accept that he come along for the sale. He knows how to be discreet, you know."

"Benjamin, don't insist," Welling said with some authority. "It's better for our transaction this way."

"You are the best judge of that," Cooker said, taking out his credit card.

"No, let me get this," Welling said, snatching the bill away from Cooker.

Cooker and Virgile said good night to Welling in front of the gates of the city hall without any excess politeness.

"Bye, old chap," Cooker mumbled, wrapping his scarf around his neck.

"Good-bye, Mr. Morton," Virgile said.

As Cooker pulled out his phone to call Elisabeth, a freezing breeze had chased the last night owls away from the Place de Rohan. The cafés had turned off their signs. The Bar de l'Hôtel de Ville was the only place still open, attracting hybrid techno animals who also milled in the deserted Rue de Ruat. High up, the Pey Berland Madonna had to be shivering. Cooker and Virgile would not yet be going home.

11

Night watch. Cooker had to ring several times before a
stooped figure shuffled over and agreed to crack open the
wrought-iron gate of the Hôtel de Villesèque. An enamel
sign above the doorbell read "Logis de France. Traveling
sales representatives welcome." The night watchman had
messy hair and tired eyes, reflecting many nights on call.
Cooker figured he had fallen asleep at the reception desk before having to open the gate. *Can't blame him for being irritated
with the two nutcases who wouldn't quit knocking at the window,*
Cooker thought.

"Let me see what I have left," the old man said, putting
reading glasses on the tip of his beak-like nose.

Only three keys were missing from the board above the man,
whose gray Scottish wool sweater gaped at the neck.

"Just one room?" the man asked with a sly smile.

"Two," Cooker said, categorical but polite.

"Will you have breakfast in your room or in the dining
room?" the man asked, addressing Cooker.

"Neither, thank you," Cooker said.

"In that case, sirs, may I ask that you pay for your rooms
up front, please."

"Certainly," Cooker said, tossing him a credit card.

Virgile stood at the counter and eyed the night watchman
write his name in the old-fashioned registry with a black cloth
cover.

"Please, two S's in Lanssien."

"Sorry?" the man said.

"My name has two *S*'s," Cooker's assistant said, taking advantage of the moment to glance at the short list of guests in the registry for Thursday, January 28.

Room number twenty-seven listed the name Wolvertem. "Paid" was carefully written in the margin.

"Don't you have any bags?" the watchman asked, handing over two keys with heavy copper plaques engraved "H.V., Bordeaux."

"The man is right," Cooker said. "Why don't we have any bags, Virgile?"

"But boss, you know that—"

"Oh, Virgile, stop justifying yourself. Let's go. I'm exhausted."

The watchman stared as the two men slipped into the elevator after saying a quiet good night. The old hotel clock read one thirty-five. The Rue Huguerie was in a torpor, which soon caught up with the night watchman. The Hotel de Villeseque's sign was no longer flashing.

Unlocking the door to his room, Cooker flipped the light switch but the orange ceiling fixture didn't go on. Propping open the door so he could see where he was going, Cooker headed to the nightstand and turned on that light. He closed the door, sat down on the squeaky bed, and slipped off his shoes. After straightening the nylon lampshade, he lay down, fully clothed and fell fast asleep.

The walls were so thin, Virgile could hear his boss's regular snoring. It took him a long time to fall asleep between the scratchy, cold, and almost damp cotton sheets. A little before dawn—which a dull concert of street cleaners announced—he started stirring. He finally surrendered to the day when the noise of Cooker washing up in the next room was too jarring to allow him to eek out another fifteen minutes of sleep. After a hot shower, he listened to the day's horror show of news, distilled by an enthusiastic newscaster who made the morning rather ordinary, all in all. This narrow, poorly

heated room with gold-flocked wallpaper and disparate furniture was putting him in a bad mood.

Bags under his eyes and his hair still wet, Virgile dressed
quickly and went to knock on his employer's door.

"Come in. Did you sleep well, Virgile?" Cooker asked without even looking at his ragged assistant.

With his hands behind his back, the winemaker was peering out the window. He was studying the activity on the Rue
Huguerie, which was blocked by a traffic jam.

"Not good at all," Virgile said. A tail of his white shirt was
hanging out from under his sweater.

"But the hotel was quiet," Cooker said, not turning around.

"That's what you say."

"You've got good timing. Take a look."

Virgile looked out the window. A German station wagon
had stopped in front of the hotel garage. The imposing vehicle
had a Belgian license plate. Its high top and dark windows
made it look like a hearse. Cooker pulled a Churchill from his
inside jacket pocket, stuck it between his lips, and lit it with
obvious satisfaction.

"You're on, Virgile. Don't let yourself be seen."

The young man had already disappeared down the hallway. Cooker saw the Do Not Disturb sign and smiled. Then
he closed the door to his room before calling the reception desk.

"Connect me to Room 27, please."

Virgile chose the service stairs rather than the elevator.
Thanks to an untied shoelace, he nearly tripped on the concrete steps when the timed light suddenly went off. The dull
sound of an engine, along with the pungent smell of exhaust,
confirmed that he had reached the basement. He pushed open
the fire escape door and found himself in the parking garage.
There were only a few vehicles. The driver of the station wagon had to try twice to park next to a rental van, which bore
the unfortunate advertising message "I go for the lowest price."
The driver was wearing a raincoat, a russet-colored scarf, and
a checked cap. Dark glasses hid a thin face. The man walked

slowly but still looked distinguished. Virgile hid behind a pillar so as not to be spotted. The man picked up his pace, then turned around suddenly and examined the parking lot, as if he sensed someone was there. Then he vanished, sucked up by the hotel elevator. Virgile felt for his phone. His breathing was heavy, and he thought he might be trembling. He tried to call Cooker, but he had no reception.

"I'm sorry, sir. Room 27 does not answer."

"Are you sure, miss, that you rang Mr. Wolvertem?" Cooker pressed.

"Yes, sir."

"That's okay," Cooker concluded after a moment of silence. "I will try later. Thank you."

The winemaker paced his room, chewing his cigar. He flicked the ashes, not caring about the carpet that absorbed his footsteps. Thick blue swirls of smoke showed his impatience. The Rue Huguerie was busier now. An ambulance siren rose above the concert of horns. The winemaker tried to reach his accomplice, without any luck.

"Jesus," Cooker said.

In a show of anger, he crushed the bulbous cigar that he had lit ten minutes earlier, but it obstinately refused to go out. The reddened tip gave off an aroma reminiscent of the day after a storm, both acidic and refreshing. Why, in his frustration, had he sacrificed such a silky pleasure? Had his Havanophile friend James Welling seen that pitiful act of destruction, he would have certainly thought it a sacrilege.

Virgile stormed into Cooker's room without even knocking. He was out of breath and bumbling.

"So?" Cooker asked.

"So, um—"

"Is he alone?" Cooker said, showing his nervousness.

"Yes. He's wearing a raincoat, a brown scarf, and a kind of cap that you can't find anymore."

"What do you mean?"

"I don't know. Kind of classy but old-fashioned. I mean, your kind of style, boss, if you know what I mean."

"That's a big help," Cooker said, exasperated. "And his shoes?"

"What do you mean, his shoes? I don't know, sir. They were, well—"

"Virgile, you should always look at a man's shoes. They'll tell you more about the person than his tie."

"Oh. He wasn't wearing a tie. That I'm sure of."

"How can you be so sure, Virgile. You told me he was wearing a raincoat and a scarf."

"I don't know. He didn't look like the kind of man who would be wearing a tie."

"Virgile! Good God, who or what did he look like?"

"Calm down, boss. He looked kind of like a cop. You know, the kind of guy you'd see in an American television series. In any case, one thing is certain. He was nervous."

"What do you mean?"

"He was in a hurry and kept looking over his shoulder."

Cooker stared at the tip of the Churchill that was burning slowly in the room's only ashtray. Virgile looked contrite and clumsy, like someone who has been judged wrongly and too quickly. The winemaker pushed up the window that opened onto a ridiculous balcony. He breathed in the city air and listened to the clamoring.

"What are we going to do, sir?" Virgile asked.

"Follow me," was the only response that he got.

Cooker walked purposefully, with Virgile in his wake. They quietly went down a floor and stood in front of the varnished wooden door of room twenty-seven. The winemaker knocked twice. A husky voice answered.

Cooker improvised. "There's a letter for you, Mr. Wolvertem." Virgile was impressed with Cooker's ad-libbing.

The door opened a crack, and the thin shape of James Welling appeared. He was dressed in nothing but a white bathrobe that was too big for him. Cooker, whose size gave him authority, shouldered his way into the room. Virgile followed.

"So, my dear friend, what should I call you now?" Cooker asked. "Morton? Welling? Wolvertem?"

The man was distressingly thin. His knees were knobby, and the tendons on his neck stood out. The top of his hairless chest looked bony. He tried to conceal it by crossing his arms. The man's pale blue eyes looked pathetic. "It's not what you think, Benjamin."

Abandoned on top of the crumpled bed sheets were an off-white Burberry, a cashmere scarf, a gray suit, and a Yves Saint Laurent tie. Cooker went to the bedside table and picked up a bottle of pills that bore the warning "Do not surpass the prescribed dose." He set it back down next to a set of car keys.

Virgile, who was also surveying the room, spotted a pink silk bra on the rug.

"Virgile, go see if the station wagon has what we're looking for. You know my weakness right now. Only Angélus," the winemaker said.

"Fine, boss. But let me check something first."

With a certain arrogance, Virgile gave his employer a serious look before staring into their victim's pitiful eyes.

"Let me explain," the man said.

"You, don't play with me! Is that understood?" Virgile ordered in a voice that stopped the imposter in his tracks. "Boss, we knew the man was quite a wine collector, but I bet he also has a thing for fine call girls. Did you see the pink silk bra on the rug?"

Virgile peered into the bathroom, where a naked woman was trying to hide behind the shower curtain. When she came out in a bathrobe, Cooker couldn't believe his eyes. She had blond hair, blue eyes, high angular cheekbones, and long voluptuous legs. Clearly, the con man had a weakness for not only Bordeaux but also Eastern European women.

In the hour that followed, Inspector Barbaroux and his team filled the Hôtel de Villesèque. The cargo in the station wagon was exactly as Cooker had suspected: a few Médocs, some rare Pomerols, a couple of Saint-Émilions, and mostly the stolen Angélus—the best years: 1986, 1989, 1990, 1993, 1994, and the mythic 1995.

Cooker and Virgile gave Inspector Barbaroux a full account of their encounters with the con man, and in return the inspector had let them hang around for the interrogation.

"John the Belgian" was a repeat offender. His impeccable Oxford accent came from his English father, who had been cellar master at Buckingham Palace. His father had married a frivolous redhead from Liège. This singular couple had given birth to twins: Eddy and John. Eddy drowned in the Meuse River when he was eight. John wound up abandoned by his mother, who vanished into the Flemish mist. His cellar master father raised him in London until the father was dismissed after some obscure scandal that brought dishonor to the house of Windsor. The father sank into alcohol and wandering, while his son became a not-very-orthodox trader of fine wines. John the imposter had a reputation as a con artist in Germany and Switzerland, but he and a few recruits fully intended to extend their influence throughout Europe.

The man puffed up his confession with references to Lafite-Rothschild, Prieuré-Lichine, and Pétrus, along with some Old Testament. But John's good manners did not impress the hardened police officer, who was perhaps a bit rough around the edges.

Morton was handcuffed and invited to change his attitude and drop the masquerade. Barbaroux used language that was as raw as wine straight from the vat: "Stop treating us like jackasses, Mr. Roberton, because we now know your real identity. Your name is John Roberton, and you were born in Canterbury on January 6, 1946. True or false?"

"True, Inspector."

"I'm tempted to believe you. The name Robert Morton was directly inspired by your real name. As for the rest of it—why James Welling and, what was the other one—Wolvertem? Is that Flemish? Perhaps an homage to your mother?"

"Sort of," the accused answered, looking down.

"So, you recruit your accomplices in Belgium, I gather?"

"If you say so."

"I encourage you to be a little more cooperative, Mr. Roberton. You wouldn't want me to use our corkscrew method on you. The bad bottles often end up deep in the cellar. Sometimes they even get forgotten, if you know what I mean."

Roberton was playing with the signet ring, as he did in Cooker's office the day he was supposedly repenting. Then he began a long monologue, punctuated by "Don't you have anything to drink, Inspector?"

Barbaroux invariably responded, "Later, later."

Yes, he was the brains behind the Angélus gang. He had accomplices, musclemen, and others, primarily recruited in Belgium. In Ostend fifteen years earlier, he had met Willem Vanderbroecq, who introduced him to a certain Gerrt Voets, who, until then, had done mostly bank heists. There was far less risk with wines. Their break-ins multiplied as orders came in from collectors around the world.

For some time now, they had worked for an individual named Ignacio Ribera de Montuño. He was a little eccentric and ran a huge family olive-oil business. He lived in a former monastery, now mostly in ruins, in Cienfuegos de las Campanas. The monastery was in a lost hamlet of Andalusia. The millionaire had an insane passion for church bells. His chapel had hundreds of bronze bells that rang out whenever there was a full moon.

The Spaniard was also a great wine connoisseur, frustrated that he didn't have a wine estate of his own. He had made an offer to purchase the Château Angélus estate, which was rejected. Now he was extremely envious of the owner of the grand cru classé Saint-Émilion, and it had turned into an obsession. He wanted to get his hands on all the Angélus he could.

He was very demanding of his Belgian supplier. Unprepared for this customer's new fixation, Roberton had tried to sell him some cases of Clos du Clocher, a very fine Pomerol, but Ignacio would not have it. He wanted Angélus. His terms were strict, and he paid cash.

Willem Vanderbroecq was in charge of finding the wine, and Gerrt Voets was supposed to step in, as needed.

"We didn't know where to find the bottles he wanted," John the Belgian explained. "That's when we started tailing Cooker. That notebook of his is famous for holding secrets. Gerrt Voets planned the carjacking. The kids weren't supposed to hurt the man."

Then Roberton's men robbed the cellars on the Place de la Madeleine in Paris, as well as La Vinothèque de Dionysos in Bordeaux. They had planned a third heist.

Ignacio had a strange sense of humor, and his way of thumbing his nose at the famous Bordeaux wine estate was sending out a cryptic message to coincide with his taking possession of purloined Angélus.

In the meantime, Roberton, ever the opportunist, continued to tail Cooker all the way to La Tortinière. He wanted to meet the man in person.

His Spanish customer insisted on making the exchange in Bordeaux, so Roberton had planned to drive there from La Tortinière. His accomplices would then head to Paris for the final heist. But Roberton had changed his mind at the last minute and had gone looking for Oksana in Tours. That decision threw off their schedule and ended up sabotaging the Paris job.

A young detective was typing out the statement as Barbaroux half-listened to John the Belgian. The deputy came in without knocking, carrying a can of beer.

"Want me to take over, Inspector?"

"No. Sit down. Mr. Roberton is going to serve us up his best and explain how he got rid of his mistress—employee is a better word—in the Loire Valley, along with her lover."

For the first time, the accused dropped his waxy face into his hands.

"Believe me, Inspector, that's not my fault. That was Gerrt. He's the one who found Oksana in Tours. He knew I was hooked on her, and her skipping out had hit me hard. But Gerrt wasn't about to be taken in by her charms. She knew too much, and he didn't hesitate. He killed her, and, to throw the cops off, he made it look like it was the concierge by faking his suicide. The concierge had never even been with her. Gerrt followed him from the hotel on one of his nightly walks and did him in right there on the riverbank."

"Don't try to get out of this, Mr. Roberton. Once you've poured the wine, you have to drink it. And yours seems to be bad two-buck chuck. Now, you said three heists, where was the third?"

"We never got to it because of the Oksana 'incident.' Vanderbroecq took the Morgan to race back to Paris to do it, but didn't make it in time for those crackpot letters. That crazy Ignacio got pissed at us. He canceled the Châteaux Angélus deal, and decided he wanted a Cave de l'Angélus— that's a rare Swiss wine from the Valais region, purplish robe and leathery aromas. So, there I was, left with all those bottles of wine to unload."

Then he added with a sheepish grin, "I thought Cooker would like them."

Barbaroux booked Roberton. After being held for forty-eight hours, the call girl was released. Although she had Baltic traits, long flowing blond hair, and big Prussian blue eyes, she was really the daughter of a farmer from Corrèze, in the middle of France.

The sky looked low. The rainfall that had intensified all day long seemed to be taking a break. The winemakers in Beauséjour, Cheval Blanc, Belair, Canon, Fourtet, Figeac, Pavie, and Trotte Vieille knew the rain would start up again before nightfall. Yet they had to prune the vines before March first. There was a saying in the Garonne valley. "By the feast of Saint Aubin, prune your vines to shape, and be assured of a plump grape."

The sun was setting, casting its final rays on the hills that overlooked the Landes forest. Workers in dull-green rain jackets were tirelessly removing suckers from the vines. The needle on the barometer fluctuated between rainy and windy. The weather forecasters were predicting a depression over the Bay of Biscay.

Cooker and Virgile were a little late arriving at the Château Angélus, but Hubert de Boüard was not a man to take offense.

"Just in time," their host said loudly when they finally climbed the château's steps. They were soaked from the storm.

Under the large front awning, Hubert congratulated them for so cleverly solving a case that had given him a lot of unasked-for publicity.

Inside the château, he had lined up several bottles that were coming to room temperature not far from a crackling fire in the hearth. Bits of grit were causing occasional mini-explosions, which interrupted the ceremonial silence. The vertical tasting promised to be sumptuous.

At that instant, the church bells of Saint-Émilion rang out the Angélus. Then the bells of the Saint-Martin church responded with equal fervor.

"France's churches are empty. For whom are the Angélus bells ringing?" Virgile asked.

"For God's children like yourself," Benjamin answered. "You know, my boy, wine, like God, is an enigma. You need to taste it many times to make a religion of it. And then—"

"And then, what?" Virgile asked.

"And then, you see, life is nothing but a succession of small miracles. Like this 1989 Angélus that awaits us."

"A miracle, yes," Hubert de Boüard said. "But also a blessing."

BOOK 3

Nightmare in Burgundy

A Winemaker Detective Mystery

Jean-Pierre Alaux
&
Noël Balen

Translated from French by Sally Pane

LE FRENCH BOOK

"O happy Burgundy, which merits being called the mother of men since she furnishes from her mammaries such a good milk."
—Erasmus

1

His head was spinning. For three hours now, he had been sitting at the table between the wife of the ambassador to the Netherlands and a film star whose name he dared not ask for fear of offending her. He vaguely remembered having seen her in a period piece where she played the harpsichord in a château full of mirrors and china. He had to lean in a bit to exchange a few words with the guests across from him. Bunches of red and yellow tulips cluttered the tables. People smiled at each other between the stems.

The dinner was sumptuous, as elegant as it was generous. You could read the satisfaction on the faces of the guests. As the feast continued, attitudes relaxed, looks of collusion replaced polite nods, and witty remarks cut the air with great panache. After savoring a duck pâté accompanied by a Bourgogne Aligoté des Hautes Côtes, perch supreme served with a chilled and fragrant Meursault, and crown loin of veal sprinkled with green peppercorns, along with a 1979 Côte de Beaune Villages, the guests thought the meal was finished. But this was underestimating the hospitality of the venerable knights of the Confrérie des Chevaliers du Tastevin. A cockerel and morel fricassee seasoned with Chambolle-Musigny added to the feast, and no one had trouble finishing it. Meanwhile, the Cadets of Bourgogne, decked out in black caps and wine-merchant aprons, had accompanied the arrival of each dish with a great many wine songs, comical tales, and jovial melodies. Beaming, with sparkling eyes and gleaming whiskers, they bellowed verse after verse at the top of their lungs.

Always drinkers, never drunk,
They go along their way
And thumb their nose at fools who grump.

Always drinkers, never drunk,
They happily proclaim
Their credo without shame.

Always drinkers, never drunk,
They go along their way!

The cheese course was announced. Platters arrived filled with creamy Epoisses washed in marc brandy and aged on rye straw, a soft farmhouse Soumaintrain cheese, mild Saint-Florentin that gave off the scent of raw milk, lightly salted and creamy Chaources, and supple La-Pierre-qui-Vire. Accompanying them were small rounds of goat's milk cheese, including an especially full-bodied tomme du Poiset. To top it off and honor this Chapter of the Tulips, the hosts had elegantly slipped in some soft Dutch cheese with amber and orange hues. Benjamin Cooker prepared a nice plate for himself, enhancing it with a 1972 Latricières-Chambertin that sensuously tickled his taste buds.

Here come the Cadets of Burgundy,
Sowers of life and of sun;
Lovers of water are mad.

Here come the Cadets of Burgundy,
A bottle in each hand!
Open the door to some fun
Here come the Cadets of Burgundy,
Sowers of life and of sun!

The chamberlain stepped to the podium. The association's slogan—Never whine! Always wine—was inscribed above it in gothic letters.

He tapped the microphone, waited for the brouhaha to subside, and greeted the assembly. He congratulated the chef for the excellent dinner and declared the meeting of the Chapter of Tulips open. Then, in a solemn voice, he briefly praised Benjamin Cooker, introducing him as the most recognized wine specialist in France and one of the most sought-after winemakers in the world. He spoke of the *Cooker Guide*, whose publication all vintners dreaded, and emphasized that the most recent edition had excellent evaluations of certain Vougeots. Finally, he invited the inductee to join him on the stage, next to the members of the association whose gold and red vestments shimmered in the spotlight.

There was a ripple of applause. Leaning on the edge of the table, Cooker rose slowly. He emptied his glass of water, discreetly loosened his bowtie, tugged down the jacket of his tuxedo, and made his way between the tables. He felt the weight of all the eyes turned toward him and slowed his pace a bit for fear of getting tangled in the train of an evening gown or tripping on a chair as he made his way to the dais. He was welcomed with a quotation recited with good-natured pomposity. The crudeness of its kitchen Latin made all the guests laugh.

Totus mundus trinquat cum illustro pinot
Imbecili soli drink only water!
So, Brother Cellarer, fill our cup
Because, as the saying goes: *in vino veritas*

Cooker was handed a chalice. He emptied it and proceeded to the dubbing, which fell somewhere between schoolboy farce and ritual solemnity. He swore fidelity to the wines of France and Burgundy and then bowed his head while the grand master of the order tapped his shoulder with a vine shoot.

By Noah, father of the vine
By Bacchus, god of wine
By Saint Vincent, patron of vintners
We dub you Knight of the Tastevin!

Cooker was then invited to take the microphone. He looked over the assembly, and a silence as thick as a wine coulis filled the room. One last clearing of the throat, and his voice resounded under the enormous girders of the wine warehouse.

"Grand Chamberlain of the Order of the Knights of Tastevin, Grand Constable and all of you, knights of the brotherhood, ladies and gentlemen, good evening!

"First, let me tell you right away how excited I am to be here among you tonight. Could I ever have imagined that I would be crowned with such laurels within the walls of this distinguished château that has so often inspired me? As a child romping in the vineyards of the Médoc and learning to swim in the water holes of the Hourtin pond, I could not see my-self playing or living in any place other than that corner of the world, where vineyards were loved with so much passion. For a long time I thought that good wines were made only there, because you know that the natives of Bordeaux are a bit chauvinist, and my grandfather never drank anything other than his own wine. I found out later that his wine was far from the best, but I must admit that for me, it still has a particular bouquet. It seems that we often pattern our lives after those first impressions of childhood.

"I like to recall that it was a child of your land, a son of Burgundy with visionary talent, who contributed to protect-ing the Port de la Lune from English invasions. The shores of Bordeaux owe so much to the three fortresses built by Sébastien le Prestre de Vauban. That was another time. The world may never be at peace, but wine abolished our borders long ago. I have traveled extensively in lands even farther from my culture than Burgundy, and I have learned that wine is a universal language. Each time a man raises his glass and empties it, I know what cloth he is cut from, what stuff he is made of. I can guess his disposition, sometimes his sense of humor, his reserve, his impatience or his sense of moderation, his wit or lack of tact. No need to talk further: the drinker reveals himself and sometimes shows what he would like to hide. The older I get, the more I believe that this is one of the greatest revelations of wine.

"To tell you that it is an honor to be named Chevalier du Tastevin in a setting as glorious as the Vougeot château would be a little banal and superficial. For me it's a sign of friendship more than an honorary distinction. I have too many good memories, between Côte de Nuits and Côte de Beaune, too many faithful readers and vigilant winemakers between Chalon and Mâcon, not to show my pleasure and my great joy in this moment. Finally, since I must conclude, and I promised not to talk too long, I will quote one of your own, Jean-François Bazin, who does honor to the Burgundian parlance and wrote this: 'The Confrérie des Chevaliers du Tastevin is like a ray of sunlight in the darkness of the cellars!' So this is what I say: I'm here in broad daylight, even if I incur the wrath of all my friends in Bordeaux."

The dining room of the Hôtel de Vougeot was still empty at this early-morning hour. With his mind still reeling from alcohol, excitement, songs, and laughter, Benjamin Cooker had slept little. A cool, almost cold shower had restored his calm, and he had stretched his legs walking among the rows of vines that bordered the establishment. In keeping with an old habit, the winemaker had taken a room in the hotel's annex behind the courtyard. He was pleased with room number nine, whose window with small panes of glass opened onto the vineyards of Vougeot.

"Did you sleep well, sir?" a waitress named Aurélie asked, dipping an Earl Grey teabag into a white porcelain teapot.

"Well, let's say I closed one eye from time to time, miss."

"Did you see what happened across the street? Some kids covered the whole café with graffiti."

Cooker went to the window, parted the lace curtains, and wiped the condensation from the glass. On the facade of the Rendez-vous des Touristes, black letters were clumsily scrawled in spray paint between a wall thermometer and some empty window boxes. He squinted.

Domine exaudi orationem meam
et clamor meus ad te veniat

Cooker read the phrase in a whisper. He had studied Latin in his youth.

"It's such a shame to dirty everything that way," Aurélie grumbled, heating up the teapot. "Especially to write such nonsense."

Cooker sat down before his plate and observed the hotel employee. He had known her as a girl and suddenly realized that she had become a woman in the two years since he had last seen her. Her ruddy cheeks had become more defined, and mascara accentuated her long black eyelashes. Her hair was pulled back and showed off her forehead. The somewhat awkward and pudgy apprentice who used to hide her eyes behind long bangs was now a lovely waitress whose precise gestures and alluringly delicate nose added to her charm.

"I know it's those boys from Dijon who did it," she went on as she placed the teapot on the table.

"Are you sure?"

"Who else could it be? The neighborhoods over there are full of graffiti like that. You wouldn't believe what it's like near the train station. And what really kills me is that it's not even French. I don't understand a word of it."

"It's Latin."

"Ah, I was sure it wasn't French."

Cooker breathed in the aroma of bergamot and took several swallows, burning his tongue. He put his cup down and slipped his coat on.

"Have a nice day, Aurélie. I'll hold onto my key, because I might be getting back late."

He crossed the road and stood in front of the defaced wall of the café. The paint was dry, and only a few letters had dribbled down the yellowish stucco. He took out his notebook and wrote down the Latin phrase, taking care to translate it accurately.

Lord, hear my prayer.
Let my cry for help to reach you.

As soon as he entered the café, all conversation stopped. Cooker sat down nonchalantly at the first table and ordered an espresso. The owner brought him a small cup of very bitter coffee, which Cooker tried to sweeten with three cubes of sugar. The café patrons started talking again, but quietly and warily. Three men who looked like retirees were filling out their trifecta sheets and muttering. At the end of the bar, two young sporty types with low foreheads and protruding lower lips sipped beer and whispered to each other. They were wearing similar royal-blue tracksuits. Next to Cooker, a homely couple sat across from each other in silence; the woman, whose triple chin spilled over the collar of a knitted vest, was shooting sidelong, slightly fearful glances across the room, while her husband was picking his nose with satisfactory results.

"May I borrow your newspaper?" Cooker asked.

"Go right ahead!"

He carefully pushed aside his cup and opened *Le Bien Public* on the table. The snowstorms in the Nuits-Saint-Georges were the lead story in the paper. Cooker perused an article on local sandblasters and the weather forecast for Easter week. On page three, he happened upon his picture, in black and white, which took up two columns. The slightly overexposed photo, taken during his speech, made him look like a jovial and cunning horse trader at a country fair. It did not at all resemble him and made him smile, as did the article's headline: "Winemaker Cooker gets toast, is spared roast at multicourse Vougeot fête."

The couple—farmers, Cooker presumed—watched him without uttering a word. The chatter at the bar grew livelier. "They're real bastards from the city pulling that shit." Gray coils of cigarette smoke floated upward in the harsh ceiling light.

"Worse than dogs lifting their legs!"

"What do you mean, René?"

From his vantage point, Cooker could see a fine foam moustache under the nose of one of the beer drinkers.

"They write their crap like they piss against a wall!"

"Ah, I get it now."

The café owner turned on the radio. It was a nostalgic channel that seemed to crackle from beyond the grave. A duo from the seventies chirped with optimism in the sputtering of the radio.

"It's taking the cops long enough to get here, as if they had anything else to do."

Then they took out a game of dice and a green felt cloth.

"All the same, if I catch those little shits—"

Everyone counted their tokens without paying attention to the refrain, in which "Venice" rhymed with "Paris." The barely snuffed-out cigarette butts continued to smolder in the ashtrays.

"The cops?"

"Hell no. The little shits who wrote all this trash—we're gonna smash their faces in, believe me!"

Cooker turned to the couple and said, "Excuse me for interrupting. Did that happen last night?"

"The scribblings?" grumbled the old woman. "We saw them this morning. Definitely weren't there yesterday, were they, Emile?"

"Can you tell me where Vougeot's priest lives?"

"There ain't no priest in Vougeot and no church, neither."

"As a matter of fact, now that you mention it, I can't remember seeing a bell tower," Cooker said, pursing his lips. "I hadn't even paid attention."

The woman rubbed her triple chin and looked at him intently. "In Vougeot, you don't get married, and you don't die."

"That seems rather reasonable to me," Cooker smiled as he stood up. He left two euros on the table, nodded politely, and took his leave.

He walked back up the main street toward the river. Slabs of frozen snow edged the road. On the parapet of the bridge that spanned the Vouge, the same black writing ran across the cement.

Non abscondas faciem tuam a me;
in quacunque die tribulor

Cooker took out his fountain pen and jotted down the phrase before translating it.

Do not turn your face from me
In my day of trouble.

He continued walking to the small locks that constricted the river, abruptly transforming it into a narrow channel. He stopped for a moment to look at the walls on the water's edge, which were covered with thick patches of moss. Then he turned around to go to the grocery store. He bought the paper, a box of cashews, and a postcard. It was only upon leaving the store that he noticed the graffiti running the length of a low wall near the ancient washhouse.

Inclina ad me aurem tuam:
in quacunque die invocavero te,
volciter exaudi me.

Again he reached for his notebook and transcribed the phrase diligently, despite the biting cold, which was numbing his fingers.

Incline your ear to listen
When I call,
be quick to answer

A gust of wind stung his face, and he pulled his collar up to his ears. In the distance, crows squawked in the vines. Their stricken cawing dissolved in a milky sky that was so low it merged with the snow-powdered earth.

Cooker shivered.

2

The tasting had already begun when he arrived, out of breath, in the large room of Vougeot's ancient wine and spirits storehouse. The experts were seated in groups of six and moving glasses around on the tablecloths in a slow and formal ballet that seemed almost contrived. Cooker greeted everyone, apologizing for his tardiness, and went to the seat reserved for him as the Tastevinage guest of honor. He went to work immediately.

Dozens of bottles were wrapped in orange silk paper and displayed on the table between stainless-steel spittoons and wicker baskets full of rolls. Each taster had a notebook for comments. There was barely any talking. Wet swishing, tongue-clicking, and elegant gurgling were the predominant sounds rising in the crisp air of the wine warehouse.

Cooker was tired from the night before but quickly managed to concentrate. He had no trouble getting into the spirit of the game. He had prepared long and hard for it back in Bordeaux by studying the Tastevin Burgundy wine reference book. Around him, nearly two hundred fifty tasters—all elite handpicked palates—were assuming the posture of expert connoisseurs, displaying the learned gestures of acknowledged specialists. He had spotted some old acquaintances, several renowned wine growers, important wine merchants, brokers, oenologists, some researchers from the university, heads of viticulture unions, popular restaurateurs, brilliant sommeliers, and a handful of knowledgeable amateurs. Among the witnesses were local officials and personalities, as well as a well-informed assembly of specialized journalists, including several leading Parisian experts whose vitriolic writing made Michelin-star chefs tremble.

The Tastevinage session had been wonderfully well orga-
nized, and the hosts from the brotherhood were seeing to its
successful unfolding without participating in the tasting. This
served to guarantee neutrality. The questions posed by the
jury were of devilishly simple precision: "Is this wine worthy
of the appellation and vintage that appear on the label? Is it
truly representative of them? Is this a wine that I would be
happy to own in my cellar and proud to offer to a friend?"
There were many fine points that were not to be influenced by
preconceptions, moods, natural inclinations, memory lapses,
or subjective reactions. Presented anonymously, each of the
fifteen bottles swaddled in opaque wrapping was slapped with
a concise label indicating only its appellation with no mention
of the winemaker or the merchant. Cooker was enjoying the
atmosphere of this ritual, which blended the sacred and the
profane. All these furrowed brows gave his fellow judges the
forbidding—some would say merciless—appearance of court-
room magistrates.

Cooker knew perfectly well that the stakes were high and
that winemakers and the rest of the profession awaited these
evaluations with a certain amount of anxiety. Initially, he
tasted the small bottles fairly quickly in order to feel them in
his mouth. His colleagues seemed surprised to see him proceed
this way: a quick movement of the glass to make the wine
speak, a swallow, and one or two swirls around the palate.
Then he would spit it out immediately. Some, convinced that
the famous Benjamin Cooker could do no wrong, revised
their strategy and imitated him. When he had finished this
preliminary trial, he took up each wine again. But this time
he lingered over the visual quality, tipping his glass to better
observe the transparency, the brilliance, the tint, and the intensity of the color. Then he would bring the wine to his nose
to capture the whole aromatic expression in a tight bundle of
details that he quickly jotted in his notebook.

After detecting the most harmonious bouquets, he swirled
each wine in his mouth with exaggerated slowness, breathing

in a little air to oxygenate the liquid. He closed his eyes and held himself straight in his chair while leaning his head slightly forward and putting his hands flat on the table. Then he would spit and start over without changing his posture. He analyzed the subtlest flavors, the astringencies, the delicacies of certain tannins, the powerful first impressions, the disappointing finishes, the acidity, and the roundness. From time to time, he would nibble a roll to cleanse his palate.

Fifteen swallows of red wine carefully swished and reswished were enough for him. The dice were cast. He put aside his notebook, cracked his knuckles, gave an enormous yawn, and stood to go stretch his legs in the welcome hall. On the way, Cooker shook some hands, patted the back of some old acquaintances, brushed past quite a few people without really excusing himself, and joked with one of the knights of the Order who was observing from the back of the room. After a few moments, he returned to his seat and quickly took a small swallow of each wine without spitting. He reread his notes, crossed out two or three words, and then rose again to join the session chairman.

Seeing him proceed this way, some people lost a bit of their assurance and kept their eyes on him. Cooker felt their cautious curiosity. A number of them seemed to be losing their bearings. They wore doubtful expressions and seemed absorbed in unspoken questions. So this was how the dreaded Benjamin Cooker operated? The man who was believed to be so serious, almost ascetic, was behaving like a dilettante with an approach that would have been considered casual if he had not proven his talent.

Ultimately, one-third of the wines tasted were worthy of the coveted stamp. The award winners would have the distinguished honor of putting the famous insignia created in 1935 by the French artist Hansi—Jean-Jacques Waltz—on their bottles. The insignia was a purple shield with a small barrel at the bottom, a knight's helmet in the middle, and, at the top, a white-bearded, red-faced member of the Order of the Knights holding a cup and a bottle. A rope of green vine leaves framed the picture. Cooker did not wait for the complete announcement of the results before taking his leave. He said good-bye to the organizers and explained that he had another business meeting. He promised to stop by and see them at the offices of the Confrérie in Nuits-Saint-Georges.

As he left the château, he checked his cell phone for messages. His assistant's hoarse voice suggested some possible bad news about an Entre-Deux-Mers estate, and he called him right back.

"Virgile, what's going on?"

"Hello, boss, you don't need to worry. I solved the problem."

"Meaning?"

"I went to Sadirac myself to do the decanting, and I brought the samples back to the lab. Alexandrine will analyze them this afternoon if she has time. Otherwise, tomorrow morning at the very latest."

"Don't take advantage of her conscientiousness. Miss La Palussière is overwhelmed these days."

"No worries, sir, I know how to handle it, and, well, she accepted a lunch date."

"Bravo, Virgile. I see you are not giving up. Aside from that, how's the weather in Bordeaux?"

"Nice, as usual. I hope we'll be able to eat outside."

"Enjoy it while you can! It's awfully cold here."

"So the life of a knight is not so easy?" Virgile could not resist joking.

"It's unbearable. I just tasted some little gems, including a Morey-Saint-Denis that was quite magnificent. I am going to have to spend some more time in this region."

As he spoke, Cooker was walking toward the village, his wool scarf wrapped around his chin. He picked up his pace to get warmer, gave a few final pieces of advice to his assistant, greeted the lab director, and promised to call back the afternoon of the following day.

As he approached the grocery store, he spotted a police van parked at the corner. Uniformed men were interrogating the shopkeeper, while some of their colleagues were taking pictures of the graffiti on the bridge.

"We can't let this drag on," one of them said. "The same thing is happening in Gilly."

Cooker kept on walking as if he had not heard anything and headed for his hotel. In the distance, the massive silhouette of the Vougeot château seemed to be dozing in the middle of a burial ground of vines whose bony limbs and gnarled stumps were packed all the way to the back of the vineyard. A thick sky was brushing against the points of the towers where the crows were performing sinister and mocking spirals.

The canvas top of Cooker's convertible was sagging slightly under the fine layer of crusty snow, and he had to scrape the windshield with the blade of a Laguiole knife that had been miraculously abandoned in the back of the trunk. It took three tries before the engine started. Cooker waited for the confident purring before getting on the road to Gilly-les-Cîteaux. Traversing the wintry Burgundy terrain in a vintage Mercedes 280SL that he had failed to have serviced only heightened Cooker's sense of adventure.

As he drove, the land became almost foreign. The highway seemed to serve as a paved border that marked the age-old conflict between the vineyards and the plowed fields, between the noble dryness of the highlands and the ordinary generosity of the lowlands. In less than ten minutes, he was in the deserted town of Gilly. He parked next to a war memorial and walked slowly around the square, where he saw scrawling on the pillar.

Quia cinerem tamquam panem manducabam
et potum meum cum fletu miscebam

He slid his hand into the inside pocket of his coat to grab his fountain pen and notebook.

Ashes are the bread I eat;
and to my drink I add my tears.

On the wall of the church, there was another message in writing that didn't seem as controlled.

A facie irae et increpationis tuae;
quia elevans allisisti me.

Cooker had more trouble translating this phrase, whose syntax seemed convoluted.

Before your anger and your fury;
since you raised me up and then cast me aside.

Finally, he approached an old house, tastefully renovated with a respect for the materials of the era. The two large panels of the entry door had been defaced with a heavily written message.

Dieis mei sicut umbra declinaverunt,
et ego sicut foenum arui.

Some of the letters were dripping between the granular veins of the oak.

My days are like the waning shadow,
and I am like withering grass.

The writing was identical to what he had seen on the wall in Vougeot. And once again, there were only two phrases, which, put together, seemed to form a coherent stanza. It wouldn't be long before the police arrived to collect evidence and take photographs. He had to clear out as soon as possible if he did not want to run into them.

Cooker put his notebook and his fountain pen deep in his Loden jacket and then rubbed his hands and blew on them. In this country of silence and mystery, he knew only one man capable of enlightening him.

3

The road stretched before him, gentle and monotonous. There was a soothing quality about the forest surrounding the Cîteaux Abbey, filled with hornbeams and oak and beech trees. Cooker put in an old Verdi cassette. The worn-out tape made the lamenting violins sound even more sorrowful. Listening to the voice undulating between smiles and tears, he imagined this *Traviata* in the faded silk of an over-the-hill courtesan, irrevocably plagued by rapid consumption. He turned down the volume as he approached the entrance to the monastery and parked under a row of poplars.

The abbey's porter, who had a room near the entrance and had greeted many visitors over the years, welcomed Cooker warmly. Eight years earlier, the winemaker had stayed in the abbey's guest room while he was writing the first edition of his guide. On the advice of a friend from Burgundy, a winemaker in Coulanges-la-Vineuse, he had written a letter to the father superior. He was hoping to get access to the Cistercian archives. The monks had consented to give this curious man from Bordeaux the privilege of nosing through the abbey's old papers. For more than a week, Cooker had bent willingly to the monastic discipline, attending all the prayer services, participating in the domestic chores, and spending his free time in the dark corners of the library. There, he had listened to Brother Clément, a small vivacious man of letters, whose humility was as impressive as his knowledge of the history of Burgundy. There was nothing he did not know about this complex and multilayered region marked by dynastic issues, feudal land divisions, the vagaries of commerce and wars, the parceling of vineyards, and the political strategies of the first wine traders. Without the support of Brother Clément, the manuscript would not have had such a wealth of anecdotes and details gleaned, for the most part, directly from Cîteaux's documents.

Cooker waited nearly a quarter of an hour in the entrance of the cloister. He paced, recalling how the silence and deliberate slowness he had expected were nothing like what he had found here. This meditative place had bustled with activity then, as it surely did now. Memories came flooding back to him—the echoes in the corridors, the blessings in the refectory, the bells, the thundering organ during Sunday Mass, the collective prayers, the rustling robes, the trundling tractor in the fields, and the clinking of dishes in the scullery. Although his business and family obligations absorbed him now, Cooker still thought about these Cîteaux monks. He was moved to find himself back within these thick walls, where minutes seemed to expand and make one forget that time was passing.

In the distant interplay of light and shadow, a small stooped man was approaching. He was taking baby steps, and his rail-thin body was swimming in the folds of a white robe that dragged along the flagstones. Cooker moved toward him.

"Brother Clément?"

"Have I really changed that much, Mr. Cooker?"

The winemaker immediately regretted having spoken so quickly and put out his hand in response.

"I don't blame you," the monk said and sighed, slipping his bony fingers into Benjamin's palm. "I can hardly recognize myself sometimes."

"You have grown very thin," Cooker said.

"My dear friend, one must depart light. Clean and light. The body empty and the heart clear. God is calling me, and I am ready. To tell the truth, I have never felt closer to Him."

"I envy your serenity, Brother Clément. If you weren't such a chatterbox, I'd mistake you for a holy man!"

"And you're just as sarcastic as ever," the monk said with a smile. He sat down with difficulty on the edge of a white stone bench. "Don't change a thing, and keep saying what you think. With your good manners, you can get away with it. I like that."

"I always wondered how you managed to take a vow of silence. To spend your whole life being quiet!"

"Who told you Cistercian monks took a vow a silence or, for that matter, that I spent my life being quiet?"

"That's what people imagine."

"People have strange ideas about monastic life. You know, there's no place noisier than a monastery. In fact, I remember you saying that when you were here the last time. At any rate, people imagine all sorts of things."

"True enough."

"You see, I think we live in a land of silence here at Citeaux, where a man keeps his word."

Cooker stood facing the monk. With the tip of his shoe, he played with a small pebble that had come loose from the flagstone.

"I believe some people think you are infallible," Brother Clément continued. "Everyone who reads your guide believes that it all comes very easily for you."

"As a matter of fact, no one suspects just how much work goes into the *Cooker Guide*. At any rate, it's never good to give the appearance that you've taxed yourself. You have to put on a smile, look inspired, and give the impression that it is all done with great ease and pleasure. Not many people are interested in knowing the truth."

"Funny calling that you've followed," the monk said and sighed. "I have often wondered how you manage not to get bored."

"You just need to have faith. But that's not something I'm going to be telling you about!"

Brother Clément chuckled and rubbed his hands together with a glimmer of mischief in his eyes. His gaunt cheeks looked like they had been carved out of marble by a divinely inspired sculptor. "In the seminary during my youth, I was very interested in the theater. My superiors did not look upon that kindly, but I would often sneak out to see a play. That's when I realized how much life is like a comedy. I still believe that, by the way. I read many articles by Tristan Bernard, who, as you surely know, was a big theater critic. One thing he wrote bothered me at the time and still bothers me today: 'If it's bad, it bores me, and if it's good, I'm a bore.' I always found that funny, and kind of pathetic."

"I think he also said, 'I never go to see plays that I have to talk about. It might influence me.'"

"At my age, I'm still not surrendering to boredom," Brother Clément said. "I'm open to a surprise or two. Why settle for the predictable?"

"I can't agree with that point of view," Cooker replied. "For me, what's predictable isn't necessarily boring. I test, and I have to come to an understanding by experiencing for myself, by seeing for myself, and even more so, by drinking for myself. I don't know why, but without that, it's not real for me."

"I've noticed! And what brings you here today, besides the pleasure of chatting with me, of course?"

"I've been meaning to pay you a visit, but I admit that I am here sooner than I expected. Some surprising things are happening in these parts."

"I know," the old man said as he rose painfully. "Burgundy will never cease to surprise us."

"You know about the inscriptions they found in Vougeot and Gilly?"

"What do you think? Just because we are enclosed in this abbey, that we are ignorant of the world around us? Be aware, my dear Benjamin, that nothing that touches the world is unknown to us."

"I've copied each of those phrases, and it all intrigues me," the winemaker said, handing his notebook to the monk. "I translated them as best I could."

Brother Clément went through the notes and took his time to weigh each word. He was wheezing, as if just breathing was a labor.

"You managed pretty well. It's actually quite good, aside from a few turns of phrase."

"I was surprised myself that I still remembered my Latin. I think I owe it more to my years as a child in the choir than to my high school teacher. At least it seems that way, because each time I see a Latin phrase, I can't help but smell the incense."

"In that case, I can refresh your memory." The monk smiled.

"Exactly. I was counting on you. I have the feeling that I know these passages, but their origin escapes me. And who do you think could have painted all of that on the walls?"

"That's another story! Follow me."

They walked through the rhythmic shadows of the cloister before slipping under an entryway and following a dark corridor where a few rays of vapid light were trying to pierce the frosty stained-glass windows. Then they stepped through a small secret door and crossed a nearly empty room furnished with only a writing desk. Another door led to an antechamber that was just as deserted, and they finally came to the abbey library. The entire time, they did not speak a word. Brother Clément was walking slowly, forcing himself to control the wheezing and coughing fits that assailed him.

"I am moved to find myself here again," Cooker said, raising his blue-gray eyes toward the high shelves. "I have nothing but fond memories of this place."

The monk did not respond but turned toward the shelves containing hundreds of works bound in cracked leather, bundles of tied-up documents, and volumes of canon law probably no longer consulted. A fine film of dust rose up as the two men passed. Cooker felt rooted in centuries of history and timeless knowledge. At one corner of the maze, Brother Clément pulled from the stack the *Breviarium Monasticum* published in 1892 under the guidance of Father Paul Delatte from the Abbey Saint-Pierre de Solesmes. He placed the massive volume on a stand, paged through it quickly, and stopped at page ninety-four. He ran his index finger slowly down the page.

"Psalm 101 from the Book of David. This text is often called 'Prayer in times of misfortune.' It's in fact the prayer of an afflicted person who has grown weak and is pouring out a lament before the Lord. The psalm is very well known and is often quoted, too. I am surprised that you didn't remember it."

"I have lapses, Brother Clément. I don't mind admitting it. And it's been quite a while since I have immersed myself in the Bible."

"Sometimes the psalm is referred to as Psalm 102, especially in the Hebrew Bible, which predates the Greek Bible and the Vulgate by centuries. Let's look at the *New Jerusalem Bible*, which most Catholics use today, where it's Psalm 102."

Cooker leaned over the narrow table to get a better look at the opened volumes. He put on his reading glasses and knit his brows.

"Indeed, my translation is not so bad," he said without hiding a certain satisfaction.

"It's well done. You did not suffer in vain on the school benches. The phrases you copied down in Vougeot correspond to the first verse of the psalm, and the ones from Gilly correspond to the fourth."

"That could mean that two are missing. They might be scribbled on some other walls. Who knows? Maybe in another village."

"Not necessarily. Maybe they were deliberately omitted."

For my days are vanishing like smoke,
my bones burning like an oven;
like grass struck by blight, my heart is withering,
I forget to eat my meals.
From the effort of voicing my groans
my bones stick out through my skin.

Brother Clement whistled with excitement. "Read the next part. Very interesting."

I am like a desert-owl in the wastes,
a screech-owl among ruins,
I keep vigil and moan
like a lone bird on a roof.
All day long my enemies taunt me,
those who once praised me now use me as a curse.

Leaning over the monk's shoulder, Cooker read the words in a low voice. His lips were hardly moving, as if he were praying and absorbed in the soothing rhythm of the chant.

"There you go. This is the passage that intrigues me the most," the monk said, straightening up with difficulty.

"This one?" Cooker asked. "Why a desert owl?"

"I suppose you wouldn't have those in your native England," the monk responded with amusement.

"I would have just translated that as a pelican." The wine-maker shrugged.

"That would not necessarily have been wrong. In medieval Europe, the pelican was thought to be particularly attentive to her young, to the point of providing her own blood by opening up her breast when no other food was available. Pelican or owl, that doesn't change the problem."

"I don't know what to make of all this," Cooker confessed in a vexed tone. "Why would someone be covering walls with verses from a psalm?"

"Maybe it should be seen as a plea, a way of addressing God or man. I don't know. This is about someone who surely has serious reasons to complain."

"Still, there are other ways to express your feelings."

"It seems all our big cities are covered with graffiti," the monk said between coughs. "Some people see it as a youthful protest, a cry for help, or even a cry of desperation. Some of it is even considered art. These days, people can find very absurd ways to express their discontent."

"It's true that the method, writing with spray paint, makes it seem similar to other vandalism, except the author knows Latin and refers to the Old Testament. You must agree, it is somewhat unusual."

"I don't know what to say, Benjamin. You'd have to study the text in order to decipher the code and uncover the hidden meaning. There must be one. At least I hope there is. In the body of the Psalter you find everything and its opposite: threats, confessions of sin, petitions, vows of chastity, grievances, gratitude—everything."

"You're right. You'd need to deconstruct this psalm in order to—"

"Take this. It's a gift," the monk interrupted, handing him a hardback fabric-covered *New Jerusalem Bible*. "I suppose you don't have one with you, since you're traveling."

"No, I don't, I confess."

"In that case, your penance will be to reread certain passages, even if it means you fall asleep doing so!"

The two men promised to see each other before the winemaker left town. Brother Clément stayed in the library, citing overdue research as an excuse, and did not offer to walk his visitor to the door. But he did point Cooker to a secret passage to use as a shortcut.

As soon as Cooker was outside the abbey, he took a deep breath and strolled among the poplars. Then he slid behind the wheel of his convertible and sat quietly, as though protected by the fog of condensation on the car windows. With his hands on the steering wheel, his eyes half-closed, and his lips moving over the verses of the psalm, he dwelled on the powerless lamentations. At last he took out his cell phone and pressed the contact button, where his assistant's number was on his list of favorites.

"Hello, Virgile?"

"Yes, boss. Is something wrong?"

"Why do you ask?"

"You told me you would call tomorrow afternoon. I am surprised to hear from you so soon."

"Do you know Burgundy, Virgile?"

"Not really, boss. Not at all, in fact. Just what I've read in books."

"Okay, then come and get a taste of it," Cooker said. "I'll expect you tomorrow."

"How do I get there?"

"Figure it out. Ask my secretary to get you a ticket."

"By train? I'll have to route through Paris. That's a long way, boss!"

"And stop calling me 'boss.' You know how much that irritates me."

"Yes, bo... uh, sir!"

4

He was dressed in a fine linen tunic and had Roman sandals on his feet as he climbed Mount Sinai on the back of a mule. Two shots rang out. In the distance, the half-nude Jesus, a chastely veiled Mary Magdalene, the faithful Emmaus, and half a dozen apostles were assembled in the shelter of an olive tree. The violent echo of the explosions faded into the night.

Cooker sat up suddenly in his bed, felt around for the light switch, and knocked the Bible off the night table. Outside, he could hear shutters banging open and several piercing screams.

Wearing a bathrobe made of wool from the Pyrenees and a pair of kidskin slippers, he walked down the steps of the annex, crossed the courtyard, and found himself on the main road of Vougeot. A group of villagers were gathered a few feet from the post office. An elderly man with a moustache was yelling from a window and brandishing a hunting rifle.

"Don't mess with the Mancenot brothers! Don't mess with us!"

Cooker cautiously approached the circle of people gathered on the sidewalk. He recognized the woman with the triple chin and her husband, as well as the owner of the Rendez-vous des Touristes, who was kneeling by a body. A rather lost-looking woman stood apart from another group of people he didn't know, all motionless in the freezing wind.

"Go get a blanket!" a small bald man shouted to a young girl with a frightened expression. "The checkered one at the back of the linen closet! Hurry!"

Cooker drew closer. A boy was lying on the asphalt, his body curled on its right side, his eyes rolled upward, legs twitching and trembling. Blood from his abdomen was streaming slowly through his jacket. The steady flow was beginning to form a thick shiny puddle on the pavement.

"He's done for, the little bastard!" the man with the moustache continued to yell, shaking his rifle.

"Have you called an ambulance?" Cooker asked as he leaned over the injured boy.

"Yes! They are coming from Nuits-Saint-George!" someone answered.

"It's better not to move him," one of the women said as she averted her eyes.

"Goddammit, is that blanket coming or not?"

"What happened?" Cooker asked, pulling his bathrobe tighter.

"One of the Mancenot brothers fired," replied the café owner. "It's that moron, Ernest!"

The man with the gun was still standing in the frame of the window, his weapon at arm's length. He had the crimson face and bewildered look of lonely old men who drown their celibacy in cheap liquor and hatred of the world. Behind him, a furtive silhouette was pacing under the halo of a bare lightbulb.

"And Honoré does not dare show his face. Look at that!" shouted the fat woman's husband.

"That's the end of them pissing us off, those assholes!" the shooter yelled, sticking out his chest. "Two buckshots full blast. I didn't miss!"

"Shut your mouth, Ernest!" the café owner yelled, his jaw tense.

Then Cooker saw another body lying a few yards away from the group. He approached the second victim, whose left cheek had been blown away by the volley of lead. The other side of his face was intact, his open eye looking dazed. The kid could hardly have been eighteen. His long hair was soaking in a bloody pile of flesh and bone shards. No one else dared to look at him. He was lying there, his head mangled, abandoned to the cold and wind. Cooker suppressed a gasp of disgust.

The girl arrived with the checkered blanket. Someone grabbed it to cover the boy whose blood continued to pool on the pavement. His legs were shaking faster and faster; a red dribble was beginning to flow from his nose.

Cooker heard the wail of sirens. An ambulance with a flashing blue light turned from the highway to cross the bridge and was speeding toward them. It was closely followed by a police car. Everyone moved aside when the paramedics and police officers leaped from their vehicles. Ernest Mancenot had disappeared from the window. The police officers walked around the victims without hiding their revulsion. The paramedics quickly decided to transport the wounded boy to the hospital in Dijon and to call for a second ambulance to take the dead boy to the medical examiner's office. They carefully slipped the curled-up boy, his legs still shaking, onto a stretcher. As the speeding ambulance disappeared, the police officers started questioning members of the crowd.

The café owner spoke up and explained briefly that the two boys had been shot down by one of the Mancenot brothers while they were getting ready to spray paint the wall of the post office. Cooker turned and then saw the black inscription on the facade, near the mailbox: "In V. . ." in round, thick letters. The victims had not had the time to write any more than that. Old Ernest had shot them down in the middle of the act. The can of spray paint had rolled into the gutter. An officer recovered it and wrapped it in a plastic bag.

"Do you know the victims?" the captain inquired.

"Cedric and David Bravart, two cousins," replied the woman with the triple chin. "One of them is from Vougeot, and the other is from Gilly. That one there is David."

The policeman glanced at the body, frowned, and raised his head in the direction of the window, where Ernest was now standing again.

"Mr. Mancenot! Put down your gun, and get out here!"

"I did my job!" the old man barked.

"I am waiting for you, sir! Do not make us come and get you!"

All eyes were focused on the Mancenot brothers' house, an austere and charmless building weighed down by its granular and graying stucco. Minutes ticked by. The police officers were waiting near the entrance. Cooker sneezed and crossed his arms to warm himself. His feet were freezing. He was thinking about going back to the hotel and putting on something warmer when the Mancenot brothers stuck their drunken faces through the half-open door. Ernest spat on the ground and looked around defiantly.

"Two cartridges, two targets! Gotta have balls, that's all!"

He was summarily handcuffed and pushed into the police cruiser, while Honoré, looking even more stunned than his brother, began to whimper. "Don't worry, Ernest. I'll take care of everything."

While a police officer went upstairs to recover the gun and the cartridge cases, the second ambulance arrived, just ahead of a rattling Citroen 2CV. Out of this climbed a man in his fifties with salt-and-pepper hair in a ponytail. He was wearing a mauve scarf and had a camera around his neck. A reporter from *Le Bien Public*. He snapped a few photos of the stretcher as it was sliding into the van, the Mancenot's still-open window, and the graffiti just barely begun. Then he questioned several of the bystanders he seemed to know well. Each one gave him more or less the same version of the story, some of them reveling in describing the state of the bodies in minute detail and reporting the old man's deranged behavior.

Cooker was about to return to his room when he heard a man call out, "Mr. Cooker?"

The winemaker jumped and turned to see who was talking to him. "To whom do I owe the pleasure? Do we know each other?"

"Well, I know you," the man responded. "My name is Bressel. I wrote the article on your induction into the brotherhood of the Chevaliers du Tastevin."

"Ah, so you're the one."

If the moment had not been so tragic, Cooker would have smiled and commented on the ridiculous headline and unflattering photo.

"Yes, I'm the one who covered the Chapter of the Tulips," Robert Bressel confirmed. "Do you intend to stay in the region for long?"

"I don't know. Why?"

"I'd love to do an interview."

"I'm supposed to leave in four or five days."

"It would be great to have the opinion of an expert like yourself on the latest Tastevinage."

Shivering, Cooker suddenly realized the incongruity of the situation. Here he was, standing in the middle of the street at five in the morning, in pajamas, bathrobe, and slippers.

"Maybe this is not the best time to discuss this," he said, holding back a sneeze. "I need to get some more sleep."

"I live in Saint-Bernard," Bressel insisted. "Last house on the way out of town. You can't miss it. If you feel like it and have the time, stop by and see me."

"I'll think about it, sir."

Cooker nodded a good-bye and walked quickly toward the hotel annex. Once in his room, he ran a scalding hot bath and soaked in it for more than an hour while reading the first thirty Psalms of David.

A waft of patchouli incense assailed his nostrils even before he had crossed the threshold. Cooker wiped the soles of his Lobbs on the horsehair doormat, took in one last lungful of fresh air, and dove into the vestibule. Dozens of little candles twinkled on a shelf that ran all along the wall and seemed to come alive under the haunting undulations of an Indian sitar.

Robert Bressel offered him a cup of green tea and invited him to sit in a heap of cushions with batik covers that looked particularly uncomfortable. The winemaker preferred a carved African stool. Several naively sculpted snakes were crawling along its base. The living room was rather large, but the motley decor devoured the space. Cooker's eyes widened at the dozens of bouquets of dried flowers, numerous oriental knickknacks, terra-cotta reproductions of Aztec gods, ivy dripping from macramé suspensions, an enormous plastic elephant painted gold, tourist posters of Sumatra tacked on the walls among yellowed posters of Che Guevara, Jimi Hendrix, and Romy Schneider, a Balinese armoire, a yellow-straw Mexican hat, a Napoleon III–era china cabinet, precariously stacked books, CDs strewn everywhere, a copper bowl full of moldy cereal, and a laptop on the floor, which was covered with oriental rugs and hemp mats. The sinuous sitar music irritated Cooker's auditory passages.

The journalist poured the tea in Chinese cups while imitating the sweeping ethereal gestures of North African Tuaregs. The mauve scarf knotted around his blond hair was hanging over a mohair sweater that bore a geometric pattern of lamas. He sniffed his cup and raised his eyes toward the ceiling.

"It's a gyokuro from Japan. The best!"

"Thank you very much," Cooker said politely from his Congolese stool.

"I prefer it to the bancha from China, which is too fibrous, and the oolong from Taiwan, which is too pale."

"I tend to stick with Grand Yunnan, like my father. Or else I make do with any Earl Grey or Darjeeling."

"It's true that it's the national drink in England," Bressel said. Cooker noted that Bressel looked a bit disappointed by his placid ignorance of fine teas.

"Yes, I drink almost as much tea as wine. That tells you how hopelessly Franco-British I am!"

"Speaking of which, I need some biographical information for a note at the beginning of the interview."

"My secretary will send you a whole press kit," Cooker said, cutting him short. He didn't care to expand any more on his personal history.

They spoke quietly, mostly about wine production. Slumped in his pile of cushions, Robert Bressel did not have a tape recorder for the interview, but instead used a big spiral notebook. Cooker gave his cautious opinion on the samples he had had the honor to taste at the Château du Clos de Vougeot. Of the eight hundred and nineteen wines from the 2000, 2001, and 2002 vintages, he admitted that he had tasted only a dozen. But the experience of the Tastevinage had convinced him that he needed to spend part of his visit in the Morey-Saint-Denis area, which he regarded as one of the finest terroirs of the world.

"No kidding?" the reporter marveled.

"I rarely joke when I'm talking about wine, unless I've drunk too much of it, which, of course, is a hazard of the trade."

The interview continued in a more or less relaxed, almost friendly tone. The sitar had ceased its soporific whirling, and Cooker poured himself a second cup of green tea. He expounded on the state of the wine business, the problems of exportation, the specificity of pinot noir—the flagship of the Burgundy grape varietals—the need to age the best wines and the care exercised in decanting, the unfairly underrated communal appellations, the heterogeneous nature of the wine-growing region of the hautes-côtes, climatic variations, the parceling of terrain, the rising values of the Mâconnais, and the new decrees of the agricultural regulatory agency INAO. After all that, Cooker could not resist the urge to ask a few questions of his own. He had talked enough about wines and the wine business. Before the interview ended, he intended to steer the discussion toward other things that were on his mind.

"And I must also say that there is no lack of excitement in the area," he ventured.

"Do you mean what happened last night?"

"Since my arrival, some very disturbing things have occurred. This graffiti on the walls, the two kids who were shot. Usually this region is rather peaceful and—"

"Pardon me for contradicting you, but Burgundy has never been a peaceful place. Admittedly, it's a good life, and I agree that people envy the apparent tranquility, but that's not the whole picture."

"Oh, really? What are you trying to say?" Cooker asked as he poured himself a third cup of tea.

"I wasn't really surprised to see that graffiti yesterday morning."

"Were you expecting it?"

"Not at all. I just think it is one more mystery among so many others here," Bressel said.

"A rather quickly solved mystery at that, mind you."

"Frankly, I find it hard to believe that the two kids could have scrawled those inscriptions, especially in Latin!"

"And yet they were interrupted while spray painting the walls."

"So? What does that prove?"

"Not much, really," Cooker said. "Have you heard anything about the injured kid?"

"He died around eight o'clock at the hospital in Dijon. I found out just as you were arriving."

"That's awful," Cooker sighed.

"Absolutely horrible. Ernest Mancenot is in custody now, but he may very well be released on his own recognizance. He had a .10 blood-alcohol level."

"That didn't keep him from shooting straight," the winemaker said without a hint of sarcasm.

"They're a family of hunters. The two brothers are old hardened boys who have nothing else to do but hunt down game, go mushroom picking, and spend their pensions on booze."

"What kind of work did they do, exactly?"

"They drove trucks for a construction company."

"And the two kids?"

"The Bravart cousins? I think they were still in high school or maybe apprentices. To tell you the truth, I don't know much about them. I should find out. But in my opinion, they were not scholars. I know the parents a little. I wouldn't think that the Bravart household read much of the Psalms of David. People would know."

"Psalms of David, you say?" Benjamin was good at feigning surprise.

"Yes, Mister Cooker, it's about two verses from Psalm 101 or 102, depending on which Bible you consult. I learned this from my nephew, Pierre-Jean, who's a librarian in Dijon."

"You don't think the Bravart boys would have been familiar with it?"

"As I said, I wouldn't think so. But who knows? And if they were familiar with that particular psalm, you would have to wonder what their motivation was, and what the texts actually mean."

"That's my opinion, too," the winemaker said, "But now that they are dead, we'll never know what they wanted to tell us."

Robert Bressel slid over his raft of multicolored cushions and made his way slowly to the stereo. The sitar resumed its moaning. Benjamin Cooker decided it was time to leave.

5

The clock struck noon. The station was almost empty when the train from Paris came to a stop on track two. Virgile jumped down from the car with his bag over his shoulder, his sunglasses pushed up on his head, and his jacket open over a fine linen shirt. He had a radiant and always-a-bit arrogant look that young men from the southwest of France have when they cross north of the boundary line drawn by the Loire River.

"You look good," Cooker said, shaking his hand.

"I am in great shape, sir. I slept the whole trip."

"So much the better. I intend to take you on a tour of the grand dukes."

"The Dukes of Burgundy?"

"You hit the nail on the head, my boy."

As they left Dijon, the winemaker decided on going the back way and took Highway 122. He followed the signs for the Route des Grands Crus and drove slowly, enjoying the purring of the six cylinders. As they passed through the winemaking villages, Cooker cheerfully narrated without ever adopting the pedantic tone that sometimes annoyed his young assistant. They went through Chenôve, Marsannay-la-Côte, Couchey, Fixin, Brochon, Gevrey-Chambertin, Morey-Saint-Denis, Chambolle-Musigny, and finally Vougeot, which they reached an hour later, even though the most direct roads would have taken them there in no more than twenty minutes.

"It is really so different from the Bordeaux region," Virgile declared as he got out of the convertible. "Little convoluted parcels of land, no chocolate-box châteaux every hundred yards, good solid farmhouses. It smells of the earth here!"

"It is very different," Cooker said. "I thought it would be good for you to experience this terroir for yourself. Traveling can be an excellent education for young people. Besides, my grandmother always used to say: 'A change of pastures fattens the calf!'"

"Thank you for taking the trouble," the assistant said as he buttoned up his jacket and rubbed his hands together to warm them. "And to think that yesterday I was eating outside. Honestly, it's beautiful here, but you freeze your butt off."

"That's also part of the charm." Cooker smiled. "I don't think those sunglasses are going to be very useful."

They dropped Virgile's bag off in the room reserved for him in the annex, which was across from Cooker's.

"You're spoiling me, sir, with this view of the vineyards and the Clos de Vougeot château!"

They both stood at the window, arms crossed, gazing over the ocean of grapevines where the silvery sparkling of the trellises met with the milky luminescence of the sky. The field hands, in groups of three and four, were bending over the rows, straightening the wooden stakes, and stretching wires to attach the branches. Others were burning armfuls of vine shoots pruned over the winter. The plumes of white smoke skimmed the earth, refusing to rise. Pointing toward the horizon, Cooker launched into a long history of the Clos de Vougeot that Virgile found fascinating.

The centuries filed by with a richness of detail and anecdotes reminiscent of alter candles and ancient parchment. Cooker enjoyed telling Virgile about the monks from Molesmes who founded the Cîteaux Abbey on the marshy grounds where nothing grew but thin reeds known as *cîteaux*. Then he described the rock quarries not far from the hamlet of Vooget, where the first acres of vines were planted at the very beginning of the twelfth century. He recounted the rivalry with the monks of Saint-Germain, who settled in Gilly, the successive land acquisitions, the donations from the lords, and the protection by those in power. He spent time explaining the construction of the Clos de Vougeot château in 1551 by the abbot of Cîteaux, Dom Loisier, who had to stand up to his Cistercian brothers because they criticized him for squandering God Almighty's funds.

"I won't go into the seizure of the château during the revolutionary period and all of the buybacks and shady financial negotiations, and how it was made into a hospital at the beginning of the Second World War, and the terrible explosion under the German occupation, which damaged the roof. Not to mention the fact that the four magnificent wine presses almost ended up as firewood. The Americans also requisitioned it to house prisoners after the Liberation, before the Confrérie des Chevaliers du Tastevin became the proprietors and undertook the restoration of the buildings. You see, Virgile, what fascinates me the most in all this history is the permanence of the traditions and the winemakers' attachment to this unique piece of land, their fierce protection of the appellation, and the level of quality, along with superior wine-making standards and the manual harvesting. And then there's the unalterable boundary of the terroir."

"It hasn't changed since the twelfth century?" Virgile interrupted.

"It's difficult to push back stone outer walls. The vineyard covers exactly fifty hectares, ninety-five ares, and seventy-six centiares, which makes upward of one hundred and twenty-seven point two acres."

"I admire your precision, sir," Virgile said with a touch of impertinence.

"Make fun if you like, my boy. I am always careful to leave nothing to chance, as Francois Mauriac wrote."

"And how many people own the Clos de Vougeot?"

"About eighty sharing a hundred parcels with sixty different vinifications."

"When you say about eighty, would that be more or a bit less?"

"Well done, Virgile. You've caught me. I don't have the exact number in my head anymore. It changes, depending on sales and divisions that take place when parcels are inherited. On the other hand, I can tell you that the vineyard produces about two hundred tons of grapes, and from that, depending on the year, two hundred and fifty thousand to three hundred thousand bottles."

"And is their quality equal?"

"Not really. The nature of the terrain obviously has a determining influence, as you would suspect. The vineyard has a gradient of just three to four percent, but that is enough to create important differences. In the upper section that you see back there, the ground is stony, mainly limestone. Toward the middle, the loose layer of earth becomes somewhat thick and dense. At the bottom, the pluvial erosion has accumulated sediments, and because the constant moisture results in a thick silt, they have to drain it sometimes."

"It's true. It's fairly flat toward the lower part, and I bet that the contour of the highway, which is a bit elevated, didn't help things."

"Bravo, Virgile. Very good deduction. The water table is not far from the surface in this spot, and it tends to hold more water. Then the construction of the highway exacerbated the problem by interfering with natural drainage. If only the civil engineers had your down-to-earth common sense!"

"If I understand everything you've told me, it is rare in these parts to have this type of château in the middle of a vineyard."

"Yes, it's kind of like something you might see in Bordeaux, but the Burgundians don't do that sort of thing. They don't ruin estates. They disturb the least area possible. The vineyard is king here, and you do not dominate it with ostentatious structures."

Cooker turned away from the window and went to his own room to get a woolen scarf he had forgotten to take with him in the morning.

"Okay, let's not dawdle, Virgile. I have other things to show you."

They climbed into the convertible and got back on the highway toward Nuits-Saint-Georges. Cooker apologized for not having offered his assistant something to eat.

"Don't worry, I had a sandwich on the train that made the trip worthwhile: tasteless ham on crumbly white bread, barely fresh butter, and a jungle-rot pickle! The worst of it is that, well, I'm a bit ashamed to admit it, but I was so hungry, I thought it was delicious!"

"Those are the guilty pleasures you should not deny yourself, my dear Virgile," Cooker replied, holding back a laugh. "You know as I do that there are wines you talk about and wines you drink. They are not always one and the same."

They quickly passed through the center of Nuits-Saint-Georges and continued on toward Beaune. They decided that Virgile would visit the Hospices de Beaune, a former hospital for the poor and needy that was now a museum, while his boss would spend that time digging up research at the Athenaeum Bookstore across the way on the Rue de l'Hôtel-Dieu. They looked at their watches and agreed to give each other an hour before meeting in front of the bookstore.

Cooker rummaged with pleasure through the shelves devoted to wine. They were arranged on a platform, as if a certain homage needed to be paid to the subject. He felt at home in this bookstore that honored his profession and where one could unearth everything published on the topic. He consulted a good number of oenology treatises, monographs on cooperage, technical publications in English, historical essays, several photo albums on Burgundy, and some guidebooks written by competitors with whom he often disagreed but whose expertise and convictions he respected. He foraged for nearly an hour and decided to buy the latest issue of the magazine *Burgundy Today*, whose main article was devoted to the rankings of the premiers crus, as well as half a dozen works by Pierre Poupon, including *A Taster's New Thoughts*, *The Fruits of Autumn*, *The Wine of Memories*, *Pleasures of Tasting*, *My Literary Tastings*, *The End of a Vintage*, and *The Vintner's Gospel*. Flipping through the pages, Cooker was struck by the poetry, irony, and erudition—there was, in these little well-crafted books, a spiritual vision of the vine and wine that he could not resist. A winemaker capable of expressing himself with such style was certainly an authentic writer. This Burgundian had as much talent as, or perhaps even more than, certain stunted writers of the Académie Française. One passage made him chuckle: "Smell, sniff, inhale—nothing that is fragrant or that stinks should leave you indifferent. Let odors lead you by the nose." Cooker would gladly use it in the introduction to the next edition of his guide.

He looked forward to delving into these simple yet lyrical pages that very night. He had noticed a particularly intriguing paragraph: "Thus, 'good news' was gradually revealed to me. A gospel intended for the winemaker is written in my heart. This Bible is open to all. Everyone can enter it, not just to gather the grapes left over after the harvest, but to harvest according to his thirst."

"Magnificent, sir! It's really worth a look! I hope I wasn't too long?" Virgile had never learned to hide his enthusiasm, and that was one of his greatest qualities. He was clearly affected by his visit to the former hospital, where the sisters of the Hospices de Beaune had once cared for the destitute in a magnificent facility that featured a religious polyptych painted by Flemish artist Roger Van de Weyden. Virgile had come away talkative and excited.

"You know that I don't believe all that Holy Cross, Virgin Mary, relics, and Bible-thumping crap. But frankly, things done in the name of God are really impressive, especially when it comes to helping the poor and caring for the sick.

It's great, I admit. And the roofing with the colored tiles is unbelievable. The altarpiece, too, is really superb."

"I'm happy that you liked it," Cooker said, amused by his assistant's contagious good mood.

"It's even very moving to see all those little beds lined up. I felt like I was crossing into another world. It wasn't difficult to imagine the sick coughing, crying, and being afraid to die or the nuns who served the meals, applied the bandages, and came by with spittoons. It must have been a hell of a place."

"Not necessarily. Maybe it was a place where people could be at peace and die in the loving embrace of the Lord, or at least under His watchful gaze."

"To listen to you, you'd think that God was present in all things here on earth."

"Precisely. By the way, I have some interesting things to tell you."

On the way back, the winemaker related the events of the two previous days. He summed up the matter of the psalms and told Virgile about his reunion with Brother Clément, his interview with Robert Bressel, and the slaying of the two cousins by old Mr. Mancenot. He omitted the gory details.

"That's pretty wild," Virgile said and sighed, a bit alarmed. "It doesn't surprise me that you found yourself in the middle of such a story. I would even say—no offense—that it's just like you."

"You're right in a way." Cooker smiled. "I won't deny that I sometimes have the feeling that this mystery was written for me."

Near Nuits-Saint-Geoges, Cooker turned right and headed toward Argencourt. They left Highway 74 behind them. Fine layers of sand spread over the icy frost were slowly turning the road into long tracks of mud.

After a few miles in the gloomy plains, the massive silhouette of the Cîteaux Abbey appeared in the distance.

"Does the history lesson continue?" Virgile asked in a slightly mocking tone.

"In a certain way."

The abbey porter had them wait in a parlor with bare walls, a bench, and three chairs. A crucifix watched over them. When Brother Clément came into the room, Cooker tried his best to hide his concern and sorrow. The monk was deteriorating by the hour, and he was walking even more slowly than he had the night before. There were shadows in his gaunt cheeks, and the curve of his back was more visible than ever. When he greeted them, the sound of his voice still had all of its clarity, but the resonance was frail.

"I've been thinking over this business of the psalms quite a lot, Mr. Cooker."

Virgile was silent. He looked impressed by the austere setting and this small exhausted man whose piercing gaze transfixed him.

"Well, I've reread the text many times and haven't deduced much," Cooker admitted with a sigh.

"And yet there must be some important hidden elements. The psalm is both obvious and enigmatic. Anyone can find what he wants in it and understand what suits him. But it's impossible to discern how this psalm relates to the two poor boys who were killed last night."

"You've already heard?"

"One would have to be deaf not to hear what is said in these parts."

"I have trouble believing that two kids barely eighteen years old would be amusing themselves by scrawling Latin sentences all over the walls of their towns!"

"Who knows? You must never jump to conclusions," Brother Clément suggested wisely. "But using the Old Testament to tell everyone that you are suffering is something that comes from another era!"

"They might have been taking advantage of the situation to add fuel to the fire, if only to frighten or irritate the townspeople. Perhaps they wanted to liven things up a bit."

"A type of game? It's possible. There's not much going on around here in the winter. The young people get bored."

Virgile was quiet and stood off to the side. He wasn't missing a word, but he seemed not to dare face the sharp gaze of the monk, who looked at him from time to time.

"They had started to paint some letters," Cooker continued. "But we can't know for sure what they planned to—"

"They managed to write 'In V.' Is that correct?"

"Yes, just three letters."

"We don't need to look too far: it must be the beginning of the saying '*In vino veritas.*'"

"What an idiot I am. I should have thought of that!" Cooker said, hitting his forehead with the palm of his hand.

"Provided, of course, that they knew some snippets of Latin," Brother Clément pointed out. "But the saying is pretty well known, after all."

"That's a theory that could hold water," the winemaker said. "You wouldn't have to be a Latin scholar. The Bravart cousins must have gone to Sunday school and were probably in the children's choir."

"What intrigues me even more is the time frame. The first writings were found on Wednesday, April sixth, and here we are in the middle of Holy Week, between Palm Sunday and Easter. Next Wednesday is the feast of Saint George, who is a very special martyr in Côtes-de-Nuits."

"I know, but what is the connection?"

"None, for sure. I'm asking questions. That's all. Etymologically, *George* means laborer. But the derivation isn't Latin. It's Greek. The word is composed of *gé*, the earth, and *ergon*, worker. So he is considered the patron saint of those who live by working the earth. But I digress, certainly."

Brother Clément was having increasingly more trouble enunciating. His voice was growing weaker, and his body was curling up, as if shriveling in pain. Cooker apologized for having come at such a late hour and suggested returning the following day.

"Don't worry. We've already sung vespers, and it's not yet time for evening prayer. I have all of eternity before me to rest."

"I wouldn't want to overstay my visit," Cooker said, throwing his coat over his shoulder to show they were going to leave. "Promise me that you will take it easy, Brother Clément, and don't concern yourself about this story."

"As you wish, my friend. But think about rereading a very interesting passage from the Book of Isaiah. It's in chapter five. I know you will appreciate it."

They took their leave as night was beginning to fall, plunging the parlor into twilight. The monk said good night with a slight nod of the head. He asked the abbey porter to give him a few minutes before accompanying him to his room. The conversation had visibly exhausted him.

Cooker and Virgile got back on the road to Vougeot without feeling the need to discuss their visit. *La Traviata* accompanied them softly in an *addio del passato* that the heartbreaking voice of Maria Callas rendered even more sorrowful each time Cooker played it. The 1953 version on a cassette in pitiful condition was so moving, it drew tears of compassion for the glory and misery of courtesans.

"Don't you have anything more cheerful?" asked Virgile.

"You're right. Maybe it's not music we need," Cooker said, turning down the volume. "Come on, let's get back on track. I think I know just the thing."

Cooker passed by the sign for Vougeot, took the road to Morey-Saint-Denis, and parked in the lot of the restaurant Castel de Très Girard so that they could fittingly celebrate Virgile's first day in Burgundy. As soon as they were seated in studded armchairs in the main dining room, they opted for the gourmet menu, which included appetizer, first course, main course, cheese, and dessert. Cooker ordered smoked salmon cannelloni in lime-flavored mascarpone on a vegetable aspic and artichoke mousse, then shrimp ravioli on a bed of fennel in chervil broth, followed by stuffed saddle of rabbit in prunes covered with bacon on a bed of spinach and tomato comfit.

258 J.-P. ALAUX & N. BALEN

Overwhelmed by the variety of the menu, Virgile finally chose the same dishes as his boss.

They ate more than they should have, calmly sipping a bottle of 1995 Gevrey-Chambertin from the Domaine Trapet Père et Fils. With a weary gesture they declined the cheese platter, but when the waiter offered the dessert menu, Cooker couldn't resist a pyramid of red fruit in gewurztraminer with peach sorbet, a wafer, and a sweet almond sauce. His assistant gave in to a chocolate macaroon with vanilla ice cream and a cocoa-bean emulsion.

While waiting for coffee, Cooker carefully took a Montecristo double corona from his cigar case. He rolled the flexible, well-veined tobacco-leaf wrapping between his fingers and then pulled out his little chrome guillotine. He took the time to prepare his vitole before lighting it. He discretely loosened his belt one notch, stretched his legs, leaned his head back on his chair, and, with relish, exhaled a thick puff of smoke toward the ceiling light.

"You may not believe me, Virgile, but this is the first Havana that I've smoked since I've been here."

"It's about time I got here, then!"

6

As soon as he awoke, Cooker dropped two antacid tablets into a glass of water, dragged himself to the shower, and stayed under its tepid spray for a good quarter of an hour. Then he gave himself a generous splash of Hermes men's cologne and slipped on a pair of wide-ribbed corduroy pants, a beige flannel shirt, and his comfortable tweed jacket, whose pockets were beginning to lose their shape a bit. He didn't have the energy to polish his Lobb country shoes while he waited for Virgile, who would certainly be a little late. Instead, he decided to consult the Bible passage that Brother Clément had referred to. He quickly found the Prophesies of Isaiah at the front of the Book of the Prophets. He briefly looked over the first pages before stopping at chapter five, verses one through seven, "The song of the vine."

> Let me sing my beloved the song of my friend for his vineyard. My beloved had a vineyard on a fertile hillside.

> He dug it, cleared it of stones, and planted it with red grapes. In the middle he built a tower, he hewed a press there too. He expected it to yield fine grapes: wild grapes were all it yielded.

> And now, citizens of Jerusalem and people of Judah, I ask you to judge between me and my vineyard.

What more could I have done for my vineyard that I
have not done? Why, when I expected it to yield fine
grapes, has it yielded wild ones?

Someone knocked at the door. Three short raps. Cooker
went to answer it, the Bible open in his hand.
"Hello, sir. Sleep okay?"
"Listen to this, Virgile," Cooker said, and read him the
passage.

Very well, I shall tell you what I am going to do to
my vineyard: I shall take away its hedge, for it to
be grazed on, and knock down its wall, for it to be
trampled on.

I shall let it go to waste, unpruned, undug, overgrown
by brambles and thorn-bushes, and I shall command
the clouds to rain no rain on it.

Now, the vineyard of Yahweh Sabaoth is the House of
Israel, and the people of Judah the plant he cherished.
He expected fair judgment, but found injustice, up-
rightness, but found cries of distress.

Cooker's trembling voice remained suspended in the air, as
if to emphasize the dramatic effect of the last verse.
"I don't understand any of it," his assistant confessed, running his hand through his short hair. "It's all Greek to me."
"Actually, you're not far off." Cooker smiled. "It doesn't
bother me all that much that you're a nonbeliever. But not to
be moved by the power of words, that always baffles me."
"Sorry, but for me, this kind of grand speech reminds me of
old Hollywood movies. You know, all those togas, Charlton
Heston playing the handsome hero Ben Hur fighting on his
chariot, and a bunch of skinny slaves in jock straps. I can see
the rows of cardboard colonnades as I speak! I love it."

"All right. I don't think I'll get anything insightful out of you on this subject. Your ambivalence depresses me."

They left the annex to go to breakfast in the dining room. The weather had become milder during the night. The frayed clouds were whitish strips that revealed patches of blue sky. Aurélie welcomed them with a pretty smile and sparkling eyes that stopped Virgile in his tracks at the door. He stared at her and stammered a shy "good morning," which was not at all like him.

"Well, what's gotten into you, my boy?" Cooker whispered as he sat down.

"You didn't tell me that the welcoming committee was so charming."

"I knew you would be impressed, but I didn't want to give everything away at once."

"She's just my type."

"I have the impression they are all more or less your type. In the meantime, Virgile, get ready, because the mission awaiting you demands concentration and quite a lot of precision. I am really counting on you."

"Thank you. I take the challenge as a sign of trust."

"Most important, you are going to save me time. Please give my excuses to Olivier Lefflaive. He's a friend. He'll understand. Tell him that I have too much work to do in Vougeot and that I'll come by to say hello another time."

"I know his reputation, and he seems to be a real character, your friend Lefflaive!"

"Yes, we resemble one another somewhat. Very unusual career paths, in any case hardly typical of what people expected of us. Olivier was active in the theater circles in Paris for a long time. He's the son of a winemaking family, but he wanted to see the world, play some guitar, write songs, experience other things. Finally, the call of Burgundy was stronger than the glitz of the capital. When he returned to Puligny-Montrachet in 1984, he threw himself into his terroir like a madman and accomplished an impressive amount of work."

"It seems that his white wines are to die for."

"The reds are not bad, either. The vineyard is a very demanding business, and it's expanding. But Lefflaive and his people are down to earth, and they respect tradition. They also have a lovely motto: 'Wine teaches us respect, and the vineyard teaches us modesty.' But I won't say anymore about it. I'd rather let you discover it for yourself."

After gobbling up every morsel of their buttered bread, cleaning out a ramekin of apricot jam, and emptying their cups of tea, they left through the back door. As they passed the counter, Virgile could not resist a conspiratorial and promising wink, making the waitress blush. Cooker shrugged as he watched his assistant. Then he handed him the keys to his Mercedes and gave him some superfluous advice on how to proceed during the tasting. He waited until his purring convertible disappeared at the other end of town before heading for the Rendez-vous des Touristes Café.

When he walked in, the welcome was notably more polite than it was on his first visit. He found the same dice players sitting in front of their green felt cloth at the far corner of the bar. He took a table near the woman with the triple chin and her unassuming husband. Cooker had the feeling that he was at a re-enactment of the scene he had witnessed forty-eight hours earlier, except today they were greeting him amiably. He was now part of the landscape. Everyone knew who he was or thought they did. The night the Bravart boys were murdered, he had been seen coming out of the hotel in a bathrobe, patterned cashmere pajamas, and leather slippers. Cooker was no longer a stranger. He concluded that just having witnessed the face of death with these people was enough to create a rapport.

Cooker ordered coffee and began to chat about the weather, but the conversation soon turned to the events of the last few days. Each person gave his opinion and wanted to share it with everyone else.

"You have the right to defend yourself, but it's despicable to shoot kids!" yelled one of the dice throwers.

"He'd better be careful, that idiot Ernest," the man next to him said icily. "If I were a Bravart, I'd make no bones about planting one between his eyes!"

"Justice will run its course," Cooker objected.

"What justice? Do you still believe in justice? It looks like he's going to get out tomorrow."

"I don't think so. He will probably be released on a bond or perhaps his own recognizance," the winemaker said. "That doesn't mean he will avoid a trial."

"He'll be watched!" the woman interjected. "And we'd better watch out, or else he'll gun down all the kids as soon as he's plastered."

"Frankly, sir, you don't kill two kids over a trifle," her husband dared to say.

"When I was young, I did worse things than write on a wall," the café owner added.

The exchange, which was growing more heated, was interrupted when a man in green overalls pushed the door open with his shoulder and barged in.

"There's firemen at Mother Grangreon's place!"

"Is it on fire?" the café owner asked, surprised.

"On ice, actually, yes!" shouted the man in overalls. "The old woman woke up under a layer of snow."

"Stop kidding, Mimile!"

"I'm serious. She was in her bed, and when she opened her eyes, she was under a layer of snow."

"What snow? It's all melted since yesterday."

"Up north, where her house is, there were still patches of snow on the slopes, and there was some near the hen house. In any case, someone dumped it on her bed. Apparently she screamed like a pig and began running all around the house. And get this, guys—all the dishes were in pieces on the floor. The furniture was turned upside down, and the curtains were pulled down. Wait till you hear the next bit: there was writing in black paint on the walls. She fainted or, I don't know, had a heart attack or something like that!"

"Writing in Latin?" Cooker asked cautiously.

"What do I know? In Latin or Chinese, who cares?"

"Is she dead?" a guy at the counter asked.

"No, but she's drooling a bit, her eyes are rolled back, and she's all stiff. It's not a pretty sight."

"Mother Grangeon never was a pretty sight," joked one of the customers.

"Let's not kid around," the café owner interrupted. "Nobody could stand Mrs. Grangeon, but we've never seen anything like this in Vougeot. Believe me, it's not a good sign!"

Cooker spent most of his day in the village, at the Bertagna wine estate, to establish a winemaking protocol on an experimental parcel of land. He had been in touch with the managers of the property for several months and had promised to spend some time with them when he came to the area for his induction. The project was exciting and still needed some adjustments, but the cellar master and the master grower were efficient and cooperative. After long consultation and a methodical test of the decanted samples, Cooker concluded that he would definitely have to come back to Vougeot to put a final touch on this limited vintage. Before leaving, he took advantage of the opportunity to taste several vintages of Clos de la Perrière Monopole, a true Vougeot wine, which was produced outside the château but whose balance he had always appreciated.

Once back at the hotel at the end of the afternoon, he allowed himself a break in the dining room for a cup of tea. Aurélie prepared a smoky lapsang souchong, which he drank in little sips while waiting for Virgile to return. The girl made some overtures to engage him in conversation. He went along, but wasn't fooled. She finally gave herself away by casually asking one too many questions about his assistant, whose brown eyes had met hers that very morning. Cooker didn't hesitate to give her the information that she was trying hard to get out of him.

"In fact, here he is!" Cooker exclaimed as he heard the familiar sound of the convertible.

Virgile walked in with the ease of a handsome guy used to making a theatrical entrance. His gaze came to rest on Aurélie's smooth face.

"So?" Cooker said.

"Nothing but good news, sir," Virgile said, his speech mildly slurred.

"But you look smashed, my boy," Cooker said, worried.

"To be honest, I didn't leave very clearheaded. It was so fine that toward the end, I didn't have the willpower to spit. But don't worry. I didn't get behind the wheel right away. I took a little nap in the car, and the cold air woke me up."

"That's not very responsible," Cooker grumbled. "I expected more professional behavior from you! Let's see what your notes look like."

Virgile took out a bundle of pages that his boss almost tore from his hands.

"Very cool atmosphere. I got along very well with Pascal Wagner. He's a super sommelier. We talked about rock 'n' roll almost as much as we talked about wine."

The assistant was effusive and joyfully related his visit with Olivier Lefflaive. The wine tasting had taken place before a nice plate of local cured meats, Bresse chicken stewed in honey, and several local cheeses.

Cooker was not really listening to him and consulted the sheets to see if they were in order.

"Well, I am going to my room to read all of this in peace. Tonight I am skipping dinner. I decided to diet today, and considering your state, I suggest you do the same."

Once in his room, Cooker raised the thermostat, took off his shoes, pulled on a cashmere sweater, and stretched out on his bed to study his employee's report. Everything was recorded according to Cooker & Co. criteria. He began with the tasting of the whites, which had been lined up in the 1999 vintage: Meursault, Chassagne-Montrachet, Puligny-Montrachet, Chassagne premier cru Blanchots, Meursault premier cru Charmes, and Puligny-Montrachet premier cru Chalumeaux. The notes were well written, both technical and perceptive, and some made the winemaker smile.

Virgile's notes were as pertinent as they were impertinent. Chablis grand cru Valmur 2000: "Rather citrusy, mineral, with a touch of sweetness, a bit creamy. Superb bouquet. (You could say fabulous without exaggerating too much.) Floral, round, balanced. Very satisfying structure." In the margin he had scribbled a note that was crossed out. Cooker could still make it out: "Think of asking Mom what perfume she wore when I was in high school. Same lemony, slightly acidic, smooth smell."

Cooker could see that the finale of the wine-tasting session had been a real joy: Puligny-Montrachet premier cru Pucelles, Corton-Charlemagne grand cru, and Bienvenues-Bâtard-Montrachet grand cru in four successive vintages. Sublime whites that brought the art of chardonnay winemaking to unexpected heights. They were sometimes difficult to spit out. Virgile had done good work. Admittedly, his conduct had been a bit less than stellar, or at least he had drunk without much moderation. But he had written an impeccable wine-tasting report that was sufficiently precise and analytical without losing his personality and refined subjectivity. Obviously, this young man from Bergerac felt comfortable in Burgundy. He understood its authenticity, its rough manners, its gruff simplicity, and its down-to-earth honesty that emphasized doing what you say, not saying what you do.

Cooker placed the notes on his bedside table, picked up his cell phone, and punched in the number for Robert Bressel, the reporter. Night would soon fall on Vougeot.

"Good evening, Mr. Bressel."

"Ah, Mr. Cooker!"

"How did you know it was me?"

"I have an ear for voices. I only have to hear one once to recognize it among thousands."

In the background, there was the muffled sound of a sitar mixed with the banging of a tabla. Cooker had no trouble imagining the heady odor of patchouli. He rubbed his nose in irritation.

"I heard about what happened last night at Mrs. Grangeon's place," Cooker said. "How is the good woman doing?"

"Good woman? Who says?"

"I don't know her, to tell you the truth. But what happened to her is still very strange."

"That old lady has a reputation as a battle-ax and nasty shrew. Mean to everyone, including family. But no one wishes her any harm. At the moment, she is still at the hospital in a state of shock. I just finished my article, and I had to hold off a bit, because the doctors don't want to comment just yet. We only know that her heart is not about to give out."

"That's good."

"Apparently, the less heart you have, the stronger it is."

"I have the impression that this latest episode completely exonerates the two boys. In my opinion, they died for nothing—just for having been smart alecks."

"That's my opinion, too, but it seems to me that the police are still on that track. I inquired myself, and it appears that Cedric was more or less a dunce, but his cousin, David, was an excellent student: baccalaureate with honors, seven years of Latin, and good grades throughout, right on schedule for catechism, first communion, and confirmation. In short, a completely plausible suspect. And besides, his name was David."

"Maybe," Cooker conceded. "But it doesn't necessarily follow that he would know all those psalms. Still, what a waste. Those poor kids!"

"Getting back to Adèle Grangeon, I think the staging is a bit crude."

"What are you insinuating?"

"As if someone meant to add a layer of complications, offer a whole new set of clues, and send yet another message to decode."

"What are you getting at?"

"Nothing, but I have the feeling that there is something to pursue here. The graffiti messages that they found at Grangeon's place correspond to the missing second and third verses from Psalm 102. I tried to reach my nephew to get some information. I already told you about him. He's the one who works at the regional library. He did his thesis on the folklore of Burgundy and the secret histories of the Côte-d'Or. I'm sure he's got something to say about this."

"What's his name again?"

"Pierre-Jean Bressel. You can find him during the day in the offices of the historical collections."

"Excuse me for belaboring the point, but there is still something strange about Mrs. Grangeon. How is it that she didn't wake up in the night?"

"It seems that she's been taking sleeping pills since her husband died. She must have been sleeping like a rock."

"I see."

The two men sketched out some more theories without much basis, then decided they had examined the case from all angles. Soon after hanging up, Cooker called his wife to confirm that he would, indeed, return home the following weekend. He missed Elisabeth, and he told her so tenderly and discreetly. Then he asked about his dog, Bacchus, and whether the first buds were blooming along the paths of their home, Grangebelle. Cooker knew that Elisabeth would pick up the melancholy in his voice and want to know how this trip to

Burgundy was unfolding. He responded vaguely. She pressed him a bit. Benjamin reassured her, "Everything is going well, my sweet. Nothing to report."

7

The dining room was deserted, the shutters closed, the tables empty, and the coffeemaker turned off. Cooker waited for a few minutes and decided to go back and awaken Virgile. When he turned into the passageway that led to the courtyard, he spotted the furtive silhouette of Aurélie hurrying nervously from the annex. She smoothed her hair before slipping through the back door.

Cooker sighed and walked directly to his assistant's room. He knocked several times without getting a response. He turned the doorknob and found that the door wasn't locked. Cooker poked his head in and surveyed the scene. The bed had slid toward the chest of drawers. The rumpled sheets were spilling onto the floor, and the pillows had been tossed to the other side of the room. The sound of a vigorous shower was coming from the bathroom, joyously accompanied by off-key whistling. Virgile was merrily butchering the melody from *The Bridge Over the River Kwaï.*

"That's right, my boy, the sun is shining, shining, shining," Cooker sang softly as he closed the door.

When he returned to the dining room, Aurélie was bustling behind the counter and putting the breakfast rolls in wicker baskets.

"Sorry, sir, I was late. Your tea will be ready in a few minutes."

"No rush," he said and watched, amused, as she laid out the tray with feverish movements that were so unlike her. "I hope it was nothing serious?"

"No, sir, just couldn't find my watch."

"Ah, Aurélie, time flies when we're having fun!" he teased.

The young woman paid no attention and approached the table with an angelic smile. Her pink face, luminous blue eyes, pulled-back hair, and round mouth gave her the honest but still mysterious look of a polychromatic virgin in a Romanesque church.

Virgile appeared in a heady cloud of Italian cologne. He waved to his boss enthusiastically. He gave the waitress a sidelong greeting that was both subtle and awkward as he walked past the counter. Aurélie blushed and lowered her head to dry a stack of saucers. Virgile focused on devouring his pastries. He drank two glasses of orange juice and served himself cup after cup of tea.

"One would think you haven't eaten in a week," Cooker said. "Build up your strength. You seem to need it."

"Did you read my notes?"

"Yes, and I congratulate you. It's quite unexpected, considering your condition last night. I hope you got your beauty sleep?"

Virgile ignored the question and asked about the plan for the day.

"We are going to Dijon!" Cooker announced as he was getting up. "And we shouldn't sit around too long."

The engine of the Mercedes was already running when the young man trotted out of the hotel, a croissant in his mouth and his jacket half on.

"You think of nothing but eating, my boy!" Cooker said. "Come on. We're off!"

Comfortably stretched out in the convertible's burnished-leather seat, the assistant pulled a stack of raisin cakes out of his pocket.

"That young girl spoils you, Virgile. Please don't take advantage of her generosity."

They arrived without mishap in the historic center of Dijon and had no trouble finding a place to park. The winemaker gave some free time to his assistant, who felt duty-bound to visit the former Palace of the Dukes of Burgundy and its fine arts museum. Cooker intended to see the reporter's nephew at the regional library, which was not far away.

Once he got there, a receptionist showed him to the office where Pierre-Jean Bressel presided. At the back, to the right of shelves dedicated to the history of Burgundy, a gray silhouette was seated at a table. Cooker approached slowly to get a good look at the archivist, who was filing piles of documents. The man was no more than thirty. He had a moon-shaped face, slightly flabby jowls, and thick bifocal glasses that distorted his face. His greasy hair was plastered to his skull. Robert Bressel's nephew seemed to belong to another era. As he rose slowly, Bressel's shoulders remained stooped, as if the centuries were weighing them down.

"Hello, sir. May I help you?" His monotone voice exhaled dust and melancholy.

"Hello, young man. I was sent here by your Uncle Robert. He interviewed me in Vougeot a few days ago, and he recommended that I meet you in order to—"

"I know," Pierre-Jean Bressel interrupted. "You are Mr. Cooker, aren't you? He called me, and I have been expecting you, more or less."

"I was in the area for a meeting in Dijon," Cooker lied with impressive composure. "I hope I am not disturbing you."

"Not in the least. I suppose that you want to talk about the events that have taken place recently."

"Absolutely. It seems that you have worked for a long time on the folklore of Burgundy and that you might be able to shed some light on certain matters for us."

"I do not know if I am able to help you, but I have, in fact, studied certain phenomena that come from legends or beliefs. Let's say mysteries, if anything."

"Do you think that what happened to Adèle Grangeon might be in your area of expertise?"

"I am just a historian and do not claim to be anything more, but it does seem to correspond with other events that took place long ago. It's not the first time that snow has been found on a bed in a home where the furniture has also been moved, and dishes have been broken. There have been many instances of this sort, most notably one that happened in 1826 in the town of Pluvet. Many houses were found this way, with snow on beds and other furniture. The residents said the devil had visited them. Some even claimed to have been hit by rocks in their sleep."

"And what did that mean?"

"We do not know any more about it."

The librarian pushed up his thick glasses, which had slipped down his nose. He smoothed his oily hair and extracted a file from a stack.

"This dissertation deals with several other matters of this sort," he said in a toneless voice that was beginning to irritate Cooker. "I will spare you the chapter on the haunted houses. There are so many of them. But one particular story might be noteworthy. Back in 1633, a Chrétien Bochot, who ran an inn on the Rue de la Bretonnerie in Beaune, was complaining of nightly disturbances. Each morning, he would find trunks and furniture turned upside down and dishes thrown on the floor. Luckily, in those days, dishes were made of pewter, so they didn't break. But the noise must have been terrifying. He also said he heard things: whimpering, chains rattling, groans, and screams from the attic."

"So, what happened?"

"After that, we don't know."

"In the end, no one knows anything," Cooker said, both disappointed and annoyed.

"We suspect some things."

"But you don't have a vaguely rational explanation?"

"By cross-referencing, we have observed that there is always a child connected to the story, sometimes several."

"Could the children have been playing dirty tricks to frighten people? A little like the two young Bravart kids in some way?"

"Not at all. It was just observed that children were in the vicinity. There are three more recent examples. In 1877 in

Chauvirey, a man who took in a little girl from a social-service agency was the target of the same type of harassment. He heard scratching, footsteps, and a terrifying racket every night for several months. They called in a soothsayer, a sort of exorcist, who concluded that the noise manifested only when the child was in bed and that it was her spirit acting up."

"And there, same thing," Cooker interrupted wearily. "You're going to tell me that we know nothing more about it."

Pierre-Jean Bressel did not respond but rather readjusted his glasses and turned some pages of the dissertation.

"We also know that in 1898 in La Roche-en-Brenil, a Mr. Garrie, who was a weaver by trade, saw his clock shake and fall to the floor and his lamps suddenly go out. He relit the lamps and put the clock back up. But the same thing happened. He called his neighbors over, and they watched as the furnishings tumbled over, and pictures came off the walls. Then a hammer sprang out of a drawer, broke a window, and ended up in the street."

"That's disturbing," the winemaker admitted, leaning over the document.

"I have some press clippings from the time of the incident. See for yourself. The events occurred over the span of several days: tables knocked over, jars of pickles smashed, sideboard upside down."

"Was there a child involved that time?"

"Yes, a youngster from the hospice who was raised by the family. As soon as he was sent to Saulieu, there were no more incidents. There were also several children in the home of Mr. Girard in Aubigny-la-Ronce. On the night of every Sabbath there were terrifying noises that everyone heard. One of them was a sound like collapsing logs, as if someone were knocking over entire stacks of firewood. It always happened as soon as Mr. Girard's daughter-in-law put the grandchildren to bed."

"And yet there was no writing on the walls, as there was in Vougeot," Cooker remarked, trying to look Pierre-Jean in the eye behind the Coke-bottle glasses.

"Indeed, that may be a new element that should be indexed."

"So there is no historical incident, proven or imagined, that involves the Psalms of David?"

"As far as I know, not one. We find many legends that revolve around the devil, satyrs, suspicious ceremonies and nights of debauchery. There are also quite a few tales of ghosts, such as a certain lady in white who wanders the countryside. From time to time, she is dressed in black instead of white. But is this really the same phantom? There is no dearth of shocking occurrences and bizarre apparitions—stories of tortured saints, trials, and stakes, talking crucifixes, fake Virgin Marys, bodies risen from the dead, what have you. Herders of wolves, goblins, spirits, and miraculous springs."

"You are talking about superstitions and rumors, whereas what we have here are not hoaxes. Your stories don't appear to be relevant."

"You should consult Lucien Filongey. He's a man who claims to be an expert in the field, and he easily invokes celestial forces. He deals with all those things that worry the common mortal."

"Where can I find him?"

"Ask anyone in Gilly-lès-Cîteaux. They'll tell you how to get to his place."

"Filongey, you say?"

"Yes, Lucien Filongey: part bonesetter, part magician, part exorcist. You won't find a more interesting man!"

"This part of the country never ceases to surprise me," Cooker said, nodding. "I was familiar, or so I thought, with its wine spirit, but I didn't know about the...divine spirits."

"That's amusing," Pierre-Jean conceded soberly. "The novelist Stendhal, who knew this region extremely well, was not very fond of our countryside. But he was a great admirer of the wines of Clos de Vougeot. Incidentally, he wrote something very true: 'As I left Dijon I stared hard at the famous Côte-d'Or, so celebrated throughout Europe. I had to recall

the verse, "Are witty people ever ugly?" for without its wonderful wines, I would find nothing uglier than the Côte d'Or.'"

"You have an excellent memory," Cooker said with admiration. "Perhaps that is why you immediately recognized
Psalm 102?"

"Stendhal also wrote this: 'At the table, Burgundians speak
only about wines, their comparative merits, their faults, and
their qualities; boring politics, so impolite in the provinces, are
left aside.'"

"I thank you for all of your valuable information, Mr.
Bressel, but I must go."

"It was a pleasure," murmured the librarian.

As soon as he had left the building, Cooker took a deep
breath of fresh air. His feet planted solidly on the sidewalk,
he stood for a long moment, turning over in his mind this
conversation, which had seemed far too rambling. He started walking without paying attention to the passersby or the
half-timbered homes and shops of the old city, which would
have fascinated him on any other occasion. His phone rang at
the bottom of his coat pocket.

"Are you finished with your meeting, sir?"

"Where are you, Virgile?"

"I'm buying mustard."

"You are?"

"Well, yes. In Dijon, it seems appropriate. I'm getting a jar of
it for my sister, Raphaëlle. She loves it. I am at the Maille shop."

Cooker walked up the Rue de la Liberté and spotted Virgile
behind the magnificent store window that had flaunted its letters of gastronomic nobility since the nineteenth century. The
fluttering salesgirls seemed to be greatly enjoying themselves in
the company of this handsome young man with an imposing
build but reassuring long eyelashes. He was bewitching them
with his distinctively southwestern French accent. Virgile
emerged, beaming.

"I also got a jar for Mrs. Cooker. She likes it, I hope."

"Even if she hated mustard, she would pretend to appreciate it, because you're the one giving it to her. Be careful, or I'll start getting jealous."

"Come on, Mr. Cooker. She could be my mother." Virgile burst out laughing.

"With you, you can never know, Virgile. No woman can resist you. Or is it the other way around?"

"You exaggerate, sir. But honestly, those women were charming," he added with a wink.

"So, what did you think of the Dukes of Burgundy Palace?"

"Not much. I decided to stroll down the streets instead."

"And no museums, either?"

"Sorry to disappoint you, but without you, it's not as much fun."

"Never mind. You're not going to get out of it that easily. We're going there right away!"

"But I had no intention of avoiding it, boss."

They quickly ate panini sandwiches with goat cheese and dashed off to the Ducal Palace. Cooker did not want his young assistant to miss any of the galleries. Without overwhelming Virgile too much with commentary, Cooker gave him an overall idea of what he needed to know so as not to die an idiot. Cooker spent some time examining the *Presentation of the Infant Jesus in the Temple*, painted by Philippe de Champaigne, while Virgile lingered even longer before an anonymous painting from the Renaissance, simply titled *Woman at Her Toilet*. They both came out of the palace inspired but exhausted.

Virgile said that nothing was better for re-energizing than a good walk, preferably at a brisk pace. Cooker went along with the idea and even decided to walk double time through the churches of Notre-Dame and Saint-Philibert and the Saint Benignus Cathedral. They found their car not far from Place Bossuet, close to the neighborhood that used to be frequented by "blue bottoms," as wine growers used to be called in Dijon. It formerly housed the wine growers trade organization.

Night had fallen without warning, and the streetlights were already lit. Cooker suggested taking a detour to the Castel de Très Girard, which Virgile could not very well refuse. On the way, they chatted like satisfied tourists, and then Cooker told Virgile about his meeting at the library. He shared his reservations about the librarian with the chubby face, shiny hair, and thick binocular glasses.

"I have a bad feeling. I almost have the impression that he was saying a lot but not revealing anything. Maybe I wasn't listening the way I should have been, or perhaps I wasn't picking up what he was saying between the lines. He was a strange guy: polite and friendly, yes, but evasive, elusive even."

"You must have been frustrated," Virgile concluded.

"Not really. It was more that I had the impression that he wanted to lead the discussion in a certain direction and not really talk about the reason I had come to see him."

When they arrived in Morey-Saint-Denis, they parked in front of the Castel de Très Girard and finished their conversation before going into the restaurant. Cooker asked about Raphaëlle, Virgil's sister. He knew that she had a serious medical condition, and he had lit a candle for her in the chapel of the cathedral that very afternoon.

"Thank you, sir. She is doing better, and we're hopeful. Between your candle and my jar of mustard, she has been spoiled today!"

The owner greeted them with open arms. "Sorry that I wasn't here to greet you the other day. It was my night off. How are you, Benjamin? It's been more than a year."

Although he had not been born in Burgundy, Sébastien Pilat was an expert in the habits and customs of the land he had adopted. An impressive understanding of wine and a decided taste for well-crafted cigars complemented his gastronomic knowledge. It was obvious that he had taken over the reins of this establishment with the goal of making it one of the best in Côte-de-Nuits. And his hard work, innovation, and high standards were paying off.

"The other night we ate entirely too much here at your restaurant," Cooker said as he unfolded his napkin on his lap. "We've come back to do penance!"

Cooker ordered just one course and a dessert, but Virgile opted for the entire regional meal. A marc de Bourgogne granita allowed him to recharge his appetite halfway through. When it was time for coffee, Sébastien Pilat invited them into the private back room, where he offered them their choice of cigars from his humidor. The winemaker chose a Cohiba Esplendido and suggested that his assistant take a Flor de Copan Linea Puros. The distinguished Honduran cigar was a final intermediate step before the Havanas of the big island. Settled in their club chairs, which were facing the fireplace, the three men watched the flames dancing while they talked pleasantly about the renovations that Sébastien was planning, which would improve this little eighteenth-century mansion even more. Then they got around to the gossip that was swirling in the villages of the Côte. Cooker admitted that he was very interested in all these stories, and in the course of the discussion, Sébastien asked them innocently, "Did you hear that Honoré Mancenot, Ernest's brother, was found dead tonight?"

Cooker and Virgile looked at him, incredulous. They simultaneously let out a big cloud of white smoke, their cigars frozen between their fingers.

"It was dark out, and a driver spotted his moped lying on its side on the shoulder of the road. The old man was in the ditch, his head smashed against a big rock. A phrase in Latin was painted on the pavement."

"What phrase?" asked Cooker, sounding worried.

"Honestly, I wouldn't know, but it was definitely in Latin. A retired professor from Morey confirmed it."

"Someone talked to me today about a man named Lucien Filongey," Cooker said, taking great care not to let the ashes from his Churchill fall on his shirt. "Do you know him?"

"Who doesn't know him? It's said that he heals burns and resets fractures. There might be some truth to it, or else he wouldn't have so many clients. Some people also say that he performs rituals that are, well, let's just say not very orthodox."

"I'd like to meet him, but I'm not sure how to go about it."

Putting his finger on his lips and frowning as if to concentrate better, Sébastien thought for a moment. "If you don't want to arouse suspicion, there is a simple solution. Just take a bottle of wine to him and ask him to release it from a spell."

"Are you serious?"

"The old people around here still resort to this practice from time to time. It's rare now, but it was common years ago in the countryside. Filongey knows all the prayers for chasing away evil spirits. He's a strange guy. You'll see. If you want to contact him without looking like a busybody, all you need to do is remove the label from any bottle. Take it to him, and have him do his prayer. Make it up as you go, and get him to talk!"

"You mean to say that I have to get a bottle of wine exorcised to worm something out of this charlatan?"

"If you really want to mine the depths of darkness, I don't see any other solution."

"It keeps getting better," Cooker said and sighed as he threw what remained of his cigar into the flames.

8

The man was wiry and tall, slightly stooped but chin up. His lean torso was squeezed into a black satin shirt. Pearl buttons shimmered under the glare of the candelabras.

His weather-beaten face, with its angular cheekbones and prominent nose, was not animated by any particular expression. It wasn't clear whether he was friendly or aloof; he seemed beyond ordinary appraisal, just simply indifferent, absent from the world.

"Welcome to the house of divine help, gentlemen."

Cooker and Virgile walked into a large room with dark velvet curtains that seemed to be breathing in the flickering glow of the candelabras. Before a wooden screen, a grinning skull and open prayer book lay upon a desk. A string of ebony rosary beads was draped around an image of the Virgin of Lourdes. Above her, a boxwood wreath was drying.

"You must be the gentlemen from Bordeaux," Lucien Filongey said curtly.

Virgile shuddered, but Cooker refused to let himself be spooked. He figured the sorcerer of Gilly read *Le Bien Public* newspaper, just as everyone else did. One did not have to be a seer to know who the two men were.

"Yes, you are aware that we are on a business trip in this region, but we find ourselves in a bit of a fix."

The man crossed his arms and stared at them.

"We've tried everything," Cooker continued, trying to sound distressed. "But this particular wine concerns me—I brought you a sample. It's evolving in a way we just don't understand. I was told you could help, and maybe rid the wine of whatever evil has possessed it."

"Your science has its limits." Filongey sneered.

"I agree," Cooker replied humbly.

"Place your bottle on the table, and stand back."

The shaman seized a vial of water, sprayed his hands, and held them around the bottle without touching it. He remained this way for more than ten minutes, in absolute silence, before declaring in a rumbling voice, "Our help comes from the Lord, who made Heaven and earth. I exorcise you, living wine, through the One who, at the wedding at Cana in Galilee, changed the water into excellent wine, through Him to whom the Jews gave wine mixed with gall, so that no secrets may be exchanged with the evil spirits, so that you may be wine that is healthful and cure all God's creatures who may drink of it. Dismiss, oh Lord, every evil spell, incantation, impotence, fracture, ague, infection, distress, curse, satanic act, convulsion, and all other infirmities of the body and soul. Through Jesus Christ our Lord. Amen."

He had delivered his entire speech in one breath. His eyes were wide open, trained on the neck of the bottle.

"Hear us, Lord, and grant your benevolence to those who ask for it, and look favorably on your creature tormented by the devil, and spread on this wine your blessings and your sanctification. I bless this wine and sanctify it in your name so that the demons will be expelled and their evil spells will be broken."

Virgile pursed his lips to stifle the laugh that was rising in his throat. He would not be able to contain it much longer. Cooker gave him a swift kick on the shin with his Lobbs. The young man paled. Filongey continued.

"You have planted the vine and have surrounded it with care from the beginning, and in times of drought, you have watered it with the divine blood of Your Son. Deign then, Lord, to bless this fruit of the grape so that it may be the wine of mercy, science, doctrine, devotion, love, and virtue to cure all creatures who will drink of it, so that it will nourish the soul and fortify faith, that it will sustain the body, that it will enlighten the mind, make the heart rejoice, chase away pain and sorrow, and destroy all evil in those creatures who will drink of it. Through You, the all powerful and everlasting God. So be it."

"Amen," Virgile let out. He could not stand it any longer and was ready to say anything to get rid of his nervous tension.

"Thank you very much, Mr. Filongey," said Cooker, who had managed to keep his British stiff upper lip. "I have no doubt that your prayer will be invaluable to us."

"I will pray for you tomorrow at the same hour. Our good country of Burgundy must be saved from the workings of the devil."

"It's true that Vougeot has not been spared, lately."

"The good Adèle Grangeon received a visit from him two nights ago. Beware—the devil may be lurking among the vineyards!"

"We will be vigilant," Cooker promised. "I would not want to suffer the same fate as that poor woman or the old man they found dead in a ditch last night."

"The Prince of Darkness strikes the pure and the impure alike. I prayed for the salvation of the soul of our good Adèle, who did not deserve such a fate. A pious woman who never forgets to go to Mass and say her prayers to the Black Virgin."

"The Bravart cousins were also devout Christians," the winemaker ventured.

Lucien Filongey turned red and waved his arms. His tunic came undone, giving him the look of a nighthawk poised to swoop down on its prey. He bellowed, "Children of cursed childbirth! Not one of them legitimate! Bastards! Detritus of whores! The Mancenot brothers are nothing but sodomites, traitors! Bigots!"

He stopped suddenly and stared at one of the candelabras as if the mere power of his lunatic gaze could extinguish the flames. Then, in a softened voice, he said, "Shh! Gentlemen, Satan is listening to us." His tone turned unctuous, making him sound all the more disturbing. "The Evil One is among us. He lurks and observes us, just waiting to find a home in malevolent spirits."

"We thank you again for your intercession, Mr. Filongey."

"The world of wine is quite wrong to deprive itself of my services. The winemakers do not know what they are missing. In the past—I'm talking about ancient times—there wasn't a single wine in this land that did not have recourse to divine protection. Do you know that it was the priests of the diocese who would save the vineyard by putting a curse on the flies, the weevils, and the *escrivains?*"

"The *escrivains*, you say?" interrupted the winemaker, who could never resist the chance to enrich his cultural knowledge, no matter where he was or the circumstances.

"Yes, it's a name they used for little evil brown and black beetles. They called them scribblers because they left little markings on the vine leaves. The Clos de Vougeot suffered much and it was a great misfortune, gentlemen! Whenever the vines were withering under the vermin, and the leaves were devoured, people would have processions. They would forbid using the name of the Lord in vain and everyone went to confession. Purifying, cleansing, and sanctifying the soul—this is what we need to bring back today."

It was time to leave, Cooker thought as he reached for his bottle. Filongey gave them an icy smile.

"Before you leave, gentlemen, I would like to offer you two excellent wine tonics that I made myself. I macerate a good quarter gallon of red arrière-côte for about ten days with about two and a half ounces of fennel seeds. And for the white, I always use one from the slopes of Beaune. I add slices of fresh kola nut with a little *eau-de-vie*. Tell me how you like it, since you are the experts."

"We won't forget," Cooker said and nodded, eager to leave.

"Every person I have given it to has benefited from it. Believe me, it's the only remedy for severe exhaustion and anemia. It's better than other tonics, even cod liver oil and horse blood. All those potions rot in the stomach and cause pestilential gas, inflammation of the uterus in women, vaginal discharge in young girls, and extreme diarrhea in young boys. I can assure you that my fortifying wines are safe! You only need to take one shot glass of it twice a day, preferably at ten in the morning and four in the afternoon."

"Many thanks, Mr. Filongey," Cooker said, faking a grin.

"May the All Mighty protect you, and don't forget to drink at least one glass of magnetized water every day."

Virgile let out an immense sigh of relief as soon as he closed the car door.

"That nutcase freaked me out!"

"I confess, he didn't put my mind at ease, either," Cooker said as he stomped on the gas.

Virgile put the two vials of Lucien Filongey's tonic in the backseat and turned to his boss, letting out a nervous laugh.

"Holy shit. I bet these two bottles will get rated nineteen out of twenty in the next *Cooker Guide!*"

9

The rounds of wine tasting in the Morey-Saint-Denis vineyards appellation would begin later than planned. Lucien Filongey's ranting was still troubling the two men from Bordeaux, and they were struggling to concentrate on the work they had to do. Before they reached the Clos de la Bidaude, they slowed down to look for the place where Honoré Mancenot had met his death. Halfway between Vougeot and Morey, they saw the writing in black paint that ran across the pavement. They stopped short on the embankment.

In his notebook Benjamin Cooker wrote down the Latin phrase that stretched in three segments across the gravel carpet.

Deus virtutum convertere:
respice de caelo, et vide,
et visita veneam istam
Et perfice eam, quam plantavit dextera tua: et
super filium hominis, quem confirmasti tibi
Incensa igni et suffossa ab increpatione vultus
tui peribunt.

"What are you thinking about, boss?"

"It must have taken a lot of time to write such a long passage."

"You can't say there's heavy traffic on this road. You could write a book in between the time two cars go by!"

"Maybe. In any case, the person who wrote this has an impressive memory and serious knowledge. There's no doubt about that."

"And you're forgetting something," Virgile said. "He believes in God."

"In God or the devil," grumbled Cooker.

"At any rate, as for the phenomenal memory, I agree with you. I don't see the guy holding his Bible in his left hand and writing with a spray can in his right. And also, it couldn't have been easy in the middle of the night, in the dark."

"Maybe he used his headlights to help him?"

"I don't know. It looks to me like he was just trying to get it down," Virgile said. "The way you just want to get something down when you observe a wine and take your notes without looking at your notebook. You see, in this spot, the writing is more spread out, as if he had to go faster. Maybe he heard a car coming. There, he hurried. Everything was written in one shot. The letters are strung together. Here, again, it's very clear. And there, false alarm: the sound of the engine must have grown more distant, and he ended less frantically. The letters are more rounded in the last words. There is even a period."

"After such an explanation, my boy, what can I add?"

Cooker checked to see if he had correctly transcribed the text and walked over to the embankment. The grass was still flat in some places. Perhaps old Mancenot's moped had slid the length of it. He had probably gone down near the distance marker. He could make out a faint sign of impact. The body had surely rolled all the way down to the pile of rocks, where there were still large traces of blood. Cooker went back to the Mercedes, where his assistant was already searching for a radio station that would spare him the umpteenth tear-jerking scene from *La Traviata*.

"I don't want to tell you what to do, but we're going to be late, sir."

"You are right, Virgile. Our work awaits us. But I forgot something in my room."

They stopped briefly at the Hotel de Vougeot. Cooker jumped out without turning the engine off and reappeared quickly with his Bible. He put the car in first, ground the gears, and headed off toward the secondary road.

The plan for the day was entirely dedicated to the terroir of Morey-Saint-Denis, and a long itinerary lay before them. Virgile had taken care to organize the visits by calling all the estates that Cooker wanted to discover or study in depth for the new edition of the guide. Their side trip to the scene of the tragedy had disrupted their schedule. Now there was no time to waste, and they had to get down to business: taste without lingering, avoid long conversations, remember to get the informational brochures for all the wineries, file the notes immediately, and, if possible, get additional samples to back up their opinions once they returned to Bordeaux.

They went from one tasting to the next with almost military rigor. Virgile spat without a single lapse of protocol. More than once, however, he did wax enthusiastic about some cru that deserved to be more closely examined.

Having read his boss's works attentively, he knew perfectly well that the village of Morey-Saint-Denis constituted one of the smallest communal appellations of the Côte-de-Nuits. At the Vinexpo exhibition and during advanced training courses given by the faculty of oenology, he had been able to taste the five particular appellations that were part of the terroir: Clos de Tart, Clos Saint-Denis, Bonnes-Mares, Clos de la Roche, and Clos des Lambrays. These five red wines alone, classified as grands crus, brought together the qualities of the two prestigious appellations on either side of them. The nature of the terrain could be tasted in the wine. They had the intensity and the power of a Gevrey-Chambertin without losing the finesse and elegance of a Chambolle-Musigny.

Virgile had never before faced so much Morey-Saint-Denis in so little time: a Clos de la Bidaude, one of Guy Coquard's Les Blanchards, several vintages of the Dujac estate, as well as Domaine Alain Jeanniard, the cuvées En La Rue de Vergy from the Lignier-Michelot winery, Aux Charmes from Pierre Amiot et Fils, Les Millandes de Palisses-Beaumont, and Henri Perrot-Minot's La Riotte Vieilles Vignes. All these terroirs, which the Burgundians called "*climats*," contained enough

aromatic marvels and richness to satisfy the most sophisticated palate. Virgile was therefore attentive and picked up
several samples in order to continue exploring when he got
back home. While he was finishing his list of small bottles
and filing the cards at the Beaumont estate's wine warehouses,
Cooker retreated to the car.

Benjamin was feeling weary. In his mouth, he could still
taste a nice vintage that had had a sustained color and somewhat woody flavor. It was becoming cooked fruit, a bit like
jam, with hints of vanilla. The nose had opened on notes of
cassis and spices. Despite the sweetness on his palate, he was
preoccupied with the writing discovered on the road. He had
been thinking about it continuously while he worked. He
pulled out his fountain pen and began translating, resolving
as best he could the problems of syntax. Then he reached for
his Bible in the glove compartment and consulted the psalms
one by one, concentrating intensely. His index finger ran
down the length of the pages with a regular cadence so that he
would not miss the passage. Many minutes went by before his
finger stopped at Psalm Eighty, lines fourteen through sixteen.

God Sabaoth, come back,
we pray, look down from heaven and see,
visit this vine;
protect what your own hand has planted.
They have thrown it on the fire like dung,
the frown of your rebuke will destroy them.

He went over the text several times in its entirety and
remembered having read it many years earlier. It was a
prayer for the restoration of Israel, a heartfelt plea for justice.
Nothing in the text where the vineyard was invoked managed
to awaken in him the least hint of a clue. He got out of his
car, pulled out his cell phone, and punched in the number for
Robert Bressel as he strode through the courtyard across from

the farmhouse. He motioned for his assistant to hurry up as he waited for Bressel to answer.

"Hello," he said simply, since Bressel claimed to have an ear for voices.

"Mr. Cooker, good timing! I just came back this minute from the police station in Nuits-Saint-Georges, and there's lots of excitement there."

"The investigation is making progress?"

"They took some photos of the graffiti and made enlargements so that the handwriting specialists could analyze them. According to my information, nothing jumped out at them."

"They couldn't say if it was the same person each time?"

"I am pretty close to the captain," Bressel explained. "But he doesn't tell me everything."

"However, that is an important point." Cooker's words remained suspended in silence. "Hello?"

"I'm still here, Mr. Cooker. I am weighing what you just said. Do you think that the latest writing on the road might not have been written by the same person?"

"It's just a theory. They don't exactly match. But maybe it's because of the way the writing was done."

"I am not following your reasoning," the reporter confessed.

"Writing on a vertical surface with a can of spray paint would have to differ slightly from writing on a horizontal surface. You understand? The act of bending over and tipping the can has to modify the handwriting. That's without even considering the conditions, which had to be challenging. There was more urgency."

"That makes sense, especially since it all happened at nightfall, around seven-thirty, according to the autopsy report. It was still early, and there was a bit of traffic."

"That's what I was thinking. I went to the scene, and if you examine everything very carefully, you notice some nuances, slight changes, compared with the graffiti in Vougeot and Gilly. Unfortunately, I haven't seen the writing at Adèle Grangeon's."

"You seem to be giving this matter a lot of thought," Bressel observed in a tone that could be interpreted as respectful, intrigued, or sarcastic.

"I can't help it," Cooker responded a bit curtly. "And by the way, I also had the chance to see your nephew in Dijon. Strange boy!"

"Pierre-Jean is a brilliant young man, but he has never had much luck. He deserves more than that job at the library, and I think he is bored there."

"He told me a lot of interesting stories, but I didn't learn anything. I had the impression that he was taking me for a ride."

"I'm surprised to hear that. That's not like him."

"What I mean is that he didn't give me any leads, and he kept changing direction. At the end of the day, I felt a bit lost."

"Pierre-Jean never says anything without a reason, so that surprises me. Perhaps he didn't have any insights."

"Possibly. Did he talk to you about our meeting?" the winemaker asked as he signaled to Virgile to put the cases in the trunk of the convertible.

"No, I haven't spoken to him since your visit."

"You don't see each other regularly?"

"Very rarely. He's pretty introverted. He lives in his books and doesn't mix with people much. He has a hard time with his looks, and I am afraid he'll end up a bachelor. It's true that he has never been attractive. He was in love once, a girl in his class, but she went off and married some wife-beater. He's good-natured, though, and remarkably sensitive. I think he never quite recovered from the blow of not getting the job of curator of the historical archives."

"That's an important position for a young historian," Cooker said.

"Indeed, and he worked very hard for it. He passed all his exams brilliantly and submitted a dissertation that received a special award from the jury. The position should have gone to him. I have always suspected some maneuvering went on."

"Who was named in his place?"

"The grandson of a prominent regional politician who's the mayor of a town near Nuits-Saint-Georges and a big wine trader. I'm sure he influenced the administrative authorities who made the decision."

"I see."

"That said, his grandson was not a bad student. He was a decent candidate, but he hadn't really distinguished himself on the exam. At any rate, the scores have never been made public. Just one mention in the *Journal Officiel*. But why am I telling you all this?"

The winemaker did not answer. Robert Bressel cleared his throat and excused himself on the pretext of having to meet a deadline for the next day's paper.

"I'll be sure to buy *Le Bien Public* to have the pleasure of reading your article," Cooker said by way of good-bye.

10

"This time they attacked the château, Mr. Cooker!" Aurélie shouted this without taking the time to greet him. She was trembling, and Cooker didn't know if she was frightened by the events or simply excited by so much activity in so few days.

"What happened?" the winemaker asked.

"There are firemen, and policemen, and other cars, and—"

"Are all those people up there? At the Château du Clos de Vougeot?"

"Yes, Mr. Cooker, they flew by, no sirens, but they were going fast!"

Cooker raced to the annex to knock on his assistant's door. After several tries went unanswered, he began to bang. Virgile finally responded and stood in the doorway in a white T-shirt and navy-blue boxer shorts with yellow polka dots. His eyes were half-closed, and his face bore the creases of his bedsheets. His mouth was frozen in a half yawn.

"You have five minutes to take a shower and meet me."

While he waited, Cooker went to drink a cup of tea without bothering to eat anything. He checked the inside pages of the *Le Bien Public*. Robert Bressel had written an evasive article mentioning only that the investigation was running its course, that some new clues had appeared, and that the police were following every lead. The journalist seemed to be trying to reassure readers, but his tone was almost clinical.

When Virgile tumbled into the dining room, Cooker did not even let him come to the table, where Aurélie had just laid out a generous breakfast. He led him directly to the road leading to the vineyard. They walked quickly without exchanging a word and soon arrived at the Château du Clos de Vougeot.

Several vehicles were parked helter-skelter, and a crowd had formed in front of the heavy door. Police officers were talking quietly with a group of firefighters, while some other men in uniforms stood slightly apart, chatting with the farmhands. Cooker and Virgile approached cautiously.

A small owl was nailed to the enormous entry door. Its wings were spread apart to reveal a cavity of brown flesh swarming with maggots. The animal was in an advanced state of decay, and its mud-stained plumage had disappeared in certain places. On the left panel of the door, an enormous black inscription was written diagonally: "Jeremiah," and on the other side, below the bird, slightly skewed near the hinges, Cooker could make out "26."

"Mr. Cooker, how are you?"

Cooker swung around and recognized the head of the Confrérie des Chevaliers du Tastevin, who was walking toward him with his hand extended in a friendly gesture. Despite the worried expression that was darkening his face, the man could not neglect his good manners and natural cordiality.

"For heaven's sake, I'm very well, my friend, if it weren't for these unusual distractions."

"Since your arrival, it seems impossible to get a good night's sleep in Vougeot!"

"By that do you mean I am a bird of ill omen?" the winemaker allowed himself to joke as he introduced his assistant.

The Burgundian was delighted to see that the specialists from Bordeaux were so interested in the productions of the Côte-d'Or. He did not try to hide his satisfaction when they mentioned their recent wine tasting experiences and announced their desire to return soon.

"I am very sorry that you happened to arrive in the middle of such business," he said, chagrined. "I don't understand any of this."

"Oh, we've seen things like this before. Haven't we, Virgile?"

Virgile gave Cooker a knowing look.

"But who could this Jeremiah be?" continued the representative of the brotherhood. "Certainly not the author of all these senseless acts. He wouldn't sign his own crimes, would he? Could the culprit have wanted to expose someone named Jeremiah?"

"Who knows?" Cooker said, shrugging.

"I don't know of any Jeremiah in the vicinity. And I don't mean to brag, but I think I know Vougeot and its environs pretty well."

They reeled off pleasantries and useless theories, all in a tone of impeccable civility. But Cooker was preoccupied and in a hurry to leave. He was grateful for Virgile's intervention.

"I believe we are expected elsewhere, Mr. Cooker."

"Indeed, Virgile, duty calls."

They said good-bye with the utmost courtesy and headed back to the hotel.

"I think I know what it is, my boy."

"I suspected as much, boss."

"Really?"

"When I saw that frown, I knew right away."

"I didn't look too unpleasant, I hope?"

"It was close, but you were okay. But anyone who knows you well could tell."

"Thanks for letting me escape honorably."

"You're welcome. I was in a rush to go back myself. I still haven't had a bite to eat this morning."

"This Jeremiah doesn't exist," Cooker said without responding to his employee's remark. "He does not exist, or at least not the way they all think. It's that '26' that put me on the right track. At first I stupidly thought that it was about a guy who was twenty-six years old or maybe about someone who was born in 1926."

"That's not all that stupid. Maybe it's a simple clue. Why complicate things?"

"But who says it's complicated? Go and have your breakfast. I have two or three things to check in my room."

Cooker got back to the annex and rushed to his Bible. He went straight to the Book of the Prophets and stopped at Jeremiah, which was preceded by the words of Isaiah and announced "The Lamentations." The text contained fifty-two paragraphs, or two times twenty-six.

As soon as he saw the drawn features and sad eyes of the abbey porter, Cooker understood that Brother Clément's health had deteriorated even further.

"Everything is going very quickly, Mr. Cooker. Since yesterday he has not been able to get out of bed, and I fear that he will not hear the bells of the next vespers."

"I do not want to bother him. Excuse me for coming so late, but I worked all afternoon at Charmots."

"I think it's one of Brother Clément's favorite Pommard wines. Do not be afraid. I know that he will be happy to see you."

They crossed the cloister and entered the large white stone stairway leading to the lodgings. At the end of a long corridor filled with shadows and silence, they came into a small cell, where a young monk was kneeling beside a bed. Brother Clément was lying on a white sheet, with a wool blanket pulled up to his waist. The porter signaled the novice to leave. Cooker walked slowly to keep the floorboards from creaking. He sat on a wooden stool at Brother Clément's bedside.

"It's good... of you to... I was waiting... for you."

His voice was extremely weak, as if emptied of all its substance, but a gleam still remained in his eyes. The winemaker leaned even closer.

"The tawny owl... the ruins..." stammered the monk, whose bloodless lips hardly moved.

"I thought about it," Cooker said almost in a whisper. "I reread the psalm many times before coming, but I still don't know what to deduce from it."

"All day long... my enemies... insult me..."

"Those who once praised me now use me as a curse," Cooker continued. He could have recited all of Psalm 102 in one breath, so much had he dwelled on it in his hotel room.

"It's... the prayer... of a... poor wretch..."

"Please don't strain yourself, Father. I have thought about all of it, and I, too, think that we are dealing with a desperate person. I also think he wanted to announce his revenge by pointing to Chapter Twenty-Six in the Book of Jeremiah. Because it can be nothing else, correct?"

Brother Clément closed his eyes twice to show that he agreed.

Cooker remained silent, wondering where the dying man was finding the energy to still take an interest in the land of the living.

With infinite tenderness, the abbey porter came in to touch the old man's forehead and feel his pulse. "He is asleep. He is still with us, but his body departs from time to time."

"The best would be if he did not awaken," murmured the winemaker.

"I don't believe so. He has always lived with his eyes wide open, lucid, and perceptive. He deserves to leave fully conscious."

"How long have you known him?"

"I was his student at the seminary before joining him in the cloister. He taught me everything. I have been entrusted with the duty of abbey porter for more than fifteen years now, and I owe this sign of trust from our abbot to the education that Brother Clément gave me. His courses were models of generosity and open mindedness. This is all that is required of an abbey porter."

"I am surprised that he talked to me about this psalm," Cooker whispered. "How did he know about the owl at the Château du Clos de Vougeot?"

"I've told you that he has always had great vision in this life. And it seems to me that he is still alive, no?"

"I am sure that he would have many things to tell me about that owl if he still had the strength."

"He would have said that it's an animal with an unfortunate reputation. It's been made an emblem of ugliness and a sign of bad fortune. In early days, you'd find them nailed like that in cemeteries or on farmhouse doors. Ignorant people believed they brought bad luck because they were night creatures. But living in the dark sharpens the ability to apprehend the unknown, to use one's mind to conquer the darkness. In a way, it's putting one's experience, knowledge, and thoughts in the service of wisdom. Men of the church are often described as crows. Some are, of course. But we others, the contemplatives who embrace seclusion and a certain solitude, we who get up at night to pray and earn the salvation of souls, we are, in a way, far-sighted owls!"

"How is it that I don't know your name?" Cooker suddenly asked.

"Because you've never asked," answered the monk. "My name is Brother Grégoire."

A door slammed in the distance. The noise, usually so mundane, had something incongruous about it, a violence that had no place in this environment. Brother Clément opened an eye and began to moan. Brother Grégoire pulled down the blanket and folded it over the end of the bed.

"He has nothing but the skin on his bones left, and the least bit of weight makes him suffer," he explained to Cooker, who was visibly worried.

"I don't see him breathing. Is he sleeping?"

"I think so. May the spirit of Saint Bernard accompany him in his sleep!"

"Are you talking about Saint Bernard, the monk at Cîteaux and founder of the Clairvaux Abbey?"

"I don't know any other by that name," Brother Grégoire replied, surprised. "Why would I pray to someone else? Saint

Bernard slept very little. He spent enough time working each night to become the patron of all insomniacs, the patron saint of dream chasers."

Brother Clément cast his right eye in Cooker's direction. Cooker drew closer again to catch the snippets filtering from his dry lips.

"Read me... the prophecies of... Jeremiah."

An old Bible was lying on the bedside table. Brother Grégoire handed it to Cooker, who put on his reading glasses. There were nearly one hundred pages in the Book of Jeremiah, and Cooker didn't know where to start.

"From the beginning," the porter instructed.

He read for more than an hour, without stopping, turning the pages at a regular rhythm like a penitent on a hard road. He read without worrying about whether his voice would soothe Brother Clément in this bare cell. He read the adventures of knowledge and violence, exile and corruption, the temple destruction, and foreign divinities. He read about promises of punishment and prophesies to the glory of man saved by the All Powerful. He read the lamentations until he became inebriated with words both nonsensical and sublime.

> Yahweh says this: Look, I shall fill all the inhabitants of this country, the kings who occupy the throne of David, the priests, the prophets and all the citizens of Jerusalem, with drunkenness.

> Then I shall smash them one against the other, parents and children all together.

> Yahweh declares. Mercilessly, relentlessly, pitilessly, I shall destroy them.

He was nearing the end of Chapter Thirteen when the bells of the Abbey of Cîteaux rang to announce vespers. Cooker shuddered and looked up to catch Brother Clément's serene gaze. He thought he saw a smile appear between the hollowed cheeks.

The dying man's lips quivered, and Cooker understood that he wanted to speak to him. He pressed his ear closer. The monk murmured a few words and then gave his soul up to God.

11

She was offering herself without shyness or modesty to Virgile's feverish fingers. He would never come back to see her, and for a moment, she must have dreamed that he would take her away from this place that she knew only too well, that he would take her to the ends of the earth. But Aurélie was a down-to-earth girl and settled for what Fate brought her. For a few days, it was this handsome boy with brown hair and brown eyes who was eagerly caressing her breasts. Virgile's fingers lingered a moment over her stomach, lightly brushing her navel, massaging the fullness of her hips. Then he slid his hands across her chest to titillate her nipples. She let him know she liked this little game of teasing by biting his earlobe. Virgile gave in to it in turn and let out a moan as soon as he felt Aurélie's hot breath between his thighs.

A few hours earlier, both of them had slipped out of the hotel to go dancing at a nightclub in Dijon whose Spanish-sounding name was not worth remembering. Cooker had been fast asleep, probably over a chapter of the Bible, so the night was theirs. They had escaped in Aurélie's tiny car and had drunk several glasses of cheap tequila, their heads already reeling from sufficiently adulterated German techno music.

Back in Vougeot, the girl told him she didn't want to end up spending the night in Virgile's bed, as she had been too embarrassed the night before coming out of his room when she ran into Cooker. She didn't want to see his amused look again. Despite Virgile's insistent pleas, she parked at the edge of town, out of sight, in the recesses of an overgrown dirt road.

Virgile was pressing tenderly on the nape of Aurélie's neck, matching her rhythmic movements. His mouth was on fire.

If there was a God, he would have to reside in the body of a woman, he thought. After performing the delicate ritual of the condom, which almost turned into a comedy, the girl seated herself on Virgile's lap, facing and embracing him. She was holding onto the seat while she straddled him, letting out frightened squeals. They hadn't found any other solution for making love in the cramped Fiat 500, whose original pistachio color and rust-dotted chrome authenticated its rare 1962 vintage.

Aurélie had snuggled against his shoulder and was nibbling on his neck. Now they were satisfied, entwined in their shared sweatiness, unable to separate. For a long while Virgile kept his eyes closed. When he finally opened them, he thought he saw a dark impression standing against a pale moon. He blinked to probe the darkness. The shadow was in profile, one arm raised on the side of a barn. He pushed Aurélie aside brusquely and threw his clothes on helter-skelter. The girl watched dumbfounded and teary-eyed as he opened the car door and started dashing toward the town. He ran full speed on the soggy path and almost slid as he rounded a patch of vines. In front of him, the silhouette was weaving between a cluster of shrubs and bolting toward the Vouge River flowing below. Virgile was closing in. The fugitive hesitated to head down the streets of Vougeot, deciding instead to return to the twists and turns of the vineyard.

"Keep going, you idiot!" Virgile yelled, energized by the memory of muddy practices on the rugby field in Montravel.

It took him just a few seconds to catch up to the man, who had begun limping. Virgile tackled him, crashing down with all his weight. They rolled in a water-filled rut. The fight was quickly over. His two knees pressed against his adversary's torso, Virgile prepared to deliver a punch, but his arm froze.

The man was a woman.

"And where were you again, Virgile?" Benjamin Cooker said, glancing at the side mirror as he pulled out skillfully, and passed a Dutch camper.

"In her car, sir."

"The green one that looks like a Burgundy escargot?"

"That's funny, I thought the same thing."

"It's an old model, rather sought-after, but not very practical for a strapping young man like yourself."

Virgile ignored the remark and continued telling his story: the chase in the middle of the vines, a tackle worthy of rugby star Serge Blanco, the scuffle in the mud, and his shock when he discovered the frightened face of Murielle Grangeon.

"The police told me her name while I was giving my deposition, but I still didn't understand any of it. They didn't see fit to fill me in."

"I got Robert Bressel on the phone while you were being questioned," Cooker confided. "Trust a reporter to find what the police don't know yet. He knew this Murielle Grangeon very well."

"Is she related to the old Adèle?"

"She's her niece, a poor girl who's been struggling for years. She started off okay, studying classical languages and medieval history. She loved that stuff. She went to school with Bressel's nephew Pierre-Jean. She was majoring in Latin and Greek and getting her master's in twelfth-century monastic studies in the dukedom of Burgundy. But then she got knocked up and married some guy from Gilly who used to beat her. It seems like he made a living doing odd jobs and selling stolen cars. He's in prison now, sentenced to eight years. So she found herself alone with two kids. She cleaned offices at night for a commercial cleaning company in Dijon."

"And the kids?" Virgile interrupted. "Did she leave them home alone?"

"No, she lived with her mother, at the other end of Vougeot."

"So her mother is Adèle Grangeon's sister?"

"No, her sister-in-law. Murielle's father was Adèle's brother. The guy died very young of a heart attack. Do you follow me?"

"Up to this point, it's simple. So, in short, the kids' grandmother was a widow and took care of them while Murielle slaved away at a crappy job."

"I imagine she must have felt frustrated having left behind her classical studies for a life of menial labor," Virgile said.

"Not only did she have to work hard, but then her mother got sick. Some kind of cancer, which killed her in just a few months. She had to leave her job to take care of the kids. With no money, no job, and mouths to feed, the first thought Murielle had was to go to her aunt Adèle. But the old lady wouldn't even put them up. Nothing, no helping hand. Door shut, get lost."

"What a bitch! Excuse me, but there's no other word."

"I agree completely."

"So she found herself on the street?" Virgile asked, worried.

"At first, not really. Some friends from school took her in here and there, but you know how that goes. After a certain amount of time, there aren't too many friends who can put up with two kids and a mother in a small apartment. She ended up in a home for single mothers and women in distress. You know the type of place. She was offered unappealing and underpaid internships. Nothing to meet her needs, and the Department of Health and Social Services put her kids in foster homes. That's when she had her first bout of major depression."

"That could put anyone over the edge," Virgile said sympathetically.

Cooker glanced at the wobbling arrow at the bottom of the gas gauge. He would have to fill the tank of his SL280 soon if he didn't want to force Virgile to spend another night under the stars. He took his foot off the gas pedal and continued driving at a more reasonable speed.

"But, Mr. Cooker, when you say that she had her first bout of depression, you mean that she had many more?"

"Yes, she was diagnosed as manic-depressive. She was treated with her fair share of antidepressants, antianxiety pills, tranquilizers, and sleeping pills. And she spent long periods in psychiatric hospitals. According to Bressel, she changed enormously during that period. She was getting thinner and exhibiting strange behavior. She seemed to be changing more and more every day."

"And the kids?"

"She saw them once or twice a month. And even then, only if her condition allowed. She did have one opportunity, though, thanks to Pierre-Jean Bressel. When he heard that a job as a guide had opened up at the Château du Clos de Vougeot, he had his uncle Robert pull some strings to get her foot in the door. Of course, she landed it easily. She knew the history by heart, and what's more, she was from the area."

"All's well that ends well, then."

"Not really. She thought things would get better. But the Department of Health and Social Services wouldn't let her have her kids back. They said her situation wasn't yet stable, that she didn't have suitable housing or a long-term contract. That didn't help her mental health, and she had several more crises. She started showing up for work late and taking sick days. Eventually, she hardly showed up at all. The château could not renew her contract."

"She must have been angry at the world."

"Let's say, rather, that her depression turned to anger. With her situation becoming more and more precarious and her unemployment checks running out, the manic-depression became more acute. She had short periods of overexcitement alternating with moments of extreme withdrawal. Murielle soon lost her sense of reality. A specialist could explain it better than I can."

"Don't worry, boss. Crazy is crazy."

"You do have a skill for distilling things," Cooker said, smiling, "even if that's a bit harsh."

They stopped at a gas station and filled the tank. While his boss cleaned the windshield, Virgile got out to stretch his legs, flirt with the cashier, and buy a copy of the sports newspaper *L'Equipe*. As they were leaving, Cooker turned on his cassette player and invited *La Traviata* to accompany them on the trip.

"That's all we need now!" exclaimed Virgile. "You know I don't care for opera, and honestly, this Maria Callas woman scares me a little. I don't know why, but she sends shivers down my spine."

"I would be disappointed if you said she didn't, my boy. Callas touches the deepest part of what we are."

"Was your diva another tormented soul?"

"I don't think so. Let's just say she had a flair for the dramatic."

"Is the whole story that you told me just the reporter's version?"

"Yes. On the other hand, it was the investigators who uncovered the rest. At least, what they were able to piece together, because even with the help of the experts, it's hard to interrogate someone like that. When she wrote her first messages in Vougeot and Gilly, she was in the middle of a manic phase, and she surely did that in a delirium of vengeance inspired by a desire to frighten people. I think she must have been angry with the whole world, but her world had been reduced to that little corner of vineyard where she endured all the suffering and humiliation."

"But why phrases from the Bible?"

"In my opinion, she must have had a mystical vision of the world. All that time spent on ancient texts, translating from Latin, steeped morning, noon, and night in obscure religious writing, stories of sorcerers, ghosts, demons."

"That couldn't have been good for her! Do you think that's why she did what she did?"

"I do. When she wanted to terrorize her aunt, all she did was reproduce some very old scenes from Burgundy folklore. She knew them inside out. On each occasion she used the situation to her own advantage. Old Mancenot, for example.

She just happened to come across him. She was getting ready to write some ominous messages when she spotted his moped on the side of the road. Honoré was so drunk, he had had a fatal accident. The findings from the investigation and autopsy confirm it. Murielle, as delirious as she was, knew how to turn the event into something malevolent. Same thing with the owl: she found it while she was roaming the town at night. The bird had already been dead for quite a while, which explains the condition it was in, but she knew how to turn it into an object of terror. I don't even want to imagine what was going through her mind in moments like that."

"What is she up against, now?" Virgile asked, somewhat worried.

"Compared to what she has been through, she's not in danger anymore. She'll be able to get better treatment. After all, she didn't kill anyone. She'll surely be charged with disturbing the peace and defacing private property. But in my opinion, her mental state will be taken into consideration."

"And yet, two teens were slain because of her, in a way. That's the worst thing, it seems to me."

"Indeed, that's the most tragic part of the whole story. Their burial is next Monday in Gilly, and there may be a big turnout. Robert Bressel will have his front-page article."

Cooker flashed his headlights to keep a Spanish truck from cutting him off while passing. The road sign announced that Bordeaux was four hundred and fifty miles away, and the night promised to be a long one.

"In my opinion, the librarian had guessed the whole thing," Cooker continued, putting on the windshield wipers. "He knew Murielle Grangeon well enough and was aware that there were few individuals capable of quoting the Psalms of David and the Book of the Prophets by heart and knowing the old local traditions as well as she did. I do not deny that I suspected him of being involved in some way. After all, he also had sufficient motives for wanting revenge."

"I personally think that it was honorable of him to say nothing," Virgile murmured.

"Maybe Brother Clément had also guessed a lot of things. Murielle had often consulted him during her research. When I think back on everything that he told me, there were actually lots of clues to put me on the right track. Pierre-Jean Bressel emphasized the presence of children in all of the haunted-house stories. Brother Clément always brought me back to the themes of the vine, sorrow, and injustice, as if he were trying to steer me in the right direction. And then there was the owl reference that could have been read as a pelican, which relates to the sacrifice of mothers. Perhaps I should have known that we weren't necessarily dealing with a man."

"What did the monk say to you when he was dying?"

"*Honora Dominum et vino torcularia redundabunt.*"

"And what does that mean?"

"Honor the Lord, and vats will overflow with wine."

"Magnificent! Imagine. His last word was 'wine.' I would love to die that way," Virgile said with a yawn.

"Not really, his last word was '*redundabunt*' because you always place the verb at the end of a sentence in Latin. As for the rest, the question is not so much knowing what you say at the moment of death but how you say it."

La Traviata took off on a thrilling flight that the violins could not bring back to earth.

"You see, Virgile, we wandered in the age of the Pharisees, in the footsteps of the apostles and the mystic Jews. We experienced the tonsure of Cîteaux and the dungeons of the Middle Ages. We even came close to believing in the devil and ghosts, and finally, it was nothing but a modern story: divorced unemployed mother no longer entitled to benefits, children taken away, court orders. Hopelessly modern!"

Cooker turned to look at his assistant. Virgile had fallen asleep. He was snoring peacefully, his mouth half open like an angel. Cooker swerved a bit as he reached for his coat to cover his passenger. Then he lowered the volume of *La Traviata* until she didn't have a breath of life left in her.

"Sweet dreams, my boy. Come the night, all is forgotten."

Thank you for reading the Winemaker Detective Mysteries

We invite you to share your thoughts and reactions on your favorite social media and retail platforms.

We appreciate your support.

MORE IN
THE WINEMAKER DETECTIVE SERIES

WWW.THEWINEMAKERDETECTIVE.COM

Deadly Tasting

A serial killer stalks Bordeaux. To understand the wine-related symbolism, the local police call on the famous wine critic Benjamin Cooker. The investigation leads them to the dark hours of France's history, as the mystery thickens among the once-peaceful vineyards of Pomerol.

Cognac Conspiracies

The heirs to one of the oldest Cognac estates in France face a hostile takeover by foreign investors. Renowned wine expert Benjamin Cooker is called in to audit the books. In what he thought was a sleepy provincial town, he and his assistant Virgile have their loyalties tested.

Mayhem in Margaux

Summer brings the winemaker detective's daughter to Bordeaux, along with a heatwave. Local vintners are on edge, But Benjamin Cooker is focused on solving a mystery that touches him very personally. Along the way he finds out more than he'd like to know about the makings of a grand cru classé wine.

Flambé in Armagnac

The Winemaker Detective heads to Gascony, where a fire has ravaged the warehouse of one of the region's finest Armagnac producers, and a small town holds fiercely onto its secrets.

Montmartre Mysteries

The Winemaker Detective visits a favorite wine shop in Paris and stumbles upon an attempted murder, drawing him into investigation that leads them from the Foreign Legion to the Côte du Rhône.

Backstabbing in Beaujolais

The Winemaker Detective is called in to help a newcomer to Beaujolais in the midst of a bitter rivalry with a well-established estate, while the entire region is wound up to ship the year's Beaujolais nouveau around the world.

Late Harvest Havoc

Christmas is in the air, while disaster strikes the vineyards in Alsace. Vintners are tense and old grudges surface. The Winemaker Detective's reputation is on the line as he must find the cause before the late harvest starts.

ABOUT THE AUTHORS

Noël Balen (left) and Jean-Pierre Alaux (right).
(©David Nakache)

Jean-Pierre Alaux and **Noël Balen** came up with the wine-maker detective over a glass of wine, of course. Jean-Pierre Alaux is a magazine, radio, and television journalist when he is not writing novels in southwestern France. The grandson of a winemaker, he has a real passion for food, wine, and winemaking. For him, there is no greater common denom-inator than wine. Coauthor of the series Noël Balen lives in Paris, where he writes, makes records, and lectures on music. He plays bass, is a music critic, and has authored a number of books about musicians, in addition to many novels and short stories.

About the Translators

Anne Trager loves France so much she has lived there for over a quarter of a century and just can't seem to leave. What keeps her there is a uniquely French mix of pleasure seeking and creativity. Well, that and the wine. In 2011, she woke up one morning and said, "I just can't stand it anymore. There are way too many good books being written in France not reaching a broader audience." That's when she founded Le French Book to translate some of those books into English. The company's motto is "If we love it, we translate it," and Anne loves crime fiction, mysteries and detective novels.

Sally Pane studied French at State University of New York Oswego and the Sorbonne before receiving her master's degree in French literature from the University of Colorado, where she wrote *Camus and the Americas: A Thematic Analysis of Three Works Based on His Journaux de Voyage*. Her career includes more than twenty years of translating and teaching French and Italian. She has worked in scientific, legal, and literary translation, including a number of books in the Winemaker Detective series. In addition to her passion for French, she has studied Italian. She lives in Boulder, Colorado, with her husband.

CPSIA information can be obtained at www.ICGtesting.com
Printed in the USA
BVOW08s0947241115

428325BV00001B/8/P